Praise for *Her Holiness*

"*Her Holiness* draws readers into a realm where nightmarish visions and ancient secrets converge beneath the weight of Vatican intrigue. While fighting for women's equality, Kate Murphy forces an age-old institution to confront its fears and failings. It's an unforgettable journey that illuminates the power of conviction—and the harrowing cost of defying tradition."

—KEN WILBER, author of *Finding Radical Wholeness* and *Religion of Tomorrow*, founder of Integral Institute, and cofounder of Integral Life social media hub

"A masterful blend of ancient intrigue and modern ambition, *Her Holiness* sweeps you from the hush of Vatican corridors to the steamy depths of Brazil. Kate Murphy's haunting visions—and the unstoppable fervor of those who fear her—drive a mesmerizing and unsettling narrative. It's a testament to the power of a single voice challenging centuries of entrenched doctrine."

—JAN PHILLIPS, author of *Stop Seeking, Start Finding*, cofounder and executive director of the Livingkindness Foundation

"The role of women in spiritual leadership has long been suppressed. *Her Holiness* is a foray into that dynamic, sparking new interest in how women can participate more visibly in the spiritual transformation now underway. The story embraces suspense, action, and provocative questions about the equality of women in religious life and leaves the reader wanting more!"

—DONNA D'INGILLO, founder of the Institute for Christ Consciousness, author of *The Women Who Loved Jesus*

"*Her Holiness* is a daring, spiritually rich, and emotionally gripping novel that explores the complex intersection of faith, love, and human longing. With lyrical prose and deeply resonant characters, Dustin Dunbar invites readers into a world where divine mystery and earthly passion entwine. It's a story that dares to question religious dogma while honoring the sacred, offering a fresh and fearless narrative that stays with you long after the final page. A powerful meditation on identity, redemption, and what it means to be chosen."

—GREG VOISEN, host of *Inside Personal Growth* podcast,
author of *Hacking the Gap*

"With fleet storytelling driven by dialogue and enlivened by welcome human touches, plus a deep sense of both injustice and possibility, *Her Holiness* stands out from the papal thriller pack."

—BOOKLIFE REVIEWS

HER
Holiness

A Novel

Dustin Dunbar

Published by River Grove Books
Austin, TX
www.rivergrovebooks.com

Distributed by River Grove Books

Design and composition by Greenleaf Book Group and Mimi Bark
Cover design by Adrian Morgan

Publisher's Cataloging-in-Publication data is available.

Print ISBN: 978-1-966629-24-5

eBook ISBN: 978-1-966629-25-2

First Edition

To my beloved Grandma, whose sixty-three years
of teaching Sunday school inspired countless hearts.

And to my two wonderful girls—Tallulah and Milly—may
you always know that you can be whatever you choose to be.
You are limitless, just like the love that surrounds you.

We are often chained like Peter in the prison of habit.
Scared by change and tied to the chain of our customs.

—His Holiness Pope Francis (1936-2025)

Prologue

The old man sat alone in the dim, unadorned church, the silence suffocating him like a shroud. Hours before, the news had pierced his solitude like a dagger—he had sent everyone away, dismissing them to an uncertain safety, knowing the emperor's men were coming for him.

This moment did not surprise him; fear was a foreign concept, a distant echo. He had anticipated this day for years. In the earliest days of the church, he had greeted each dawn with the grim possibility of martyrdom lurking just beneath the surface, yet the sunset always found him alive and breathing.

They had been betrayed—betrayed by the Empire that had silenced their leader and scattered the flock like autumn leaves. The belief that the movement would wither away without its leader had proven to be a naive illusion. They had gone underground, their beliefs transforming into whispers in the shadows. Some ventured to far-flung provinces, forging tiny congregations, establishing clandestine lines of communication. He had traveled first to Antioch and then to Rome, recruiting the devout, assembling small cells of faith that met only under the veil of night, hidden in the bowels of caverns and secret chambers.

Their numbers had swelled quietly, all while the Empire clung to its disdain. They were seen as criminals—convenient scapegoats in a world hungry for blood. They faced gruesome fates; torn apart by wild beasts in the Colosseum, nailed to crosses, set ablaze, crushed, drowned . . . the emperor and his footmen seemed to devote their waking hours to devising fresh torments for the followers of this burgeoning faith.

The old man pushed thoughts of martyrdom aside, kneeling on the unforgiving stone floor as he prayed. Each crack and ache in his knees brought sharp clarity to his mind. He gazed upward, whispering the sacred words so many of his brethren recited without knowing the name of the one they truly addressed. The heavy wooden doors of the church creaked open, shattering the quiet. Soldiers entered, their armor glinting ominously in the faint light. "Stand up," roared the leader, his voice a tempest of wrath.

The old man had heard that particular brand of fury for nearly four decades, yet he could never grasp its roots. His church was meant to embody peace and love, ideals that stood in stark contrast to the rage surrounding him. He rose slowly, exhaustion weighing down his bones, his body groaning in protest.

They seized him roughly, one soldier striking him across the face with a laugh laced with cruelty. "The emperor will rid us of you all soon enough," the leader spat, eyes ablaze with hatred. "He knows you set the fires. You think to undermine the Empire with your cult? He'll see you dead before that happens."

The old man remained silent. He went limp, offering no resistance, surrendering himself to their grip as they dragged him away. They confined him in a cramped cell, a solitary window casting a narrow beam of light across the rough stone wall. He couldn't climb to peek outside; instead, he sat on the cold floor, lost in the labyrinth of his own thoughts.

It had been so long, his journey filled with trials and betrayals, yet the memory of his greatest shame loomed over him like a dark cloud. Years ago, they had gathered in a quiet garden after supper. Their leader had slipped away to pray, leaving the old man and two others to drift into slumber. When their leader returned, he had roused them, but soon they succumbed to sleep again, weariness overwhelming them. And then the soldiers invaded, just as he had dreaded. He had followed in their wake, a ghostly shadow, as they dragged his leader toward the high priest's palace.

He witnessed the brutal spectacle—his leader spat upon, struck, condemned as a blasphemer. The flames of injustice flickered in his chest as he turned away to find warmth by the palace fire, the cold night air biting at his skin. But warmth was fleeting. One of the palace maids confronted him, eyes sharp, accusations ready on her tongue. "You're one of his men," she charged. He denied it vehemently, retreating to the porch, desperate for the solace of shadows.

Outside, another maid pointed a finger, echoing the accusation, and again he protested. Yet the crowd began to swell, suspicion twisting like a vine around his heart. "Look at him! He has the same accent," someone shouted. Panic gripped him, morphing into anger as he hollered back, proclaiming he knew nothing of the blasphemer they spoke of.

Then, the rooster crowed. It was the second time that night, its voice slicing through the dark like a blade. And in that moment of revelation, he recalled his leader's words: before the cock crows twice, you will deny me three times. Overwhelmed with despair, he fled the palace, tears tracing down his weathered face.

Nearly forty years had passed since that harrowing night—the crucifixion, the resurrection, his ascension as reluctant leader of the church. He had journeyed to distant lands, spreading the word, facing the wrath of sovereigns more than once. This was not his first prison cell; Herod had confined him too, but he had escaped. Yet he never truly believed he would perish peacefully in his sleep.

The specter of danger was a constant companion. And now, it seemed this Emperor—Nero, a name synonymous with madness—would be the architect of his end. Whispers spread like wildfire through the streets, embers of unrest ignited by the devastating fires that had ravaged the city for six long days, leaving destruction in their wake. Rumors claimed Nero had orchestrated the infernos himself, watching the flames consume the city while he strummed his lyre. The people, hungry for a scapegoat, turned their fury upon the old man's church, and the noose of blame tightened inexorably around his neck.

They left him in the cell for more days and nights than he could count, his sense of time warped into an indistinguishable blur of despair. Eventually, he abandoned the effort to remember. It was a grim and desolate existence, punctuated only by the slop of food that arrived intermittently, insufficient to stave off the gnawing hunger that consumed him daily. He became a specter of his former self—skin stretched taut against bone, mind dulled by the cruelty of his surroundings.

Finally, the soldiers came for him again, their laughter echoing darkly off the cold stone walls as they dragged him, weak and disoriented, into an open cart. The jostling of the vehicle rattled through him, a cruel reminder of the life he had led before this nightmare.

He was taken to the Circus—the massive arena that had seen the cruelest spectacles of entertainment, where the masses reveled in the suffering of the faithful. It was a place where cries of despair transformed into the roars of a bloodthirsty crowd. As they unloaded him at the foot of a looming obelisk, a surge of recognition struck him. Spectators packed the stands, their faces a medley of excitement and malice, howling and jeering at the sight of him—the condemned.

At the base of the towering monument, a crude wooden cross awaited him, stark and foreboding against the canvas of their revelry. Panic rose within him as he caught sight of it, and he struggled against his captors' grip. Laughter erupted around him, jagged and cruel. "Stop wasting your energy, old man," one of them taunted, tightening his hold. "I am not worthy," he gasped, his voice cracking, hoarse from disuse. "Do not crucify me as you crucified my Lord." The guards merely smirked. "You are going to die on that cross, old man. Now be silent and face your fate with some dignity." He could feel his heart pounding, the weight of his pleas hanging heavy in the air. "Do not!" He shouted now, desperation coloring his words. The eyes of the crowd turned toward him, curiosity morphing into a darker hunger.

The leader of the guards sighed, annoyance flickering across his features. "What would you like us to do with you, old man? How should we kill you?" He closed his eyes for a moment, gathering what little strength he had left. "You may crucify me if you wish. I cannot stop you. But hang me . . . upside down." His voice was barely a whisper now, laced with a reverence he could not shake. "I am not worthy to die as he died." The guard shrugged, laughter spilling from his lips like venom. "Dead is dead."

He waved a hand at two of the men, and they stepped forward with a grim eagerness. "Upside down it is." With a chilling efficiency, they laid him upon the cross, nailing his hands and feet, securing him to the brutal instrument of his execution. He felt the sharp surge of pain with each blow, but he offered no resistance, no cry of anguish escaped his lips. They lifted the cross, hoisting it high until its base struck the ground with a dreadful thud. His head hung low, nearly touching the earth, while his feet rose into the air—an inverted position that felt like a mockery of everything he stood for.

As the crowd roared and the sun beat down mercilessly, memories flashed through his mind—moments of laughter, love, and fervent faith. He thought of his wife, his daughter, and his Lord, contemplating the love that had inspired him to endure so much for the sake of others. Time stretched painfully, each agonizing minute a reminder of the suffering he had seen inflicted upon others.

Yet amidst the torment, a profound peace washed over him as the hours passed, the pain blurring into a distant hum. In those final moments, as darkness encroached upon his vision, he summoned the last vestiges of his strength. With every ounce of love that had filled his heart across the decades, he breathed his final words in Latin, a prayer woven into the very fabric of his soul. "*Ignosce, diligatis envicem, nunc coepi.*" Forgive, love one another, now I begin.

And as his spirit slipped away, he felt a weight lift, a liberation into eternity, surrounded by the echoes of love that transcended pain. The shouts of the crowd faded into the background, and in that moment, he became one with Christ.

I

THE POWERS OF HELL

Chapter 1

Dublin

THE NOT-SO-DISTANT FUTURE

Everyone assumed they would marry. After all, they had been best friends since Catholic grade school. But instead, they chose to give their lives and their love to God and the church. He was enrolling in seminary to become a priest, and she was joining an abbey to become a bride of Christ.

Over their years growing up in Ireland, they had strengthened each other, resisting the temptations that often ensnared the young and the virtuous. Although their righteous choices had set them apart from their peers, they didn't care. They had each other.

When temptation hadn't come to them, they had gone to it. They had found moments to be alone together, and with intentions that were nothing short of holy, they would touch each other in the most innocent of ways—a gentle caress on the cheek, a soothing head massage, or a comforting foot rub. They would trade off playing the role of the tempter. If one could endure a simple back rub without succumbing to sinful thoughts, the tempter would intensify their efforts, progressing to a chaste kiss or a breath in the ear. Each step had been more arousing, a further test of their resolve.

On the eve of taking their separate paths, they decided to play their ritual one last time. They both knew this time was different. This was their last chance to know the sins of the flesh. It was their last chance to affirm their choices so they could never look back and wonder "what if." But most importantly, this was their last night to know each other.

And so they did.

The result was far from what they expected. Years of denial and curiosity culminated in an act of lovemaking that was nothing short of miraculous. They had secretly hoped for the experience to be awkward, brief, painful, or even repulsive, allowing them to move forward on their chosen paths without regret. But over the years of driving each other to distraction, they had unwittingly gained a profound understanding of each other's desires. Their intimacy transcended the realms of the physical. It was a moment of irreplaceable connection, enviable to even the most seasoned couples.

When it was over, as the angels of their innocence flew sadly away, they held each other and wept. Their tears were not for the sin they had committed but for the revelation that this act between those who loved each other could never be sinful. They wept because—having eaten the fruit of the tree of knowledge—they knew they were meant for one another. The paths they had chosen had been, just yesterday, innocent and perfect. Now they wept for the realization that those paths had become, in a heartbeat and a quiet gasp, heartbreakingly wrong for them. Yet, they could not abandon their commitments. They might see each other again one day, but never again like this.

In their innocence, they had veiled their eyes from learning about reproduction, fearing that even talking about sex could lead to sin. Thus, they believed the old wives' tale: You can't get pregnant the first time. So as she left him that night and stepped into the confines of the nunnery the next day, her mind and heart were filled with doubts and regrets—but she was not yet aware of the being beginning to fill her body.

◆

SHE HANDED HIM her baby with great hesitation, running her finger down the soft skin of the child's arm one last time. "Goodbye, love," she said and let him take the girl into his arms. He swaddled the child in a thick cotton blanket and cradled her against his chest. The mother fastened the buttons of his voluminous black coat, enveloping both him and the baby in its warm embrace. This was all secret; no one must know. She stuffed the empty sleeves into the coat's pockets and watched him walk away.

The past twenty-four hours had left the young seminarian emotionally numb. Now, as he leaned into the bitter, wet wind and trudged toward the remote monastery, he went over the past day again in his head. *Perhaps none of this had happened, and he had simply fallen down a flight of stairs and knocked himself into a coma full of hallucinations?*

Maybe "emotionally numb" wasn't quite correct; he could still feel the horror and the heartbreak, the ecstasy and the devastation. Above all, he felt the weight—the incredible burden of the tiny life he was responsible for. What he felt was not numbness after all but rather dissociation from the world around him. He might have gotten up and bathed, eaten and brushed his teeth, gotten dressed, and checked his mail, but it was as if he was merely watching himself follow his routine. Cotton bunting enveloped his senses.

He boosted the baby higher under the thick wool trench coat—a graduation gift from his mother.

"Every good priest must have a fine wool coat," she'd said, beaming, her Irish accent making even these simple words sound more like a song than a statement. "You'll be asked to call on people at odd hours, and you can't have the Irish damp gettin' in your lungs," she'd explained, brushing bits of lint and paper off her son's broad shoulders. He could tell she was trying not to cry. His father had died some years before, and now, with him leaving, she would be alone. "You're a noble man," she had said, patting his arm and wiping her eye. "You were quite the child too. Never fussed. Never gave me trouble or fought with the other boys." Her chest puffed out, and she raised her head. "You were always different. A special child, you were."

Now here he was cradling his own child in his arms, and he found himself chuckling. He recalled his mother's words about his own quiet babyhood. In almost two hours of walking in this bitter, wet, cutting cold, this baby hadn't made a peep.

"She gets that from me," he said out loud, then suddenly halted. "My little one. She's like me, inheriting my wee ways. I am her father, and she is my daughter. And she's quiet, like me. Or . . . she's dead, and I've done her in?"

The sudden fear sparked a primal protective instinct within him. Panicked, he started to struggle with his coat, desperate to see his daughter and reassure himself that the Irish cold had not killed her, and this fabric prison had not suffocated her.

As he spun, madly trying to free the coat sleeves that had been tucked into his pockets, a terrifying, unfamiliar voice deep inside began taunting him. "She's dead, and you've killed her. You'll go to hell and deserve it, you baby killer. This is your punishment for your ways with her mother."

His panic escalated, and he spun forcefully, trying to bite a sleeve now with growling determination and gnashing teeth. The young seminarian was like a black cyclone twisting across the wet, muddy plain.

Just then, a monk hustled around the corner, going to fetch water from a quickly freezing well. His first thought was to run away from the rabid Sasquatch that had apparently wandered near the monastery and was now grunting, growling, and flying in circles, trying to bite at its own arm. Instead, as monks are known to do, he disregarded his own safety in compassion for the poor creature's plight.

As the monk slowly crept up close enough to the beast to see through the icy fog, he saw that this was not a rabid Sasquatch but instead a man in some strange distress. Not taking any more chances than compassion required, he kept his distance and began beating the water bucket with its wooden ladle. His lifelong vow of silence was being tested like never before.

The sight of the monk sent the man to his knees. "Please. What if I've killed my baby? I've carried her in the cold too long, and I cannot get to her."

The monk rushed to his aid, silencing him with a finger to his lips as he quickly began to unbutton the coat. A warm cloud of trapped air escaped and hit both of them like a wave, carrying the most powerful scent known to man: that love potion babies produce from every pore. Both men gasped as this blast of pheromone-charged air hit them, and of course, that deep breath cemented their intoxication.

The next instant, the monk saw a slideshow of images.

the world upside down

the world *on fire*

blood dripping into eyes

red hair

the Ring of the Fisherman

a baby

the man in front of him

The monk's eyes flew open again in time to watch as the man pulled back the blanket, revealing a pair of large blue eyes mirroring his own.

"My daughter." He gently stroked the baby girl's cheek. "My life."

Chapter 2

Dublin

Rebecca Murphy was packing up her home in Dublin, one room at a time. At least, that was what she meant to be doing. She stood in the front room, a vase in one hand and a piece of butcher paper in the other, staring out the picture window onto the road. Men and women walked purposefully, children straggling behind or running ahead. One, a young girl with red pigtails, caught her eye and made her feel like she had butterflies in her stomach. No, the wrong age. It had been three years since she'd given up her child and left the abbey, her heart torn in two. Giving birth to that baby girl had changed her; she knew then that her life's goal—to honor God—would follow a different path than she'd planned. She must be a mother.

Justin had remained in seminary, fully devoted to his first love, though Rebecca could never understand how, once he saw those blue eyes looking back up at him, he didn't melt and change course on the spot. Their night of passion and their child born of love were both pleasant and painful memories.

When she had met Simon during her first semester at Trinity College, his sense of humor and bright smile had won her over immediately.

She was ready to laugh, ready to be swept up in something other than longing for the past. He was a graduate student, she an undergrad, and despite knowing it might scare him off immediately, she'd brought up children on the third date.

"I understand this is forward. I'm sure it sounds crazy, actually . . ." They sat on a bench near East Campus.

"What?" Simon asked, pushing his hair from his eyes. The day was unseasonably warm, the slanted light shining through the trees.

"I—I'd like children. I mean, I'd like them quickly once I marry."

Simon chuckled. "Yes indeed, that's a bit forward of you, I'd say." She was worried he'd hop up and leave, this man she felt drawn to, whose easygoing ways set her anxieties at rest. But he didn't. Instead, he wiped her own hair from her eyes, then kissed her on the cheek, then the lips, soft and slow. "I don't mind a forward girl," he had said then. "I'm flattered. I don't mind at all."

Rebecca shook herself from her stupor and finished wrapping the vase, then placed it in the box on the table. She looked around the room at photos of their life together so far, still hanging on the walls.

They'd married in the spring, the cherry blossoms in the Rose Garden at Trinity in bloom, and the picture of that day hung above the couch: Simon in linen slacks and a vest, Rebecca in a simple white A-line dress with lace overtop. There had been a strong breeze, and her hand held the veil in place on her head as the tulle fluttered to the side. It had been a glorious day—all the promise in the world.

They'd tried almost immediately to conceive, but nothing. Months and months of nothing. She finally visited the doctor, who confirmed that due to complications with her first birth, she would not conceive again. To help Justin, she told everyone including Simon that the father was from another town and wanted nothing to do with her or the baby. Simon was heartbroken about her infertility, wanting children himself, but kind.

"I have you, my darling. That's enough."

And while he seemed to move on, Rebecca's deep desire to have a child quickly turned to depression. She kept up with her studies and tried her best to remain upbeat around Simon, but inside, she was in a pain she could not describe to anyone. No one understood. If only Justin was there. They would simply give one another a look, and that look would communicate multitudes.

Simon finished school the same month Rebecca graduated, and as he began looking for work as a professor, Rebecca pushed to leave Ireland. She suggested Rome—far from the constant reminders of her childless state and close to the epicenter of the Catholic Church: her beloved Vatican. Though she had lost her child, she had not lost her faith.

She stood now with the gold crucifix they kept above their door in her hand—Simon's concession for what he knew meant so much to Rebecca. Although Simon had been raised Catholic, he questioned everything to do with religion, calling its followers "sheep." He respected Rebecca but pushed back against her devotion, enjoying the hot fire he could spark in his wife when challenging her beliefs. She, for the most part, found Simon's elitist nonsense endearing. Though their Dublin friends and family thought there had never been a more philosophically odd couple, they were in love, no matter their differences.

Simon had agreed to the move, hoping that it would ease Rebecca's sadness and sense of pressure. "We'll have a new start," he'd said, his arms wrapped around her. Then he pointed at the cross. "We'll put this above our *new* door. Right down the street from the *big boss*."

Rebecca had laughed and kissed him over and over again, thrilled for a new beginning, for this loving man.

She wrapped the crucifix carefully now and put it inside the box marked "sitting room." Tomorrow, they would say their farewells, lock the door, and leave for their exciting new life in the historical center of Rome.

◆

ROME

Simon had been slightly reticent about leaving home, though Rome's rich art history was certainly a draw. Most of all, though, he wanted to give Rebecca a reprieve from the constant reminder of her infertility; in the end, he agreed that Rome would offer them both proximity to their passions.

The first thing he noticed was the light: so much brighter than it had ever shone in Dublin. The warmth on his skin, the heat rising from the pavement, the way the sunlight hit the statues and fountains with such brilliance was an entirely different mood from the dark, rainy streets of his hometown. Rebecca seemed to revel in it, too, instantly happier, distracted by the Eternal City.

The Murphys' apartment building stood in an ancient section of Rome, near the lively and charming Piazza Navona. On long walks, they enjoyed the echoes of the buzzing city bouncing between the stone buildings, the sound of water splashing in sculpted marble fountains, and the greetings from neighbors to shopkeepers cascading from windows and doorways, a chorus as pleasant as birdsong.

Their new apartment was small but cozy, an inviting, cool place to return to after each day of discovery. The shuttered window of their living area looked down over the narrow, black-cobbled street, and they woke each morning to the sounds of the city. They would open their eyes, remember their good fortune, and look at one another with bright smiles like children on Christmas morning. Simon was pleased to have the old Rebecca back—full of life and hope.

One evening, she was practically floating when she met Simon at the door.

"Oh, Simon! It's a sign, for sure! The good Lord has shown us that Rome is where He wants us!" Her hand was unconsciously making gentle circles on her stomach. "I'm certain God has many blessings in store for us here in Rome. You won't believe it!" she bubbled.

She led him down the hall and into their living room, where a dark-haired man sat. The man was so strikingly handsome that even Simon noticed, but before suspicion or jealousy could take root, he caught sight of the man's priesthood collar.

"Simon," Rebecca exclaimed, smiling like she was about to surprise him with the perfect gift. "This is Father Kelly. I ran into him today when I was looking for our home church."

Father Kelly rose, and a warm smile lit his face as he leaned in and shook Simon's hand. The men exchanged polite greetings while Simon tried to determine why Rebecca was quite this excited. He understood her passion for the church, but next to finding a redhead in Ireland, finding a priest in Rome had to be one of life's easier challenges.

"I'm sorry, I don't . . ." Simon mumbled, scratching his head. He looked at his wife in time to see her snap out of an adoring gaze that had not been aimed at him. His initial suspicions flared again, but Rebecca's laughter quickly doused the flames.

"Simon, my darling, I'm sorry. I'm still in shock myself. Father Kelly and I went to school together back in Ireland!"

Father Kelly laughed and looked at Rebecca. "And we were both going to enter God's service, but—" Father Kelly's smile flickered just enough to show that there was regret within this fond memory.

"But . . ." Rebecca continued, her smile turning to a bitten lip. She turned to Father Kelly and their eyes met, but quickly, she shrugged and turned back to Simon. "It wasn't meant to be," she said. "But none of that matters now! Because here we are, and here you are, and praise God, it truly is a miracle."

Simon stood flummoxed and silent.

Father Kelly steadied him with a hand on his shoulder. "Rebecca, do you have a drink for two parched fellas?" he asked.

As Rebecca scurried off to fetch the drinks and give the men a moment to themselves, the tall and impossibly handsome Father Kelly turned to Simon, who was still trying to sort out which way was up.

"Simon, my friend?" Kelly queried.

Simon found himself staring at the black buttoned-up chest of Father Kelly, and as he raised his eyes to the priest's face, he felt like a kid at the base of a redwood. Simon knew he could never compete with this man. Not only was the priest tall, but he was also broad-shouldered and small-waisted, with alabaster skin pulled over cheekbones so chiseled that even in his eighties, he would look fifty.

Simon would learn later that the teen girls called Father Kelly "Father What-A-Waste." He would never correct them for making fun of Father Kelly because they weren't wrong. Simon agreed. Here was a mountain of good DNA going to waste.

Simon would also learn that what wasn't being wasted was the purity of Father Kelly's heart. It wasn't just his beauty that was so disarming; it was also his aura—the feeling that exudes from the truly pure of heart who suspect no one and see only good in everyone.

But for now, Simon was still dazed.

"Simon! Friend!" Father Kelly's laugh snapped Simon back to some of his usual ability to speak.

"Aye," Simon mumbled. "Were you born or were you carved?"

"What?" Father Kelly laughed.

"You look like one of those damned marble statues they've got all over this damned city—forgive my language—but look atcha. Smile for me again."

Father Kelly obliged, his smile even more endearing this time.

"Stop it, for all that's holy! It's too damned much, Kelly. Could you at least have a cavity or somethin'? Maybe let me break your nose to put a bump in it."

Father Kelly laughed even harder.

"Well, if you're here for my wife, I can't stop her."

Kelly stopped laughing and put both hands on Simon's shoulders. A jovial seriousness came over him, and he spoke to Simon in the way only the pure of heart can. "Simon, no. That's why I wanted to be alone with you."

"Oh God," Simon groaned with a slight smirk showing through. "It's me you want!"

"Now, hold on." Father Kelly laughed.

"Let me get my bags and tell poor Rebecca. It turns out the dreamy priest has a crush on Simon, and I'm off to live with him now. Who knew divine intervention included two-timing?"

Rebecca walked in with drinks to see Father Kelly bent over with laughter. "My—What on earth?" she asked.

Simon relieved her of the drinks and ushered her back out of the room. "Give us another minute, love."

"Simon," Father Kelly panted, still holding his stomach, "now you've got to promise to stop. You're going to kill me right here, and you know it's a mortal sin for an Irishman to die with an unfinished drink."

"Well, so it is," Simon relented and handed Father Kelly his glass. "*Sláinte*."

"Simon, and let me get this out, you hear me? Your wife and I were good friends. Very good friends. But that is all." Simon saw something flicker in his eyes. "She was always excited by all things Catholic and it seems that hasn't changed, so you know that to her, a coincidence— no matter how mundane—is a miracle worthy of being reported to the Vatican."

"Aye," said Simon, taking a seat on the couch.

"So, I agree it's a blessing we've found each other again, and I pray you will become my parishioners, and I can have my first true friends who think of me as Justin first and Father Kelly second. But it is still 'Father,' Simon."

Simon raised his glass in acknowledgment.

"I took my vows of celibacy when I was ordained, and I take them very seriously. You can always know without a doubt that I do not, will not, and cannot ever have any motivation toward your wife other than a loving friendship. All right?"

"All right," Simon said, grateful that Father Kelly had addressed the issue head-on, which reassured him that this was a man of his word. "I thank you for that. We'll be friends, then. The three of us."

"Grand," Father Kelly said and raised his glass in return. "*Sláinte*."

Chapter 3

Rome

Under a radiant blue Roman sky, Father Kelly was hastily cross-ing St. Peter's Square when he heard his name shouted across the grand plaza. He turned to find Rebecca and Simon, who had been members of his Santa Maria parish for the past year, waving him down with beaming smiles.

Bouncing on Rebecca's hip was a little girl with a blaze of sunset-colored curls.

"Who is this little darling?" he asked, noting that the girl's gaze seemed drawn to his clerical collar.

"Katerina," Rebecca said, shifting the child's weight. "Katie, to us."

Her answer only added to Kelly's confusion. The girl was beyond toddler age; she must have been born before he had taken his orders.

As Rebecca set the girl down on the cobblestones, the child spun around, taking in the bustling crowds.

Simon, seeing Father Kelly's bafflement, teased in a thick brogue, "She's our daughter. Ye old immaculate conception, Father."

"What? I don't understand?"

"Simon!" Rebecca elbowed her husband, rolling her eyes at his sacri-legious streak. "The adoption—"

"Adoption?"

"Yes, it was finalized last week," Rebecca said. "We've been a family for exactly six days."

"Congratulations! I had no idea." Father Kelly waggled his eyebrow with a ruffled look.

"We didn't want to get our hopes up too much," Simon said. "Or yours."

"Yet here you are—parents! I couldn't be more pleased!" Father Kelly finally broke into a grin. His heart had ached at the sight of Rebecca with a husband that first day they had met in Rome, and now Rebecca was with a *child*. A girl that would be about the same age as theirs, and even looked like what he envisioned their daughter would look like now, but he was happy for her. It was bittersweet, but he knew he was destined for this work. If only he'd been allowed both—heavenly dedication and earthly love.

He knew that doctors had concluded that Rebecca would never conceive again. Father Kelly recalled her trembling hands, tears of frustration, and shame.

When Simon had agreed to join one of their counseling sessions, Rebecca had wept, "We've tried everything. Simon, I'm so sorry that I can't have your baby!" Sliding from her chair and curling into a ball on the cold floor, she'd clenched her grandmother's rosary beads in white-knuckled hands.

Father Kelly had pushed down the urge to rush to her. Instead, he'd waited to see how her irreverent husband would respond to his wife's grief.

Simon had fallen to his knees beside Rebecca, kissing her fingers with the rosary still threaded through them. He pulled her to his chest, not saying a word, pressing his wife's cheek to his heart until her sobbing gave way to quieter tears and deeper breathing. Simon stroked his wife's raven hair, pushing wet strands from her cheeks and curling them behind her seashell ear. Finally, he said, "Becca, I will always love you no matter what, and we will have our child in God's way."

Rebecca pulled back, eyes widening. "Is this a cruel joke?" her raised eyebrows seemed to ask. Even around Kelly, Simon rarely talked about God unless he was criticizing religion. Rebecca had thought he had only come to Santa Maria to please her.

Softly, she inquired, "What do you mean, in God's way?"

"There are many ways God gives people children," Simon had replied. "Becoming pregnant is only one possibility." Father Kelly labored to reconcile these words with the aggressive disbelief in religion Simon had always displayed. Perhaps, as Rebecca had always hoped would happen, Simon was beginning to open up to God and the church.

Regardless, Kelly knew that he could not have expected more compassion from even the most religious of husbands in his parish. If Rebecca had said anything in response, Father Kelly couldn't recall it; what he remembered was the relief that had crept across her face. It was like the first streak of light that pierces a bleak, stormy sky.

Simon had said, "We will have our child in God's way," and here was that child pulling on Father Kelly's cassock and pointing to the sky. The fact that his faith was being bolstered by Simon, of all people, made Father Kelly's head spin. There was something familiar about her button nose, her quick eyes that seemed to take everything in, and the fiery ginger hair that curled in tiny ringlets around her ears.

He reached down, scooped up the giggling miracle, and planted a kiss on her cheek. As she continued pointing upward, he followed the girl's fingertip to the top of the towering granite Egyptian obelisk that stood in the center of the square, eternally reaching for the sun and the sky in one of man's ancient attempts to touch the divine.

"Yes, child, isn't it spectacular? It's over four thousand years old. At the very top, there used to be a metal ball that contained the ashes of Julius Caesar. That piece is in a museum now. Caesar probably feels betrayed because he no longer gets to sit up there and look down on us. *Et tu, Brute?*"

It was not unusual for Father Kelly to sprinkle his speech with Latin. He had fallen in love with the language in seminary, so he believed he was merely being clever, quoting Shakespeare's version of Caesar's last words.

But his mouth fell open when Katie looked him in the eye and answered, "*Nocent mihi.*"

The priest glanced at Rebecca and Simon for an explanation. His peripheral vision was filled with a hundred and forty saintly statues, all seeming to stare down at the girl. "How does she know Latin?"

Simon and Rebecca shared a look of astonishment. "Latin? She rarely says a word. How could she possibly know Latin?" Rebecca asked, taking the child from Father Kelly.

Father Kelly barely noticed as the girl slipped from his hands into her mother's. Then his logical mind stepped forward and reminded him that Simon had a history of getting a laugh in at what he called Father Kelly's "superstitious side."

"Oh, I see what's happened here." Father Kelly grinned and began talking to the child in his best Irish brogue. "It was a wee leprechaun up to all sorts of shenanigans that came to visit you, now, wasn't it?" He cut his eyes at Simon. "A wee mischievous leprechaun must have sneaked into your room at night, and while your dear sainted parents slept away in the other room, he taught you Latin phrases so that you could both have a good laugh at the silly, superstitious priest. Well, b'gosh and b'gorry, you can tell that little leprechaun you both got me. You got me good!"

Simon stepped toward Kelly. "Seriously, Father. I swear. I've not taught her anything. She rarely speaks at all."

Father Kelly cocked his head. "Stop teasing," he said. "Simon, you've been tutoring her. Admit it! You've brought her to the square before and—"

"No," Simon replied. "This is her first visit. When in the last six days would we have had the time to plan something like this, even if we'd wanted to? She knows a few Italian words because she was found at a monastery, but we were told the monks mostly spoke to her in English. They told us to be patient, and she would open up in her own time."

Anxiety began to color Rebecca's face. "That was gibberish, Father. It must have been. It didn't sound like Latin to me."

"Becca, I read from ancient scriptures every day. I'm one of the few people left in the world who's actually fluent in Latin. And Katie just said—"

Rebecca interrupted him, crouching in front of her daughter. "Katie, tell Mummy the truth. Do these words mean anything to you?" She asked Father Kelly to repeat the Latin phrase.

"*Nocent mihi,*" he said, watching the girl for any reaction.

"Katie? Did you hear Father Kelly?" Rebecca asked as Simon knelt beside her.

Katie didn't flinch or shrink from their inquisition. She looked from one parent to the other before focusing on Father Kelly. Finally, in a soft but certain voice, she said, "They hurt me."

Simon, obviously protective no matter how recently this girl had become his daughter, looked ready to do battle. His face was grim but composed as he reached for Katie's hands. "Hurt you? Who hurt you, sweetheart? Tell Daddy."

Rebecca swept Katie into her arms. "You're frightening her, Simon."

"She doesn't look frightened to me," Father Kelly said excitedly. "She just translated *nocent mihi* into English." He continued, "*Qui vobis noceat?*"

Simon protested, positioning himself in front of his wife and daughter. "Come on, Father Kelly, she's only four years—"

But Father Kelly repeated, "*Qui vobis noceat?*"

When Katie didn't respond, Kelly, undeterred, tried English. "Who hurt you?"

"That's a translation too?" Rebecca asked.

"Yes. Who hurt you, Katie?" Kelly repeated, drawing closer.

The child studied the faces of the adults, then answered, "Many people."

Father Kelly pulled back, thinking furiously.

Rebecca was amazed. "This is the most she's spoken to anyone since we've had her. Right, Simon?"

"It's the most she's spoken at all!" her husband cried. "But what is going on? Where is the Latin coming from? Does she have some kind of—psychic—?"

"Never use that word!" Father Kelly's rebuke clearly stunned Simon and Rebecca. "I'm sorry," he backpedaled. "But it's not—it's just—it's not safe." He was now stern as stone.

The tense moment was interrupted as the bells of the greatest church in all Christendom began to ring, signaling that Mass would soon begin. With the peals of the bells echoing between them, the curving colonnades flanking the square seemed to sweep believers and nonbelievers alike into the maternal arms of Mother Church.

"What do you mean it's not safe?" Simon asked. "Do you know what she means, Father?"

Father Kelly looked around at their public surroundings, then quietly said, "Follow me."

◆

IN SILENCE, PARENTS and child followed their priest, who led them down the towering central nave, between the marbled walls, past sculptures and tombs, beneath the enormous semicircular vaults, to the Chair of Saint Peter. Father Kelly ushered them into a pew, seating himself behind the new family. It never failed to fill him with awe:

the mass of golden angels and sculptured rays of light that seemed to burst through the stone walls above the throne, with a stained glass dove—representing the Holy Spirit—at the center. The sense of lineage expressed physically in this place reminded him of his purpose.

He watched Katie as Simon pointed to the suspended ancient wooden chair where, according to lore, St. Peter had actually sat while preaching to the Roman faithful.

"Isn't it beautiful, Katie?" he said. "Do you know who sculpted the bronze casing that holds the chair? I'll give you a hint: the same artist who designed the bridge we crossed on our way here."

"Angels," the child said.

"Yes. Good! The one with the angels. Remember the artist's name?"

"Angels."

"Yes. Six hundred years ago, he carved angels on the bridge, as well as on this altar. He's my favorite artist; do you remember his—"

"Angels! Angels!" the little girl repeated. "Angels!"

Simon's mounting exasperation was stilled by Rebecca's hand on his knee. She gave him a look that said, *She's a child, Professor Murphy.*

He was clearly startled when Katie shouted, "I see them! Angels! Angels!"

She pointed to the air all around, her finger swooping and curving above her.

Simon and Rebecca blushed as parishioners turned toward them, some clearly annoyed by the disruption and others delighted by the presence of a precocious child. Father Kelly, however, saw only Katie's gaze.

He believed her and wished desperately to see through her eyes. Normally, Bernini's art thrilled him—the sun above the gilded bronze statues that surrounded the Chair of Saint Peter made it look as if the chair were drifting through soft clouds—but now he had an unusual sense of disappointment. He too wanted to see the angels.

Once the sonorous, centuries-old ritual of Mass began, echoing up through Michelangelo's richly decorated dome, there were no further outbursts from Katie. She sat perfectly still between her parents, seemingly transfixed. Behind the trio, Father Kelly tried to concentrate on the liturgy, the words that had inscribed themselves on his soul when he was a child himself. But he found himself contemplating the riddle of Katie's outbursts.

When Mass concluded, the family joined the crowd shuffling toward the sunlit square, but near the exit of the Basilica, Father Kelly made his way to a pair of intricately sculpted white-marble Baroque cherubs, who were holding a font of holy water. "May I bless your new family?"

Rebecca and Simon agreed, likely relieved that Mass had returned him to his usual pleasant demeanor. Father Kelly dipped his right thumb into the water and made the sign of the cross on the couple's foreheads. "May the peace of the Lord be with you and your family always."

Next, he stooped to gather Katie in his arms. As he rose with her, the girl reached for his rosary, turning its crucifix upside down. "This way," she said.

"No, my child, this is the proper way." He smiled, gently readjusting the crucifix.

Simon quipped, "She enjoys turning things on their head, I guess."

"Ugh, just like her father," Rebecca said, a smile playing on her lips.

Father Kelly dipped his thumb back into the holy water. Katie met his gaze and once again reached for the cross, flipping it upside down and pushing it against his chest. Their eyes locked, and he hesitated, but decided to let her have her way. He touched his thumb to her forehead. "May the peace of the Lord be—"

Those waiting their turn to touch the holy water would later describe the scene to anyone who would listen: the young priest suddenly screaming out in pain, his body in spasms, his eyes wide with shock as though he had been electrocuted or stabbed. The parishioners would also remark that the child was oddly still—she did not cry, protest, or even squirm.

In the days that followed, Father Kelly would spend feverish hours journaling in a tormented attempt to articulate his experience. His words were repetitive, sketchy, and thoroughly inadequate. Not even Latin would provide any relief.

"Father! Somebody, help!" Rebecca shouted, snatching Katie away from the priest.

Worshippers swarmed Father Kelly, propping him up until his pained face relaxed. After a few slow, deep breaths, he seemed to regain his composure.

"Father! What happened? Are you all right?"

Disoriented and flustered, the clergyman nevertheless brushed away Simon's concern. "Yes. I—I'm sorry. I was—I didn't feel well for a moment. Forgive me."

"We'll walk you back to your quarters," Simon said, offering a hand.

"No, thank you. No need. I have business here still. Let's just—may I finish?"

The surrounding parishioners pressed forward to watch Father Kelly dip his thumb into the font once more. He brought his trembling hand to Katie's forehead, pausing for a moment. The crowd held its collective breath until he had completed the sign of the cross.

"May the peace of the Lord be with you, Katie—*sempre*."

After the blessing, Rebecca asked Simon to take Katie outside so she could make sure Father Kelly was okay in private.

"Justin, are you okay? What was that all about?"

"I'm not sure. I need some time and space to process it," answered a very shaken priest. He leaned closer to Rebecca, his voice barely a whisper. "She's the same age our daughter would be now. And she . . . she looks like what I remember."

Rebecca's smile trembled, a rush of emotion flooding her. "A mother knows her child's face," she said, her voice thick with devotion. "A mother never forgets. Not for a single moment, and now it seems a father doesn't forget either." Joy surged through Justin, overwhelming him, and tears swelled in his eyes.

"But to put any lingering doubts to rest, I also had DNA tests done. She is 100 percent ours," Rebecca said as he pulled her into a tight embrace.

"Justin," she murmured, her voice steadied with certainty, "I made you a promise back then, and I make it to you again now: I won't tell a soul until you say it's okay. I'll carry this secret to my grave if I must."

"Thank you, Becca," he said, his heart pounding with a mixture of relief and shock.

Chapter 4

Rome

Standing in their cramped foyer with her phone pressed to her ear, Rebecca watched Simon and Katie playing on the living room floor. His manner was easy, and his inquisitiveness as he edged closer to the girl, surrounded by building blocks, somehow made her think of their time at Trinity.

In those carefree student days, late nights at the pub had been balanced by early-morning study sessions over strong tea or milky coffee at a favorite café. When they'd first met under the arches of the college's old library, Simon had been working on a master's degree in history while Rebecca had been studying child psychology.

The nostalgia she felt for the hours they'd spent working in agreeable silence was quickly followed by a twinge of guilt. Their lives were different now—in exactly the way they'd wanted for so long.

On the other end of the line, the phone rang three times. Rebecca turned away and whispered, "Please be home, Maly. Please."

The move to Rome had been good for them. Simon had earned his doctorate in art history at Sapienza University and then became a faculty member. Rebecca had found her dream job: working with children at the acclaimed Bambino Gesù Hospital. Her work there had elevated her already strong sense of purpose and furthered her resolve to have a child of her own. It had also brought her a new friend and confidante, Dr. Maly Rin.

The tiny Cambodian doctor walked the hallways of her hospital with composure and compassion. Things got done under her rule. She found solutions to knotty problems, burned through bureaucracy, and did everything possible to improve the lives of Rome's children, one family at a time. Rebecca secretly thought of her not as head of pediatrics but as Champion of Child Wellbeing.

Indeed, without Maly, the Murphys might never have become parents. One day over lunch, when Rebecca had shared her disappointment over being childless, it was Maly who had delicately suggested adoption. When the Murphys had agreed, her deft hand made swift work of Katie's adoption process.

"Mummy, Mummy, look!" Rebecca turned to see Katie pointing excitedly at a tower of blocks. The girl had to stand to add blocks to the precarious structure. Simon clapped his hands, enjoying their daughter's handiwork.

"Oh! Would you look at that? Keep going, sweetheart," Rebecca encouraged. She listened to the phone ring and watched Katie ease a yellow triangle into position atop the tower.

"Easy does it," Simon cautioned.

"It's so tall," Rebecca said admiringly.

"Hello?"

Rebecca turned away to talk to Maly, only to be startled by a commotion behind her. She turned back to see the blocks—a present from Maly herself, who had said all children should have at least one wooden toy—crashing to the floor. Katie's squeals were a mix of delight and disappointment.

"Hello?"

"Maly, it's Rebecca."

"Oh, lovely. I was just thinking about you. How did Katie like St. Peter's? Perfect weather for a visit, no?"

"Oh, well . . . you know, it was—" Rebecca searched for words. Behind her, Simon and Katie were gathering the blocks, and Simon was asking Katie if she could make the tower even taller this time.

"Overwhelming for a child, maybe," Maly suggested.

"Yeah, and for adults too. It was—"

As Rebecca retreated into the kitchen in silence, Maly filled the gap with casual chatter. After Rebecca made a few meager attempts to respond, Maly hesitated and asked, "Becca, is something wrong?"

"Well, we hope not," Rebecca said, relieved to get to the point.

"Tell me. What is it?"

"Maly, is there anything about Katie's past that I don't know? Should we have asked more questions before bringing her home?"

"More questions?" Maly echoed.

"Look, I don't want to sound ungrateful."

"Not at all," Maly reassured. "Never, Becca."

"We love being parents."

"I know you do."

"But I—Simon and I—we need to learn more about Katie."

Maly had told Rebecca that information about birth parents could shed light on temperament or health concerns, should either arise, but she'd warned that in this case, Katie's past was a dense forest and they would be navigating without much information.

"Becca, you sound . . . has something happened?"

"Is it possible the monks know more? Would they be willing to meet with us?" Rebecca pleaded. "Perhaps if they know Katie has found a good and loving home—if Simon and I could ask them ourselves— they'll recall something that could help us."

"Those old souls, bless their hearts, dwell in a realm of their own. They are so steeped in faith that they are more likely to think of milk as coming from God than from a cow. So they know exactly where she came from."

"Where?" Rebecca asked, involuntarily holding her breath.

"God," Maly said.

"Well, of course!"

"Becca, I understand that adoption is difficult, and rest assured, I will help all that I can. It's typical to be flustered by the onslaught of challenges. I know it's overwhelming."

Maly was clearly trying to help, but her calming words would not be enough.

"We have to speak to them. Or to someone. We have to know more, Maly."

◆

MONTE CASSINO

FOUR YEARS EARLIER, a monk at Monte Cassino pulled open the medieval monastery's thick wooden door to fetch the morning paper and, in the predawn darkness, nearly somersaulted over a milk crate. Anyone else would have cursed. But not Paolo, who for decades had lived under the monastic Rule of Saint Benedict.

Sitting where he'd fallen on the dewy stone path, the monk did a quick inventory of body and soul, reckoned he had survived the tumble, and blessed the occasion as another sign of God's providence. He then turned his grateful attention to the milk crate, which was most likely a charitable offering from a local farmer.

Pulling away the thick blanket, he discovered an infant gazing up at him.

"Praise the Lord!" he exclaimed. As he stood to survey his surroundings, he called out in faint hope that whoever had left the child might be nearby.

"*Buongiorno?* Hello?"

Only the baby answered, gurgling and cooing from within its swaddling. The old man leaned closer, admiring the baby's pure white skin, patches of red hair, and alert eyes. "What on earth?" he asked aloud, wondering how one such as this had come to be in Italy. With a weathered thumb, he gently touched the child's chubby cheek lightly dusted with freckles.

Serenity overwhelmed him—the kind of peace a monk seeks through decades of prayer and meditation. He smiled with his five remaining teeth as he dropped to the ground again, though more gently this time.

Closing his eyes, he breathed deeply, savoring the purest moments he had ever experienced. A vibration coursed through his body, and he trembled with ecstasy. He was transported through a vision of his life, beginning with his first arrival at Monte Cassino as a young, breathless monk.

Tears filled his cloudy eyes as the euphoria faded. Then he put his hands together in prayer and touched them to his forehead, bowing to the infant. "*Grazie, piccolo angelo caduto.* Thank you, little fallen angel," he said.

The morning was cold, and Paolo hurried the child inside to be near the fire that was struggling to heat the decrepit monastery.

◆

ROME

"As far as we know," Maly explained to Rebecca, "Paolo and his abbot quickly contacted the local authorities. There was an intense search, but Katie's parents were never found."

Maly had delivered Katie's scant biography before, and the latest recitation was once again not what Rebecca was asking about.

"But there has to be an explanation," Rebecca pressed.

"An explanation for what? Becca, you have to tell me what's going on."

Maly tensed as she listened to Rebecca's account of events at St. Peter's Square. Social service records had shown that many couples had considered adopting Katie as an infant but had failed to follow through. One couple had admitted that they both felt strange when holding the baby. Others had simply moved on, looking for someone different.

As the string of rejections had mounted, frustration had festered among Katie's caregivers. They found her remarkable and knew from experience that as she grew past her toddler years, her chances of finding a home would quickly dwindle. Adoptive parents preferred the experience of nurturing a child through the early stages of life.

Months before, when Rebecca had confided that she could not bear children, Maly had immediately thought of Katie, who was under her care as a physician. Cautiously, she had probed for more information. "You and Simon would be amazing parents. Are you open to other options?"

Rebecca had nodded and tucked her chin, recounting Simon's acceptance of her infertility and his suggestion about "God's way."

"If God wants it so," Rebecca replied wistfully, her eyes drifting skyward.

That day, Maly had found herself excited at the paired possibility: a family for the little girl who had become dear to her with only a few office visits and the fulfillment of her friend's greatest wish. When Rebecca first met the little girl at the monastery, it was the happiest Simon or Maly had ever seen her. Now, however, she feared that her matchmaking might have done the desperate couple a disservice. What had happened at the church was startling.

As Rebecca explained, Maly's gnawing concern grew. She faltered, then blurted, "Becca, sorry to interrupt, but you and Simon aren't considering annulling the adoption, are you?"

"No! We love Katie! I would never give her up again!"

"Again?"

"I mean . . . that . . . uh . . . she has been passed around so much. She is here to stay with us now and forever."

Relieved, Maly shook her shoulders, releasing the tension from her body. "I'm sorry, Becca. Some couples get cold feet. I had to ask."

"That's okay, I understand. But how do we help her? She's been having nightmares. She cries out, but when we go to calm her, she's sound asleep. I have a degree in child psychology, Maly. I should know how to help her, but I don't."

Maly recalled the little girl's unusual composure in her office and began to sense that Rebecca's concerns were valid. But as a doctor she needed to follow findings, not feelings.

"I know a little something about nightmares, Becca. Let's set up an appointment. Bring Katie in, and we'll run every cognitive and psychological test that we can. I know she's physically healthy. Let's make sure there isn't something else going on."

"Thank you, Maly."

"Give Katie a hug for me."

◆

HANGING UP THE phone, Rebecca joined Simon and Katie in the living room. She perched on the sofa as he rose from the floor and made a show of stretching.

"I think I could use some fresh air. Do you mind, Becca?"

"Where are you going?"

"Oh, just a walk," he shrugged.

"Just?"

Simon feigned innocence, but Rebecca quickly caught on. She knew him. "Cannoli!"

"Cannoli?" he countered, still playing along.

"Is that all you think about?" Rebecca asked, laughing and curling her legs under herself.

Simon walked over and laid his hands on her shoulders, looking into her eyes with a devilish grin. "You know it's not. There is also tiramisu!"

Rebecca let him lift her upright, but before their lips could meet, a glance past Simon revealed Katie watching them with the seriousness of a tiny judge in a courtroom. Simon followed his wife's gaze and reluctantly loosened his embrace.

"This is what mummies and daddies do when they love each other, sweetheart," he said, planting a rerouted kiss on his wife's cheek.

The little girl smiled, then returned to the wooden blocks that had begun to rise from the rug again like the obelisk in St. Peter's Square.

"You go. But don't forget to bring back something sweet for us," Rebecca said, giving her husband a friendly push before positioning herself cross-legged on the floor beside their daughter.

"Always," Simon promised, locking the door behind him.

Chapter 5

São Paulo

The temple in the heart of São Paulo held ten thousand worshippers, and on this sweltering Sunday morning, every seat was filled. Thousands of LED lights on the ceiling blinked in programmed patterns, creating a shimmering illumination over all the ecstatic, expectant faces.

The crowd swayed, sang, and prayed together, wild with excitement and spiritual fervor. Their God was good to them; they believed He had brought many of them material success, and in Brazil, that was no small thing. This belief, what those Northern Hemisphere snobs called the "prosperity gospel," was simply the truth. God loved His people, they had suffered enough, and now, He wanted them to succeed.

Finally, it was time for the sermon. A thin, middle-aged man in a dark suit with a white rabbinical-style shawl draped over his shoulders strode to the center of the dais and gazed out over the crowd. He raised his hands into the air to bestow blessings upon them. He smiled beatifically at his wife, a blonde woman seated in the front row and dressed immaculately in white. Then he gestured for silence, calming the murmurs of excitement that had greeted his entrance.

"My children, my people," he began in Portuguese. "May the light of Jesus shine upon you."

The assembled worshippers chanted the line back at him.

"My people, our time is at hand," he said. "For too long, Brazil has been ignored by those above. They call us—and our brothers and sisters in Africa—the global south. The brown people who are here to serve others. In Mexico, the people of the global south work on the farms and in the *maquiladoras*. Here in Brazil, we work in the mines. In the United States, the immigrants work in the homes of the rich, cleaning their toilets, making their food, raising their children. They are the very people without whom the entire society would collapse, and yet they are treated as garbage.

"But every day, the numbers tilt more and more in our favor, the balance shifts in our direction. My people, your faith is what makes you strong, and their lack of faith is what makes them weak. They believe in God, but only in the entitled way that the idle rich believe that life will simply work out for them. We know differently. We know that God loves us, but we also know that He rewards us for our faith. That faith is real and can be turned toward our goals. And the more people learn this message, the more powerful it becomes.

"My brothers and sisters, you must go forth into the world and spread the Word. You must tell the people who do not believe, and especially the people who hold false beliefs, that you are in possession of the truth. We must bring the truth from the global south to the misguided people of the north! We must, and we will!"

He went on in this vein for some time, speaking as if inciting them to a crusade. After thirty vehement minutes, he returned to his seat and allowed the service to continue, broadcast to millions of viewers across Brazil on the church's own TV and radio channels.

When the service was finally over and ten thousand followers were streaming out into São Paulo's sunbaked streets, he rose from his seat and disappeared down a private, dimly lit corridor to a small, unassuming door.

He opened the door and slipped quickly inside, locking it behind him. There, he carefully took off his shawl and folded it, placing it on a shelf above his head. When he turned around, he was smiling broadly.

In a voice so much softer than in his sermons that his followers might not have recognized it, he said, "It is so good to see you, *minha querida*."

"You were marvelous, Edhir," Djiana said, rising from a couch on the far side of the room, her dark hair flowing around her shoulders. She gestured to a large monitor that took up most of one wall in the lushly appointed office. "I watched the entire service. Your sermon was thrilling."

She moved forward to embrace him. When he pulled her close, Edhir could feel that she wore nothing beneath her floral-patterned silk dress. He growled in the back of his throat and ran his hands up and down her body as they kissed.

When they broke their embrace, he leaned against his desk and took a moment to slow his breathing.

"We are preparing them, my dear," he said, his voice filled with craftiness and self-satisfaction. "The time will not come for many years, but it will come. One day, La Igreja Universal do Deus will control all of Brazil, and after that, we will absorb the Catholics and make them our own. We will take our rightful place above all other faiths. And you, *minha querida* Djiana, will be by my side in our hour of triumph."

He stood and opened his arms, gazing up and down her body. Tugging softly at a knot of fabric, she dropped her dress to the floor in a shimmering heap and stepped toward him.

Chapter 6

Rome

Simon enjoyed strolling the ancient cobblestone streets of his adopted home, relishing the scents of sweet and savory dough baking in wood-fired ovens, the ancient buildings' reminders of their history, the sounds of a city so alive. These walks also nourished him with ideas for his lectures at the university. Rome was a living museum, a treasure trove of world art and history that constantly fueled his never-ending urge to enlighten.

While this section of Rome was rife with tourists, it suited the Murphys because their daily necessities were all within walking distance. This included Simon's favorite restaurant, Bella Ciao, located a pleasant fifteen-minute walk away in Trastevere, a picturesque medieval area south of Vatican City on the west bank of the Tiber River.

Walking there, Simon pondered one of his most fundamental issues with Catholicism: Why in the world wouldn't the church swap those dry, tasteless Communion wafers for the best cannoli any mortal could ever hope to taste? "Is sweetness not its own form of enlightenment? It's practically a holy experience!" he would often joke to Rebecca, rubbing his belly and licking his lips. "If only Jesus had served cannolis at the

Last Supper, the Blessed Sacrament would be both spiritually elevating and sumptuous."

Rebecca would reply, "Do you say these things just to make me crazy?"

"But of course, my love! It is my divine calling." He grinned, winking at her like a naughty cherub.

Rebecca had her own reasons for choosing their locale, of course. Basilica di Santa Maria, also in the heart of Trastevere, had been the first church ever to offer Mass to the public.

Bella Ciao was loud with diners and filled with the heavenly scent of pastries. Simon purchased one small box of his favorite dessert for his family before deciding that a second box might smooth the path of a visit to Father Kelly.

Simon's sense of kinship with the priest had continued to grow despite their differences in belief, and he appreciated the man's steady ability to take a joke rather than taking refuge in stone-faced indignation like so many other churchmen. This connection brought Simon to Santa Maria with delicacies that he hoped he might trade for some answers.

He knew Rebecca had been seeking the same thing on her call with Maly. He also knew his wife's training would be both a blessing and a curse when it came to understanding Katie's behavior. Neither he nor Rebecca wanted to use words like *psychic* or *paranormal*, but they were both struggling to make sense of Katie's strange interaction with Father Kelly.

Simon marched through the Piazza de Santa Maria, ignoring its eateries, bars, and street performers to head straight for the Santa Maria church.

"Simon." Father Kelly put down his pen and consulted his watch, looking absentminded rather than surprised to find a visitor at his office door. "Forgive me, but—"

"No, I don't have an appointment," Simon interrupted with a smile.

"Oh, good, so I haven't entirely lost my mind." Father Kelly rose to properly greet his visitor.

Simon noted that the usually impeccable Kelly looked unkempt. His hair was in disarray, and the top button of his cassock was undone. As Simon glanced at a journal that lay open on the desk, the priest hastily shut it.

"Sorry to intrude," Simon said. "But Becca insisted I thank you for your blessing today."

"Not necessary," Father Kelly said.

"We insist." Simon presented the box from Bella Ciao and waited as Father Kelly lifted the lid and the aroma of fresh cannoli infused the air.

Father Kelly closed his eyes and inhaled. "Oh my. Please give Becca my thanks. Can you visit a while?" he asked.

"Just for a little while," Simon fibbed. He sat down and wondered how he should begin. Rebecca usually took the lead when it came to discussions with the priest. Finally, he asked the obvious question. "Are you feeling all right? After the blessing and, you know, the way it affected you?"

Father Kelly remained silent, his eyebrows pinched.

Simon pushed, "Father, it's obvious something happened. I didn't want to discuss my daughter in public, but it wasn't just the blessing. It was also your reaction in the square when I said—"

Father Kelly cut Simon short. "You need to be careful with your choice of words, Simon. I meant no disrespect, but—"

"No, tell me. I was joking, mostly, when I said it."

"We can't joke about some things. Not in this climate," Father Kelly insisted.

"What climate? What are you talking about?"

Father Kelly grabbed his journal as though it might bring him stability. Rubbing his palm along the binding, he began, "It was not so long ago that one of our highest-ranking leaders, beloved in many circles, caused an uproar."

"Who?"

"Cardinal Carlo Martini, the Archbishop of Milan. Know the name?"

"No," Simon admitted.

"He was once a papal candidate, but the conclave rejected him, and I'm not sure he ever recovered."

"Many are called, few are chosen."

"Hmmm, yes, well, this was different. On his deathbed back in 2012, Martini could no longer curb his displeasure with Pope Benedict. He spoke harshly about the philosophical direction the pope had taken and—this is the part that outraged the Vatican—he scolded the Catholic Church, saying it was behind the times by at least two hundred years."

"Ha! Two hundred feels generous," Simon scoffed. "At this point, they're still debating if they should upgrade to the printing press or just stick to stone tablets!"

"This is serious, Simon. We have to be careful."

"Careful of what?" Simon exclaimed, throwing his hands in the air.

"For Katie's sake, please!" Father Kelly fell silent.

Simon took a breath to calm himself. "You've told me nothing."

Father Kelly continued in a lower voice. "Simon, there is a war in our church. It is fairly quiet now. But—"

"Factions, you mean. Politics." This was familiar territory for Simon. His aggravation subsided a little.

"All right, we'll use your words. Yes, factions. Cardinal Martini was loved and respected because he walked among the poor and rejected any sort of personal material wealth. He never even owned a car. He preferred to take his meals with the indigent because he saw that they were constantly overlooked and forsaken. And yet he fervently believed that they were the true future of the Church."

"And therefore, I shouldn't say *psychic* in public?"

Father Kelly opened his journal, searched through several pages, and then apparently had second thoughts; he closed the book again and stood. "Did you know that my father was a high-ranking officer in the Irish Defence Forces?"

"No," Simon replied.

"These days, I think of him a lot, and I struggle with his beliefs—his conscious choice to raise the sword, so to speak, his insistence that force must be met with force."

"You're losing me, Father."

"A quest for purity . . ."

"Whose quest?"

"There is a faction within our walls that is becoming, in my mind, the kind of force my dad would surely fight against, if for no other reason than to gain some leverage, create some balance of thought and purpose. But I don't have that in me. I don't want to fight against my own people!"

"How on earth does this relate to Katie?" Simon asked, on the verge of losing his patience.

Father Kelly stood and stepped close to his friend and parishioner, hushed and intense. "They'll come after you, Simon. They'll come after your family! They won't tolerate whatever is going on with Katie."

"What? Who are you talking about? She's a child!" Simon was incredulous.

"She's a threat," Father Kelly insisted. "And she'll be a target if we don't do something—now—to protect her."

Simon used all his professor's gravitas to keep his voice even as he begged Father Kelly to explain. "None of this is making sense. Please tell me what you think is going on with Katie."

"I was not completely honest with you after I blessed Katie," the priest began. "Something happened that shook me, and I needed some time to think before speaking with you and Becca."

He returned to his seat and opened the journal, where Simon could see page after page of fervent handwriting intertwined with rough drawings and Latin phrases.

"So I was right. When you touched Katie—?"

"A vision stormed my mind. I saw it as clear as I see you standing before me now. I couldn't see anything else. I couldn't think. The real world was gone, and the vision took over."

Incredulous, Simon insisted on hearing every detail. Father Kelly demurred at first, still struggling to find the words to describe his experience. Finally, he closed his eyes and spoke.

"I was in Rome and it was burning, the air thick with smoke and ash. I was in a kind of oval stadium full of people watching an event. Ancient Rome, it had to be. Civilians were dressed in white, and the soldiers were in red uniforms. In the center of the stadium was the same Egyptian obelisk that stands in St. Peter's Square."

Father Kelly opened his eyes but stared past Simon as he continued. "Next to the obelisk was an old, gray-haired man. He was in agony, covered in blood. Just barely alive. He had been crucified. But the cross and the body . . ." The priest took a deep breath to steady himself. "They were turned upside down."

Simon recalled Katie fidgeting with the crucifix Father Kelly wore.

"The old man turned his head and looked directly at me. He had to blink the blood from his eyes. Then he whispered *diligatis*—which means 'love' in Latin. And then he died. But the last thing I saw, Simon—and I don't even know how long the vision lasted—seconds, maybe? But I can't shake it. I can't . . ." He shuddered at the memory.

"The last thing you saw was—?"

"Two Roman soldiers removing the man's body from the cross. A white sign was fastened to the cross with wire, and I could see written in Latin *amicus INRI, petrus.* Which means 'friend of Jesus the Nazarene, King of the Jews—'"

"Saint Peter!" Simon knew enough Latin to understand that the word *petrus* meant "rock" but also the name "Peter." "So what the hell—sorry— what does this all mean?"

"I haven't had much time, but I've done a little research on St. Peter's death, and I plan to visit the Vatican Apostolic Archive again to have a fuller look."

Simon's eyes went wide. "I've heard rumors about the Apostolic Archive, but I didn't think they were true."

"They were one of the main reasons I moved to Rome. You should see the books and parchments they hold," Father Kelly confessed. "His Holiness has given me full access, and I go as often as I can."

"I don't suppose you could sneak in a friend?" Simon asked.

"I wish I could. I could use some help, but it's virtually impossible to gain access to any of the ancient documents unless you are a member of the clergy."

As he had done several times since moving to Rome, Simon asked himself, *Why imprison information?* But he kept that particular frustration to himself and simply asked, "What do you expect to find there?"

"Let's start with what I already know. There are incredible similarities between the records of the events of St. Peter's death and what I saw when I touched Katie's forehead."

"Like what?"

Father Kelly looked into his friend's eyes. "Everything. Every detail we have recorded was present in that vision."

"I'll admit, that's fascinating. But now I have more questions. How is my daughter connected to this? Why did the vision come when you blessed her?"

Father Kelly closed his notebook, leaned in, and whispered, "I have the feeling St. Peter is trying to tell us something."

"Through Katie?" Simon's voice bounced off the stone walls of the office, amplifying the question's improbability.

The priest made hushing motions with his hands. Chastened, Simon lowered his voice. "Surely, she's just a young girl who picked up a little Latin by being in a Catholic orphanage. Maybe she doesn't even have anything to do with your vision. Maybe you would have had it no matter whom you blessed today."

"Let's baptize Katie. Immediately," Kelly offered. "Likely, the monks at the monastery performed the rite. But I can't find any record of it, so let's make sure your wonderful child is blessed by God, in our parish, for all to see."

To Simon, the suggestion felt more like superstition—like throwing salt over their shoulders—than the sacrament of sanctifying grace.

Chapter 7

Rome

Half an hour later, Simon found himself crossing the Ponte Sisto pedestrian bridge, walking thoughtlessly past historic monuments that would normally have caught his interest. Their enduring presence offered no comfort to a mind consumed by new revelations.

Despite their similar Irish Catholic upbringings, Simon didn't share his wife's faith. Without those beliefs to fall back on, he was at a loss to fathom his conversation with Father Kelly. For the first time since they had settled into their adopted home city, Rome felt alien to him.

His thoughts swirled with the emerging possibility of Katie's spiritual gift—if that's what it could be called. Father Kelly's suggestion that the Church's clandestine factions could be dangerous to the family rather than simply internally divisive was alarming. The idea that his four-year-old daughter could be even peripherally involved seemed preposterous, but he had witnessed Father Kelly's dramatic, inexplicable reaction to touching Katie that morning.

The priest's concern for the Murphys, careful note-taking, and organized plan to visit the archives didn't suggest to Simon a man whose grip on reality had loosened. Father Kelly seemed to be purposefully seeking understanding, logically moving toward truth after an experience that had left him disheveled and drained.

The idea of baptizing Katie as some sort of superstitious insurance policy was not appealing to Simon. However, he could see the logic of the priest's suggestion, even if putting the clergy at ease was usually the last thing he cared about. Plus, Rebecca would be thrilled to see Katie formally and officially welcomed into the Church.

Simon dimly recognized his own street and tried to blink away images of Rome on fire, bloodthirsty soldiers, and a brutal crucifixion. Not yet ready to see Rebecca or Katie, he continued walking past the apartment's entrance.

His review of Father Kelly's grim visions was interrupted by the sound of footsteps behind him. Hackles up, he spun around but was further unnerved seeing no one else on the street. He shuddered at the thought that Katie might really be in harm's way. He wondered how he could gain access to those Vatican archives. Research was what he knew, the way he made sense of his world.

The walk was doing little to quiet his mind. He slowed his pace and considered returning home. Feeling both invisible and conspicuous at once, he leaned against a wall near an alley. Focusing on deep breaths, he failed to detect the hand reaching from the darkness behind him until it gripped his shoulder.

He cried out, flailing his arms and spinning wildly to free himself from the thick, dirty fingers grasping him.

"What the hell!"

"Sir, I was only . . ." The stranger stepped from the shadows to reveal his haggard form.

"Who are you?" Simon demanded. "Have you been following me?"

"No, no. I was just wondering . . ." the beggar said, cupping his hands and lowering his head in supplication.

Simon felt stupid and rude. He had been so focused on the supernatural that he'd failed to notice what was around him, what was real. He muttered an apology to the man, who stood bowed in silence, and shoved the box of cannolis into the man's grimy hands. The beggar's face brightened as he looked up at Simon.

"Bless you, sir. Bless you," he said and stepped back, again consumed by the darkness.

But Simon was already striding purposefully back toward his apartment building. He knew now what he would tell Rebecca: nothing. At least, nothing about St. Peter's death or the war within the Vatican that might be the undoing of their small family.

The emerging picture of Katie's perception, or ability, or whatever it was, hadn't yet crystallized. So he would not go looking for trouble. Instead, he sought sanctuary in what he knew to be real: the comfort of home and the warmth of his wife.

Simon quietly let himself into the apartment and found his wife in the rocking chair. Katie was nestled in her arms, her head resting on Rebecca's shoulder. She tucked curl after curl of vermillion hair behind Katie's ears, easing the girl into sleep.

Simon knelt beside them. Before he could speak, Rebecca whispered, "Xenoglossia."

"Pardon?"

"It's when a person is able to speak or write a language they haven't acquired by natural means," she said. "I did some research earlier while Katie was building."

Simon waited, welcoming any salve for his anxiety, even from an online encyclopedia.

"There are a lot of cases of children and adults speaking other languages without knowing them—and lots of explanations, like the collective unconscious and past lives—"

"Past lives?" Simon interrupted.

"Well, obviously most scientists don't give that much credence, and even when xenoglossia happens, the empirical evidence is extremely rare. It's spontaneous. Nobody is prepared with a recorder, so there's no real proof these people said what they said. That must be what happened with Katie today," Rebecca continued as she slowed the rocker to a gentle stop. "See? There's no reason to worry."

Simon nodded, trying to ignore the ringing of Father Kelly's words in his ears.

The rocking chair creaked as Rebecca carefully stood with Katie in her arms. Before carrying the girl to her bedroom, she cast a stern glance back at Simon.

"What?" he asked hesitantly, afraid his wife could see right through him.

"Where is my cannoli, Mr. Sweet Tooth?"

Chapter 8

Rome

Katie had already begun to understand sleep and recognize its patterns. Shallow slumber was her favorite, and it enveloped her as she lay in her mother's arms. She heard a door latch, footsteps, and a male voice, which mingled with street noise to compose a vague, soothing lullaby.

She felt her body rise as she was carried to her bed, still hearing the blend of sounds that accompanied the reassuringly familiar gestures of her parents. Wrapped in her blanket, she lingered in this condition for as long as possible, determined to cling to the simple sensations she found so pleasurable.

Mummy singing.

Daddy stroking her hair.

The soft thud of wheels on cobblestones.

She knew she would not be able to hold on. Unlike sleep itself, this was a part of existence she struggled to understand. Everything ended—both good things and bad things.

The next stage of sleep was deeper and, by degrees, darker. Initially she felt safe, if not altogether carefree, floating in an empty and soundless dimension, suspended between strata of unconsciousness. She could not hear the street or her parents any longer. She was far, far away, gratefully deprived of stimulus and expectation.

But that state of grace could abruptly end for no reason. The darkness could implode and Katie could plummet to a remote, suffocating, hellish depth. On this night, the descent was savage.

In an instant, Katie found herself walking through a dense inferno of fire and ash. People were screaming. At first she believed she was alone, and in terror, she witnessed ancient soldiers swinging their weapons with utter contempt for human life and dignity.

Then she realized that her parents were with her, and this gave her the disorienting sense of spanning two lives—her dreaming memories and her waking life. The three of them walked through ancient wreckage, yet neither Daddy nor Mummy seemed aware of the horror that surrounded them. Instead, they laughed and joked about art, the way they so often did when they all went out together.

Mummy teased, "Rome has nothing on Paris for history and art. How many dark oil paintings of baby Jesus and Mary can a person look at? The Impressionist and contemporary art in one Paris museum blows away the medieval and Renaissance art in Rome."

Daddy retorted, "Keep your Musée d'Orsay. My beloved Bernini could take your Monet any day!"

"As a sculptor, yes. I'll give you that. But no contest as a painter!" Mummy replied.

Daddy spun and stumbled as if struck in the chest, his elaborate antics a mockery of defeat. "*Touché, mon amour!* Argh! Katie, she really got me that time—right in the heart!" But then Daddy sprang upright and gleefully shouted, "Hey, but wait—Monet didn't even sculpt, except for maybe the bushes in his garden!"

Their banter continued as Katie breathed floating ash, witnessed horrifying acts of bloody violence, and grew more and more alarmed that her parents could be so indifferent. Even when they passed the ominous, black-hooded sculpture of Giordano Bruno lording over the Campo de' Fiori Square on the exact site where he was burned at the stake for heresy, Daddy joked, "Don't be afraid, my little cupcake. He looks scary here, but in real life, he wasn't scary at all. He was a really smart poet and philosopher who said a lot of things the Catholic Church didn't appreciate."

Daddy pointed in the direction of the Vatican. "See how Bruno's statue stares directly at Vatican City? It's his historical revenge and remains an open wound for the Church."

Katie suppressed screams as the sculpture came to life and stared into her eyes. Bruno opened his book, pointed at her, and proclaimed, "The soul is not the body, and it may be in one body or in another, and pass from body to body."

But Daddy smiled and said, "Goodness, darling, Bruno was hardly the first person to talk about reincarnation. Unfortunately, his timing could not have been worse. *Ciao*, wagging tongue; hello, body on fire!"

As Bruno continued to speak, a group of angry cardinals—exemplars of the Roman Inquisition—swept forward and seized him. They slashed the artist's tongue from his mouth and dangled the bloody trophy in Katie's face before torching Bruno. Flames sizzled sickeningly and the smell of burning flesh enveloped them.

Still, Daddy continued his lecture. "It was Emperor Constantine and his power-hungry mother who decided to sever reincarnation from Christianity around AD 350. It was a smart ploy. Banish the idea that human beings might have more than one life, and gain a stranglehold on the masses with the Church's *one life, one chance* doctrine." He flung his hand toward the Vatican in disgust. "Egotistical priests declaring that only they could know the truth. It has been over 400 years since Giordano Bruno was tortured and executed for his unwavering commitment to free thought. Yet, here we are, still awaiting an official apology for this monumental injustice." He paused briefly, allowing the gravity of his words to settle.

"It took over 350 years for Galileo to receive an apology," he said, a note of frustration creeping into his tone. "One can only hope that the recognition of Bruno's contributions to intellectual freedom will follow soon."

By now, Katie was desperately tugging on Daddy's sleeve. "Daddy, stop. Please stop!" But Daddy didn't hear her or notice their terrible surroundings.

"The question we could explore is the nature of God's forgiveness and the depth of Its love for humanity. Rather than viewing God through the low-level lens of judgment or punishment, we can recognize that eternal, unconditional love extends to all, regardless of differing beliefs or theologies."

As Daddy added layer upon layer of historic fact, mixed with iconoclastic commentary, they strolled together through the ancient hellscape. In the near distance, Katie saw all of Rome erupt in flames.

Emperor Nero's soldiers began relentlessly torturing trapped Christians. Katie saw a man's arms being severed from his torso. A woman fell to her knees pleading for help, then was suddenly beheaded by a blood-soaked legionnaire.

It was unbearable, but Katie had learned that the terrors of sleep would eventually disintegrate. Finally, she heard herself scream for help while she struggled against the entrapment of her blankets. Although she recognized the pattern, the hopeless feelings still coursed through her: all was lost, there was no escape, she would be mauled by fire and hatred and—

"Katie! Katie, baby, what's wrong?"

She soared into the air, landing softly against Mummy's breast. Together, they swayed gently in the darkness until Daddy appeared and wrapped his long arms around them both. "Oh, sweetheart. It's okay. We're here. It's only a nightmare," he said.

Katie was at peace again. The final stage of sleep had been achieved: rescue. Her only worry was that Mummy and Daddy's soft assurances had made her feel drowsy again, and the whole thing might repeat itself.

Chapter 9

Rome

The man licked his gooey fingers one by one as the last morsels of crisp dough and buttery cream melted in his mouth. The unexpected late-night treat was more satisfying than he had anticipated. He had almost tossed the half-flattened box into a garbage bin, but a quiver of gratitude had reminded him that God's gifts should never be wasted. He'd made the sign of the cross before scooping out the first mouthful.

It was nearly midnight. He leaned against a darkened storefront and scanned the street for anything of even fleeting interest. He heard a familiar melody and hunched his shoulders. Ignoring his phone was not an option, but first, he took one last lick of his thumb and glanced warily up and down the near-empty street.

"Ciao."

"Where are you?"

"Where you told me to be."

"And?"

"And what?"

A heavy sigh. "Carlitos, is there anything to report?"

"No. The guy wandered all over the place; he didn't even notice his apartment building. Just kept on walking, then suddenly ran home and—nah. Nothing."

The handler he had never met paused before asking, "You say he suddenly ran home?"

"That's what I said. Yes."

"Why did he run?"

"I should know?"

Another sigh. "Yes, Carlitos. I was hoping."

Carlitos's deeply furrowed brow gave the impression that he was always deep in thought. This was not so. But he was often annoyed, especially by this particular caller's questions.

"I can't say. I mean, not exactly, but—"

"Yes?" the caller pressed.

"The guy—"

"The dad, you mean?"

"Who else we talking about?" Carlitos mumbled.

With a sound like swallowing a peach pit, the man on the other end of the line said, "I was merely seeking clarity."

Carlitos sniffed and ran his sleeve across his mouth. "Yeah, the dad, the guy you have me following. He's drifting around muttering to himself, and then suddenly he yelps. I see he's in some kind of fight."

"A fight? With whom?"

Whom? Carlitos hated this fancy prick, *whomever* he was. "It was nothing. Some old beggar, I guess."

"We didn't send you out there to guess, Carlitos. Maybe it was a ruse."

"A what?"

"Maybe the father was meeting secretly with someone of importance who was pretending to be—"

"He was a beggar. The dad gave him a box of pastry to get rid of him," Carlitos assured the caller.

"How do you know it was pastry? Perhaps it was—"

"I know because—" Carlitos stopped himself. Maybe he'd be criticized for eating on the job. He moved the phone from one sticky hand to another and changed his tone. "I know 'cause I opened the box to make sure it wasn't, like you say, a ruse?"

"He let you have the box?"

Carlitos had followed the father to the apartment building, then turned to find the beggar retreating into an alley. "Not at first. We had a . . . you know." Carlitos stopped, certain his caller would understand his implication.

"No, I don't know. What happened?"

"I hit him." Carlitos recalled the sweet satisfaction of felling the man with a single blow. The stomping and kicking that followed had also been invigorating. Power was so much more fulfilling than thinking. Violence was its own reward.

"Carlitos, are you still there?"

"Yeah, yeah. I was saying, the guy wouldn't give me the box, so I put him in his place, which did not work out so well for him."

"Carlitos . . ."

"I was very nice at first. He should have realized."

The caller was silent. When his voice returned, the tone was stern. "Did we ask you to do harm?"

"Don't I sometimes have to take care of things?"

"Only the Lord takes care of things, Carlitos."

"Okay, sure, but the sermons always say, 'He works through his followers.'"

Another sigh. The man began to speak, but Carlitos interrupted. "Hey, wait. Something's going on up there."

"In the apartment?"

"Yeah. A light came on."

"Can you see anyone?"

"A shadow on the window shade." Carlitos stepped into the street but felt exposed there, like he'd blown his cover. He eased back against the building.

"Is it him?" the man on the other end asked.

Carlitos didn't think so. The silhouette was too short. It gently bobbed, turned, and then—"There he is," Carlitos said as another, taller shape appeared.

"The dad?"

"Must be. Maybe the kid woke up."

"Can you hear a child crying?"

"From down here?" Carlitos knew he was stepping out of bounds, but it was the stupidest question yet, and his curt response served its purpose.

The apartment quickly went dark again. "The light went out," Carlitos related. "They're in for the night, I think." He felt a flicker of hope at the prospect of returning early to the shabby rooms he shared with five other immigrant men. There was food there and a cot.

"Nevertheless, you should stay," the caller ordered.

Now it was Carlitos's turn to let out a heavy sigh. The cold night was nipping at his nose and feet. He had chosen his only set of good clothes for this assignment. In an open-necked shirt, slacks, and decent loafers with no socks, he looked like a tourist from Brazil, but now he knew he had miscalculated the weather. "Okay. But when's someone gonna tell me what I'm supposed to be doing out here?"

There was a gruff exhalation before the man shot back, "If you no longer wish to serve a higher purpose—"

"I didn't say that."

"—or obey the Catechism and protect the Holy See from—"

"I'll stay! I'll stay! I was just asking."

"Do not ask, Carlitos. Just do. Do as you are told."

When the cell phone went silent, Carlitos cursed, stuffed his thick hands in his pants pockets, and began to stroll down the street to cast a glance upward at the third-story apartment. His furrowed brow tightened irritably.

His mind came to attention when he saw a small group of people further down the street, arms aflutter, voices yelping as the kid's father had done earlier that night.

Carlitos spun and began walking in the opposite direction. Someone had likely found the body of the beggar. He hadn't intended to kill the man, but he felt no remorse. It wasn't his fault old bones crushed so easily.

◆

CARLITOS COULD BARELY remember the face of the first person he'd killed. In the *favelas* surrounding São Paulo, where he'd grown up, death came daily and in an instant.

He'd been raised on the third floor of a house that had been built in stages. The first floor held an *açougue;* the smell of searing meat and frying beans and yucca permeated the two floors above, which each housed families of as many as a dozen.

The outside of the building was slipshod and rough, with air-conditioning units and satellite dishes protruding like growths. The roof was a sheet of corrugated iron; it held three water tanks, one for each floor.

Carlitos had five brothers and two sisters. His father was a miner who was rarely home; it seemed to him that the old man only came around to impregnate his mother. She traveled into one of the city's wealthiest neighborhoods every day, one of a team of maids who cleaned the high-rise apartment of a family who had more money than Carlitos's entire neighborhood. His mother said they were searched on the way out every day to make sure they hadn't taken anything, and the building had armed guards at the front door and in the parking garage.

Even with both parents working full time, there was never enough. Food was sometimes scarce, and all of Carlitos's clothes had belonged to two brothers before him. His sisters constantly sought ways to make themselves pretty without money for makeup or fashionable outfits.

Still, there was fun to be had. Life in the *favelas* was hard, but it was exciting. Every family had as many children as Carlitos's, if not more, so roaming gangs of boys rampaged through the narrow streets. When Carlitos was eight or nine, he began to run with a group that ranged in size from ten to fifteen boys, every one as skinny, ragged, and hungry as himself.

They played traditional children's games, kicking a ball in the street when someone could find one, running aimlessly or hiding from each other when there was no ball. But they also stole. Fruit, candy, or drinks—whatever the owner of one of the *favela*'s hundreds of small stores might have left within a child's reach, his attention diverted by a paying customer.

And sometimes, they got into fights with gangs of children from other neighborhoods. The *favela* was vast, and it was unwise to walk far in any direction without permission or an escort. Carlitos soon found that the fighting skills he'd developed as the middle brother of five served him well in the streets; he could punch hard and fast or sneak a kick to someone's ribs when they were already down.

One day, strangers came to the neighborhood. Vast numbers of them all headed to the small plaza that would have functioned as a town square if Carlitos had grown up in a small town instead of a close-packed warren of hand-built brick buildings with stolen electricity and improvised sewers. He and his gang followed along, eager to see if anything of note was happening.

It was something like a political rally—a concept that was only familiar to Carlitos from TV—but instead of a politician, the man at the podium was wearing a white shawl over his shoulders and talking about Jesus Cristo. He was telling the people that if they believed in Jesus Cristo, their faith would bring them money and prosperity and they would no longer be poor.

Carlitos looked around at the people watching. It didn't seem like any amount of prayer would lift them out of the *favela*. He didn't even think they believed it. But they all had smiles on their faces and were waving their hands in the air and praying with the man in the shawl.

When the praying and singing stopped, Carlitos thought the show was over. But then the man in the shawl asked for what he called "offerings." The people watching the speech took out money and began dropping it into wooden baskets that men were carrying through the crowd.

Carlitos couldn't believe it. Hadn't the man just finished telling these people that their faith in Jesus Cristo was supposed to bring them money? And now they were giving their own money away—to this crazy man!

He was even more shocked to see how much money they were giving away. Not coins, but bills. And not a single bill from each person but multiple bills. The price of a meal, if not more. Carlitos began to think that perhaps talking to people about Jesus Cristo was a good way to make a living.

Just then, there was a shout and an uproar, and the crowd parted. A skinny, dirty blond-haired boy Carlitos didn't recognize shoved through the crowd, running as hard and as fast as he could right past Carlitos and his friends, and disappeared up the cement steps that led between two buildings—and he was carrying one of the baskets of money! Two men were following him, shouting at top volume with eyes full of shock and rage.

Carlitos's friends Max and Igor, two brothers who always seemed to be up to something, exchanged a silent glance. Then Max shoved Igor as hard as he could, propelling him down to the ground directly in front of the running men, where he landed on his hands and knees. The men tumbled over him, and he cried out in exaggerated agony. They picked themselves up and turned their attention to the crying boy, who was clutching one knee in both hands.

Max grabbed Carlitos. "I saw where he ran," he hissed in his ear. "Come on."

Without a backward glance, they launched themselves up the cement steps after the thief.

They found him in minutes, tucked between two buildings, eyes wide and shaking like a rabbit, clutching the basket. When he saw them, he tried to get up and run, but they were already on him.

They never learned his name. They learned how loud he could scream, though. And the money in the basket bought food and clothes for close to a month.

Chapter 10

Vatican City

Father Henryk Lemski closed his disposable cell phone and suppressed the urge to toss it against the wall or crush it underfoot. He felt chilly and alone as he paced in his remote Vatican City office.

He didn't like his work. He didn't like Carlitos and the other dregs of humanity he "managed." He really didn't like the clandestine nature of his appointment, which made him feel detached from his best impulses and deepest beliefs.

Still, what was the alternative? A Catholic Church laid waste by heresy, led by rebellious young pastors whose vain, self-righteous blogs championed artificial insemination, homosexual rights, and marriage within the clergy? Degradation. Sacrilege! He had watched Poland, his once deeply devout homeland, succumb to doubts born of sensational standoffs between Vatican rule and these provocateurs, clergymen who professed a deep concern for "the people" while destroying the people's only chance of a merciful eternal peace.

Thugs like Carlitos would never know Lemski's true identity, and that was some comfort, but he was just as ignorant of his own supervisor's name or face. He undoubtedly worked for some high-ranking

Vatican functionary whose political ascent might be harmed if his real work became public, but he had no idea who.

The disposable cell phone was his only conduit to guidance and instruction. He had been told to use it sparingly. Sometimes, though, all he wanted was someone to talk to.

"Our Father who art in heaven . . ." Lemski dropped to his knees, seeking a solace that rarely came these days. As a parish priest, he had never known such burdens. He had been there to serve the people, and he had done so with vigor and joy.

In those years, he had received as much as he had given. He was carried through many an ordeal by the grateful faces of devotees whose burdens seemed to ease with his prayers and encouragement. Now he served bishops and cardinals who appeared to be ignoring the needs of the flock while engaging in church matters that were internal and covert.

"Dear Lord . . ." he began. The words would not come. When they did, they sounded morose and self-pitying to him. Disgusted with his weakness, he stood and returned to his desk.

As he sat, Lemski could no longer disguise the true source of his vexation. It was not Carlitos or his fellows nor the solitary confinement of his commission. "The little girl," he muttered. She was not the only one he was watching. But she was local and current, and her notoriety was growing.

He awakened his tablet and tapped open the girl's file. It was significant enough that someone barely four years old had already drawn Church attention. The first entry seemed innocent enough:

From: Monte Cassino. Benedictine monk discovers infant at doorstep. Parents not known. Paolo De Fiori, monk, reluctant to release child to authorities. Monastery stricken with unusual illnesses and general grief following departure of infant. Abbot authorizes medical and psychological intervention.

"Heartsick hermits," scoffed Lemski. Such an incident would have held no interest for the Vatican if not for the social worker's comments. A Catholic, of course, she had felt compelled to report the behavior of this Paolo fellow and the "unsettling sense" that the baby seemed to express something like compassion for the old man. When pressed for more details, her response was, "I had this strange feeling."

Lemski trusted this woman because he knew the feelings of the faithful. The excitements of the unblessed, on the other hand, verged on unholy hysteria. Such ecstatic expressions were at the core of the Church's war against false visionaries, witchcraft, and idolatry. Then came what would send Lemski over the edge. He read the pope's personal testimony:

> The abbot of the Benedictine monastic community shared with His Holiness the profound experiences he and the other monks had following their time with the young girl. Despite her tender age of two, she left a significant impact on them. After a private and personal meeting with her, the pope reported in a letter to the abbot that he had undergone an existential crisis, accompanied by wild hallucinations, nightmares, visions, and deep spiritual awakenings that followed in the weeks after their encounter. Given the intensity of his experiences, the pope requested that the abbot keep him informed about the child's growth and whereabouts. He expressed the sentiment that the abbey's motto resonated deeply with what he felt after meeting her: *Succisa Virescit*, which translates to "cut down, it grows anew."

"The little girl," he whispered through clenched teeth. The child had almost vanished after leaving the monastery until a nurse at Bambino

Gesù Hospital began providing a stream of evidence that put Lemski and his team on the highest alert.

> From: Bambino Gesù Hospital. Nurse Amedea Negrelli reports abnormal child, prone to fits of "emotional instability" throughout the night; precociously adaptive to stimulus with an "unnerving awareness" of adult moods and contrivances.

Curious at best, Lemski had thought when he'd first read the interview. But when questioned again weeks later, Nurse Negrelli had revealed that prospective parents were rejecting the child based on unflattering intuitions:

> From: Bambino Gesù Hospital. Nurse Amedea Negrelli reports that a woman admitted that her husband suspected the child was "possessed." Another couple claimed holding the girl was "stressful." One would-be mother was afraid to look into the child's eyes.

A footnote also mentioned hints of "clairvoyance" in the little girl's conversations. One adoptive couple returned for a second visit with the child and were discovered asking for "predictions of the future." When confronted, the husband used the words *psychic* and *medium* to describe his impression of the girl. Their adoption application was denied.

Strange indeed, thought Lemski. Perhaps the adoptive-parent candidates intended to supplement their income by offering up their child to all the desperate seekers who believed fortune-telling could save them from sin and remorse.

Lemski pushed away from his desk, struck again by the stabbing pains of his discontent. Heading the de facto Supreme Sacred Congregation, a modern-day Roman Inquisition, was not what had originally brought Lemski to Rome. He had coveted a Vatican appointment. But after being interviewed, praised, and served lunch with important functionaries, including the private secretary assistant to the pope, he had been passed over.

The rejection had stung deeply. Upon returning to Gdańsk, he was noticeably irritable with parishioners and increasingly uninterested in his charitable work.

Then the call came. Unexpected, but welcome. "Father Lemski?"

"Yes."

"I'm calling from the Vatican."

The V-word took Lemski's breath away. Had there been second thoughts, a change of heart?

"Hold, please, for the Monsignor."

Lemski did not exhale until he heard the voice of a man he would probably never meet and whose title he had come to suspect did not actually exist.

"Hello, Father Lemski. Forgive this late-night intrusion."

"No intrusion. How may I help you?"

The question had made Lemski popular among his flock. It showed a humility that was, in this case, calculated. He was determined to contain his enthusiasm, afraid that he had appeared too eager and unctuous during his previous stay in Vatican City.

"I regret not introducing myself during your recent visit to Rome, Father. Your exemplary service to His Holiness is commendable and much needed in these evolving times."

"You are too kind."

"Perhaps, but I am also correct in recognizing your value to our Church. Though I fear I may be wasting my time with this . . ." The Monsignor trailed off, bemusing Lemski further.

"Yes, Monsignor?"

"Your devotion to Gdańsk is nearly legendary. Despite your Vatican campaign, we are wondering if another type of position in Rome is even worth mentioning."

"We?"

"Yes. Forgive the generality. But the undertaking I wish to discuss with you demands utter secrecy and discretion. I say this now for the sake of brevity. I won't waste your evening if you harbor hopes of a more public role in the Holy See."

Anything—anything—to be called to Rome.

Lemski gripped his emotions tightly. "Monsignor, I serve only the church, not my personal hopes and wishes," he said.

"Excellent. I was told to expect such a response. But before I go on, can you assure me you are alone and available to speak with me for the next hour or so?"

Thus began a string of conversations that continued at odd hours, over several weeks, and always with a different personage. The Monsignor was replaced by other men of vague titles whose names Lemski never found on the official Vatican City registry. At times, he felt as though he were shadowboxing. A conspiratorial excitement would flourish in him, making him feel vain and important. But then he would kneel in his church late at night, a lone pilgrim praying for illumination.

When nothing as obvious as a mission or an order seemed to come from his conversations with the Romans, Lemski made lists of questions. "Will I be housed in Vatican City?"

"Oh, yes. We've prepared a priest's apartment for you in the Apostolic Palace."

His heart burned with excitement. "Will the pope know of my appointment?"

"His Holiness is overwhelmed with his calling, but he will welcome you with a title we have constructed that suits your position without publicly revealing your undertaking."

"The secrecy, though—"

"Does it alarm you?"

"In some ways, yes. It's just that, well, perhaps I'm not quite grasping the mechanism by which I . . ." He did not want to sound stupid. He groped for a way to articulate his confusion, and today's "Monsignor" helped him.

"By which you receive?"

"Precisely. How do I remain invisible and still gather information?"

"Our legions are vast," the Monsignor explained. "This is our strength. Rivers and tributaries, a natural network that is centuries old. Every day, throughout the world, we invite testimony and promote input as the duty of good Catholics everywhere. Sightings, blasphemies, maledictions—the conjecture that pours in will alarm you by its sheer volume. But not one of our flock knows how the Church uses this information. Nor is it specifically—with some exceptions, which I'll explain later—directed to your branch of activity."

"Resourceful."

"Ever."

They also discussed the enormous challenges facing His Holiness, the uphill battle to repair the damage done by one of his "progressive" predecessors, Pope Francis. Father Lemski had embraced the ascension of the new supreme pontiff from the beginning, and so in the end he decided that his purpose in Gdańsk had been fulfilled. It was time for something new.

"I am honored to be chosen. I take this vow consciously and with an unwavering wish to serve His Holiness," he had told his final inquisitor, the Cardinal-Deacon.

Now, sitting in his catacomb-like office, Father Lemski was momentarily buoyed by thoughts of the pope. Even if he did not always enjoy his work in Rome, he truly had never wavered in his faith and belief in his Roman pontiff.

The wheels of his chair squeaked as Lemski resumed his review of the little girl's electronic file. He swiped forward to the testimonies that had arrived earlier in the day and were the reason he had engaged Carlitos.

> From: St. Peter's Basilica. Dominique and Jacinthe Bonfils, French citizens on holiday. Encouraged by friends to share their story with Vatican officials after witnessing a blessing offered by a Father Justin Kelly that appeared similar to an exorcism. Priest reacted as if "electrocuted" and then feigned "dizzy spell" to distract the curious.

That same event had brought forth a church employee whose contribution added weight to the Bonfils' observations.

> From: St. Peter's Basilica. Caretaker Roberto Franza observed Father Justin Kelly with a red-haired girl and her parents. Franza witnessed the girl pointing into the air and claiming that she could see angels.

How blessed is the Vatican, thought Lemski, *to be protected by the millions of faithful Catholics who know the difference between the sacred and the profane.*

On the corner of his desk, the cell phone's vibration was moving it in a slow circle.

He answered quickly, his breathing shallow. "Yes?"

The voice was unfamiliar. But many in the church knew his phone number, if not his name. "A baptism at Santa Maria Trastevere. The little girl."

"No!" Lemski felt as though his hair had caught fire, which took his mind to Nurse Negrelli, who claimed the redheaded child's hair sometimes flared with the blinding light of a torch.

"We'll know the day and time soon enough. They cannot hide from us."

"How did you come by this knowledge?"

The silence that followed was no surprise. Calls he received often ended abruptly.

Lemski stood, his will and purpose restored, and called his superior.

Chapter 11

Rome

It was not unusual for a nurse to enter the office of a physician or department head. Most information was shared electronically, but face-to-face communication was often easier.

Senior nurse Amedea Negrelli stood outside Dr. Maly Rin's office, holding a folder and pretending to study its contents before knocking and entering.

The orderly space was empty, as she had known it would be. A trusted receptionist had alerted her when Dr. Rin had exited through the hospital's lobby for a lunch appointment. Although Negrelli assumed she had at least an hour, she also knew it would look suspicious if she stayed too long.

Negrelli was a skilled and severe presence at Bambino Gesù Hospital. She had only been there a short time but had earned the trust of staffers. She made it her business to master the complexities of medical data and patient care—and to memorize the habits of administrators and doctors.

She stood before Dr. Rin's computer, hoping that she had not logged out of her hospital account. Many busy doctors considered it a waste of time to continually sign in and out throughout the day.

"God is good," the nurse whispered when she found the computer wide open and spotted the file she sought three entries deep in the document history. As expected, Dr. Rin had referred to it earlier in the day when Rebecca Murphy and her daughter, Katie, had visited to discuss test results.

Dr. Rin had invited Negrelli to view some of the findings, but she hadn't been able to memorize it all. Now, she sent the file to print. About to search for other records of interest, she spotted the physician's personal datebook open beside the keyboard.

Negrelli tensed when her cell phone began to ring. She decided to ignore the call so that she could sift through Dr. Rin's schedule and then return to her regular duties as a purposeful presence in the hallway and a competent assistant in the examination room.

Her eyebrow twitched with excitement when she spotted the entry. Yes, of course! It was only natural that the doctor would be invited to the baptism.

Nurse Negrelli had ushered mother and child into Dr. Rin's office earlier that morning, offering pleasantries. "How is your little girl this morning?" she had asked while looking at a subdued, even suspicious-looking Katie.

Rebecca had hesitated. *A sure sign*, Negrelli thought, *that something was amiss*. Perhaps the adoptive mother was truly innocent of Katie's profanation and was hoping for proof of a neural disorder that might explain her odd behavior.

Negrelli had let it pass. "The doctor will be with you in a moment. Tea? Water?"

"No thanks, Amedea."

The nurse lingered, stealing glances at the girl, ready to memorize spontaneous gestures or conversations to further prove that the child was a danger. As she shuffled files and pretended to be preparing for the doctor's arrival, Katie's eyes followed her. Negrelli finally stopped her useless chores, turned, and smiled.

Katie's arm jutted out with her forefinger pointed directly at Negrelli. "You!" Her voice was hushed but forceful. Her finger remained still and arrow-straight, her face unmoving.

Negrelli would later report that it felt as though a projectile had entered her body. She briefly felt faint but forced herself to smile wider and inquire, "What is it, child?"

Katie only repeated her mysterious accusation. "You!"

"Sweetie, it's not polite to point," Rebecca said, pushing the child's arm down. "Sorry, Amedea."

"Not at all. She's . . . unique."

The remark did nothing to defuse the tension. Instead, both mother and daughter now gazed at Negrelli with an unnerving curiosity.

Dr. Rin's entrance broke the tension. "Hello, Becca. Sorry to keep you waiting."

Negrelli exhaled as the doctor sat behind her desk. She moved toward the desk with the intention of assisting, but the doctor dismissed her. "Thank you, Amedea. That'll be all."

"Of course. Nice to see you, Rebecca."

Rebecca had nodded but had not smiled, instead reaching for Katie's hand.

Now, as Negrelli hastily jotted a date and time on a piece of paper to slip into the folder, the memory of Rebecca's expression distracted her. There was no good explanation for her caution and defensiveness.

Had she been discovered? Would there be ramifications? If she were confronted, Negrelli knew she must lie and deny all allegations. She had a higher purpose that would not be derailed by an overly protective mother.

Lost in her head, she didn't hear the voices in the hallway over the sound of the printer humming. She jumped when her cell phone chirped again. At the same moment, the office door opened.

"Amedea?"

Negrelli turned cold. "Dr. Rin."

◆

THERE WERE DAYS when Dr. Maly Rin wanted nothing more than to sit in silence in a fine restaurant. She relished the escape from sterile hallways and cramped examination rooms. Today, she had planned a solo lunch for herself.

Crossing Piazza di Sant'Onofrio, walking briskly along the Passeggiata del Gianicolo, and soaking up the majesty of the Eternal City, she nodded occasionally to familiar faces among her fellow pedestrians. She knew that her appearance was that of a confident, energetic woman. But a look into her soul would reveal conflict, scars, and doubts.

"Why can't we find anything? Good God!" Rebecca had been nearly beside herself earlier in the day as Katie played quietly with toys kept in the corner of Maly's office.

The "comprehensive cognitive assessment" of a preschool-age child like Katie was designed to evaluate physical, social, and emotional delays in development so that medical professionals might intervene as necessary.

"As a physician, I find myself in the odd position of envying the illnesses I can diagnose and treat in the other children here. Becca, I've scoured these test results looking for any indication of neural issues, and the only thing I can possibly guess at would be selective mutism. This is where Katie could have an anxiety disorder where she won't speak in specific situations or to specific people, but it usually coexists with shyness or social anxiety, or—" Maly shrugged her shoulders and shook her head. She couldn't go on with more empty clinical descriptions. There was simply nothing here.

"Come on, Maly," Becca had said. "You know I know about S. M. What about the nightmares, speaking in Latin, and the unwillingness to communicate verbally with me or her dad?"

Maly herself still suffered with disrupted sleep decades after the traumatic catastrophe of her own family's rupture. In her dreams, she regularly saw the mother and father she had left behind the night she was forced to flee Cambodia. She would speak to her parents and believe they had been reunited, only to have the morning yank her from their embrace.

"The problem is, we can't know what events Katie experienced after birth."

"She probably felt deserted. Her parents left her," Rebecca said.

"She was an infant," Maly offered as a meager defense.

"But she knows now, doesn't she?" Becca challenged, searching for something, anything, to explain her daughter's behavior.

"Well, yes, but—"

"Could they have abused her?" Even saying it out loud had filled Rebecca with despair; she dropped her head into her palms.

Katie noticed and rose from the corner, slowly but certainly. She placed a comforting hand on her mother's shoulder. Rebecca looked up to meet her daughter's eyes and burst into tears, pulling Katie close.

"Can you come to the baptism, Maly? Would you, please? It will be short and simple. We don't want to draw attention and . . ." More crying had suffocated her words.

On the street, Maly realized it had begun to rain. She paused, weighing whether it was wiser to continue or run back for an umbrella. The hospital was closer.

As she rushed into the lobby, her main concern was keeping her footing in her wet shoes. She took no note of the receptionist, who turned pale and frantically dialed the phone as she passed. Nor did she expect to find Nurse Negrelli in her office.

"Amedea?"

"Dr. Rin—I . . ."

Before Negrelli could say more, Maly's eyes turned to the papers spewing out of the printer.

"I was making a copy of the test results you requested."

Maly hesitated before responding, "What request?"

"For your appointment with the Murphy child."

"Rebecca and Katie?"

"Yes. Exactly." Forcing a helpful smile, Nurse Negrelli stepped to the printer and lifted the stack of pages.

"But, Amedea, that appointment was this morning."

Negrelli brought a hand to her forehead. "Oh! *meu Deus*! Of course, of course. I'm so sorry. I was confused by your request and should have asked before you . . ."

"But I made no such request."

Negrelli shook her head, muttering, "Confusion, confusion. I apologize, Doctor. I'm not myself today."

"A touch of a cold?"

"Perhaps. Or old age." Self-deprecation was a tried-and-true deflection. The nurse apologized one more time, tucked the pages into a folder, and exited with them.

In the ensuing silence, Maly sat and scrutinized her desk, but could find nothing out of place. Even so, she decided to skip lunch. *I should cancel my reservation*, she thought, and reached for her personal datebook where she had jotted the phone number of the restaurant.

But no number was visible. The page had been turned to the next day, when she had only one pressing appointment: Katie Murphy's baptism.

Chapter 12

Rome

Katie heard her parents' every word. She understood their desire for her to communicate. She wanted to speak. She knew how to speak. Words, however, were difficult to muster. Her mind was a tumult, an intrusive parade of images that left her mentally exhausted.

Unexplained faces, events, and repeated phrases—"I am not worthy of being crucified in the same manner as my Lord"—echoed within her from dawn to dusk. Sometimes, she felt almost capable of understanding them. The feeling was not much different from the way a word would sit on the tip of her tongue, almost ready to escape her lips and please her parents.

At those moments, she would stand perfectly still, feeling that if she could let the images click into place, she could find their meaning at last. But those moments were rare and often interrupted by well-meaning adults, who found her steady, unblinking gaze unsettling.

Just that morning, Daddy had tried to engage with her over breakfast as she stared past her food, her hands in her lap.

"Remember the nice priest you met when we attended Mass at St. Peter's Basilica?" he said.

Katie wanted to answer before his look of anticipation dissipated. Finally, she managed a single word: "Yes."

Daddy and Mummy seemed overjoyed, their eyes meeting across the table and their smiles lifting their cheeks. Katie wanted to shout, *I know how to say things. I want to say things.* But explanations were too much work. Even now, a fresh wave of sounds and sights was rushing at her.

"That's good because we're going to visit him today. He wants to see you again and do something nice for you."

Daddy was grinning as he moved his hand over her head like a magic wand. Through the internal assault on her senses, she heard him whisper to Mummy, "Let the brainwashing begin."

"Simon!"

"If we would leave her alone, she would probably turn out to be the most spiritual person on the planet." He shrugged.

Katie wondered what that meant as she lifted her spoon to eat some oatmeal.

Mummy smacked him playfully on the arm. "You be nice today, Mr. Anti-Everything."

"I'm always nice," Daddy said, winking at Katie.

"Like when you forgot the cannoli?"

Daddy shifted in his seat. "I told you I gave them to a beggar."

"A likely story," sighed Mummy.

"And for the record, I'm not anti-everything. I just don't blindly follow a bunch of outdated Biblical tenets. I mean, what's next? Will the Catholic Church ban me for being metrosexual? Will I be excommunicated because I pluck my eyebrows and look good in an Armani suit?"

Mummy giggled despite herself. Katie ate more oatmeal.

Daddy pushed back his chair and scooped Katie up, spinning her until she squealed with glee while he kissed her again and again on the cheek. "But I am not anti-you, my sweet little chubby chunk of love!"

For a moment they were suspended in a private joy that was entirely removed from the troubles of recent days.

"More!" Katie demanded, throwing her arms wide and her head back.

Simon and Rebecca rejoiced to see their daughter exhibit silliness and fun. In that moment, Katie's body seemed solely hers, and she occupied it with childlike happiness.

As she spun and spun, Katie discovered something new: wild play could momentarily shut out the disturbing visions. Stillness wasn't the secret—fun was. "More! More!" she cried.

Daddy obeyed until he was too dizzy to continue. As he lowered Katie to the floor, she held on to his neck, and they laughed together as he steadied himself.

Chapter 13

Rome

"Sunday is the preferred day, of course."

"Yes, Bishop Parker. I know," Father Kelly agreed.

"The celebration of baptism during the Sunday Eucharist celebration is strongly encouraged so that children and families learn more about our church and its traditions."

"That would be ideal." Kelly nodded briskly.

"And yet here we are on a Thursday, preparing for an afternoon event that likely will draw little attention among the multitude, so to speak."

An unexpected visit from Bishop Parker, who had taken Father Kelly under his wing when he'd first arrived in Rome, was usually a pleasant event. The large, middle-aged man, whose forehead was swept with a wave of graying hair, had a way of encouraging younger priests without being overbearing. But today, Father Kelly was beginning to feel cornered, even outdoors in the Piazza di Santa Maria.

"Also, I see no godparents listed—"

Kelly quickly countered, "Yes, well, no godparents have been chosen. Though I understand a close friend and physician from Bambino Gesù Hospital will attend." He felt defensive, as though he were rushing to baptize the girl. Which, of course, he was, but he couldn't possibly share his reasons with the bishop.

"Good. And the parents, have they confided what they expect from God's Church for their child?"

"Expect?" Kelly felt simultaneously jumpy and sluggish. "Well . . . safety, for sure, and—"

"Safety?" Bishop Parker said quizzically.

"Protection is the word I meant to use," Kelly covered.

"Protection from . . .?" The bishop's hanging question was clearly an invitation for him to be more specific or candid, and preferably both.

Father Kelly ignored it. "Bishop, if there is a problem in the scheduling . . ." He let the question hang.

"No. Not that I'm aware of," the bishop muttered.

"May I inquire, then, what your concern is at this late hour?"

The bishop paused and averted his eyes. Father Kelly glanced around the square and noticed a man sitting idle on an adjacent bench. A tourist, he assumed, capturing images of a church with his phone held aloft, aimed past the bench where he and the bishop sat.

"Father, when we bring families into our embrace, we do have some expectations of our own. Do we not?"

"Most certainly."

"Such as?"

"The parents must accept some responsibility for training their child in the practice of the faith. God's commandments are not to be ignored," Kelly said.

The bishop carried on his Socratic-method sermon. "Yes. Very good. And the parents of this little girl, have they expressed how they will fulfill their duty after the baptism?"

"They are lovely people, Bishop," Kelly said, more defensively than he intended. For a moment, he felt the pang of envy he'd experienced upon seeing Simon at his door the other day. The same sensation had shamed him when Rebecca and Simon had presented their daughter to him in the square. Despite his ironclad vow to the Church—and all the reassurance he had given to Simon upon meeting him—Father Kelly quietly hoped that priests might be allowed to marry in his lifetime. Seeing Rebecca with their daughter—after what they had been through, after what he had given up, and those red curls, that little nose, and the piercing eyes of his child—all of it made him wonder. *Might he lay with a woman he loved and not sin? Would he be a good father to the children who surely would be born of his marital bed?* Part of him longed to know.

"You know them well," the bishop said. A statement, not a question.

Father Kelly felt challenged. "I—Bishop, if I may, I'm sensing that you have doubts about my ability to anoint this child."

"Not at all."

"Then what issue are we dancing around?" He had never before spoken to his mentor in this manner, but his patience was wearing thin.

"Your future," the bishop said.

A cloud passed over the sun, throwing a long shadow across the square. Yet the chill Father Kelly felt came from within.

"My future?" Father Kelly felt the smooth marble fountain under his left hand. Legend said that on the night of Jesus's birth, a geyser of oil had miraculously appeared from the earth here and flowed into the Tiber River. The Jewish community in Trastevere had interpreted it as a sign that God's grace would soon flow into the world, and because of the spring, the spot became a meeting place for the first Roman converts to Christianity.

"Father Kelly, you are a rare talent. You might help carry our Church forward. We must shepherd you, guide you as best we can. But one obstacle in the road has the power to forever alter a man's path. Your associations, your encouragements, your—"

"Are you suggesting that I cancel the baptism of this child?" Kelly interrupted, no longer interested in guidance or approval.

Bishop Parker's face darkened as he turned away. His head was down, and his lips moved as though in prayer. When he looked back up, he gazed out over the square. "The child, any child, deserves the blessings of Christ. The parents, though . . . I hope they fully appreciate how and why our Church functions in the way that it does. In the way that it must."

At this, the bishop smiled, patted Father Kelly's knee, and rose. The conversation was over.

Father Kelly watched the bishop disappear around a corner as sunlight returned to the square. Although he intended to go back inside Santa Maria, he stopped walking when he noticed the same tourist sitting on a different bench and again fiddling with his cell phone.

The man looked up even as his fingers pressed buttons, and it was apparent to Kelly that behind dark sunglasses, the man's eyes were on him. The priest changed direction. He hastily followed in Bishop Parker's footsteps, rounding the same corner before ducking behind a newsstand.

Moments later, a thickset man with deep wrinkles in his forehead passed. The tourist.

As he rushed back to the cathedral, looking over his shoulder all the way, Father Kelly wondered, *Why am I being followed?*

◆

VATICAN CITY

Father Lemski changed out of his cassock into a plain black suit, wrapping a dark scarf around his neck. He added a dark gray fedora and stood before the bathroom mirror. He saw an utterly ordinary man, possibly a longtime resident of Rome, a cipher among the throngs who went about their business every day.

Although the secretive nature of Lemski's work in Vatican City often made him feel insignificant and unappreciated, he now savored the thought of anonymity. How grand to stroll about the city of Rome with little fear of detection by other priests or their minions.

Even his flock of undercover agents, who might recognize his voice, would never be able to spot him in a crowd. That included Carlitos, who, it seemed, could not carry out the simplest assignment without going astray and requiring additional intervention on Lemski's part. Maybe this time, though, the lunkhead's incompetence had actually done him a favor.

"He got away," Carlitos had reported by phone half an hour earlier, without embarrassment or contrition.

"What do you mean?" *How hard could it be,* Lemski wondered, *to follow one man?*

"He took off from Piazza Santa Maria, and I lost him."

"Did you check the church?"

"No, but—"

"Well, perhaps he circled back."

"Maybe, but—"

"But what?" Lemski fumed. What was so hard about keeping your eyes and ears open? Could this brute from São Paulo not tie his own shoes without tripping headfirst into the sewer?

He calmed himself with the thought that his operative's ineptitude only proved his own superiority. "Where are you now, Carlitos?"

"Um. I don't know."

"How can you not know, my son?"

"A lot on my mind."

Lemski tried again. "All runners stumble. Don't let this little mistake—"

"I didn't fall . . ."

Lemski's fury returned. He pulled the phone away from his ear and squeezed it in his hand. With difficulty, he got himself under control again. "Carlitos, listen to me. Return to the church. He probably ran an errand and—"

"I think he might have seen me taking pictures," Carlitos interrupted.

"So? He doesn't know you. You're a tourist, remember? Return to the church and enter when the baptism begins. No one will notice another visitor wanting to attend such a special service."

Father Lemski reminded himself to be grateful that for every under-achiever like Carlitos, there was a Nurse Negrelli, who, in his mind, was fast approaching sainthood.

> From: Bambino Gesù Hospital. Nurse Amedea Negrelli reports baptism Thursday, 2 p.m. Mother distraught. Cognitive tests do not reveal source of child's strange behavior, including a frightening accusatory gesture in doctor's office. Mother too exhausted to properly discipline little girl.

The update had come with enough time for Lemski to devise a plan. He hoped he could count on Carlitos, who was becoming demanding.

"I need to get paid. Today. Can you get me the money I earned so far?" Carlitos blurted out.

"You know how our payment methods work," Lemski replied patiently.

"Yes, but—"

"Stop saying 'yes, but'!"

"Okay," Carlitos said, his tone suddenly shifting. "But don't say I didn't warn you."

"About what?" Lemski asked. Carlitos, though bumbling, had at least been predictable. This new attitude suggested more of the potential that had been detected when he was recruited but might be harder to deal with.

Carlitos paused. "I might have to disappear for a while."

"You're in trouble?" Lemski said, masking his hopefulness.

"Maybe . . . and maybe you too."

Lemski's shoulders tightened. "Perhaps you should tell me what's going on, Carlitos."

"Perhaps you should give me my money."

Good God, Lemski thought. *Blackmail's bad enough, but attitude too?* "You're not happy with your assignment, Carlitos?" he growled through gritted teeth.

"It'll do." A short pause. "But *Polizia di Stato* don't seem so happy."

"Police? What have you done?" Lemski groaned in frustration at being expected to figure out the situation through these thinly veiled threats Carlitos was lobbing at him.

"You know what I've done!" The accusatory voice was quiet but forceful. Despite himself, Lemski began to feel vulnerable.

"Somebody must have seen me or something," Carlitos continued, just vaguely enough to heighten Lemski's concern.

"Will you please tell me exactly what we're talking about?" He was tired of playing cat and mouse with this knuckle-walking street thug.

"Why? You never tell me anything."

"For reasons I've already explained, Carlitos," Lemski said, "This is a highly sensitive—"

Carlitos interrupted. "Then I guess that's what I'll tell the police when I give them your phone number."

"How dare you threaten me!"

"I want my money," Carlitos reiterated, his tone even.

"You know I can simply dispose of this phone and get another." Lemski liked the authority he heard in his voice. In a magnanimous tone, he offered, "Listen, I'll make arrangements for delivery after the baptism. But outside, away from the gathering. Understood, Carlitos?"

"How do I know you won't call the police instead?"

"What purpose would it serve for me to cheat you, Carlitos? Do you want your money or not?" Lemski knew he had the oaf with that.

"I'll be there."

"After the baptism. Outside on the square."

"I got it," Carlitos said.

After ending the call, the priest sat quietly at his window and crossed himself. He would attend the baptism incognito. It was essential that he stop relying on this disastrous thug and see the mysterious little girl with his own eyes.

Chapter 14

Rome

Dr. Maly Rin sat quietly in Santa Maria Church as the pews behind her filled with people. Unlike others, who whispered and stared at the splendor around them, which she had seen before—the wide marble columns, the intricate Cosmatesque floor, the colorful mosaics rimmed in gold—today, the doctor was not aware of her surroundings. Test results occupied her brain like an invading army.

Page after page of Katie's medical file stated, essentially, nothing. Rebecca was desperate to account for the child's behavior, and Maly could offer no explanation. She wondered whether the mess involving Katie was her long-awaited penance for fleeing and not returning to her own parents when they'd called out to her.

She'd always reassured herself that her mother and father had been urging her and her younger brother onward and away, to safety, to freedom, to a future. But lately, she'd found herself wondering whether they had, in fact, been calling out to her to turn back and come to their rescue, to weather whatever came next as a family.

Her work had always driven away the nightmares; the facts and figures in all her medical files were solid and specific and reassuring.

Just last night, though, she had dreamed of sitting curled in her mother's embrace. When her mother moved to adjust her position, Maly did the same and only then noticed the pink lines cutting across her mother's arms like rivulets, running to a delta of scarring. Maly had been afraid to lift her eyes to her mother's face, terrified of the mass of burned tissue she would see. The dream was the worst she'd experienced yet. She'd never woken before with the smell of smoke in her nostrils.

No chart could distract her from the piercing guilt. Had she missed something about the girl? And what would account for her ever-more-frequent dreams of Cambodia, a place she'd vowed never to think about again?

Maly had even considered calling her brother. She'd read about people who continued to search for loved ones even years after disasters. But Maly hadn't looked back. Even before they'd fallen out of touch, she'd never mustered the courage to ask her brother what he had seen when he had glanced over his shoulder as she had reached for his hand to hurry them along.

The Bambino Gesù Hospital was not just a haven for children with exceptional medical problems. It had rescued Maly. She continually threw herself into her work, overseeing tricky convalescences and marveling over unexpected recoveries that made her proud to serve humanity through medicine. But her inability to unravel the mystery of Katie Murphy was starting to unravel her. Maybe it was guilt that had led her into medicine, but she could not pretend it could provide forgiveness.

"May I join you?" A male voice interrupted Maly's thoughts. She was immediately comfortable with the presence of the large white-haired man, even as he sat almost too close beside her. She watched as he settled in and suspected he was not as old as his hair might suggest. He smiled gently at her, and she found his mixture of dignity and kindness attractive. Maly's mind wandered to wondering why there was no man in her life to comfort her after the nightmares. Most days, she accepted that there was simply no room for one.

"We're drawing quite a crowd, it seems," the man said, looking over his shoulder.

"Hm?" Maly turned to discover that clusters of people had gathered. What had started as a trickle was now a deluge. "Why?" she asked, more to herself than to the man next to her.

"Yes. Why indeed?" he replied with an almost impish grin. "Perhaps we should sell tickets—a charitable offering, of course."

"Are you a friend of the family?" she asked.

"A colleague of the priest, actually. I am Bishop Parker. And you?"

Maly hesitated. "Yes, a friend." Then, her spine tingled as it had when she'd discovered Nurse Negrelli in her office the day before. She thought back to the senior nurse's curiosity about Katie, the way she loitered during the child's appointments, and Rebecca's discomfort during their latest visit.

"What's wrong, Becca?" she'd asked when it was obvious her friend was holding something back.

"I don't know. Is . . . Is Amedea acting strangely today?"

"How do you mean?" Maly had asked, quietly pleased to hear her suspicions echoed by someone else.

"Maybe it's me. I'm so . . . she's just . . . I'm uncomfortable."

"She's thorough," Maly had said. Truthfully, though, she had wanted to ask if Becca also felt that the nurse was searching: every question an insinuation, every remark a criticism.

"She's oppressive." Rebecca described how Katie had pointed a finger at the nurse, who had recoiled before recovering with a broad, false smile.

"Like she was acting?"

"Yes. Like it was a mask, that smile."

Maly thought back. Before she'd dismissed Negrelli so that she could speak to Rebecca in private, the nurse had leaned over the desk as though to assist. What had caught Maly's eye was a silver crucifix that slipped out from under the woman's collar. It struck her as a talisman of sorts, not intended for the sight of others.

In sudden nervousness, Maly's hands lost their grip on her handbag, which rolled onto the floor with an embarrassingly long series of clinks and crashes. Bishop Parker started, then helped her gather the items that had rolled under his feet.

"Are you all right?" he asked, his hand gently touching her forearm.

Maly ignored him and slowly examined the faces of the numerous strangers who filled the church. Nearly every pair of eyes challenged her with pious indignation.

When she settled into her seat again, Maly was grim.

"My dear, you're trembling," the bishop said, placing his hand over hers.

Maly pulled away. The steely eyes of the strangers were unsettling yet familiar. She had seen that same look from the political insurgents who had swept through her country as though they were entitled to maul and mutilate and burn anyone who challenged their creed.

◆

DADDY WAS LECTURING again, but Katie could tell his heart wasn't in it. Her parents had indulged her wish—which they correctly interpreted from her soft, disjointed phrases—to visit the Ponte Sant'Angelo. It was the opposite direction from Santa Maria, but they agreed it would be fun to take a taxi to the church on such a special day.

She felt beautiful in her white dress and stockings, leather shoes, and the special bracelet Mummy had slipped around her wrist before they'd left the house, just after she had tightened the bow in Katie's hair and smoothed her own skirt.

"Honey, here we are! You are now on one of the oldest and most famous bridges in the world." As Katie walked, the bridge stretched before her, long and wide. She could see the river through the diamond-shaped openings along the sides. "Look at the iron balustrades," Daddy said, pointing.

Mummy chuckled. "Balustrade. Dear, that's a big word for a little girl."

"Start them young, that's what I say," Daddy said. "In fact . . . Katie, the Roman emperor Hadrian had this bridge built out of travertine marble around two thousand years ago, in 134," Daddy said, but his enthusiasm seemed make-believe. Katie had only known him for a week, but she could tell there was no fire or passion in this speech.

"Yeah, yeah, yeah," Mummy said. "Get to the good part." Her arm was threaded through Daddy's; her hand held Katie's.

"My erudition *is* the good part." Daddy smiled, and Katie felt better. That was the Daddy she knew.

"Oh, 'erudition.' Now you're really getting going," Mummy said.

"Before the seventh century, the pilgrims named this beauty the Bridge of St. Peter because it was the main way from Rome to the Basilica."

"Tell Katie about the angels," Mummy urged when they arrived at the crest of the walkway over the Tiber River.

Katie looked up to see her mother's face alight with excitement and anticipation, then up to the giant statues that loomed above her; from her viewpoint, their wings looked like they touched the heavens.

"But I've told her," Daddy replied. "At the Basilica, remember?"

"More. More," Katie said.

Mummy smiled as she squeezed Katie's hand.

"First, you have to tell me the name of the artist," Daddy challenged Katie with a wink.

"Simon, she's a child."

"She's our child, and we are educated—"

Katie interrupted with a sound she repeated in various tones and cadences as if she were trying it out. "Brrrr—brrrr—"

"Are you cold, honey?" Mummy knelt to button the top of Katie's coat. But before she could finish, Katie shook her head and blurted, "Berni."

Mummy and Daddy looked at each other with delight.

"So my little pebble does remember Bernini!"

◆

THROUGHOUT THE MORNING, Simon had reviewed his doubts about the baptism. Had he agreed too quickly? Would the ceremony actually do anything helpful, like calming Katie's nightmares or revealing more about what troubled her? He'd made a personal vow during one of his earliest counseling sessions with Becca to continue expressing his skepticism, but respectfully and with humor. He now owed that to his daughter.

He continued explaining that in the year 1535, there were six huge statues standing on each pillar of the bridge—the likenesses of Adam, Noah, Abraham, Moses, St. Peter, and St. Paul, who were still present and posed as if they were teaching from their Bibles. It wasn't until the mid-1600s that Bernini asked ten angels to fly down from heaven and land on the bridge so that he could sculpt them.

"The gorgeous and colossal angels really liked Bernini," Simon said, picking Katie up and spinning her in a slow circle, her arms spreading apart in the crisp air. "So they agreed to his request and soared down and perched on the bridge."

"Angels!" Katie said and pointed upward with both hands.

"Yes, sweetie. But now all we have is marble likenesses. After Bernini finished his great work, the angels flew back to heaven, where they lived happily ever after."

"Angels, angels!"

The excitement in Katie's voice drew stares from passersby.

"Do you remember what else Bernini asked of the angels?" Simon asked. "Look at their hands." He lifted Katie higher as he slowly passed a statue. Each angel displayed a significant item: a cross, nails, whips, a crown of thorns, a sponge, a lance, a throne, a facecloth, a scripture, and a garment with dice. "Do you see the dice, Katie?" he asked as he positioned the girl on his shoulders.

"Dice," she repeated as her fingers stretched upward as if she could reach them.

"Yes." Simon moved closer and stretched Katie's arm for her, but the girl's fingers couldn't even graze the bewildering shapes. "Strange to see dice related to Jesus, eh?" he asked, turning back to Rebecca with a raised eyebrow that suggested he was coming close to finding his usual form.

Rebecca interrupted, "Simon, she doesn't need to hear all this. Not today."

"She does, especially today, I would think," he replied. Rebecca's face fell. Katie reached down for her mother's cheek and laid her hand there like a blessing.

Rebecca took the consoling hand into her own and kissed it. "Not today, Simon," she repeated.

"I'm only—"

"Please, Simon!"

Simon lowered Katie to the stone walkway and looked out over the river, silent but smoldering. His patience for false decorum was thinning. Speaking the truth was not a sacrilege; it was a responsibility. When you join the Church, you should be told everything. Everything.

"Once Jesus was nailed to the cross, the Roman soldiers gambled for His clothes by throwing dice. Can you imagine?" he continued in a softer tone.

Rebecca opened her mouth when another voice in a heavy British accent responded, "All the things the angels are holding are known as the instruments of the Passion." A young man with cropped blond hair stared up at an angel while sketching with ink on a broad pad. He spoke with zeal before looking up with a smile and asking, "Are you tourists?"

Katie's shrill voice overpowered Simon's attempt to reply. "There, there!"

Rebecca groaned to see the source of her daughter's outburst. "No, sweetheart, you cannot have gelato. You're wearing your church clothes."

"Maybe just a taste." Simon grabbed Katie's hand and ran toward the pastel-colored stand.

"But she'll drip it all over her pretty coat and dress," Rebecca cried.

"Jesus will understand." Simon smirked. Katie giggled as she tried to keep up.

Rebecca shot the young man a chagrined shrug, then followed her husband and daughter toward the mobile gelato stand as Katie and Simon decided together which flavor would cause the worst stain.

◆

AFTER PURCHASING A small cup with gooey, dark-colored flavors, the three crossed St. Peter's Bridge toward the Castel Sant'Angelo, where they hoped to hail a taxi. Father and daughter hurriedly swallowed the remnants of their treat.

As the family disappeared from view, the young blond man pulled out a burner phone. In a hushed voice, he shared every detail of what he had observed. "He seems so eager for blasphemy. And the child, my God, she is a sponge for his every indiscretion."

"You have done well, Stefan. You are a blessing."

"I'm honored, sir."

The artist glowed with pride. He longed to meet his advisor, enjoy the fraternity of church leaders, and rise in the security ranks as fast as possible.

Father Kelly greeted the Murphys at the church entrance and escorted them to his office. He complimented Katie's beautiful dress and was acknowledged with a perfectly normal, shy smile that eased his nerves. He had cleared his mind of the tourist who had seemed to follow him earlier in the day and thought only of what he had said to Bishop Parker: the Murphys were lovely people.

He felt the tension between Simon and Rebecca but didn't want to push the issue before the ceremony. He asked simple, indirect questions, hoping to draw them out. In return, he received an assortment of monosyllabic answers, nods, and forced smiles. So he focused on Katie.

"Where did you get such sticky fingers, little one?" he asked.

"The angels."

The child's reply was so sincere he laughed, and looked to Rebecca and Simon to join in. But instead, their eyes seemed to avoid meeting his.

"The angels? Well, I hope you'll tell me where they were serving treats so I can have sticky fingers too."

"Berni—ni," she said as her arm rose and pointed one finger to the heavens.

Father Kelly chuckled. "Admit it, Simon. You've been tutoring her again."

Simon replied, "*Mea culpa*, Father," but without his usual good cheer.

Father Kelly pushed on, explaining that if Katie's baptism were being performed during Mass, he and Rebecca would have been asked several questions before entering the nave. "But since this is a private gathering, we'll save those questions and use them to begin our ceremony. Shall we go through them once before we go to the altar?"

◆

In his handsome disguise, Father Lemski stood beside the fountain in the square, believed to be the oldest in Rome, and observed individuals and couples entering Santa Maria Church. It was a good sign that the baptism would not be kept secret, but he felt suddenly conspicuous. *The eyes of Christ witness the actions of every deceiver.*

Around him, strangers grinned and posed for photographs, unwittingly capturing him in the background or at the edge of the frame. But he could find no good reason to move away.

As he stood self-consciously in the suit that was beginning to feel too long at the wrists and ankles, he was struck by the sudden recognition that perhaps Carlitos's work was not as simple as he had thought. Trying not to be conspicuous made him feel like a painted bird fluttering among sparrows. The longer he stood in place, the more he felt the curiosity of others around the fountain.

Rationally, he knew he looked like nothing more than a single man who was uncomfortable being alone. His anxiety, Lemski realized, stemmed from the notion that perhaps he wasn't alone. His role meant that he was among the thugs and spies he handled. But was he also being handled? Was someone charged with keeping him in sight?

A sudden fear struck Lemski: might he and Carlitos actually recognize each other via some sixth sense—or worse, because Carlitos was privy to information Lemski wasn't, making his identity no mystery at all? Lemski had no knowledge of the couriers who dispatched the Vatican's cash, but they too might know him. He was embarrassed and ashamed at his naive belief that a change of clothing could hide him.

An elderly woman whose black hat clung like a bee's nest to the back of her head stood beside him. She shielded her eyes with her hand as she looked up at him. "Excuse me, sir," she said. "Do you know if Mass will be offered today?"

"How should I know?" he replied. Realizing that he sounded harsh, he tried to backtrack: "I couldn't possibly know, madam, as this is my first time visiting the city."

As the woman squinted up at him, he continued, "It must be a special occasion. People are entering the church early as if they know seats will fill."

"Oh, are you a member?" she inquired.

He unconsciously patted the scarf that lay where his collar should be before backpedaling again. "It's just a guess. I overheard a gentleman. I'm merely a tourist myself."

The woman nodded. "Thank you, sir. Be well."

"And you," he said, doffing his hat clumsily, then feeling ridiculous for doing so. He knew he should head for the church, find a small space in the back, and watch the ceremony.

Then his heart skipped, and he sucked in what felt like his last breath. The physical sensations that overtook him challenged his vow of chastity with such force, he found himself stumbling forward a step.

A slight young man with blond hair had stopped before the church, pulling a sketch pad from his satchel. With pen in hand, the beautiful creature bent his knee and began to draw.

The slender limbs and graceful, delicate gestures tortured Lemski. The way he lifted and lowered his head, the sweeping movements of his creamy arm—it had been years since Father Lemski had pined for anyone.

To combat the intense feeling, he forced himself to turn away. In this moment, there was no Carlitos, no money to be paid or leaders to answer to; in this moment, there was only his desire and this beautiful young man, oblivious of being so intensely watched. Lemski bowed his head and whispered, "Forgive me, Father, for I have sinned."

But he could not help looking back as the artist changed position, this time standing with his focus fixed upward. The clock in the tower behind the entrance told Lemski that he must enter the church soon or walk away.

He could not walk away. This time, he would not walk away.

He strode toward the modest arched opening of St. Maria Basilica, stealing glances from under the brim of his hat. When the artist knelt again, Lemski could not suppress the urge to peek at his drawing. He didn't realize how close he was until he noticed his shadow on the pad. As he stepped back, the young man turned to look at him.

"I am so sorry. I didn't mean . . . to interrupt," Lemski stammered.

The young man rose and offered a generous smile. "Not at all," he said, holding his sketch pad out to Lemski. "I was trying to capture the contrast between the bright natural light and the shadows within the entrance. Small things to notice and enjoy. There's so much to see here."

"There truly is," Lemski replied, only to realize that he was staring at the way the boy's mouth moved when he spoke, his lips plump and smooth. *Christ save me,* he thought. *How vulnerable even the strongest among us are.* "Well, your talent is a blessing," he managed as he returned the pad. "Best of luck to you."

"Thank you, sir," the young man said, removing the graphite pencil from its place behind his ear once more.

By the time Lemski found a seat midway down the long, narrow nave, he was sweating and his hands were shaking. He lowered himself to the kneeling bench and inhaled deeply. Only when he heard the priest speak did he raise his head.

Chapter 15

Rome

"What name have you given your child?"

An enormous mosaic full of yellows, blues, and greens, and wrapped in gold, depicting Mary and baby Jesus, loomed above Rebecca's head as she replied, "Katerina." Her own voice sounded unfamiliar. She was amazed to be baptizing her daughter in such a glorious place; what a blessing.

She sat in the first pew, with Simon and Katie on her left. They all stared up at Father Kelly, who stood at the edge of the dais. She felt a comforting hand upon her own. It was Maly, who sat on her right.

"What do you ask of God's Church for your child?"

Simon had suggested that Rebecca answer the priest's questions. It was an olive branch she'd accepted with a weak smile. When she faltered, however, Simon whispered, "Eternal life."

Rebecca appreciated the cue and considered her words carefully before answering, "I want my child to always know and feel the grace of Jesus Christ."

Father Kelly nodded and smiled warmly. He knew how difficult it was for parents who were not public speakers to be singled out in a crowd, especially among so many strangers. There had been no time to process the surprise of entering the nave and discovering thirty or so unknown faces looking back at them. Rebecca had gasped, and it was Katie who had offered support with a reassuring squeeze of her mother's hand.

"You have requested to have your child baptized. Does this mean that you, Rebecca and Simon, accept the responsibility of—"

Perhaps none of the strangers noticed. They might have thought Father Kelly merely paused in his recitation. They might not have detected the sudden, slight widening of his eyes, the twitch of recognition.

But Bishop Parker, still seated in the front pew, noticed. He had moved several meters to the left of the Murphys so as not to intrude on their sacred moment but stayed close enough to witness anything that might take place.

He kept his eyes on Father Kelly and waited for him to resume the ceremony. When the silence lengthened, the bishop turned to look back at the parishioners, hoping to spot the distraction. Stern, unsmiling faces met his gaze, except for one. Toward the back, the bishop noticed a young man fiddling with a cell phone held low in his lap. *Technology be damned,* the bishop thought, not for the first time. *Give your eyes and ears to God!*

What irked him even more were the deep, wide wrinkles in the man's forehead that suggested his phone deserved the same solemn attention as the ceremony at the altar. Tourists! What was he doing here if he couldn't tear himself away from this modern idol?

The bishop's ire diminished when he heard Father Kelly speak again, his voice a note higher.

"Does this mean that you, Rebecca and Simon Murphy, accept the responsibility of training your daughter in the practice of our faith and—"

"Yes," said Rebecca, breathy and tense.

She looked up at Father Kelly. He nodded almost imperceptibly toward her and continued. "—and know that it will be your duty to raise Katerina to keep God's commandments as Christ taught us, by loving God and our neighbor? And do you clearly understand what you are undertaking?"

"We do," said Rebecca, her voice more confident with the sense of purpose that was hers to claim.

Bishop Parker was touched by the woman's devoutness.

Father Kelly stepped down from the altar and moved toward Katie with outstretched arms. "Our Christian community welcomes you with great joy, Katerina," he said, his pride apparent. "In its name, I claim you for Christ our Savior by the sign of His cross. I will now trace the cross on your forehead and invite your parents to—"

But before the priest's fingers could reach Katie's face, she lurched out of the pew with a cry of pain and backed away from the altar with stilted, robotic movements. She turned a terrified look from her parents to Dr. Rin and finally to the priest.

"I am not worthy!" she shrieked, her eyes wild. It was not the voice of a child. The sound shattered the sacred space like a bombardment.

Father Kelly moved quickly to reassure Katie and rescue the ceremony. "Christ our Savior claims you, and by the sign of the—"

"I don't know him!" Katie shrieked, her hand groping behind her back as if looking for something solid to hold on to.

"Katie!" Rebecca reached out as the congregation began to whisper, the sound causing Katie's gaze to fly about as she continued to move backward, cowering.

"I don't know the man. I don't know him!" she sobbed.

Simon, equally stunned, moved to comfort his daughter. But Katie avoided his grasp, suddenly dashing toward Father Kelly. When she reached the priest, who still seemed willing to welcome her into his embrace, she clutched at him, tearing the crucifix from his neck and holding it aloft and upside down for all to see.

"I am not worthy! I am not worthy!" she screamed.

Hysteria overtook the crowd. Parents attempted to shelter their children from the sight of the apparently possessed Katie and put hands over their children's ears, while others rose with calls for Father Kelly to do something.

One voice rose above the angry din. "How dare you deny Christ's blessing! Heresy. Heresy. You speak for Satan!"

The parishioners quickly took up the man's call, their denunciations evolving into a crude chant. "Exorcise her! *Esorcizzare il demone!*"

Simon turned from the altar and saw a man in a black suit standing on a pew, pointing at Katie. Enraged, he leaped for the man, attempting to lunge over pews and drag him to the stone floor, but he was pushed away as the chanting continued. "Exorcise her! *Esorcizzare il demone!*"

"Goddamn you!" he screamed from the floor, where he was pinned down. He fought but could not rise. "Come down here and face me like a man, you fucking bastard!" he spat.

"Simon, no!" Rebecca moved to push the crowd away from her husband.

Appalled, Bishop Parker turned to his protégé. "I tried to warn you. How could you let this happen?"

Simon finally broke free and rushed up the center aisle to the man who stood at the center of the angry crowd. "How dare you!" he yelled, even as he felt hands grabbing him again. He managed to wrench himself free and grab the suited man by the lapels, continuing to curse him. The spectators closed in and dragged him off, which allowed the man in black enough time to run toward the exit, pulling the fedora down over his eyes.

"Stop him! Stop that man!" Simon continued to shout hopelessly.

Carlitos had taken part in many brawls, including some he'd personally organized, but he had never seen anything like this happen in a church. After he moved with the rest of the crowd to block the father from reaching the old man in the ill-fitting suit, Carlitos climbed over the pews himself. Standing behind the rows, he knew he had to call his boss and report what he was observing. This time he wouldn't be accused of failing to pay attention.

When the shouting made it impossible to hear, he stepped outside the entrance. As he pressed the phone to his ear, still able to see inside or spot anyone leaving, he thought he heard another phone ringing behind him.

Carlitos turned and saw the man in the black suit, the one who had been standing atop the pew and enraging the crowd. He was running away. The sound of the phone faded as the man disappeared into the square, but Carlitos gave it no thought because two municipal policemen were rushing toward the church. Pretending to have a casual conversation, he sauntered around the corner and disappeared.

The young man with the closely cut blond hair observed everything from a distance. He had not entered the church, although he was there to spy on the irreverent father of a very peculiar little girl. He had decided to wait outside once he recognized the voice of the man who had stopped to praise his artistry.

It had taken only one word, spoken with an Eastern European accent, to convince him that he was in the presence of the very man whose fraternity he craved.

Stefan saw his leader dash out of the basilica and followed. It wasn't hard to keep up. The man was almost twice his age and breathing heavily, his legs unsteady. The running soon devolved into a brisk walk, then a ponderous stroll, and finally lapsed into intermittent rests that eventually took both men to the soaring walls of the fortress known as Vatican City.

Stefan panicked when he realized he did not have access to the glori-fied city-state and would soon lose contact with his advisor.

Then he laughed at his foolishness, reached into his pocket for his phone, and dialed. "Sir? This is Stefan."

Chapter 16

São Paulo

Edhir Souza was still in bed when the phone rang just after 10 a.m. To reach it, he had to stretch across Djiana's naked body, only half covered by a white sheet. He couldn't resist kissing the nape of her neck as he grabbed the phone. She stirred with a slight groan as he answered, "*Olá?*"

The voice on the other end belonged to one of his administrators. Many Evangelicals had gone forth from Brazil to make their way in the world, but they still retained strong ties to their church. They tithed with money orders and electronic funds transfers, and they reported on events that seemed to show the influence of Jesus Cristo in the world—or the opposite. When a particularly interesting story was brought to the church's attention, it was forwarded to Edhir.

He listened to what the man had to say, thanked him for the information, and hung up. Flopping backward onto the bed, he laid one hand on Djiana's back, slowly caressing her from shoulders to hips with his fingertips until goosebumps rose on her skin and she shivered. She rolled onto her back and looked at him, wakefulness slowly filling her deep-brown eyes.

"Good morning," she said in Portuguese. "Who was that?"

"Andreas," he said, smiling at her. "He had quite an interesting story to tell. Something happened in Rome."

"What?" She rose up on one elbow, making it extraordinarily difficult for him to focus on her expression of curiosity, rather than her marvelous breasts.

"A couple from Ireland were in St. Peter's Basilica with their daughter, attempting to have her baptized, and the girl threw a fit," he began.

"So? Babies cry when you splash water on them. Why is this important?"

"No, no, *minha querida*," he said, placing one hand on her shoulder. "This was no baby and no mere cry. It was a little girl of about four, and when the priest began the ceremony, she screamed out in a voice that was not her own, and the woman who saw it, the one who called Andreas—she said the girl denied Christ. She said the priest retreated from her and the crowd began to demand exorcism, and then the girl's father attacked the man who was leading the protest. It was havoc."

Her eyes widened. "Wow, that is something. Did the witness know anything about the family or the child?"

"No, she was there by pure luck," he lied. Edhir enjoyed Djiana's company, but there were things she did not need to know yet. "But perhaps I should have Andreas send her something for her trouble and to encourage her to keep her eyes open."

"You think it was madness? Or something more?"

"I don't know," he said truthfully. "It could be possession. But it could be a frightened little girl who shouted something that sounded demonic to a church full of superstitious Catholics." He laughed, a sound like gravel shaken in a box.

"Better to know than not know, though," Djiana said in a serious tone.

"Exactly," Edhir agreed. "If she has power, she can be of use to us in our struggle against the *Católicos*."

Djiana smiled. He knew she was happy to be told his plans, to experience this intimacy. It was certainly nothing he would say in the presence of the flock. "You think she could be?"

"Perhaps. But she is just a child. We will keep our eyes on her and watch for more signs. If she emerges as a true instrument of God's will, then we will be ready to employ her in our cause." He leaned toward Djiana and kissed her, first on the lips and then down her neck to her shoulders. She exhaled deeply and wrapped her arms around him.

Chapter 17

Rome

Katie sat on her bed, listening to her parents argue. They had been whispering angrily at each other for days. A tense quiet would settle over any room Katie entered, only to erupt in more whispers when she left.

She longed desperately to have parents to love her; it was crushing to think that she might be responsible for their apparent loss of love for each other. Any time she left the apartment, she liked to look at a picture on a table in the entry hall. In a silver frame, it showed Daddy's arms wrapped around Mummy's waist and her hair whipping in his face. It was clear to Katie that before she had come into their lives, love had been easy for them.

Nighttime was the worst. Despite their best efforts to keep their voices low, she knew that they'd grow angry and yell, and then one of them would come into her room to make sure she was still asleep. Their gentle smoothing of her bedcovers did not dim the feeling that more trouble was to come.

"How could you, Simon?" Mummy hissed.

"How could I what? Defend our daughter?" Daddy yelled back, not even attempting to whisper. "Who the hell were all those people in the church, anyway?"

"Catholics!" Mummy snapped.

"Well, that's the problem. Blind followers are no help to us," Daddy said. To Katie's ears, she was the problem that the Catholics were no help with. "I shouldn't have agreed with Father Kelly so quickly."

"Why are you bringing him into this?" Mummy cried. "He didn't do anything wrong."

"He turned Katie into a spectacle!"

With those six words, Katie felt the weight of everything that had worried her for as long as she could remember. She thought of herself standing atop that pew and holding Father Kelly's crucifix upside down as the mouths of angry men and women stretched into ugly shapes and made frightening sounds.

"How could he know Katie would say those things?" Mummy asked.

"Those things" had rippled through the community at an alarming pace. The phone rang endlessly as people called to ask her parents questions, and one lady even asked to come and speak with Katie. Italian tabloids published sketchy stories—"Brawl Rocks Baptism"—and local bloggers used the event to argue about Vatican policy.

Katie knew all this only because these people's opinions caused even more arguments. Daddy would tell Mummy what he'd read, and Mummy would keep repeating, "How could you?" back to him. Most nights, these words were the last thing Katie would remember, though she never knew whether it was because she had fallen asleep or if Mummy couldn't think of anything else to say.

This morning, though, Katie heard her parents in a different way. She felt an odd energetic feeling coming on. For the first time, she heard more than the real voices of her parents or the tortured voices of the past: she heard the future.

◆

POLICE ARRIVED AT the apartment door. The banging startled Katie. Two uniformed officers and a third man in a tailored suit were waiting in the hallway. The man in the suit inquired, "Simon and Rebecca Murphy?"

Daddy said, "Yes, I'm Simon," with a hint of surprise but no concern.

"We are from *Polizia Giudiziaria*," the man in the suit said.

"The judicial police?" Something crept into Daddy's voice, a tone Katie didn't recognize and didn't like.

"Correct. My name is Frosino Azzara. I apologize for the intrusion. But we were hoping you might have time to answer some questions about recent events in your neighborhood."

Daddy invited the man into the living room. Azzara took a seat in the chair that creaked while the officers remained standing.

"Look," Daddy said, a little defensive. "We know the baptism got out of hand. But all I did was shout. It got a little noisy, that's all."

"Baptism?" Azzara said, sounding confused. The man's surprise felt to Katie like a puncture to a balloon that was starting to expand.

"Isn't that why you're here?" Daddy asked, now puzzled too. "Somebody called the police," he explained. "They had to, you know, disperse the crowd, so to speak."

"No, Mr. Murphy," the policeman said, sounding annoyed. "I'm afraid something more troubling brings me to your door." The chair creaked as the man leaned closer to Daddy. "Were you aware that a man was killed in your neighborhood about a week ago?"

Mummy moved closer to Daddy, with a worried face.

"We've been . . . preoccupied lately," Daddy said, turning to look at Mummy. "So no, I wasn't aware of a death. Rebecca, did you—"

"No, I haven't heard anything," Mummy responded.

Azzara presented Daddy with a blurry photo of an elderly man. "Recognize him?"

"No," Daddy said hesitantly.

"You're absolutely sure?"

"Well, I—no, I don't think so. Does he live in the neighborhood?" Daddy asked.

"No. But he frequented your street, and to be a bit more direct,"—he glanced at Mummy—"we have witnesses who say you engaged the man in conversation on the night he died."

"Me?" Daddy faltered.

"Yes, Mr. Murphy," Azzara replied flatly.

Daddy continued to respond with questions of his own: "And this was when? Where? Who would say that they saw such a thing?"

"Last weekend. At night. Perhaps if you take a closer look at the photo—"

Mummy interrupted. "Simon, the cannoli."

"The beggar?"

"Who else could it be?"

Daddy joked, "And to think you didn't believe that I'd given away your pastries." For a moment, Katie relaxed; Daddy sounded like himself again.

"So you do recognize this man," Azzara accused more than asked.

"Well, all I can tell you is a beggar startled me while I was on a walk. I guessed he wanted money, but I gave him a box of cannoli from Bella Ciao in Trastevere," Daddy explained.

"So you walked to Trastevere and returned home, and at that time, you encountered this man?" Azzara asked as he took out a small notepad.

"Well . . . not exactly. I visited our priest before walking home."

"The priest who performed the baptism?"

"Yes."

"Do you remember the time?"

"Of my visit?"

"Yes, and the priest's name."

"Father Kelly. Justin Kelly."

"Hmm. Go on."

Daddy looked at Mummy. He seemed uncomfortable. "Go on with what?"

Azzara smiled. "Whatever you can tell us will be most helpful, Mr. Murphy." He closed his notebook and lifted his head as if he knew he was finished writing, that no new information would change his conclusions.

"It, uh, grew late," Daddy answered. "We had a lot to talk about."

"You and Father Kelly," Azzara clarified.

"Correct. And when I left—the time, I don't know, my head was filled with so many—I had a lot on my mind."

At that, Mummy swallowed so loudly that it sounded painful.

Then, the thrust of the interrogation became suddenly clear, and Daddy exclaimed, "You can't be serious! Why would I hurt an old man?"

"Yes. Why?" Azzara asked coldly.

Daddy's words staggered out. "I'm a professor. I teach young people. I—"

"Your behavior was described as violent by parishioners at the baptism. Shameful words shouted in the house of God."

◆

KATIE UNDERSTOOD WHAT she was witnessing: the powers of hell.

The police would be visiting her new family not because the preposterous accusations would stick. They didn't need to stick. They only needed to ruin a reputation.

Katie's mind continued to flash images of her father, now at work.

◆

"SIMON, THERE IS no delicate way to say this. I regret to inform you that the rector has instructed me to postpone your position at the university."

Daddy was shocked but kept calm. "Postpone my position, but not me, I assume."

"Well, you see, yours was a temporary appointment, which we fully explained at the start of our relationship with you, and—"

"You continually praised me and assured me that funding would allow me to continue on."

"There, perhaps, is the rub. The rector had hoped that funds would give us the luxury of extending your stay, but—"

Daddy interrupted, "Student reviews of my teaching have been good."

"Very good. You're our most popular newcomer, by far," the department chairman agreed.

"Then surely I can expect to stay on in some other capacity?" Daddy asked.

"Well . . ." The department head was uncomfortable, shifting in his chair.

"Is it a complaint of some kind? Or seniority? Maybe competition with a colleague?"

"No."

"Don't tell me I'm being let go," Daddy asked incredulously.

The man seemed somewhat bolstered when he said, "And yet you are."

"But why?"

"Simon, we've been informed by *Polizia Giudiziaria* that you are a suspect in the unfortunate death of a homeless man in your neighborhood. We cannot be associated with such a scandal." By now, the department head was propelled by something outside himself, speaking in clipped, precise tones. "We shape young lives here—"

Daddy wouldn't let him finish. "Damn you!" he shouted before departing the campus forever.

◆

DADDY'S OUTRAGE HURT Katie's heart. As she lay perfectly still on her bed, her eyes began to brim with tears even as more visions coursed through her mind's eye.

◆

"THESE KINDS OF withdrawals from the Vatican Bank could bring unwanted scrutiny to the Supreme Sacred Congregation, Father Lemski," someone said over the telephone to the man in black, the man who had stood on a pew in church to shout at her.

"The disappearance of one of our agents has left us with no choice but to sweep up his mess," Lemski began. "Carlitos, if that's his actual name, confessed to me a violent, regrettable act that brought the police much too close to our activities. An unusually expensive program was implemented, somewhat hastily, I'll admit, to protect the Holy See by laying blame for the death on the shoulders of another man."

"One would think that in this situation it would be prudent to curtail surveillance while matters settle down," the superior said.

"I can understand your assumption, though it is not quite so simple," Lemski explained with a hint of condescension.

"Is that so?"

Lemski's assurances did not seem to satisfy his superior.

"The agent named Stefan—I see he now receives compensation that rivals the salary of a Vatican guard."

"His skills and commitment are exceptional," Lemski explained. "We must recruit more like him. Remember too that some of those funds are not intended as salary but are more appropriately defined as a per diem for other matters . . ."

◆

KATIE WATCHED BUT did not understand.

All of this was swept away by a new sensory overload that threw Katie onto her back. Staring at the ceiling, she suppressed the urge to cry out.

◆

Father Kelly walked quickly past the Vatican's dusty archives and into a dark tunnel that led him past hundreds of stone and terra-cotta engravings. He stopped at a gravesite and was startled when a man stepped from the shadows.

In the dim light, Katie recognized the big man, who pushed his graying hair out of his eyes. She had seen him in the church the day of her almost-baptism too.

"Bishop Parker. How did you . . .?" Father Kelly asked, relaxing.

"I was in the neighborhood."

Both men smiled.

"To think that we now stand where Constantine found the red rock that marked St. Peter's grave."

"Upon which he ordered the construction of the first basilica, which stood until . . . the fifteenth century?"

"Very good, Justin. Layers of blood, tradition, and sacred history. The new basilica now stands on the exact same spot. Here we are, about ten meters below the very center of St. Peter's Basilica, two men who embrace a rich, storied past while also reaching out, it would seem, toward very different futures. Am I correct?"

Father Kelly seemed reluctant to answer. He moved to the wall and flipped a switch. Spotlight beams shot down, illuminating the tombs. He walked to a well-lit white marble tomb and pointed to an inscription that read βράχος είναι μέσα.

"The actual Greek translation is 'Rock is within,'" the young priest said. "Imagine . . ." he said with great effort, "this is where early Christians would gather in secret, at a time of persecution in Rome, to pray over Peter in secret."

The bishop nodded.

"Is that the future you want, Bishop? Factions of Catholics worshiping in secret for fear that their questions will set off another era of persecution?"

"Of course not," the older man responded, though he didn't seem entirely committed to his words.

"Then why am I being followed?" asked Father Kelly sadly.

"Followed?"

They both looked down the hallway.

"After we met, before the Murphy baptism, I discovered a man—a man pretending to be a tourist—following me."

"I know nothing of—"

"That same man was in the back of the church during the ceremony. Now, here you are. Coincidence? Intuition? Or have you been following me too?"

The bishop looked at his protégé with alarm. "I had hoped I could protect you, Justin. I came to your defense initially. But your . . . paranoia . . . and apparent willingness to perform circus tricks in the name of Jesus—"

"She is a gifted child," Father Kelly replied, reading between the lines.

"Or a hysteric."

"She has access to other worlds."

"Sacrilege, sin, evil damnation," the bishop retorted with conviction.

"We should work with her."

"She's a carnival barker! Why would you risk your position in the church, and possibly your own salvation, to defend her and her parents?"

Father Kelly changed the subject. "So, this is why you followed me down here? To bury me?"

"To tell you that you'll be reassigned."

"Where?"

The bishop's broad chest heaved. "Far from Rome, that much is certain."

Father Kelly looked as if he'd suffered a slap to the face. He asked, "Now that I know my punishment, may I also know my crime, Bishop Parker?"

◆

KATIE SAW THE bishop stare long and hard at his protégé, then walk away without answering.

She could not bear any more pain and slid off the bed until her feet touched the floor. She walked into the living room but stopped when she heard her parents quarreling. They weren't even trying to hide it this time.

A moment later, Mummy saw her and the tears that stained her ruddy cheeks. "Honey, what's wrong?"

Daddy towered over them but reached down to lay a comforting hand on Katie. In the silence, Katie privately bid farewell to her family's life in Rome and wiped away her tears. Then she looked toward the apartment entrance and pointed.

Daddy, confused and curious, moved toward the door as the knocking began. He opened the door and discovered two uniformed officers and a third man dressed in a tailored suit.

"We are from *Polizia Giudiziaria* . . ."

II

DILIGATIS INVICEM

Chapter 18

Jerusalem

Fourteen years later

The professor enjoyed the challenge of keeping up with her new student's questions. The girl was inquisitive and self-possessed, with a mature grasp of complex papal and social issues.

She was also stealing the show.

Professor Nadia Jamira was a renowned theologian and archeologist with ten years of experience teaching Biblical Archeology at Jerusalem University, but she sometimes felt as if she should sit down and listen to this young student.

The girl's wide eyes dominated her face, and she didn't wear a touch of makeup. Her clothes were equally nondescript: a long-sleeved black shirt and baggy jeans. Her lack of care for her appearance did little to hide her inner confidence.

Her desire for knowledge and clarity was evident, though if she was hoping to inspire her classmates to debate and query, she was falling short. She knew how to stimulate a lively discussion but not when to hold back so that others might contribute.

Perhaps even more interesting was the way her intensity affected others in the lecture hall. Nadia was intrigued as she stood on the small stage of the amphitheater, looking up at concentric tiers of students.

The first Black pope had been elected over the weekend, creating an unavoidable subject of discussion. The professor explained that some Vatican observers had expected this historic event to happen long ago. There were three hundred million Black Catholics around the world, after all, and didn't they deserve representation and a sympathetic voice from the papal throne?

From one of the lower tiers, a young man asked, "Why did it take so long?"

"That's a good question. But let's set aside Catholicism and religion in general for a moment and see the Vatican as a purely political entity. In this past decade alone," Nadia replied, "a large percentage of Black Catholics have left the church."

"So the conclave was just being pragmatic?" another voice called out in response.

"Maybe. Like any political group, they need to maintain or strengthen their constituency. Pope Francis came to power at a time when the Catholic population in Latin America was dwindling."

"So should we expect Black people from all over the world to flock to the Catholic Church?" the original student asked.

"We'll see."

The professor glanced at the clock as several more hands shot up. She acknowledged a student from Kenya. "Yes, Anasa."

"In our history lessons, we were taught that there was a pope in the fifth century who was from Africa. Yet all I've heard reported is how the new pope is the first Black pope in history."

Nadia smiled. "Officially, the church and the world now recognize Zubair Madiba of South Africa as the first Black pope. But you are correct that there is a slight chance that he may actually be the second Black elected. Pope Gelasius led from 492 to 496, and he was certainly of African descent. But it is unlikely he was Black. Can anyone guess why?"

The hall hummed with private speculation, but no one chanced an answer until a familiar hand shot up.

The professor was not surprised. "All right, Kate . . ."

Kate Murphy paused as if to steady herself while reaching into a vast well. Nadia had observed this in previous classes, so she waited. Her student would become so still that others might think she had gone into a trance, only to revive an instant later with a peculiarly brilliant response.

"Around the year AD four hundred, there were two different parts of Africa. The Roman Empire ruled the northern portion, and Latin was spoken there. In fact, *Africa* is a Latin word that refers to the very northern section of that continent."

As she listened to Kate, Nadia watched the other students. While they might have been in awe of such an erudite answer coming from a classmate they liked, with the isolated Kate, their reactions were more remote. Kate seemed not to notice the other students around her, as if this were a one-on-one conversation.

"The other portion of Africa, I hesitate to call it the Deep South— sorry, Professor, couldn't resist . . ."

Nadia managed a weak smile and interrupted to explain the term, which referred to the southern portion of the United States, where slavery of Africans was infamous thanks to the Civil War that dismantled it. "Go on, Kate," she finished.

"Yes, anyway, this southern portion of Africa was called *Aethiopia.*" Kate finally seemed to remember her fellow students. "Sound familiar? It refers to 'Black Africa.' Getting back to Pope Gelasius, I don't know exactly where he was born, but I'm guessing he was a Roman who hailed from northern Africa. So even though he was African, he was more of a

Roman and probably not Black. That's why Zubair Madiba will likely keep the historic footnote as the first Black pope." Kate leaned back in her seat.

"Yes," Nadia said. "Let me add that the part of northern Africa Kate is referring to is now Morocco, Algeria, Tunisia, Libya, and Egypt. But as she has said, at the time, Black Africans were referred to as *Aethiopes*. Historical records contain a letter written by Gelasius, in which he referred to himself as *Romanus natus*, which in Latin means 'Roman-born.' But we still do not know for certain if he was Black, White, or purple. Anybody know why?"

All eyes, despite themselves, turned to Kate, who deadpanned, "He couldn't take a selfie and post it online."

Nadia was grateful for the laughter that followed Kate's quip. It wasn't typical of the response Kate got in class, but it offered a glimpse of the kind of influence she could have if she tried.

Kate was clearly uncomfortable with social interaction outside of class. When Nadia had heard fellow students invite her to join them somewhere after class, she always replied that she had to study or that it wasn't her thing.

Nadia couldn't deny that the girl was an exceptional student, but her social skills were so lacking that she had decided about two weeks earlier to call Kate's secondary school principal. She would need interns for her next dig, and Kate had potential. The professor wasn't above seeking advice on how better to channel the girl's energy. Thankfully, the man had been chatty and candid.

"I'm not surprised to receive your call, Professor, and I'm happy to share whatever I can about our Red Rock star."

"Red Rock?"

"It's a nickname some students gave Kate but didn't dare say to her face."

"Why not?"

The principal had laughed. "Well, besides her hair, how can I explain? Let's start with graduation day. You probably know from her records that Kate was our valedictorian."

"Yes."

"She was constantly in the library. I often wondered if she hid in the archives at the end of the day so the janitor would lock her in. Her thirst for knowledge is unmatched by anyone I've seen pass through these halls, before her or after."

"A reason we're thrilled to have her here," Nadia admitted. "Are her parents academics?"

"Yes, but, well . . . it's a complicated story that Kate will not discuss at length. I've heard rumors, but I suggest you avoid the topic."

"Sounds like a warning." The professor thought she was about to learn more about what made Kate tick.

"One of several worth heeding," he replied. "I gathered her parents have a rather strained relationship with authority, and as a result, the family was somewhat nomadic throughout Kate's formative years, though I believe they have returned to their roots in Dublin."

He paused as if to collect his thoughts. "As impressed as I was with the time she spent in the library, sometimes I wondered if she wasn't just hiding."

"From what?"

A long pause followed. "Trauma? Her own inner conflict?"

The professor jotted notes as the principal spoke. She had no patience for teachers' pets who turned out to be afraid to get their hands dirty. Kate was the obvious choice for the upcoming dig, but Nadia would need more information first.

The principal continued, "Kate's father once told me a story about something that happened in her childhood that I will never forget. But they should be the ones to tell you about that."

Now this was intriguing. "Okay, any other warnings you can share?"

"Yes, well, Kate is full of surprises."

"Such as an encyclopedic grasp of history?" the professor offered.

"If she chooses. Everything is on her terms. She won't be pushed by O-P-E."

"I'm not familiar with the acronym," Nadia conceded.

"Other people's expectations. On graduation day, we were all looking forward to her valedictory address. I had praised her in my introduction and even thanked her for being my teacher on certain subjects."

Nadia's laugh was genuine. "Yes. I've already had the honor as well."

"So you can understand why we were all anticipating her speech. There were probably a thousand people in the audience. But Kate stumbled up to the podium in heels that her mother had surely forced her to wear that day, and she looked out and said, 'In Latin, the phrase is *diligatis invicem.* In Italian, it is *amatevi l'uno con l'altro.* In English, the phrase is—'"

"Love one another," the professor interjected.

"Very good, Professor. Yes, she said love one another and then sat down. End of speech."

After the phone call with the principal, Nadia had sat thinking, thumping her desk with a pen, before finally deciding to call Kate's parents. Simon and Rebecca, not surprised to receive a call from one of their daughter's professors, told her several stories about how lovely Kate had been as a child. When she gently persisted, they reluctantly decided to share the story that the principal had hinted at.

◆

DUBLIN

"I'll tie the rope around your wrists, and you'll look like Jesus on the cross."

Meghan looked back at her house for reassurance.

Seven-year-old Katie reassured her, "It won't hurt."

"But isn't it a sin?" Meghan asked.

Katie began lugging two pieces of wood nailed in the shape of a cross that they'd found while playing near a construction site. They were near her new home in Dublin, where they had moved after leaving Rome.

Together the girls leaned their makeshift cross against an old stone building that neighbored Meghan's yard. Meghan slowly, carefully, pressed her back against it. Katie used some twine she'd found in a drawer at home to tie her friend's wrists snugly to the horizontal piece. Meghan squirmed, the coarse material irritating her skin.

"Let me loose, Katie," Meghan said, causing herself more pain as she wriggled to pull free.

"Why?"

"It hurts."

"Christ felt pain," Katie replied solemnly.

"Then let me tie you up," Meghan offered.

Katie ignored the suggestion and stepped back so that she could admire what they had created. She was a bit startled when her friend disappeared and Jesus hung from the cross in her place. Jesus was writhing in agony, drenched in blood. Then he stopped and looked directly into Katie's eyes, and his gaze poured pure compassion into her.

Meghan's eyes grew wide when Katie began to speak in a strange voice, as though the yard were filled with other people.

"Forgive them, Father—"

"Katie, what are you talking about? You're scaring me."

"—for they know not what they do."

"Stop it!" Meghan yelled.

But Katie grimaced and cried out as the peace of Christ left her and turned to mortal guilt. "No! Please God, no!"

She witnessed soldiers taking the deceased Christ down from the cross, removing his crown of thorns, and handing it to a woman who had been praying at his feet. Aghast, the old woman swiftly wrapped the bloody crown in cloth and handed it to Katie.

"Hide it! We have to hide it somewhere safe!" Katie spoke desperately.

"Katie! Please stop! Please stop!" Meghan yelled.

"But we have to hide it, or, or . . ."

A firm hand seized Katie's shoulder. She looked up and discovered Meghan's irate father. He shook her hard, said something she could not hear, and then ran to free his screaming daughter. He untied her wrists and carried her home, leaving Katie to stare into her empty hands.

Chapter 19

Jerusalem

A student in the front row turned today's lecture back to the new pope by asking more about his heritage.

"I heard that the new pope is a direct descendant of Nelson Mandela," she said. "Is that true, and can you elaborate on who Mandela was? We weren't taught about him."

"Well, huh. I wonder why." Kate's interruption momentarily quieted the room, but as heads turned in her direction, she seemed to recede, hiding behind a shrug. It wasn't the only time anyone had heard her say something sardonic, but it was the first time she'd seemed aware of their reaction.

Nadia glanced at the Red Rock and decided to delve deeper later, despite the secondary school principal's warnings. "Yes, this is true. Zubair Madiba's bloodline goes directly to Nelson Mandela, which leads us to another important historic event. We already know why he is considered the first Black pope. But he is also the only pope in history who has been allowed to choose a papal name that is not that of a Catholic saint or derived from his baptismal name."

She continued, "Immediately after a new pope is elected and accepts his selection, he's asked, 'By what name shall you be called?' Imagine if you were asked the same question and you could choose a name that would represent you and your religion for the rest of your life. What would it be?"

"I know what my name would be."

Once again, all eyes were on Kate, who blushed as if she had revealed an intimate secret.

Then another female student spoke. "You can't be pope. Only the guys get to choose a name."

There were some half-joking protests. The girl debated her point until a storm began to brew in Kate's eyes, and she pulled her glasses down from her face. "I'm Kate," she said. "What's your name?"

"Lisa."

"It's nice to meet you, Lisa. My dad always said that if people aren't laughing at your dreams, then your dreams are too small." She continued passionately, "As a female, don't you agree that we are equal to men?"

"Of course we are," Lisa answered.

"Not in the Church, we aren't," Kate replied back.

"Great point, Kate. So what about it, both ladies and gentlemen, what would your names be?" Nadia asked.

The young Kenyan man offered, "Adroa."

"That's interesting," the professor responded. "'God in the sky, God on the earth.'"

"How about John, Paul, George, and Ringo?" another voice shouted from the back.

A few snickers followed as a student in the back said, "No rock bands, porn stars, or movie stars allowed!"

Other names were tossed into the arena, some sacrilegious, others deeply sincere. Nadia pushed her students to think in terms of roots, legacy, and political will. "Remember, once you've been named pope, the senior cardinal deacon will appear on the balcony of Saint Peter's to tell the world the name you've chosen for your reign. Think about it. How did you feel when you learned that Zubair Madiba had chosen Nelson?"

"Does he deserve the name?" Kate asked to a chorus of groans.

An Israeli student was swift to challenge. "He can choose whatever name he wants. What's wrong with Nelson?"

"Nelson Mandela was a revolutionary," Kate answered. "He revolted against White supremacy and the suppression of equal human rights. He gave most of his life to the cause and never sought revenge against the people who tried to silence him with twenty-seven years in prison. He was a living, breathing—if imperfect—saint of the universe."

"And Pope Nelson? What is he?" Nadia followed the cue, aware that Kate was creating an energy she had not witnessed in her class before.

"We don't know yet," Kate said. "Will he crush progress or inspire it? African and Asian nations have already shown a bias toward radical conservative interpretations of Church doctrine. Is Pope Nelson an open-minded leader . . . or a fascist?"

As the classroom erupted, Nadia pictured Kate reassuring her friend that it wouldn't hurt to have her wrists tied like Christ's.

The young Kenyan was outraged. He leaped up and began a passionate defense. An Asian student rose to argue about respect for leadership. Other opinions were offered in loud, unyielding voices that volleyed back and forth until accusations and threats were heard.

Nadia tried without luck to return civility to the debate. The angriest seemed to band together as they lambasted Kate. But she didn't seem intimidated, and her peaceful non-reaction only further incensed those who were arguing vehemently. Nadia realized that Kate had meant the question honestly, not in the incendiary way it was being taken.

"Some of you seem to have interpreted what Kate said in a rather charged manner, but I believe her question was posed sincerely and with openness. Now, let's please maintain a little quiet. Is there anyone who would like to ask Kate a question, and please, let it be expressed kindly?"

A hand shot up from the side of the room. "Why do you consistently use the term 'Universe' instead of 'God'?"

Kate rose from her chair and replied, "I think the German teacher Eckhart Tolle articulated this beautifully when he stated that God is the eternal one life underneath all forms of life.

"I use 'Universe' in the same way that Tolle uses the terms 'Consciousness' and 'Being.' The word 'God' has often been misappropriated by individuals who have never truly experienced the sacred or the infinite expansiveness that this term embodies.

"Claims like 'My God is the only true God' have ignited countless wars throughout history, stemming from that flawed belief. The term 'God' often leads people to envision a separate being outside of themselves. In contrast, 'Universe' offers a more inclusive perspective, preventing us from confining the infinite to a finite entity."

She then stood on her chair, bowing gently to the class with her hands pressed together in a prayer gesture by her lips. "I'd also like to apologize, I know I can come across as brash," she added. As she stood tall and confident, sunlight streamed through the lecture hall's windows, illuminating her cardinal feather–colored hair, and a profound silence enveloped the room.

"Your protests remind me of a Latin phrase, *diligatis invicem*. In Italian, it is *amatevi l'uno con l'altro*. In English, the phrase is—"

"Love one another."

A shiver traveled up Nadia's spine as she finished the translation for a second time, and it ran all the way to her fingertips when Kate looked down at her and nodded with a peaceful smile.

The class broke up in a flurry, students separating into groups of three and four and flooding out into the sunlight, still arguing. Despite having lost control of the room, never mind the lesson, Nadia was thrilled. There were too many days when students nodded off in class only to be startled awake when everyone else left. Not today.

Kate did not join any of the groups, and no one invited her to continue talking. She climbed down from her perch, stuffed her possessions into her backpack, and made her way toward the door with her eyes on the ground.

Nadia caught her attention before she could get away. "Kate," she called.

The girl turned, eyes half-fogged like she was coming out of a trance.

"Come see me at my office hours tomorrow. I have something to discuss with you."

Kate nodded and walked out, letting the door swing shut behind her.

◆

KATE WAS HEADED back to her student apartment more slowly than usual, letting the dusty heat seep into her body, when a hand gently touched her elbow. She jumped and spun around; her eyes were as wide as a rabbit's.

The hand belonged to a tall, leanly muscular young man with olive skin and a grin that split his face nearly in two. He probably told himself that the scruff on his chin was a beard; meanwhile, his hair was clipped short nearly to his temples, where it erupted into unruly waves he swept back with his fingers.

"That was something, huh?" he said with a smile. "I'm James." He extended his right hand to Kate. She noticed that both his black jeans and his white Depeche Mode T-shirt were quite tight. Embarrassed at where her eyes had gone, she shook her head slightly, then shook his hand with some reluctance.

"Kate," she said.

"So you think women should be allowed to be priests, huh?" he asked with no preamble. "If they could, would you sign up?"

"Ha! Me? No," Kate replied stiffly. "But shouldn't I have the option? Shouldn't any woman have the option?"

"But why would you want to have the option? Have you looked at a Catholic priest lately? Do they look like they are living some kind of awesome life?" He laughed, and despite herself, Kate smiled.

"Maybe not," she conceded. "But if it was a life open to anyone, maybe it would be a better life for everyone."

"And do you believe the pope is a fascist?"

"I don't know. I think he could be."

"Based on what?"

"I don't know—based on the fact that he's risen to the top of a church that has demonstrated its authoritarianism at about every opportunity for hundreds of years? I mean, the papacy isn't a position that everyday Catholics get to vote on. In order to be nominated, you have to be someone the rest of the cardinals think is right for the job."

"Maybe direct elections of popes, then?" James shifted from one foot to the other, accentuating his lean hips. She very nearly took a step backward and shook her head again, trying to stay focused on the conversation.

"There's no way that would work," Kate said with a smile. "You'd have to have runoffs, because each continent would have a favored candidate. There'd be an African, an Asian, a European, an American."

"At least the first American pope didn't come off of reality TV shows like some of their presidents did." James snorted, laughing.

Kate laughed too, then her expression sobered. She needed to get home and study. She began to turn away.

"Wait," James pressed, momentarily halting her escape. "Come with me. I know a great hangout. We can get coffee."

"Thank you, but no," she replied, her manner formal. "I should get home and study. It was nice meeting you, though."

As she walked away, some part of her knew he was watching her. And another, newly awakened part was happy about it.

Chapter 20

Jerusalem

The next day, Kate slowly circled Nadia's office, her hands clasped behind her back as if conducting an inspection. Nadia knew it was more like a museum or art gallery than the cramped quarters of a professor, and intentionally so. If she was going to spend more time here than in her apartment, she might as well make it as comfortable as possible. She also wanted her students to feel inspired, not stifled.

On dark wooden shelves were artifacts, rare books, soil samples, and antiquities testifying to the past. Framed prints, paintings, and photographs covered the walls.

Kate's eyes devoured everything the professor held dear. The student's study of her life's work was a bit intimidating.

As Kate scrutinized everything, even group snapshots of no archeological significance, Nadia recognized the root of her visceral reaction to Kate. It was envy. She admired the girl's ability to be unapologetically herself, to shun societal expectations.

"I might be off base here," Kate murmured.

"Yes?"

"I was surprised yesterday when the Asian girl got so angry."

"Her name is Jin-yeon. She was raised in Korea," Nadia finished.

"Mm. Would she also be angry, do you think, if women were suddenly ordained as deacons in the Church? I mean, what is her objection, Professor? Why would a woman object to the possibility of my—"

"Presumption?"

"If that's what you want to call it. But . . ." Kate paused when Nadia put on her reading glasses and opened the Bible that lay on her desk.

"This isn't a modern dilemma, you know," Nadia said. "The argument for female ordination dates back to when Jesus was alive. Did you bring your Bible? Open to Luke 10:38–42."

Kate took the chair on the other side of Nadia's desk, reached into her shoulder bag, and pulled out her own well-worn Bible.

"Mary's sister is complaining to Jesus about Mary not helping her in the kitchen, and Jesus replies, 'Mary has chosen what is better.' Obviously, Jesus didn't hold stereotypical female kitchen duties to be a better place for women than the calling to serve God. His apostle Paul felt the same way. Turn to 1 Timothy 3:11."

Kate flipped to the page and began to read aloud. "Women are to be worthy of respect, not malicious talkers but temperate and trustworthy in everything."

"Indeed. Paul had a female deacon named Phoebe, known today as St. Phoebe, who helped him with *everything*. One of the most striking examples is when Paul entrusted Phoebe to personally deliver one of his epistles to the church. This is the same epistle included in the thirteen books written by Paul in the New Testament. Of all the people he could have chosen to handle these important documents, Paul chose Phoebe," Nadia said, leaning back and interlacing her fingers behind her head.

The two women shared a speculative look.

Nadia continued. "In Romans 16:1, you can see that Paul called Phoebe a *diakonos*, which translates to 'deacon.' See the line?" She looked up as the girl raked her hand through the curls that hung over her forehead. "I commend to you our sister Phoebe," Nadia quoted, "who is a deacon in the church in Cenchrea."

She had lectured about the roles of women in the ancient church many times, but never so intimately. She was ready and willing to explain that four hundred years after Paul described Phoebe as a deacon, seventeen male bishops gathered in France to declare that women should not and would not be ordained as deacons, but she sensed that this connection had already been made by her student.

"From the time of Christ to AD 441, the value of women declined dramatically, and they were eventually banned from being ordained." Nadia removed her glasses and waited for Kate to meet her eyes. "This gives me an idea. Would you like to earn some extra credit?"

Kate's face lit up. "How?"

"Do some research and write an essay telling me why the enlightened time of Christ led to an epoch when church elders banned the ordination of female deacons."

Kate instantly deflated, and Nadia tried not to feel like she'd failed to impress.

"But I already know why," Kate said flatly.

"Oh?" Nadia leaned forward to rest her elbows on stacks of student papers.

"The male ego."

Nadia's laugh was robust, and Kate joined in. Then Kate reached into her canvas bag and pulled out a hardbound notebook. It looked like the kind of book given as a graduation gift, and Nadia thought of Kate holed up in the library. The pages held voluminous notes written in black ink.

"I've already done some research," Kate said. "Let's start with Mary Magdalene."

"What about her?"

"She is not the person the Church made her out to be in the years after Christ died."

"True."

"I can't believe how much women were put down and continue to be put down even today," Kate said. "They were neglected in the early writings of the Church. Only a few female names are even mentioned. But women were obviously everywhere, and they were extremely involved and prized contributors. Then . . .?"

"Yes, Kate," Nadia agreed. She paused for a moment before continuing, "Women were prevalent in Christ's life, and then they were turned into objects of sin."

Kate nodded. "Mary Magdalene."

"Right, and yet . . ." Nadia was about to cross a line that would either end the conversation or deepen it—and irrevocably alter their relationship. She decided that it was worth the risk. "Yesterday in class, when you stood on your chair, you had everyone's full attention—male and female. No one questioned your right to stand and speak, no matter your gender. Kate, what made you stand?"

Kate tensed and began to stuff her books clumsily into her bag, dropping the notebook on the floor.

"Don't go, Kate," Nadia said, rising and extending her hand in entreaty.

"I didn't ask for the attention," Kate huffed as she slung her bag over her shoulder.

"Then why did you stand on the chair?"

Kate moved toward the door but paused.

"It's a simple question," Nadia said, knowing the word "simple" would be a hot button: Kate wouldn't be able to keep herself from answering.

"I don't know why!" she cried as she turned to Nadia. "I mean—I do know, but . . ." She started to run her fingers through her hair again but seemed to forget about them and left them there, so her face was protected by her arm as she said quietly, "It's something I can't control."

"Standing?"

"Announcing. Proclaiming." Kate sighed.

"Leading," Nadia pushed.

At this, Kate's face twisted, as if her worst fears had been confirmed. "Sometimes I want to disappear, Professor Jamira."

"Nadia."

"Nadia." Kate took a shaky breath. "Just vanish and become an archivist or librarian. Somebody nobody really sees. I feel like there's always someone watching, like I never go unnoticed. I'd be happy with that unobserved life. Really, I would. But . . ."

"Go on. You're safe here," Nadia said and meant it.

It took a long moment, but Kate finally spoke. "Sometimes, like yesterday . . . a . . . an energy invades my body." Here, she cast a look at Nadia, clearly looking for a sign that it was safe to continue. "It wants—it demands things from me. I've tried to suppress or deny it. But how do you stop a waterfall or an avalanche?"

The last sentence resonated. "Or a rocket launch."

"Yes. Yes!" Kate's shoulders relaxed and her eyes sparked. "That's exactly how it feels. My body . . ." She hesitated.

"Your being," Nadia suggested.

"Yes! Suddenly, I'm compelled to do things that go against my wishes."

"Or fulfill them?" Nadia asked.

Kate looked at her and whispered, "Do you understand? Can you help?"

The professor spread her arms as if to acknowledge the presence of others—the photos, commendations, artifacts, and fine art that surrounded them. Together, they considered the collection and its implications.

"The other students were definitely right," Kate said. "You have so much—stuff. Great stuff. Historic stuff. Lifeblood stuff."

Nadia recognized but also welcomed Kate's attempt to change the subject. "Thanks. This office is my temple."

As if Kate could read her mind, she said, "And legacy."

Nadia savored the moment of mutual respect.

Then Kate admitted, "I don't know what to do."

"That's okay," Nadia said. "I'm here to help."

Chapter 21

Venice

DeBray Ayalaz had a decision to make, and his vocal, opinionated parents back in Spain were not helping. His mother was proud that her son was considering the priesthood, but she also wanted to pass her thriving shoe design business on to him. His father, on the other hand, found nothing particularly divine about a life in the Church.

"Why would you want to live with a bunch of pedophiles?"

"So I don't end up like you or Grandpa."

DeBray had watched his father bloody his mother too many times to count, and he knew the same had happened to his grandmother.

Crying in the bathroom at age five, DeBray had realized he was not afraid for his own safety. He was angry that he could not protect his mother from the drunken monster that lived with them. That anger had grown within him. At age twelve, his dad gave him a twenty-gauge shotgun for hunting in the Montserrat mountains. But he gave little thought to hunting. Instead, he thought about shooting his father and ending the torture.

Neither his grandmother nor mother divorced the violent drunks they married, even though DeBray pleaded with his mother after each beating.

"I know you're upset, DeBray, but I made my vows in church on our wedding day. In the eyes of God and the Church, my soul is eternally bound to your father's by the sacrament of marriage."

DeBray swore a vow back to his mother: "I will be the one who breaks the chain of monsters in my family."

As a young man, DeBray was determined not to continue the abuse into a family of his own. He began a slow burn of internal questions. The first one was: *How is it that women have been put down for so long—not only in marriage but also in the Church?*

The next day he put it to his Dutch friend, Hendrik, who was already in seminary. "So, what do you think of women being priests?" The two walked along the Grand Canal.

"What's that?"

It wasn't the usual chat from DeBray, who was typically focused on finding sustenance. But the idea had stayed with him.

"Women becoming priests, what do you say?"

"I'd say that's against the order of things," his friend replied, clearly keen to drop the conversation or at least move into the shade. DeBray had stopped in the open, sunlight glaring down on them.

DeBray couldn't leave it alone. "It seems more like fear to me."

"Fear?"

"You know, keeping women down."

Hendrik wiped sweat from his forehead. "Where's all this come from, mate? It's lunchtime!"

"It's got me thinking."

"What has?"

"Just things. Life. From what I've seen, the Church is more afraid of women than of the devil himself!"

"Well, I don't know about that." Hendrik was looking at him sideways, clearly skeptical of this change in his easy-going friend. "Next thing, you'll be saying you want to be a priest *and* get married."

DeBray knew he couldn't do both and that he shouldn't want to—not the way his family was. And yet, he couldn't help but find a snag in the standards. Celibacy was clearly a rule made up by the Church.

"It's the way it is, always has been," Hendrik went on, navigating his friend toward the shade.

DeBray stopped again. "But that's the thing though. It's not. It isn't something Jesus ever spoke about or St. Peter. Obviously, St. Peter was married with children, as were almost all popes and priests up to around AD 900."

"What's your point?"

"My point is, even St. Peter lived the opposite! Women have been pushed out, and all of us are happy to keep doing it."

"Man, something's got into you."

"It's just a question."

"Something or *someone*." Hendrik nudged DeBray on the arm. "What's got into you, bud?"

"Must be hungry." DeBray threw out his face-splitting grin, and the moment was diffused.

"That's more like it," said Hendrik, slapping his friend on the shoulder and finally moving with him into the shade of the trees.

The young men went in search of iced drinks and sandwiches. DeBray kept further thoughts to himself.

Chapter 22

Jerusalem

Kate's mentoring sessions with Nadia began immediately.

"Did you take a good look at this photo?" Nadia asked, gesturing to a standing frame. "Allow me to introduce you to Sister Theresa Kane."

Kate walked to a glass case containing a blue armband. Beside it was a group photo of nuns standing at a podium, each wearing a similar band.

"Who are these people?" Kate asked.

Nadia pointed to a woman with a round, friendly face and short hair. "That's Sister Theresa. In 1979, she gathered with fifty other nuns in Washington, DC, to lead the Leadership Conference of Women Religious. At the time, the organization represented eighty percent of the nation's one hundred and forty thousand Catholic nuns."

"They're all wearing armbands," Kate said, pointing toward the glass.

"Yes," Nadia said, picking up the frame. "The bands symbolized the ordination of women in the Church. On the day this photo was taken, the sisters officially requested that the Vatican include women in all ministries of the Church. Sister Theresa is known as the nun who challenged the supreme pontiff. With Pope John Paul II sitting behind her, she looked out into the faces of her fellow sisters and said, 'The Church, in its struggle to be faithful to its call for reverence and dignity for all persons, must respond by providing the possibility of women as persons being included in all ministries of the Church. I urge you, Your Holiness,' she said, 'to respond to the voices coming from the women of this country who are desirous of serving in and through the Church as fully participating members.' The armband you're looking at is the one Sister Theresa wore that day."

Kate's fingers traced the glass. "Tell me more."

"First, let me ask, are you Catholic? With a name like Murphy, I'm assuming you are."

Kate chuckled. "Yes. My parents introduced me to the Church. I was baptized—sort of—while we were living in Rome." At this, Kate withdrew her hand, as if she suddenly feared her touch was somehow harmful to the relic.

"Sort of?"

"Well, among other things, I'm—I'm adopted."

Nadia was surprised that Kate's parents hadn't mentioned this. "Adoption doesn't preclude . . ." she began, without much of an idea of where she was going.

"I know, I know," Kate said impatiently.

"But it's complicated?" Nadia probed, hoping that Kate would fill in the blanks.

Kate nodded.

"I'm a Catholic as well," Nadia offered.

"Yes, I know. You're one of the reasons I chose this school."

Nadia was surprised. Her research and tireless archeological digs were not done for fame or prestige. Each excursion was an attempt to leave something valuable for the next generation of scholars, but she'd never considered that she herself, and not just her legacy, would be of value.

"Well, I'm flattered," she said into the awkward pause. "Now, back to the blue armband. Sister Theresa and the nuns were rebuffed by Pope John Paul II and the Vatican. The leaders didn't appreciate the armbands or the protest, so they started pushing back with new rules and restrictions. In 2005, Pope Benedict XVI was elected following the death of John Paul II. The German pontiff stayed the course with conservative views, and in 2012, he called for a complete reorganization of the Leadership Conference of Women Religious. Some American media called the Vatican's decision a hostile takeover. To justify the action, the Vatican accused the Catholic sisters of radical feminism. The nuns were also accused of failing to focus on issues such as birth control and same-sex marriage. They did, however, say the nuns were doing quite a good job on poverty and injustice."

"The male ego." Kate shook her head.

"You're right, of course. It was a pat on the head. The Vatican didn't like women telling them what to do. The armbands were an affront. I suspect they could see that the ordination of women might create a domino effect. Once women were deacons, they would want to be priests and serve Mass."

"And then be eligible to be pope," Kate finished.

"Exactly." Nadia waved her hands in the air, mocking Vatican fears. "Oh no! Not a female pope! Not that!" She laughed. "Can't you see all the cardinals scurrying around the Vatican in their little red and white lace dresses and frilly hats, worried about females being equal to them? A bit ironic, wouldn't you say?"

"More than ironic," Kate laughed. "And I think it may also be why priests are still not allowed to marry."

"How do you mean?" Nadia said.

"It's not the sex. Not really." Kate didn't blush, but she hesitated a moment over the word *sex*. Nadia wondered for a moment whether Kate had ever been in a romantic relationship. "It's the potential influence. A wife has the ear and respect of her husband—it's true for corporate leaders, politicians, and royalty. The wives always know where the money is buried. What would happen if priests married? Can you imagine? When a pope denies marriage, he does so fully aware that he continues to suppress the voices and ideas of women. It's a protective measure that can't be jeopardized."

Nadia enjoyed Kate's forceful, exciting ideas, but the fervor seemed personal. She ventured another question. "Is there someone in your life who . . . let me ask this another way: Would you want to be the wife of a priest?"

"No!" Kate said, shaking her head. "But I do have friends in the Church who those limitations have harmed. I felt as though Pope Francis unlocked the door for women to be ordained, yet I find myself struggling to grasp Pope Leo's statement that '"clericalizing women" doesn't necessarily solve a problem, it might make a new problem.' What exactly did he mean by that?"

Nadia replied, "I never understood that comment from Pope Leo either. What new problem could be more distressing than the horrific problem of pedophilia? Women are not the ones to commit such monstrous acts, and their inclusion within the clergy could truly help solve the problem. When children come to the church seeking spiritual guidance, they deserve to be greeted with compassion and protection rather than the threat of predatory priests. By ordaining women, we could provide a nurturing presence within the church that better safeguards our children. I often wish I could go back in time and ask Pope Leo what specific new problem he was genuinely worried about."

"Me too." Kate nodded. "But here we are with Pope Nelson, who was probably elected after making promises to those who would suppress fundamental human rights. When will we finally break through? When will the Church finally acknowledge the divine feminine, as it should have ages ago? Are we all going to be Mary Magdalenes forever?"

Nadia was thrilled to learn more about her student's personal motivations. "This armband and those nuns were the beginning of a revolution. It will take more time. But their courage in voicing their opinions directly to the pope and the Vatican was a significant event. This was bigger than that speech that day." Taking a step toward Kate and resting a hand on the girl's slim shoulder, she said, "Help finish what they started, Kate."

"What do you mean?" Kate asked, clearly captivated but hesitant.

"Don't hide in libraries or behind books," Nadia urged.

Kate turned once more to examine the faces of the nuns in the photo and touched her fingers to the glass. She turned to her bag and pulled out her notebook, flipping through pages until she found a neatly scrawled quotation. She began to read: "The Gospel of Mary exposes the erroneous view that Mary of Magdala was a prostitute for what it is—a piece of theological fiction. It presents the most straightforward and convincing argument in any early Christian writing for the legitimacy of women's leadership."

Nadia knew the passage, written by Karen King, a Harvard professor and authority on women's roles in the ancient church. "Professor King is one of my favorite writers too. Her colleague is the one who coined the controversial term 'Gospel of Jesus's Wife.' In 2012, the two of them announced the existence of an ancient papyrus that says, 'Jesus said to them, "my wife . . ."' They weren't concerning themselves with whether Jesus was in fact married. They were exploring the much more profound issue of whether women who are wives and mothers can also be disciples of Jesus. Maybe Jesus would have married."

"The apostles saw Mary Magdalene as Jesus's favorite, and they were envious. She was never an adulteress or a whore," Kate added.

"It is an abomination. Slut-shaming, *in perpetua*. She was an extraordinary woman, Kate, but so are you. Already, at your young age. And in a century where attacking a woman who transgresses accepted codes can't take root so easily—at least, I hope it can't. We can continue to make academic arguments for the inclusion of women all we want. But who will stand up and actually make it happen? Who will take the torch from Sister Theresa, a devout girl who looked at her brother, the altar boy, and asked herself—asked her God—'Why not me too?' Not instead of, but as well."

"I can't," Kate said, dropping her notebook to her side.

"Why, Kate?"

"Things have happened before . . . when I have . . . things have happened to people I love." She hung her head. "I can't presume that I . . ." Kate began, blinking.

"Not you alone, Kate," Nadia coaxed. "But if gifted people like you won't do it, who will? In some circles, women are still considered to be evil, just as Pope Gregory the Great once proclaimed about Mary Magdalene. Thank goodness, after hundreds of years, Pope Paul VI finally rejected the statement Gregory made in 1060. But how much did it help?" She pressed her hand on Kate's notebook. "There are still a lot of Marys in the world, Kate."

Nadia could tell Kate was listening. If she walked out of the shadows and into the light, how far could a young woman like this go?

"Kate, you can't do it all in one afternoon. But when you get back to your dorm, why don't you start by making a list? A list of people who might help you, join with you, counsel you. Start with one name. Can you think of somebody who would not hesitate to contribute to your effort?"

"My effort to do what?" Kate asked flatly, still caught in some pensive state that made Nadia hesitant to push. But she needed to get through to Kate.

"To open doors to Catholic women who are not content to serve only as nuns."

At this, Kate finally looked Nadia in the eye, fully present. After a moment, she took a deep breath, flipped to the inside of her notebook's front cover, and showed Nadia the inscription.

Dear one,

There is only one graduation day. When you finally accept who and what you truly are.

Father Kelly

Chapter 23

Dublin

Simon did not want Kate to fly to Cambodia to visit Father Kelly. "It's dangerous, and you'll be traveling alone," he argued uselessly.

Yes, she'd graduated from secondary school at the top of her class, and he'd promised her a trip to celebrate. Why not see Paris, safari in Africa, or climb Mount Everest? Anything rather than reconnect with a man who, after she had touched him as a child, seemed permanently changed in heart and mind. Had she not been so obstinate, Kate would not have found Father Kelly's secret that would come to haunt her.

"The Universe will be with me, remember?" Kate said, and her parents' smiles told her she'd hit the mark.

"You're a city girl, Kate," Simon said. "To reach Father Kelly, you'll have to leave Phnom Penh for his territorial jurisdiction, which is the countryside, the backwaters. It's different over there, you know, not all modern and safe."

There was the cost to consider too. The family could afford a one-way ticket to Jerusalem from Dublin, but adding additional flights to the Far East was prohibitive. Simon's career had never been the same since he had been ostracized from his professorship in Rome, and their resources were limited.

"I'll be nearly halfway there when I land in Israel," Kate argued. "If I don't see him now . . ." She didn't finish her line of thought as she didn't like the feeling she got when she thought of not seeing him again.

The tables turned in Kate's favor some weeks later when a package arrived from Cambodia. Inside, the valedictorian had found an embroidered notebook and an envelope filled with cash, which the ever-resourceful priest encouraged her to put toward her first year at university. Simon had relented then, but only if the parish would send an escort to help Kate make the journey into the countryside.

◆

COUNTRYSIDE NEAR LUMPHAT

Now, Kate wished she had listened to her father and not been so stubborn.

The South Asian humidity nearly felled her before she made it halfway to the apostolic prefecture—a dilapidated mission, as it turned out—where the Catholic population was not yet large enough to deserve an actual diocese. Kate had survived adolescence with very little: her father's series of "visiting scholar" appointments and mother's social work pay were not a prescription for wealth. Even so, her modest means had not prepared her for the poverty that greeted her.

The church itself was made of wooden planks, with a thatched roof, though it did have a wooden door, unlike most structures, which used large pieces of cloth to add privacy but allow for airflow. Everything—the floors, the cloth, the children that ran through without shoes—was covered in the area's fertile red dirt. All structures were raised on stilts to avoid the annual flooding and cobras, and there were very few furnishings: woven mats stuffed with cotton for sleeping, raised wooden areas for sitting, and plastic and clay pots for gathering water and cooking.

She felt almost ashamed of her comfortable youth in comparison. The people here lived a difficult life, but they smiled at the new stranger. Along with the locals' warm welcome, the brightest jewel amidst the rubble was Father Kelly's smile as he ran to embrace her.

"Aren't you a sight!" he declared, holding her at arm's length for inspection before pulling her close. He held her for a long time as though her vitality might recharge his rail-thin body. His hair was long, and he wore white linen garb, relief from the sweltering jungle heat.

A small room with a thin mattress had been cleared for her, and the parishioners greeted her as though she were royalty. All the attention made her wary, and her level of discomfort must have been evident. Even Kate knew she was terrible at masking her emotions.

"Sorry you came?" Father Kelly asked.

"Not at all," she said. "Are you sad they sent you here?"

"Not even remotely," Father Kelly said frankly. "Being here is a blessing. Hearing the confessions of these gentle souls is like being stoned to death with popcorn."

Kate laughed. "I see you haven't lost your sense of humor." She paused. "It's been a long trip. But I'm happy to find you so fulfilled."

Father Kelly smiled weakly before a cloud of melancholy darkened his face. "It's not exactly St. Peter's, is it?"

"Well," Kate mused, "considering our past, I'd say that's a big improvement."

He laughed. She laughed, too, and the pleasure of their camaraderie carried them through several difficult days of service. Up at dawn, preparing food for hours, gathering palm fronds for thatch, boiling water, helping to build a new outhouse and cook hut. By the end of each day, Kate's body ached, and her feet and clothes were caked in the same dirt as the locals. A far cry from the cobblestones and ancient art of Rome. But then, a different concern arose, and its ramifications went far beyond poverty.

"She's very beautiful," Kate said after a community gathering over shared food and children's games. She had noticed the way a woman of the group let her hand brush Father Kelly's and linger when she passed him a bowl of mango, how she watched him as he blessed the children—the same way Kate's mother looked at her father sometimes.

"Who?" asked Father Kelly, almost before Kate finished her statement.

"The woman who loves your smile so much and enjoys all your Latin wordplay."

"Oh—Ava."

She mocked, "Oh, Ava. As if she's nobody." Earlier in the day, Ava had engaged Kate in conversation. She was educated and drily funny. And at one point during the church event, Kate had watched Ava tease Father Kelly so mercilessly that he blushed crimson.

Father Kelly took a moment to appreciate the transformation in Kate—her perceptiveness, already keen as a young child, had grown—before glancing at the woman in question and confirming, "You're right. She's quite special."

Later, when night had fallen, Father Kelly suggested a walk under the moon and stars. "Everything here is beautiful at night. In my early years, the constellations were my only source of—transcendence?"

"How could they punish you so harshly?" Kate blurted out, guilt suffusing every word.

"Well, your parents have probably explained, right?" sighed the priest.

"There is no explanation. Since when is baptizing a mouthy child a sin?" Kate argued.

"You know you're more than that, and so do your accusers and mine."

"Accusers. What right do they have?"

"They have no right. But they have power."

"Or they did."

"Kate," the priest warned as he gestured to a path toward a river inlet, where they sat on rough-hewn benches. "You have no idea what they are capable of—the depths to which they will go to protect their ideology."

Father Kelly described what he'd found upon his arrival in Cambodia. A burning need for spiritual authority, but a Catholicism rife with impediments and strictures that did no one any good. "There was no salvation in the harsh edicts of the Apostolic Vicariate of Phnom Penh. As far as I'm concerned, the leadership is a bunch of scheming, punitive thugs. Your mother's friend Dr. Rin warned me. She all but begged me to leave the Church rather than sacrifice myself to this country's spiritual crisis."

Kate listened quietly before breaking in. "But what are they so scared of, Father? What does all this have to do with me?"

She had seen Father Kelly only twice since Rome. Years earlier, he'd attended a conference in Austria. Simon had been teaching in Berlin at the time, so the family made the trip. Another visit, during a short stint in Indonesia, had inspired a candid and private correspondence between the two that lasted throughout Kate's secondary school years.

Father Kelly gazed at the stars for a long moment. "I can't wait any longer, Kate."

"For change, you mean?" She, too, was looking up at the sky.

"For love." He ran his fingers along the edge of the bench. "Pope Francis was a beautiful new light to the world. His teachings inspired me to become a priest, but what changed? Even back then, millions of Catholics ignored the Church's doctrines on sex and contraception." He looked off toward the water. "I gave up things . . . *a woman* . . . for this life of service." He bowed his head and added in a near whisper, "Why not me? Why should I remain a prisoner when I long to break free?" Desperate to tell Kate that he was her father but still unable to until he told Simon the truth, which he had planned to do the next time he saw him in person.

Kate did not know anything about Father Kelly's past—the woman to whom he referred—and did not ask. She asked only about his new love. His romance with Ava had started like anyone else's, he said. An immediate attraction, followed by secret glances and casual curiosity, which eventually led to the pleasure of human touch. Kate felt a thread of envy tug at her heart. She'd never had a serious boyfriend or dated like her female friends. She had male friends, but the idea of emotional or sexual intimacy seemed beyond her.

Father Kelly said, "I've asked Ava to be my wife, and she has accepted me as her husband."

"But Father!"

"We've been very discreet."

"Really?" Kate disagreed. "Everybody here already knows. How could they not know?"

"I thought you, of all people, would understand."

"I'm not judging you," Kate said as she grasped the priest's hand. The river flowed before them and eddies formed near a log stuck by the edge of the water, an apt image, she thought, of his choices. "I'm afraid for you. They ruined you once. They'll do it again."

"How? What wretched corner of the earth could the Vatican send me to this time?" Father Kelly said, his voice rising. "Do they even know I'm here?"

After a painful silence, Kate inquired, "Tell me about her."

Father Kelly shared that Ava had fled a family of considerable wealth to seek a purpose in life. Ava's quest to avoid her family's intrusions and manipulations had brought her to the apostolic prefecture.

"The money I sent you was hers. She insisted. I'd told her so much about you and your family's travails. I won't let them win. I'll fight them. I'm fighting them now, even though my defiance is quiet. I feel more committed than ever to the beauty of the scriptures and the hope they inspire in people who have nothing else to rely on. But I wouldn't feel so strongly if I hadn't found Ava. Christ sent the disciples out in pairs, you know."

"Yeah, but that doesn't mean they were going out," Kate said, and Father Kelly chuckled.

With a smile, he conceded the point, then went quiet again. After a moment, he said, "Your parents hung on. They continued loving each other despite their opposing views. This encourages me."

"Yes, well, it certainly hasn't been without its struggles."

"I'm certain."

"But what if Ava becomes pregnant?" Kate asked.

"No," agreed Father Kelly. "We can't let that happen. Not yet, anyway. Let's pray that God protects us. That the powers of hell do not succeed."

Kate was startled at the mention of this, what she had long known was the reason for her family's troubles, for Father Kelly's—the powers of hell at play within the Church itself. What she knew, somewhere deep inside, was that she was meant to fight.

"We must not let them win." He spoke with conviction, but his words were tinged with sadness. It was a feeling that stayed with Kate, even after her plane landed in Jerusalem.

Chapter 24

Jerusalem

When she learned that Nadia had scheduled a new archeological dig in Mount Zion for the following month, Kate begged to be included.

"It's not glamorous work, you know," Nadia warned, "and we'll have to focus solely on the work. No talk of, well, anything but the dig."

"That sounds great," Kate said with genuine excitement.

Nadia recognized the desire to lose herself in work, but she wanted Kate to know what she was getting into.

"You can't just walk up and pull things out of rocks, like King Arthur and his sword. The truth is archeology is very much like being a librarian. It is quiet and tedious work."

"Perfect. My class voted me most likely to succeed—as a library nerd."

"All right then," Nadia said, feigning hesitation. "I will put you on the roster for the Mount Zion dig."

Kate threw out her arms and surprised Nadia with a hug.

As Kate turned to leave the office, she noticed a large framed photo of Nadia with a group that she assumed was a team of archeologists. She had seen the photo on previous visits, but it had paled in comparison to

Sister Teresa and her armband. This time, she came to a halt when she read the title, "Sea of Galilee."

Nadia noticed and explained, "That was when we were looking for King David's tomb and treasure in Galilee. Of course, we didn't find that or anything else, despite our beloved St. Peter's promise that it is still here with us."

At this, Kate's body bristled, but not noticing, the professor continued, "Notice the placard we're holding?"

Kate leaned in and read Peter's words from Acts 2:29: "Let me freely speak unto you of the patriarch David, that he is both dead and buried, and his sepulcher is with us unto this day." Suddenly, she was struck in the temple by a sensation like a searing hot bullet. She cried out, and her head slammed forward and shattered the glass. Her body began to shake. She stood, head bowed and blood dripping from a gash near her hairline, as Nadia leaped to her aid.

The professor grabbed Kate and spun her down into a leather chair. Kate lay back against the headrest with a scarlet stream making its way down her face, her limbs trembling.

Kate's eyes rolled back as she shouted, "It's not there!"

"What? You're bleeding!" Nadia cried as she fumbled for her phone under a mound of papers. Instead, she found tissues, so she moved to apply them to Kate's wound, but the young woman erupted again. This time, her entire body went rigid, and the voice that sprang from her throat was deafening. "IT'S—NOT—THERE!"

Dumbstruck and helpless, Nadia stared at Kate with a newly emerging fear. She didn't hear the knock at her door or see Dafna, her new admin assistant, run into the room.

"What's wrong? Are you all right? Does she need a doctor?" the plainly dressed woman blurted as she took in the scene.

When the traumatized Nadia offered no answer, Dafna turned

in time to witness Kate's remarkable transformation from physically stricken to inquisitively calm.

Perplexed, Kate ventured a smile. "Was somebody shouting?"

"Uh . . . yes," Nadia said.

With one glance at the professor's face, Kate pointed at herself and mouthed, *Me?*

Nadia nodded slowly, and Dafna stood stunned.

Kate murmured, "The tomb and treasure are not there."

"Not there? Not where?" Nadia asked.

"Galilee." Kate pointed toward where the photo had stood, only now realizing the havoc she had wreaked. "Oh, no. Not again! Did I do that?"

"What do you mean again? Tell me what happened to you," Nadia pushed, the tissues now balled up in her clenched fist.

Kate's eyes widened as she leaned forward, looking as if she might vomit, but instead, she released a breathless exclamation. "He was buried in Bethlehem."

"What? Who was buried in Bethlehem?" Nadia asked, now kneeling to look Kate straight in the face.

"David. Weren't we talking about King David? And the tomb and—?"

This time, Kate seemed to drop away completely. Her eyes looked straight through Nadia and Dafna behind her, and she began to converse, though not with anyone in the room. The dialogue was frustratingly incomplete, a spattering of words and phrases in a strange, deep voice.

Nadia released her grip on the reading chair and pointed to her desk. "Dafna, grab my recorder."

The older woman didn't move.

"Dafna," Nadia said. "My recorder!"

Dafna reluctantly retrieved the small digital recorder, her eyes never leaving Kate.

As Nadia hit the record button, she wordlessly ushered the dumb-founded Dafna out the door.

◆

"KATE, YOUR VOICE changed. It became two voices, and one of them seemed to be speaking an ancient language."

Kate nodded. "Aramaic. That was my guide. He showed me where Mother Mary gave birth, and then he took me far inside a cave deep underground. Somehow, we were able to walk through a tunnel to another cave. It was dark, but we had two torches. The guide, in Aramaic, said, 'Look at the tomb.' It was enormous but plain. Then he said, 'King David wants us to have this for the Church.'"

Nadia had returned to her desk. She removed her reading glasses. "Are you trying to tell me that you just saw the tomb of King David?"

Kate sighed. She had been through this often enough to know that her mentor's two easiest options were these: believe that she was one more insecure student trying to make an impression or write her off as a head case. "Yes. That's what I'm telling you."

Nadia paused, then laughed heartily at Kate's expressionless response. "Now that's—that's good. For a minute there, I thought you were serious."

Kate frowned, touched the bandage on her forehead, then pulled herself out of the leather chair.

"You're *not* serious—are you?" Nadia stammered, urgency rising in her voice as she watched Kate prepare to leave.

Kate didn't bother to answer. Instead, she headed for the door, heavy with defeat. She had been here before, but this time—in this place and with this woman—it was too much to bear. Pity instead of understanding, followed by ridicule. *No more. I can't do this. I'm done,* she thought.

"Whoa, wait a minute." The professor rose to stop Kate. "Sit with me so I can understand what just happened."

"But you won't. Ever."

"Please, Kate."

"You can't."

"I want to be sure I understand. You want me to believe that you—"

"Thanks for the first aid. But it's been a long day, Professor."

"Kate. Wait," Nadia said as she felt herself lunge to the door.

"I don't want to be mocked anymore! And to have it come from you, of all people? Check the facts on what I just told you. That's what Mom and Dad always did—and my priest. Sorry, but maybe now you know why I'd rather be a librarian."

"Check what facts?" Nadia asked, her body still blocking the door.

"Start recording again."

At this, the professor rushed to her desk and her recorder.

Kate closed her eyes and went over her vision once again. Her flat tone sounded as though she were reciting the phone book.

"A man guides me to a cave and to the spot where Mother Mary gave birth, then leads me beyond it. There are a lot of rocks that have been moved recently to open a tunnel down into a cave much farther underground. As we descend into this tunnel, our torches light the way. We walk very far into the tunnel and are hunched over the whole time. It is pitch black and extremely claustrophobic. Suddenly we come to an opening in the cave where we can stand easily. My guide raises his torch to light the cave so we can see the size of the room.

"There is an immense white stone structure in the center that is about twenty meters wide, long and tall. My guide walks up to the tomb and holds his torch close to it to show me a small iron door. We go in and discover one giant room. There are gold and silver coins in piles everywhere. They are stacked to the ceiling and have burst through the old bags where the fabric has decayed away. I pick up one of the thick gold pieces and look at my guide, who says in Aramaic, 'King David wanted us to have this.' We walk to the center of the tomb and find a black bronze sarcophagus in the shape of a human. On the side are the words engraved in Aramaic, 'King David of Israel.' My guide warns me, 'Do not say anything to anyone about the tomb. You will return to claim it for the people when it is safe to do so.'"

When she finished, there was a long silence. Then Nadia said, "I'll speak to your parents."

"Be my guest. But I'll be gone by the time you come to any conclusions. Nice knowing you. Maybe Notre Dame still wants me."

"Kate, please. I've given you a lot of my time. Humor me for a few more minutes."

Kate wearily pulled a phone from her bag and hit the speed dial. "Hi, Dad. Yes, I'm good. How's the weather? Yeah. Dublin. Got a minute?"

Chapter 25

Bethlehem

The church was ten kilometers south of Jerusalem University, so it would only take about fifteen minutes to drive there. Kate watched for the signs that would direct them to "City of David/ Bethlehem" while Nadia steered the car with one hand and held a cell phone to her ear with the other.

"Dafna, I know you're busy this morning, but I'm hoping you can finish transcribing the recorded conversations I've had with Kate this past week. We need both versions on file—and you've confirmed our tour time, right?"

Nadia listened, her brow furrowed, to the muffled voice on the other end. Kate thought the answer seemed unusually lengthy. After the call ended, Nadia still clutched the phone as if she expected it to begin chirping again.

"The private tour Dafna scheduled for us starts at half past noon. But before we find the largest treasure known to humankind, let's go to Mass. You okay with that?"

Kate hesitated. Her relationship with ritual was complex and predictably unpredictable. But "when in Rome" (or Bethlehem) . . . "Yeah, sure. At least I'll enjoy my visit with the angels."

Nadia eyed her companion. "Angels?"

"Private joke," Kate said as she turned once more to watch for signs. It was no joke, of course. But Kate had learned through the years that it was best not to explain everything.

They found their turn, and Nadia chuckled at the street sign. "Look at that. Manger Street. Get it?" She began to sing in a not-so-melodic voice.

"Away in a manger, no crib for a bed, the little Lord Jesus lay down His sweet head."

"Yikes," Kate said, playfully putting her fingers in her ears.

The church on the main square opposite a mosque looked more like a fortress than a place of worship. Defense had been a bigger concern than aesthetics two thousand years ago. This structure was actually a combination of two churches with a crypt underneath. A third section in the back was said to be the grotto where Jesus was born.

The women drove toward a cliff at the back of the church, where they hoped to get a perspective similar to what Joseph and Mary might have seen from the cave.

"Incredible," Kate said as she got out of the car. "I love how the view spans the desert and most of Jerusalem. Everyone wondered why I wanted to go to college out here. I couldn't explain it, but now that I am here, I know that I feel very much at home."

Nadia nodded, equally in awe. "But where would the cave be? Maybe it's along that ridge wall over there? Underneath, I mean."

Kate tried to call up a vision, but nothing came. After all these years, it was still frustrating. When she wanted to be interrupted by something awesome and inexplicable, she was left entirely alone. "We'd better get back to the church," she reminded her mentor. "It looks like Mass is starting."

They walked across Manger Square, admiring the church's quaint bell tower crowned with a cross. Centuries after construction, the travertine marble was still white.

The scent of burning incense engulfed them as they passed through the iron door. Inside, the air was cool, insulated by the five-foot-thick stone walls. The church was dimly lit throughout, except for the sunlight beaming through a stained-glass window behind the altar.

Kate inhaled the aromas and, looking up, nodded to the angels.

The church was nearly full, but two spaces were available in the back pew. Nadia picked up a missal while Kate peered up at the ceiling, where the large brass incense canisters hung from chains wrapped around stout wooden beams.

The Mass began, and for a moment, Kate was at peace with the world. Her experiences with church services were spotty at best, but she felt the draw of the Mass with its rhythm and ritual. But before she could lose herself to a meditative state, Nadia whispered, "I'm having trouble understanding the Latin. How about you?"

"I can hear fine. Oh, but—do you want me to translate?" Kate said.

A humbled Nadia declined the offer and chose to sit quietly through the remainder of the service.

❖

SISTER DEBORAH BOWMAN was suspicious when Father Maric explained why he had decided to lead the private tour himself. He had spoken to the two visitors after Mass and was supposedly impressed with the university professor's credentials and the keen intelligence of her student.

"Yes, Father. Of course, Father," she said. But the plump protector of the priest's time and health was wary. She knew that the twinkle in his eye and the quick change into more comfortable clothing—the black short-sleeved shirt with clerical collar, pressed slacks, and black sport coat that made him look so dashing and younger than his sixty-four years—meant only one thing: he was smitten.

"Will you want dinner at your usual time, Father?" she asked.

"Yes, yes, of course. As usual," he replied absently.

But she knew that when his attention was caught, a lecture or counseling session might extend past its appointed time and well into the evening.

Attempting to draw him out, she commented, "She's lovely, that girl. So friendly yet keeps to herself. Something serious in her soul, don't you think?"

"Insightful, Sister. You are so right. A light within guides her, I'm sure of it. But I won't be long. A simple tour. As usual."

The sister wasn't fooled.

And so it was that Sister Deborah was the last to see Professor Nadia Jamira and Kate as they followed Father Maric through the door leading to a staircase.

◆

THE COOL, DAMP passage narrowed as they descended into an underground room.

"It's good you reserved a private tour of the church and grotto," Father Maric said. "Too many people in a tight space make the walk uncomfortable."

He was chipper as he guided Nadia and Kate into the room. Its white marble floor was inlaid with a fourteen-pointed silver star. The walls were also covered in marble and accented with red tapestries.

"The church is beautiful," Nadia said. "It's rare to see one built in a cave."

"It is certainly unique, as it should be," Maric agreed. "This is, after all, where our Savior was born."

Nadia looked to Kate and said, "Does anything look familiar?"

"Familiar?" Maric said. "I thought this was your first visit to the church?"

Nadia remained silent, deferring to Kate's experience working her way around awkward questions.

"Do you believe in dreams, Father?" Kate probed. "Or—visions?"

"Certainly. I believe that Spirit or the subconscious tries to speak to us and, on occasion, lead us," the priest admitted.

"Then I guess you could say I've been led to this place by a vision," Kate replied. "But nothing feels quite familiar. Do you know what the cave looked like before the floor and the ceiling were installed?"

"How old do you think I am?" the priest joked. "Why do you ask?"

"I'm looking for the actual birth site of Jesus, and this does not seem right," Kate said. "But I can't really tell with all this marble covering the cave now."

Father Maric looked at Nadia with raised eyebrows. "Is she serious?"

Nadia held her breath. But the priest deserved to know the truth. "Yes. Very serious."

Maric gave this some thought, then turned to look Kate directly in the eyes. "Does Jesus live in you?"

Her blue eyes pierced him. "Yes, He lives in all of us, Father. We just have to be willing to receive His love."

Maric nodded his approval, and Nadia released the breath she'd been holding. "What did the cave in your dream, or vision, look like?" she asked.

"It was very dark and not vivid at all. I remember it being a small cave with a low ceiling. The only distinguishing thing was on a white limestone wall—a formation, a symbol, I guess, that looks like a jagged, tilted Z. I sketched it last night."

Kate reached into her pocket and pulled out a piece of paper. Maric's eyes widened with surprise when he saw it. "Yes," he said. "I've seen this symbol on one of the stones here. But . . ." He studied the women before walking to a small door, which he unlocked with a touchpad. He withdrew electric lanterns from the closet. "We'll need more light. The symbol is deep in the cave, behind the walls of the church."

Maric pulled back one of the red tapestries to reveal a thick steel door embedded in the rock. He entered another combination, and the door opened. "Watch your step—and your head, please. Follow me."

Kate and Nadia exchanged electrified glances. As they walked slowly into the cave, the ceiling gradually dropped until it was mere centimeters over their heads. Kate stopped suddenly, placed her lantern on the floor, and closed her eyes.

"Are you okay?" Nadia asked.

"I—I can hear him and sort of see him," Kate whispered.

Alarmed, Maric interjected, "See who?"

Nadia calmed him. "She's remembering what she experienced with her guide."

"I think we are in the same place," Kate ventured, opening her eyes and looking around.

"Think?" Nadia said softly.

"It was dark because he held the torch at eye level so I could see his face. The brightness kind of blinded me to the cave, but . . . I think . . ." She took a few steps farther on. "Yes. Here."

Maric stooped and lit seven large candles with a pocket lighter. "Come have a look."

Once their eyes adjusted to the light, Kate and Nadia saw cushions and pillows near the candles. Father Maric explained that this was a favorite place for clergy to sit and pray in peace. "This spot has always had the most peaceful spirit," he said.

Nadia nodded, smiling, and then gasped, stepping over to the rock wall where the tilted Z shimmered in the flickering light. Nadia held up Kate's drawing next to it. It was a perfect match.

Father Maric let out an involuntary, "Holy Moses!"

Nadia explored the wall's surface with her palms and announced, "It's pink and white limestone. All the ancient buildings are made of it. They call it Jerusalem stone."

"This is the place," Kate said, now resolute. "This is where the guide brought me."

Maric spoke slowly. "I have always felt like this was the best, most comforting place in the cave. Giving birth here makes sense. I've often wondered if the builders of the church knew that this was the actual spot where Jesus was born. But maybe they also knew that it would be difficult to have people come and worship on this spot. The ceiling is so low. It's cramped. So they went out where the ceiling is higher, where the silver star is installed in the floor. It is more comfortable, in some ways, where the star is. But the energy is so much better in here."

Kate and Nadia liked the priest. Despite his age, he had verve and an open mind. He was still willing to explore new possibilities—and seemed pleased to be doing it with them.

"I agree, Father," Nadia said. "Thank you for bringing us here."

Kate nodded, her heart full of gratitude. "I was told by the guide in my vision that once we arrived at this point, it was fourteen *amahs* from the symbol in the rock to the tunnel."

"What are you saying?" Maric said.

Nadia stepped in. "In Biblical times, they used the Hebrew measurement system throughout this entire area. The amah is an ancient Hebrew measurement based on the span of the hand spread wide, from the tip of the thumb to the tip of the pinky finger."

"That's fine. But what does that have to do with the symbol on the wall and a tunnel?"

"In my vision, after the guide showed me the shape on the rock—the Z—he showed me a tunnel that led to King David's tomb," Kate said.

And just like that, Maric seemed to have reached his limit. "Come on now. We've had all kinds of religious fanatics in here searching for this or that. But believe me, there's no tunnel or tomb around here," he said. "Most especially not King David's tomb."

Nadia scanned the wall in both directions with her lantern as the priest spoke. "He's right, Kate. If anything is beyond this rock wall, it is going to take some serious blood, sweat, and tears to get through it. We'd need some help."

With a self-deprecating smile, Kate said, "Humor me a little longer? Please?"

Unable to deny his innate curiosity, Maric sighed and sat on a cushion near the candles. "I have time," he said, his right hand sweeping across the tight space. "Be my guest."

Kate began by moving along the wall, to the left of the Z, pressing one hand after the other on the wall to serve as her ruler. Then she stopped. "Something isn't right." Hunching over, Kate walked the edge of the entire cave, holding her lantern close to the stone. Nadia followed while Maric watched from his cushions.

"Trust me, ladies, there are no tunnels or tombs around here. If there were, the Church would know about it."

Kate returned to the point about fourteen hand-spans to the left of the Z symbol and placed both hands on the wall.

"There is something different about this wall. The soil and stone appear the same, but if you look really closely, this area juts out at an angle."

Nadia raised her lantern and quickly agreed. "She's right. Come see, Father. When you look closely, you can tell that this part of the wall is not a natural part of the cave."

Father Maric begrudgingly got to his feet and joined the women. "What are you two talking about? I don't see anything strange, and my goodness, this is just a cave, not modern architecture. Not everything is proportionate or symmetrical."

"No," Kate insisted. "This is not a cave wall. It's man-made, and it looks like the builders went to great lengths to blend it in with the soil and stone native to this area."

Maric looked to Nadia, who stated, "I have been on hundreds of digs, Father. I'm quite certain Kate is right. This wall has been here a long time, but it is man-made."

"Then why have we never noticed it before? How could no one have known?"

"They did an incredible job disguising it, and I would imagine that no one was looking for it," the professor answered.

"Where does it lead?" Maric asked, looking at Kate.

"Maybe nowhere," she said. "Maybe it was built for support. But I'd sure like to find out. Wouldn't you?"

Chapter 26

Bethlehem

Father Maric was suddenly immovable, stern as the stone under their feet. "What are you suggesting?" he asked, incredulous. "I can't let you dig up a historic site! And what would you use, spoons?"

At this, Nadia pulled a titanium rod from her bag. The device was about the size of a police baton. "Thankfully, the spoon has evolved over time," she said.

The priest cried out, "You can't use explosives in here!"

"This isn't dynamite, Father," she said, holding the tool out for his inspection. "It's an extremely sensitive and highly advanced piece of technology. It's based on geophysical diffraction tomography."

"What in St. George's name does that mean?" the beleaguered priest asked.

"This device will tell us how thick the wall is, up to fifty meters. Care for a live demonstration?"

Nadia drew out a stand that allowed her to set the rod upright on one of the limestone blocks in the floor.

"I promise, Father, this will not damage anything," she said, pressing a button on the end of the rod and watching as digital numbers appeared on the side of the instrument.

The wall measured three meters thick, but there was more to tell. "There's about ten meters of open space—maybe a room or a passageway—on the other side of this wall," she exclaimed.

Kate moved closer and peered over her professor's shoulder. "How does it fracture a hole in the wall?"

An alarmed Maric said, "Wait, what's this about a fracture? You just said it measures." Nadia explained that the instrument was also capable of sending out an extremely high-vibration signal, fracturing solid material into particles that could be shoveled away. "I determine the diameter of the hole," she said, "and there is no spillover—just what we need and no more."

Maric wrung his hands. Nadia and Kate knew he felt caught between wanting to protect this ancient, sacred place, and being present for a potential discovery. Kate hoped the description of her vision would be enough to sway him.

"Tiny. Tiny, please," Maric pleaded.

"Well, since this structure is only two meters high and two and a half meters deep, I'll want to clear a diameter of two meters," Nadia said as she considered the numbers on the instrument.

"Two meters? Hold on there!" Maric's eyes widened in panic.

Kate understood instantly. "Large enough so we can crawl through?"

"Right. If we keep it close to the ground," Nadia said, rotating the digital tool to aim it carefully at the wall. "But not so big that we inadvertently collapse any part of this wall."

"Collapse. No. No. That is not good!" Maric cried out, though Kate and Nadia ignored him.

"We'll need to do the procedure twice to get through two and a half meters," Nadia continued.

"Countdown," Kate said. "Ten, nine, eight—"

Distraught, Maric shouted out, "Wait!"

"You said this was a good place to meditate," Kate said in response.

"It is!" the distraught priest replied.

"Then say a little prayer, Father," Kate said. "We're going in."

"Everybody stand back," Nadia warned.

Father Maric ducked and covered his head with his arms. But there was no explosion. Stone and soil were pulverized with little more than a pop. As the cloud of dust literally settled in the cool, dry cave, a perfect circle appeared behind it. They stared at the result.

"Incredible! A perfectly neat hole," Maric said in amazed consternation. "Maybe I should go get the spoons now?"

"Or a broom," Kate said.

"Spoons would be helpful, actually," Nadia said while moving to the circle that was full of debris.

"There are shovels in the closet where we store the lanterns," Maric recalled. "But you'll have to do the cleanup. My back is—or I could go and find you some help?"

"Let's keep this private for now," Nadia said, looking at Kate. "Good thing I signed that contract, eh?"

Before the women had driven to the church, Kate had produced a printed document and handed it to the professor. "I'll show you where I think King David's tomb is, but before we go, we need to have an agreement. One hundred percent of all items that are found with my guidance must immediately be given to the Catholic Church, without exception."

Nadia had laughed, signing quickly after teasing, "If I were in this field for the treasure, I'd have quit by now."

Nadia pulled gloves from her bag and began moving rubble, while Kate went with Maric to help fetch the small hand shovels, but also so that he wouldn't find himself alone and start thinking that it was time to fetch the gendarmes instead.

Handing a shovel to Nadia and setting to work herself, Kate engaged the nervous priest. She asked, *"Quomodo sacerdos fieri? An quia Latina docuisse patrem?"*

Father Maric's demeanor changed in an instant. "Oh my goodness, young lady. Your Latin is superb. *Vere, quia me Pater meus pater quod erat meus."*

Wiping sweat and dust from her face with her arm, Nadia asked for a translation.

"I asked how he became a priest," Kate said.

Father Maric sat on one of the cushions and took up the story, in English. "I was playing with my young sister Sara in an abandoned house in our neighborhood. As I chased her, she ran full speed through a sliding glass door, thinking it was open. Her whole body was badly cut. But she severed her jugular vein. She bled to death in my arms."

Stunned, Kate and Nadia stopped working as Father Maric continued. "I was in shock, of course, and covered in her blood. Screaming. Then out of nowhere, a pure peace came over me. I heard Sara say, 'Don't be afraid. It is wonderful here.'" He paused. "You see, I experienced my own vision, or dream, or whatever we might call it. My sister, smiling, stood before me with an angel. An angel I believe was Mother Mary. They held hands and then disappeared. In town, no one really believed me, of course. About the vision, I mean. But I suppose you both know a great deal about doubters?"

Nadia smiled. "At one time or another, I suspect most people of faith are accused of being a little . . ."

Kate crouched in front of Father Maric and placed a tender hand on his shoulder. "Touched?"

"I was thinking delusional," Nadia said, laughing before quickly adding, "Sorry. I'm Catholic, but I'm also a scientist."

"A sense of humor never hurts, Professor," Father Maric said as he watched a handful of dirt slip through his fingers. "And the truth is, sometimes it does feel like we're all digging in the dark."

After the dust cleared from the second diffraction, Nadia pointed a flashlight through the hole and could see that there was indeed a large open space on the other side of the wall. She illuminated the space for Kate before crawling through the dust ahead of her. After a moment of indecision and a quick sign of the cross, Maric slowly and painfully, it seemed, lowered himself to his hands and knees.

But when they clambered to their feet, shone their lights throughout the space, and discovered that it was empty, their hearts sank.

"Looks like the grave robbers got here first," Maric said.

"This is not the spot, but we're closer," Kate said.

Those words would ring in her ears throughout the remainder of the day as more holes were cut, all leading to dead ends or restrictive enclosures. The priest's easygoing demeanor was fading, despite his apparent faith in Kate's vision. They all suffered bumps and bruises, and once nearly plummeted into the darkness.

Finally, hunger began to gnaw at their strength and patience. Filthy and thirsty, they spat dirt and dust from dry mouths. They quarreled and then apologized.

But small breaks begat bigger discoveries. A splintered wood floor cracked open and provided a view to a lower level. The trio slid down as though into a rabbit hole and discovered a tunnel not more than a meter and a half tall and half a meter wide.

Kate spoke the words they all had been waiting to hear. "This feels familiar. This feels right."

It was too late for Maric, who fell to his knees. "I can't go on."

"You didn't have to follow us!" Nadia didn't mean for it to sound like a reprimand. "I'm sorry, Father—without your help, we wouldn't have made it this far."

Kate added, "We'll be fine if we stick together." Extending her hand, she asked, "Father, do you need a moment to rest?"

"Only a lifetime." Maric grinned ruefully. "Who are you, child?" he asked.

Kate was surprised by the question, and a little worried for the priest's health. "What do you mean? My name is Kate."

"Yes, yes. But who *are* you?" He breathed heavily. "A divine messenger . . . covered in dust?"

"That's it!" Kate's sudden exclamation was so assured that she stood upright and slammed her head into the ceiling. Her yowl echoed down the tunnel.

"That's what?" Maric asked.

"In my vision, when I had had too much, I told my guide that I was feeling . . ."

"Claustrophobic?" Nadia offered.

"Yes. Then he said it was only a little farther."

Maric rose with a groan. "Lead on, my dear. Don't worry about me."

The path they followed turned downward and was so steep that the muscles in their legs screamed for relief. The temperature dropped, too, and damp clay began to stick to the soles of their shoes. Maric could not hold his footing, and when he slipped, he mowed down his companions. As they tumbled into darkness, their lanterns were jarred from their hands, scattering and sending shafts of light helter-skelter down the slope.

The ground finally leveled off, and their descent came to a halt. The three had been thrown together like a pile of old rugs. They checked for broken bones and mumbled thankful prayers. They had survived. But where were they?

"I can't see," Maric said.

Kate crawled to a still-shining lantern that lay on its side. She grabbed it and pointed it back at the priest and Nadia. "Everybody okay?" she asked.

"Breathing," said Nadia.

"Barely," added Maric.

Kate rolled onto her back. The lantern light splashed against the ceiling, and they all realized that it was about twenty-five meters high. She moved the light in various directions, mapping the chamber with her eyes.

"Wait, stop, go back, Kate," Nadia ordered. "On the wall. What are those?"

Kate retraced her movements, and after a moment, the light revealed objects that were stacked in rows nearly twenty feet high.

"Amphoras!" Nadia eagerly stepped forward to examine the shapely containers, each about a half meter tall. Each had a long neck with two handles for pouring. The bodies swelled and then tapered into a narrow bottom. Many of them were cracked. "They were used to carry water thousands of years ago and are usually made of thick terra-cotta. Typically, they hold about two gallons of water."

"I could use a few gallons right about now," said Maric. "Look at all of them! The entire wall is covered. There are hundreds."

"How old do you think they are?" Kate asked.

"I'm thinking around three thousand years," Nadia answered.

"With all of these jugs, someone was planning for a big drought," Maric said, pondering the collection while resting his hand gently on one amphora. Without warning, the tip broke off, crashing to the floor.

"Careful," Nadia said, suddenly severe.

Maric picked up the piece of terra-cotta, then looked back at the broken amphora. "Sorry, but—oh! Something solid and shiny is inside."

Kate brought the lantern close. "It's a golden color." She whipped off her shoe and struck the damaged amphora, cracking it open to reveal more.

"Gold! The entire jug is full of gold," Maric whispered.

Kate and Nadia looked at each other in amazement.

"Could they all be full of gold?" Maric attempted to lift another amphora, but it was far too heavy. "My goodness, it weighs a ton."

Nadia and Kate took turns lifting, and they came to the same conclusion. "They were planning for a drought all right, but not a lack of rain," Nadia said. "If all these are full of gold, the fortune would carry a community through decades of financial problems." She stood back and examined the wall of amphoras.

"Something tells me this is only the beginning," Kate said as she turned, pointed the light in the opposite direction, and began to walk toward the middle of the cavernous space. There, she came upon a hard sand floor. Forty steps more put her near the corner of what seemed to be a gargantuan white structure.

"What is it?" Father Maric asked.

Kate did not hesitate to answer. "King David's tomb."

Chapter 27

Bethlehem

Before she rounded the corner, Kate hesitated. Every intrusive and debilitating vision, every failed connection with another person, every off-kilter moment of her life that couldn't be explained by social ineptitude or isolating intelligence might be justified by whatever she found on the other side.

During his reign over Israel, King David was obsessed with building a great temple. Of all the wealthy biblical heroes, David excelled the most in riches and left behind him greater wealth than any other king in the history of the world.

Kate was not accustomed to *pausing*. She had always rushed head-long into situations and had usually made a mess of them. But her next few footfalls could not be misplaced; what she was to find would explain what had made her different but would also wipe away her easy excuses for that difference. Discovering King David's tomb would set her even further apart from others. No longer would she be able to hide her premonitions behind aloofness and academic prowess. By unearthing the tomb, Kate would have to stand in her truth and stop trying to be invisible.

Her entire life felt like it had been leading up to this moment, and she was almost paralyzed by the thought of what came next. This was leading to something greater than a lost treasure. Once she stepped into her apparent destiny, what mantle was she about to assume?

"It's stacked marble," Nadia announced. She reached her hand out as if to touch the cool surface, then pulled back in amazement and respect. "Each piece must be a meter and a half wide and a meter tall."

Kate followed an excited Nadia and Maric as they rushed along the length of the tomb.

"It has to be twenty meters long!" Nadia cried out.

"And a hundred tons," Kate said without emotion. She'd been led to this tomb, but she knew the route back into the world would not be as clear.

"Do you think Goliath is buried in there too?" Maric asked.

Nadia laughed, but Kate remained serious. She breathed in and conjured her earlier vision, drawing on its peace and certainty. Lifting her lantern high, she said: "We need to find a small iron door. That's next." She opened her eyes. "It's here somewhere."

She started to pace the length of the tomb, Nadia and Maric following behind. They paused when she did, awaiting her inspiration. No one dared say a thing; they knew that time was precious. Kate couldn't shake the feeling that someone, something, would be lurking in the dark, waiting to pounce. But she couldn't remember ever not feeling that way.

It was not until they had walked around the entire tomb that she allowed herself to consider her future if they *didn't* find what they were looking for. And then she saw it. "There!"

Nadia rushed forward to inspect the small door. A closer look with her lantern revealed a large iron lock. She hesitated, then pulled out her knife to pry at it, but it was useless: the lock was rusted solid from centuries of disuse. "I hate to do this, but I think this lock has served its purpose."

With the butt of her knife, she smashed it, and the lock crumbled and fell to the floor.

Something about watching the lock dissolve into powder heightened Kate's anxiety. Still, she knew there was no way but forward. She nodded. "Okay, everybody. Let's push."

With Kate and Nadia on one side and Maric on the other, they angled their shoulders into the iron and pushed. Their feet began to slip before the door did.

"It's not moving," Maric said, doubling over, his hands on his knees.

"Push harder," Nadia groaned, her body still pressed into the door.

Maric righted himself and tried again, this time using the other side of his body.

"Harder!" Kate grunted.

After a moment or two of additional pressure, the ancient hinges exploded with a muffled *whomp*. Kate, Nadia, and Maric stumbled backward to avoid falling inward with the door. Stunned, they pulled themselves to sitting positions to see what lay before them.

Together, they used their lanterns to illuminate the high ceiling of the enclosure. Perhaps they looked up first in devotion or perhaps because they wanted to savor what would greet them, but deep down, there was also fear.

They were too stunned by what they saw to speak. Gigantic, ancient sacks that spilled gold coins everywhere. But it was what they noticed in the distance that drew their gaze: a long black shape that rested on an immense rectangle of glimmering white marble.

No one moved. Finally, Nadia stepped forward, followed by a hesitant Maric. Kate was last, but only because she didn't need to see the tomb up close. She knew what she would find. It was a sarcophagus crafted in the shape of a nude male figure, arms crossed over his chest, eyes closed.

"If this isn't David's tomb, it was certainly someone extremely rich and important," Father Maric whispered.

"It's David," Kate said with confidence, her voice causing both Nadia and the priest to flinch.

Nadia stepped forward. "Hello, King David," she whispered as her fingers hovered over his arm; her archeologist's caution returned after the recklessness of burrowing through walls and breaking locks. Ever the professor, she next bent down to discern whether anything was chiseled on the marble slab beneath.

"It's Aramaic."

"What does it say?" Maric asked, looking over Nadia's shoulder at the sloping symbols.

The professor pulled a thick paintbrush from her shoulder bag and began cleaning the surface, but before she could finish, Kate joined her and read the inscription. "King of Israel David of Bethlehem placed here for eternity. If another king shall disturb this tomb, may his throne and rule be ripped away."

Maric gave Kate a look of bewilderment. "How could you possibly know . . .?"

Kate gazed back at him with a calm humility. "I just know, Father."

Maric sucked in a quick breath, but Nadia fell to her knees and began to weep, exhausted and overcome by the significance of their discovery. After a few moments, she looked up, tears of joy streaking through the dirt on her face, and said, "Forgive me, Kate. I am so sorry."

"Forgive you?" Kate asked. "Forgive you for what?"

Nadia reached for Kate's hand. "For ever doubting you."

Chapter 28

Bethlehem

Djiana Felice Gomes raised her designer sunglasses. She typically did this to appraise an object's worth, but not this time. This item—a framed photo of a little girl—would be of immeasurable value to someone, but to her, it was annoying. Worse, it was without financial value.

"Sister, who is this child?" she asked without looking away from the frame.

Sister Deborah, who sat in a straight-backed chair, was reluctant to answer. She had seen the way the priest looked at that image. How it held his attention on bad days, when it was kindest to simply leave his meal on his desk and retreat, and even more so on good days, when perhaps he wanted to share some sense of pleasure or contentment with the little girl.

This girl, her story, belonged to the priest, and Sister Deborah took seriously her pledge to protect Maric. Her hands throbbed. Her cheek stung. The corners of her mouth felt dry and crusty.

"Don't be afraid," Djiana prodded. "It's just a question."

But Sister Deborah was indeed afraid. She was afraid of the ropes holding her hands tightly behind her back. She was also afraid of being hit again. The thought of a fist striking her mouth, the way it could again draw blood from between her lips, terrified her. It was not just the force but the frequency with which the blows had come; they had made it clear that there would be no time for prayer, that the middle-aged woman with the golden-brown streaks in her dark hair would see to it that the sister had no one to rely on but herself as she endured this interrogation.

Unable to stop herself, Sister Deborah asked, "Why do you want to know?"

The woman leaned her hands on the wooden arms of the chair. Sister Deborah noticed that her nails were not manicured, yet her fingers were adorned with gaudy rings that seemed tight enough to cut off circulation. "Ah, aren't we inquisitive?" the woman said as she observed how the nun's eyes fell on her jewels. "Like what we see, do we? What of your vow of poverty, Sister?" She released a laugh that sounded practiced. "And a little protective, too, eh? Do you have a thing for your priest, Sister?"

Djiana's smile looked as manufactured as her laugh sounded. Behind her overfull lips were capped teeth that even the nun knew must have cost thousands. This woman was clinging to her youth with steely resolve. Still, Sister Deborah's ribs could attest that the woman had no reservations about using her fists. She felt that she had no choice but to reply.

"I don't have a 'thing,' whatever that is." She breathed in and prepared for what was to come. When no blow arrived, she continued. "I have a responsibility."

"I'm touched," Djiana snarled. She pulled the photo off the desk and pushed it toward the nun. "I was just wondering," she said and took a step back, the frame still in her hand. "She reminds me of someone."

Djiana and her three henchmen had arrived at the church just as Sister Deborah had concluded that Father Maric would, indeed, be late for dinner. Their accents sounded Spanish, but the nun was certain that the woman who was torturing her was not from Spain. Mexico, perhaps, or South America.

The three men appeared restless and impatient. One had a pock-marked face, while another was tall and fairly handsome. The third, who apparently outranked the others, was built like a battering ram. His tight black clothing clung to a massive back and shoulders. His tiny, hard eyes, too close together, were barely visible beneath a short-brimmed cap and behind an incongruously stylish pair of glasses.

"How much longer do we have to wait?" he said.

Something about these three men was gnawing at the nun. What was it about them and their relationship with Djiana that seemed of some import? The men had hung back while Djiana had approached the nun with a warm smile, her expensive handbag hanging from her arm; they'd only made a move once that handbag had been swung at Sister Deborah, its gold buckle catching her temple.

Djiana turned to the man. "Relax, Fernando. They have to come up for air sometime. And when they do . . ."

Sister Deborah's spine cringed. She had to find a way to warn Father Maric. But how? Like so many other times in her life, prayer was her only ally.

Fernando scowled, checked his watch, and prowled about like a feral dog. "The time, Djiana. Do you see the time?" he said.

"No, my darling," she said, visibly checking back into her surroundings. "I don't see the time. I feel it. Yes? And the time is right, wouldn't you agree? The hour is ripe. They are late, I agree, but why? Tell me, my sweet, why are they late?"

Sister Deborah waited for a reply, but none came. Fernando merely grunted, and the other two men exchanged glances as though daring each other to speak up. There was no need. Djiana twirled an overstyled length of hair around a finger and continued to speak.

"They are late, my love, because they have found something. No. Not something. Something is not why we are here. They have found *the* thing. The treasure that will send us to new heights of pleasure and power. Can you wait? Does one more hour really matter?"

Fernando removed his cap and cleaned his sweaty brow. Thick wrinkles in his forehead added to the impression that he could be the kind of man who entertained deep reflection. Yet in the hours she had spent with her captors, Sister Deborah had witnessed nothing that suggested a contemplative soul in any of them.

"But what if they don't stop here first?" he asked.

With the assurance of someone who already knows the answer, Djiana asked, "Where would they go?"

The smallest of the three men offered, "They could call the Vatican or somebody on their way here."

"Yes, they could," Djiana replied. "Very good. Thank you. But they won't."

"You don't know that—"

Djiana turned on her heel, but Sister Deborah couldn't tell whether the man was intimidated.

"I know people, my love. The priest would insist on the privacy of his own office to make such a call. He might need to reflect a bit, put his feet up—in triumph, you see—and pour himself two fingers of the port wine he keeps here in the bottom drawer of his desk. What a little sneak, this one! I bet he smokes on the sly too."

Sister Deborah couldn't stop herself from crying out, "Oh, no! Never Father—" before being silenced by Djiana's laser eyes.

"Excuse me, Sister, did I ask you to speak?" Djiana said.

Sister Deborah shook her head in silence, her inner turmoil closing her raw throat.

Chapter 29

Bethlehem

"King David bragged to everyone that he had provided a hundred thousand talents of gold and a million talents of silver," Nadia said jubilantly. "But later, he corrected his boast in a public announcement written in the book of Chronicles."

"1 Chronicles 29," Father Maric interjected.

Nadia smiled and continued. "Yes, precisely. He said he actually gave three thousand talents of gold and seven thousand talents of silver—his personal property—and the people of Israel contributed another five thousand talents of gold and ten thousand talents of silver."

"So how much is that, and do you think it's all here?" Maric asked, looking at the bulging sacks.

Nadia swept her flashlight across the room. "It will take a team of valuators and accountants to appraise the findings, but I'm guessing it is."

"I know we will figure out the worth of the gold and silver," Kate interrupted, "but how can anyone put a price on King David's sarcophagus and tomb?" Her fingers gently brushed down David's right leg.

"Indeed," Nadia said. "The material wealth, the gold and silver, mean nothing compared to finding David."

Father Maric laughed and shook his head. "God is lucky the two of you made this discovery. All I can think about is the enormous amounts of gold and what it will mean for the church and her people. I just read that the Vatican's net worth in gold is about six billion. All of this will easily triple that value, don't you think?"

"I think we can do some rough calculations right now," Nadia said.

The three moved through the tomb in an attempt to take inventory. Nadia began to snap images with her phone. At the same time, she called out numbers that Maric entered on his phone's calculator.

They also returned to the wall where they had made their first discovery, breaking an amphora every ten feet or so to confirm what they suspected were the contents. Silver, gold, and more silver. More than any earthly soul could imagine.

"Include all this with the average estimate of the tomb's contents in the Bible that I calculated for our other dig, and we get—Jesus! Sorry, Father. A total of about seven hundred billion!"

The priest crossed himself as he exclaimed, "Mother Mary and Joseph! That is about triple the worth of the entire wealth of the church!"

Kate smiled, rose, and hurried back to the tomb.

When she returned, she held two large gold coins from the sacks inside the tomb. "You each deserve a souvenir. This will look good on your desk, Father," she said, holding the coin out. "And if anything, it might be wise to keep some proof of this on us. We might need it."

"Do I dare?" he asked, though he had already taken it.

"You took the risk of bringing us here," Kate said, turning toward Nadia. "And, Professor, imagine this in your office."

Nadia beamed. "Absolutely. Next to the blue armband, as soon as I get back. What about you, Kate?"

Kate thought for a moment before deciding. "I may take a couple for gifts. My dad will faint when he sees one. But nothing more." Her expression darkened. "I've been carrying all this stuff my whole life."

There was a pause before Father Maric asked a question that made his voice quiver. "But now what?" he asked. "Shouldn't we notify the Vatican? Frankly, this is starting to make me really nervous."

"Why?" Kate asked, though she was relieved that perhaps her concern was shared.

"Thieves."

Kate relaxed. "Oh, come on, Father. It's been safe down here for three thousand years. Thieves obviously can't find it." She took the leap into even more mundane matters. "I'm hungry. Anyone else? We should probably make our way back. Don't you think, Professor?"

Nadia shook her head. "I can't. Not yet, anyway." She looked up and shrugged. "You two go. I want to spend some time down here absorbing it all before it turns into another tourist attraction. I feel I owe it to myself."

"I can assure you, Professor, you'll have all the time you need," Maric said. "And I wouldn't feel right leaving you down here by yourself."

"I appreciate your concern," Nadia replied, "but I've been on far more dangerous digs than this one. I know the safety procedures. Please don't worry." She looked at Kate. "Please?"

"I can stay with you," Kate offered.

Nadia pondered the situation. "We only have two lanterns now. You two take one, and I promise not to stay down here too much longer."

"Okay, but what if your lantern goes out?" Maric asked.

"Then David and I will have a nice long talk with each other in the dark. We'll be fine. I'm not alone."

Chapter 30

Bethlehem

When Maric and Kate passed the Z symbol on the tunnel wall, they each took a deep breath, contemplating the return to a world that was about to awaken to startling news—their news.

"I can't wait to tell the priests in the rectory," Maric said. "The looks on their faces will be priceless."

Despite her apprehension, Kate laughed at the thought of these holy men taken aback by what two young women had achieved. "They'll think we've lost our minds."

"Indeed."

"And then they'll lose their minds. King David's tomb?"

Father Maric stopped before climbing the stairs. His mood changed from giddy glee to something darker. He stared at the gold coin in his hand. "Maybe we shouldn't tell them," he said quietly.

"Why?" Kate asked.

"Not yet, I mean," he amended. "I'm afraid they aren't prepared to handle it. If we let them know first, the news will get out and spread too fast. We can't suddenly be inundated by the curious and devoted."

"And the looters," Kate added.

The priest started to agree but tempered himself. "We'll lock the door to the cave as soon as your professor returns. Not that looters could retrace our steps anyway." He chuckled. "I'm not even sure we'll be able to."

"No problem," Kate said as she tapped her right temple. "It's all right here."

Father Maric smiled and took her hand. "Thank God for you," he said. "Let's go to my office, shall we? We'll call the Vatican first. They'll know how to handle security and a proper public announcement."

"Good thinking," Kate replied. "But will even the Vatican be prepared for this?"

"Oh, yes. This church is a sacred site, so I have access to a list of people I can call at any time. But I've never had a need—until now, of course. Do you think finding David qualifies?" He raised his eyebrows and grinned.

The hallway leading to Father Maric's office was understandably empty at this late hour. Yet Kate was sure she heard voices. A few seconds later, Father Maric seemed to stop to listen.

"What's that?" she asked.

"What?"

"You didn't hear it? It seemed like you heard voices too."

"No. It's probably this old building creaking," the priest reassured her. "No one would be around at this late hour other than Sister Deborah, and I'm hoping that her time with me hasn't led to her talking to herself just yet." The priest smiled and gave Kate's hand a squeeze. "Just this old building, my dear."

Still unsure, Kate ventured, "I thought it sounded softer. Vocal."

"I hear voices all day long around these grounds," Maric said. "Comes with the territory, Kate."

Angels, she thought.

"It's so late that the other priests have gone to their quarters. I'm actually assuming Sister Deborah has retired, too, and a little annoyed that I missed dinner."

As soon as he pushed open his door, Father Maric's assumption was disproved. Shocked by what he saw, he couldn't even cry out and simply stood as all color seemed to drain instantly from his face.

Kate shouldered her way past him. Sister Deborah sat bound to a chair, a floral scarf stuffed into her mouth, her swollen, bloodied face glistening with gashes and bruises, her eyes filled with terror.

Before Kate or Maric could react to what they were seeing, they each felt something heavy strike their heads and shove them forward. As they tumbled onto the office floor, the gold coin sprang out of the priest's hand. He desperately reached for it, but his groping stopped when the pointed heel of a well-tailored woman's shoe came down on his wrist. He looked up to see its owner staring down at him with gleefully cruel eyes.

"Welcome back, Father," she said. "We've had such a lovely visit with Sister Deborah here." Maric tried to shift his gaze to his colleague, but she was out of his view.

"Who are you?" he managed.

"We will get to that, Father. Oh yes. But first . . ."

The woman crouched, picked up the gold coin, and ran her finger along its edge, mesmerized.

Kate, seemingly forgotten, sat slowly upright and began to edge for the door.

One of the men closed in quickly, handgun pointed at her head. She wondered if his gun was the one that had struck the back of her neck.

"Ah." The woman turned to her. "You must be Kate. I've heard so much about you. The pleasure's all mine," she said, nodding her head. "Now, tell me. How was your little journey in the catacombs?"

Kate's heart dropped, and her stomach knotted. She had been correct in feeling that there was someone crouching around the corner. "I don't know what you're talking about," Kate growled. "We took a tour."

"Oh, I'm sure you did. And lucky you, it appears that you stumbled onto a treasure. I do hope you're the type who likes to share," the woman said as she held the coin up to the light. "It's the Christian thing to do, you know."

The largest of her accomplices growled, "We don't have time for this!"

"Hush!" the woman ordered.

The muscular man with the thick wrinkles in his forehead froze, and not because his minder hissed at him. No, the eyes of the young woman with red hair had targeted him. He felt their heat. As he took in her defiant glare, he thought of the pale little girl whose powers he'd witnessed in Rome years earlier when he had gone by the name of Carlitos.

"Now, Kate, I want you to know that all of us in this quaint little office can count," Djiana interrupted. "Only two of you came through that door, but three of you went searching for a very special treasure. Where is the professor, Kate?"

"Professor? There's no professor here," she replied too quickly.

With the grace of a cat, the woman leaped and smashed the back of her hand across Sister Deborah's face. The scarf shoved down the sister's throat did little to muffle the sound of her pain.

"What the hell are you doing?" Kate was on her feet and reaching toward the nun when Fernando grabbed her shoulders and forced her heavily back down. Kate's knees felt like they shattered as they hit the stone tile, the pain making its way up her spine to meet the throbbing lump at the base of her skull.

Father Maric begged, "No more. Don't hurt this child. Tell us what you want."

"What we want, Father?" the woman said. "Is that not clear by now?"

"Who are you?" Father Maric asked hopelessly.

"Yes, introductions are in order. For now, let me say that I am the future of Christianity—and you, kind sir, are the past. A past that will quickly be forgotten if you don't start answering simple questions. So I repeat, where is Professor Jamira?"

"What good will it do to know?" Maric protested. "It's impossible to find her down there."

Fernando was on the priest in two paces and began to pistol-whip him. As the old man's nose, cheeks, and forehead began weeping blood and tears, Kate again shot to her feet, flailing wildly at Fernando. When her fist nearly found his nose, he threw down his weapon and subdued her with two hands around her throat. She went limp and was close to losing consciousness when the woman spoke.

"May I ask, Fernando, do you intend to kill the golden goose? Because if you do, I will be forced to shoot you in your head." She pressed the tip of his own gun into his hair. "Is that a fair trade, *idiota*?" She pushed the gun harder into his skull. "I said, is it fair?"

Fernando let go of Kate. She fell to her knees, gasping for air, and appeared as if she might pitch forward. Djiana grabbed her hair and tugged so hard that Kate's head snapped back, forcing her eyes upward.

"To be truthful, Kate, this hair is a disaster. But we'll save girl talk for later. Yes? Now, this is my offer. Can you hear me? Hum your favorite song if you can hear me."

Kate spat, and although most of the saliva found its way back onto her own face, some dotted her captor's tailored blouse.

Wiping at the silk, the woman shook her head. "I should have known. No manners. And I thought these boys were bad."

The glare in Djiana's eyes cooled when a rhythmic melody began to pulsate in her pocket. She moved away as she brought the phone to her ear and spoke. "*Deus é bom. Si.*"

Kate was startled to hear her utter "God is good" in Portuguese. She stole glances at Father Maric and Sister Deborah as her mind went into overdrive.

Who are these people?

How could they have known about our visit?

Why do they know my name?

Her conversation finished, Djiana handed Fernando back his gun. "The time is now to get the money for the real church. Shoot the nun in the head, Fernando," she ordered. "And try not to make too much of a mess. This little bitch has already ruined my blouse."

"We'll need lanterns!" Kate cried. When Fernando stepped back from Sister Deborah, Kate continued, "And food and water for Professor Jamira, or she'll be too weak to help you."

Fernando lowered the gun, and a satisfied smile spread across Djiana's face.

Turning to Djiana, Kate continued, "We are going into a long dark tunnel." Now looking for a way to stall, she asked, "But do you really think you can just haul out the loot and hop into a getaway car?"

Djiana's contempt twisted her face into a grotesque mask. "Let us worry about the logistics, little girl."

Us. She wasn't referring to the silent lackeys who surrounded her, Kate realized. *Us* meant an organization of some sort. And the woman's knowledge of her and Professor Nadia Jamira suggested that this was about even more, somehow, than King David's tomb. Frighteningly, this felt personal. Kate had just stepped into the destiny her visions had seemed to augur all her life, and now this happened?

◆

In the cave, using the codes Father Maric provided, Kate opened the closet where lights were stored. Two of the henchmen accompanied her, and she moved slowly and tried to use her time to gain their sympathy with hesitant movements and small smiles, but the man with the facial scars was obtuse and uncommunicative. The tall man with pleasing features amused himself by cursing at her.

"I don't know how you guys think you're going to haul everything out," Kate stated simply when she saw that these two weren't buying her act.

"When did we say we would move it?" the scarred one said with a shrug.

"Oh. I get it," Kate remarked.

"No, you don't," came the reply.

"Okay, I don't." Recognizing that the window to make a move, any move, was closing, she simply said, "I just hope you guys are ready for—"

Scarface spoke again. "Get her to shut up, Tomás!"

The better-looking one smiled at his companion, then turned to Kate. "You're getting on his nerves. You don't want to do that. Trust me." Lifting his gun once more, he ordered, "Now move."

Chapter 31

Bethlehem

Nadia's lamp was dimming, but there was still enough light to continue examining the chamber and taking notes. She worked in the way that she loved about being a historian: in solitude, in quiet reverie.

She was near the tomb entrance when she heard footsteps and felt relief that Kate and Maric had returned. She knew she didn't have enough lantern power to make it back to the office. But then she heard what sounded like yowls of amazement—from voices that weren't Kate's or Maric's.

Before she allowed herself to panic, Nadia assured herself that she must have misheard in the acoustics of the giant space. In fact, she nearly called out. Then she heard the voices again.

"Holy shit!"

"The mother lode!"

Nadia realized that she was no longer alone, and that things were not right. This was confirmed when she heard Kate's voice tensely addressing the men. If Kate was not alone, who was with her? Until she knew who her visitors were, better to move deeper into the tomb, past the sarcophagus.

As she tiptoed quickly into the shadows, Nadia watched a beam of light erratically exploring the walls and floor. Others appeared and chased one another across the chamber. Nadia turned off her lantern and waited in the dark.

"This is it," Kate said, looking over her shoulder at the men. "From here on, it's basically more of the same, gold and artifacts."

"But where is the professor?" one of the men asked.

"How do I know?" Kate asked. "Maybe her lamp died out."

Then Nadia heard Kate howl and saw one beam of light fall to the ground.

"What the hell! Stop hitting me!" Kate cried out. It took everything inside Nadia not to rush out.

"No more games, bitch," another man ordered. "Find the professor—now."

Despite her fear, Kate scoffed. "I don't have a floor plan. This is only my second time down here," she said, pushing her luck.

"Don't make it your last," he said. "Find the teacher. Now."

To gauge distance and movement, Nadia watched the flickers of what seemed to be three lamps. The group was fast approaching King David's resting place.

One man's voice shouted, "What the hell is that?"

"What do you think?" a shaky-voiced Kate said. "This is a tomb, you know."

A low chuckle. "Be nice, bitch."

"Of course," Kate retorted. "You've set such a fine example."

Kate spoke in a tone and pitch that was higher and more intense than usual. Nadia knew that her student was trying to give her warning, no matter how far away she was.

"Are these bags all full of gold?" said a second male voice.

"No. Jelly beans," Kate chortled. "What's your favorite flavor?"

The first gruff voice again: "Smart ass!"

There was a short tussle, then some grunting and movement.

"Chill, Scarface," the tall one said.

"You're supposed to be on my team."

"Why are you so sensitive?" Kate asked, her voice full of disdain.

"Shut up!" he ordered.

She persisted. "But why? You've found your treasure. Take what you want, and you'll never work another day in your lives. Are you telling me you aren't tempted? That you're not—"

"We're not telling you anything," the second voice cut in.

"Sorry," Kate said sarcastically. "You probably already know that I read minds."

A howl of rage was followed by another struggle; Nadia watched as the lights danced like demented fireflies.

One man finally took command. "Shut the hell up! Everybody: no more talking!" After a short silence, he demanded, "Where is the professor? Tell me."

"She's probably in the next tomb," Kate lied, her voice returning to normal pitch, Nadia thought, to suggest to her captors that she was now telling the truth.

"There are two of these things?"

"That's all we found while I was down here," Kate said. "But maybe she's found more."

The men groaned.

Kate's guts impressed Nadia. Even so, she knew the young woman couldn't fool the men for much longer.

Nadia sat leaning against a bag of gold, thinking. Finally, she dug into her bag and pulled out the silvery, cylindrical device that had fragmented the stone and mortar.

She set the mechanism's timer and diffraction dimensions, thankful that the screen only emitted a soft blue glow that she could hide by keeping it close to her body. Then she crossed herself. Finally, she switched off the digital tool and carefully tucked it into the back waistband of her pants. She searched her bag again, quickly found a knife, took a deep breath, and waited for the men to approach.

Then she heard a sound that frightened her more than shouted threats. Having been on countless digs in the desert, she knew this sound unmistakably. The soft rustle of snakeskin, the hiss of warning.

She felt her blood run cold as she sat in the dark, but it was the movement inside the coarse cloth of the bag she rested against that forced her to act. She lunged away with an involuntary cry. Desperate to avoid poisonous fangs sinking into her flesh, she started to crawl.

The hissing grew louder, and she rolled onto her back, kicking out into the dark. When she heard nothing, she scrambled to her feet, disoriented and afraid.

A voice crawled out of the ensuing silence: "Come out, come out, wherever you are, Professor, or we will kill your favorite student."

Nadia clutched the antique blue scapular around her neck and prayed. Finally, she shined her rapidly dying lantern on the bag where she had heard and felt the snake. With a swipe of her knife, the bag opened and disgorged its slithering contents.

Fighting the panic that rose in her throat, Nadia called out, "Don't hurt her. I'm over here." Then she turned off her lamp. "My light doesn't work anymore."

A beam of light hit her in the eyes. She raised her hand to block the brightness, fearful of what would emerge from the shadows.

"There you are," a tall man said as he approached.

The thug was holding Kate at his side. His roughness with her made Nadia grit her teeth. Kate simply wore an expression of disappointment.

"If you have any weapons, you need to throw them down now," he said, pulling Kate closer at the mention of weapons.

"I only have a few archeology tools and a knife," Nadia replied. "See? I'm dropping the knife." Releasing the blade wasn't easy for Nadia.

She was no longer simply vulnerable; she was completely exposed. The blade rang against the floor as it fell. "Happy now?" she said.

The man didn't seem to register her contempt as he lunged to retrieve the weapon. He stood upright and pointed his gun at Nadia. "Get your hands up where I can see them. If you make any sudden moves, you'll both be dead."

"This isn't necessary," Nadia said. "I dropped the knife." Despite her effort to sound assured, her voice betrayed her.

"I'll tell you what's necessary," the man said before shoving Kate toward Nadia, who shuddered when she saw the blood smeared across her student's face.

"My God, Kate, what have they done to you?" she said.

"It's not my blood," Kate started to explain. "It's . . ." She paused, so Nadia filled in the gap.

"Father Maric?"

"Yes, and Sister Deborah. We need to cooperate to keep them safe."

Another hiss. Nadia heard it. Kate looked at her—she'd heard it, too, but neither of the thugs had; they were preoccupied.

"We have to execute them now," the scarred man insisted, moving closer. "No witnesses." He lifted the gun. "We can't have witnesses."

Nadia's stomach dropped, a cold sweat covering her body.

"Will you relax?" the taller man replied. "We need them . . . for a little while, anyway. Djiana has plans."

From the corner of her eye, Nadia saw the glitter of snakeskin in the reflected light as two large vipers slithered toward Kate.

"We'll let you give us the tour," the taller man said. "Then we'll see."

Nadia summoned the courage to make a demand. "If you're going to kill us anyway, at least tell us who you are."

"We are the future," the man said. It sounded practiced.

"What's that mean?" Kate chimed in, clearly picking up on Nadia's attempt to keep the thugs occupied. "Everybody's the future," she said.

"Not you," the acne-scarred man said, moving forward. "Not your pitiful, primitive religion."

Kate took her chances. "Is this something Mummy dearest taught you? It sounds like what she would brainwash her pawns with."

"Shut up bitch!" he said with such force that both women recognized Kate had hit a nerve. He grabbed Kate and pushed the barrel of his pistol against her head. "Let's go."

Despite herself, Nadia whimpered when she felt something slide over her shoes. The man laughed, assuming her fear was because of him. He shoved both women forward, still laughing as he stomped after them in his heavy-soled boots.

The taller man said, "Okay, enough, let's go." Then his voice changed. "What the hell—what the hell is that?" He jumped back, recoiling from the muscular shape that had rolled under his boot. A moment later, he slapped desperately at his ankle. Finally, he began to scream. "Help me! It's biting me!"

He turned a terrified look to his scarred accomplice, who began to flail around with his light, not yet aware that the poison of a desert viper was coursing through his counterpart's veins.

"What?" he shouted. "What is it? What's wrong?"

"Kill it!" the tall man wailed. "Kill it!"

Finally, Scarface aimed his flashlight, revealing the snake with its fangs deeply embedded in his compatriot's flesh. He struck erratically with his flashlight, which only caused more agony for the man, whose face was by now sweaty and red.

Finally, Scarface's flashlight connected with the reptile. When they heard the bones give way under the blow, he grabbed the tail and pulled it free with as wide an arc as he could manage. Twirling the long snake overhead, he tossed it into the darkness.

Meanwhile, all color had drained from the taller man's skin, and he collapsed to the dirt floor.

"Tomás! Tomás, get up! Get up!" Scarface cried, dropping to his knees beside his accomplice.

There was another hiss. Scanning with the flashlight, he saw a second snake, coiled and ready to strike. He screamed and began shooting wildly at the floor. As the sound of ricocheting bullets danced around them, Nadia grabbed Kate's hand, and together they ran for the tomb's doorway.

But they weren't fast enough. The man stopped shooting and lunged for them, dragging Kate to the floor. Nadia felt Kate's grip on her hand tug and then release completely.

With his gun to Kate's face, Scarface demanded that they revive the tall man. "Help him! Help Tomás!"

Nadia shouted, "Don't shoot! Look at me!" She waved her hands, looking directly at the panicked man. "I can help him."

The man stared at her, still pointing the weapon at Kate, though his chest was heaving and his grip on the gun was weak.

Nadia pulled the titanium bar from her waistband.

The man reacted instantly, swiveling his gun to point at Nadia. She held out her free hand in a non-threatening posture and said, "It's all right."

"What is it?" Scarface demanded, his eyes narrowing.

Nadia pressed the button on the cylinder. "It's a container of anti-venom," she said, hoping the man wouldn't wonder why it had a lighted display. "I always carry some when I dig." She extended her hand, the tool in it. "Take it. Go ahead. He needs it now!"

The man took it from her cautiously.

"Now!" Nadia repeated. "He's running out of time!"

At this, the man turned to move. But then the tool beeped. Startled by the sound, he nearly dropped it.

"What the—?"

It beeped again. The man looked closer. "This is not medicine. What is—"

Before he could say anything else, Nadia interrupted. "It's an electronic preservation container. Now get it to your friend before—"

The man snarled and lunged at Nadia. "You're lying to me!" Suddenly his head and body flew back, mid-lunge, as Kate came in from the side with a vicious swift kick that landed square on his mouth and nose. As he fell into darkness, still grasping the bar, the women ran.

This time, they were fast enough.

A second later, the titanium bar finished beeping. There was no explosion to be heard, only a dull, pulverizing thump and the soft splattering of human tissue and dust. The tomb fell silent.

Frantic, with fists still clenched ready to fight, Kate screamed into the air, "Thou shalt not steal, jerk!"

"Whoa! Kate! He is done. It's over now. You kicked him into orbit! Where did you learn that?"

Kate bent over, panting heavily. "Back home it was Muay Thai every Tuesday," she said, then deadpanned, "plus an elective: Knockin' People the Hell Out 101."

Hands shaking, Nadia couldn't help but grin, a mix of shock and sheer delight washing over her as she marveled at the whole scene. She was in awe—not just at the unexpected mayhem but at the sheer ferocity of Kate's kick.

"Someone call the UFC," she said, then wiped the tears of joy and relief from her eyes.

"What happened, Kate?" Nadia pleaded. "Who are these guys?"

"They have a plan, Professor. And I have a terrible feeling that a lot of people other than that woman are involved," Kate said.

Confused, Nadia asked, "What woman? How could they know we were here?"

"I have no idea," Kate said. "I heard the guy who's still upstairs say something about Brazil, but the woman shut him up. I'll tell you this much, they don't like Catholics." She stopped herself. "We have to hurry." She turned to run, but Nadia held her back.

"Wait. I'm assuming they're also armed, right?"

"Yeah," Kate replied.

"Then we'll need guns," Nadia said, looking back toward the tomb.

They stared into the darkness. "Maybe one of their handguns survived," Nadia said. "I'll go look."

"No," Kate said, clutching her professor.

"We'll need protection."

"But what are we going to do? Barge in and start shooting?"

Nadia understood Kate's struggle. "Let's not forget," she said, "King David believed in an eye for an eye."

Chapter 32

Bethlehem

Above ground, the women huddled in a corner of the church. Both of them were shaken at what had happened and what they would still have to do.

"Who could they be?" Kate wondered out loud.

Nadia thought for a moment. "Based on what you told me about them, my best guess is neo-Pentecostals."

"What?" Kate said, taken aback at the single-word explanation. "You mean Bible thumpers? Like they have in Mississippi or wherever?"

Nadia was traumatized but still a teacher. She explained, "More likely an extreme sect of third-wave evangelists. Prosperity theology is their religion. They sermonize about God and material wealth, but the only ones who are getting rich are the so-called spiritual leaders who make billions from the poor. Money is their God."

It was Kate's turn to feel disoriented. Finally, she gave up trying to understand. "We have to go on. We have to save Father Maric and Sister Deborah from—look at their blood on me."

"We'll notify the Vatican, and they'll help," Nadia said.

Her words failed to calm Kate, who protested, "But those phone numbers are in the office."

"I have those numbers, too, from my previous work!" Nadia recalled. The higher ground meant her phone would work, so she dialed. It seemed to take forever until a man with a British accent answered.

"Yes. Hello," a relieved Nadia began. "My name is Professor Nadia Jamira. I'm calling from the Church of the Nativity in Bethlehem. I must speak to Vatican security immediately."

The conversation was frustrating and surreal. Nadia first had to convince authorities that she was not a crank by sharing her credentials. When that didn't work, she resorted to pleading. She tried to convince the man she was in danger, but when he suggested that she call for police help, Nadia confessed that a discovery of immense importance had been made and that security had already been breached.

"Excuse me, Professor," the man said. "But we have no record of your plans for another dig. This is highly irregular, and the circumstances you've described strike me as preposterous."

"Two men," Nadia said, her voice a staccato rhythm punctuated only with deep breaths. "They tried to kill us. Two others are now holding a priest and nun hostage."

The man's hesitation betrayed him. "We have no alert from local authorities about any such disturbance."

"Will you believe me when the bodies are discovered?" Nadia cried. "Or will you dismiss it as highly irregular?"

More questions followed. Nadia began pacing. "We have reason to believe a sophisticated, highly organized group with possible ties to the Americas intends to attack the Vatican by taking control of this fortune," she said.

When the exchange seemed deadlocked, Kate said, "I'm running for help. We need help."

Nadia stopped her. "Don't you dare! You don't know who or what is out there. Local police won't have the power we need."

"But the Vatican isn't listening, and Father Maric is going to die. Sister Deborah too. Their blood will be on our—"

The man on the phone began to shout to regain contact with Nadia, who put the phone back to her ear, only to be interrupted again by Kate, who had been shoving her hands into her pockets in frustration. "The coins!" she exclaimed as her fingers found one. "Switch to video and show him the coins and the way we look—show him the blood on my hands and face!"

Multiple Vatican voices finally patched into Nadia's call. Kate watched as her mentor provided a swift, impromptu lecture on the significance and size of the find. This time, the questions were precise and clear:

"Can you verify that this is an ancient Israeli coin?"

"How many have you found?"

"Is the tomb intact? Can you estimate dimensions?"

"How many troops will be needed to secure the area?"

Finally, the British man's voice took charge again, this time with instructions. "Professor Jamira and Kate Murphy. I have looked through Miss Murphy's file. Security personnel will arrive in Bethlehem in about twenty minutes. We need you to stay where you are until they arrive."

"An eternity!" Nadia yelped, then turned to Kate and asked in a whisper, her hand over the phone's speaker, "They have files on you?"

"That is the best we can do," the Brit said. "In a few hours, you will also have our air support. Pilots and crews have already been dispatched from Rome. Do not, I repeat, do not attempt to engage the terrorists in any way. Local law-enforcement personnel are now in the process of creating a perimeter around your location, and international forces have been notified."

◆

FIFTEEN MINUTES LATER, Kate and Nadia heard vehicles in front of the church. Some kind of tactical force dressed in black swarmed out of several SUVs and took up positions to secure the plaza. An officer entered the church with a team.

Nadia stepped forward, keeping her hands visible. "I'm Professor Jamira. This is Kate Murphy."

"I'm Lieutenant Thornton. Do you have immediate medical needs?"

"We're shaken up, but nothing serious."

Thornton was familiar with the church and had already dispatched pairs of men to surround the entrance to Father Maric's office.

"When was the last time you spoke with the priest and nun?"

"Hours ago," Kate said. "And they weren't in very good shape. The—the terrorists beat them badly before sending me away with two . . . escorts."

"And where are those two now?"

"Dead," Nadia said. "In the tomb."

"And the two in the office have guns?"

Kate nodded.

"Are there any others besides the two dead and the two in the office?"

"Not that we're aware of," Nadia said.

"And no communication between the office and you when you were underground?"

"No. It wasn't possible," Kate replied. "The men were sent down to verify what we'd discovered."

Lieutenant Thornton kept his eye on the door as he dialed Father Maric's office. They all heard the phone begin to ring. No one answered.

Though he had troops positioned near an exterior wall adjacent to the office, there were no windows that might offer a glimpse of the interior. What was going on behind those walls was a mystery.

A negotiator approached the office door, announcing the presence of armed security forces. He detailed the many reasons the captors were trapped and advised them to answer the phone the next time it rang. "It will be better for everyone if you speak with us," he said.

The negotiator nodded to Thornton, who dialed again but to no avail.

When the ringing stopped, the negotiator tried another tack. "Are the priest and nun conscious? Can they walk? If so, let them come out safely. We'll stand away from the door. Just let them come out, and then we'll talk about your options. The men you sent underground are dead. Do you hear me? They are dead."

From a distance, Kate could hear the voice of the negotiator but no response from the office. Perhaps Djiana and her last henchman had taken their own lives too. She began to cry.

Nadia put an arm around her. "It's not your fault, Kate."

"No one would have been hurt today if I hadn't . . ."

"And no one could have guessed that we'd be followed and threatened," Nadia insisted.

Thornton and the negotiator conferred. "We'll have to go in," the lieutenant said.

After that, everything happened quickly. Security personnel barreled through the unlocked door, shouting commands and aiming weapons. After a few tense moments, Kate and Nadia heard, "We've got them!"

What they discovered were two very frightened and bloodied members of the clergy. Djiana and Fernando were nowhere to be found.

Everyone exhaled until gunfire exploded outside, and stray bullets hit the church tower. A bullet strike on the bell tolled as though summoning the faithful to Mass.

◆

THE SKIRMISH IN Manger Square began when a Vatican security team leader saw a man dressed in black and a heavyset woman rush across the open street, partially obscured by the dark of night. They ignored his order to halt, so he turned to his troops.

"Stop them! And I want them both alive!"

Armed security swarmed toward the couple but were slowed in their pursuit when the fleeing man began firing an automatic weapon as he sprinted toward the narrow confines of an alleyway, dragging the woman. Her screams could be heard between the bursts of gunfire.

"Shut the hell up!" Fernando cursed.

Djiana only got louder. She pounded his back and pulled back toward the square.

"Stop fighting me! What are you doing?" Fernando screamed.

Djiana continued fighting and cried out repeatedly, "Help me! Help me!"

"Be quiet! I'm trying to get us out of here!"

Fernando stumbled when Djiana's legs entwined with his and the weight of her body toppled them both as the first of the Vatican security team reached them.

"He was kidnapping me!" Djiana cried out as she clutched her chest. "He has a gun, and he tried to . . ."

She was hysterical. It took three soldiers to subdue Fernando, even though they had snatched away his weapon before he could recover from the fall.

Djiana put her hand on the arm of the soldier standing guard nearest her and pressed herself timidly toward him. "Please, take me away. Somewhere safe."

The team leader nodded his approval to move the woman away until medical help could arrive. "Try to calm her down. Get what information you can," he ordered.

Around the corner of a stone building, Djiana was a model of gratitude. "Thank you. Thank you so much. God is good. God is good."

"Okay, ma'am, we've got you. You'll be secure here."

"But, officer, how can I ever thank you?" she said, even as she pressed her gun into his head. "I want to thank you. Really, I do."

The team leader heard a single gunshot and saw his soldier crumple to the ground from behind the corner. In his confusion, he lost precious seconds and didn't see the car waiting at the end of the alley to whisk Djiana away.

Later that night, they found the belongings she had shed like a snake: a small framed photo of a little girl, a crushed disposable cell phone, a pair of dark black sunglasses, a bodysuit that had made her look much larger, and a dark wig streaked with highlights.

Chapter 33

Bethlehem

Father Maric and Sister Deborah were rushed to a hospital. The priest had suffered a concussion and broken nose, while the nun had a fractured cheekbone, several broken ribs, and a retinal tear that had blinded her right eye.

Kate also spent the night in the hospital after an examination revealed severe swelling on her neck, multiple lacerations on her head, and deep bruising across her lower back. She spoke to her parents and, in a usual flicker of longing, wondered what it might be like to have someone else to confide in as well. Nadia had no serious injuries and was taken to a secure location for food and sleep.

Throughout the following day, all four were visited by psychological counselors, whose effectiveness was hampered by several intense debriefings with law enforcement and Vatican officials.

The shootout in Manger Square had drawn international attention. There were also rumors of a momentous discovery that would be of great interest to Christians and Jews alike.

"It has to be Rome," Nadia said, quick to lay blame for the leak. The professor and her student sat in a windowless hospital conference room. Vatican security personnel, a hospital liaison, and a cardinal surrounded them.

Cardinal Parker, in his late seventies, had a thinning mop of silver hair that draped across his forehead, giving him a boyish appearance. According to his internet bio, he was a revered mentor and former diocesan ordinary whose star had risen after he helped quell a public debacle caused by a rebel priest in Rome.

He smiled in a friendly manner before responding to Nadia's accusation. "Surely you have facts to back up your brash assumption, Professor. You are, after all, an academic of considerable distinction."

Nadia couldn't tell if the smile was genuine. It didn't falter. "I've seen how these things go, Cardinal," she countered. "Rome loves to play one side against the other."

"What sides are you referring to, if I may ask?" Cardinal Parker probed.

"Truth versus public relations."

Kate found it difficult to suppress a grin. *Go, Professor!* she thought.

"When I called the Vatican to report our discovery, the more I explained, the more voices I heard. People patching into the call to verify our credibility, saying they had files on Kate. What files were they talking about? And any one of them might find it helpful to leak a little news and create some buzz for the Vatican, don't you think?"

Finally, the smile slipped. "As far as the files we have on Kate, maybe it is best you ask her about that sometime. And as you know, Professor, we have a new pope. We hardly need any more *buzz* than we already have."

"Really?"

"What are you suggesting?"

"Did the accession of Pope Nelson improve your popularity worldwide, or did you see a dip in your polls?" Nadia challenged.

Cardinal Parker stared at Nadia without answering. Then he nodded to his assistant, who stepped forward with a folder of documents.

"Professor Jamira, when was the last time you spoke to your new admin, Dafna Brisker?"

"Well, actually," Nadia said, "I haven't been able to reach her today."

"When did you speak to her last?" Parker repeated.

Kate almost blurted out the answer because she remembered the conversation in the car as they approached Bethlehem. Finally, Nadia remembered for herself. "Yesterday morning."

"And how did she sound, Professor?" The cardinal's smile was creeping back.

A Vatican security official with a British accent interrupted them. "Are we crossing borders here, Cardinal Parker?"

Though he had not identified himself, Nadia recognized the Brit's voice.

"How so?" the Cardinal inquired, his gaze fixed on Nadia.

"Unless I have misunderstood your credentials, you are a priest, not a security-enforcement professional or member of the Swiss Guard, sir."

The tension was palpable.

"Ah. My apologies," the Cardinal replied, his eyes rolling upward before locking onto the other man. "Perhaps it is time for you to . . . intervene."

The Brit wasted no time. "Professor, can you verify the timeline of your discussion with Ms. Brisker yesterday morning?"

"And your name is?" Nadia said.

"Call me *sir*. To repeat my question—"

"I heard the question, Your Sirness. Yes, I can verify the timeline, if you'll kindly return my cell phone. The call log would be the fastest way of tracing our conversation."

"Quite right," the man said without moving a muscle. "But I'm wondering about your memory."

"My memory?"

"How good it is."

"You're doubting me?" Nadia raised an offended eyebrow.

"Procedure, Professor. Just procedure. For security reasons."

"I'm the one who called in the discovery," Nadia said. "I risked my life. And now you're—"

Cardinal Parker interrupted. "Why don't you tell her!"

The Brit glanced at the priest. "Professor Jamira, I regret to inform you that Dafna Brisker is missing, and we have every reason to suspect foul play. My goal now is to determine if you are linked to this event in any way."

"Of course, I'm linked," Nadia responded incredulously. "She is my admin assistant, a colleague." Her voice began to tremble. "Dafna—missing. How? Why?"

"It is our assumption—and I will use this terminology until every speculation has been verified—that Ms. Brisker was the reason you were trailed and very possibly the source of the rumors about your discovery."

"You think she leaked the information?"

"Or was forced to," the man said.

"But I called her at the office."

"Yes," the Brit concurred, "but that call was forwarded to her cell. She was probably not in the office when you spoke with her yesterday. For now, we believe she was being coerced and is either being held hostage or is dead. But it is also possible that she was part of the attempted robbery."

The uncertainties and suspicions stung the air. The joy of finding King David was now shrouded in a shadow of loss and perhaps betrayal.

Nadia was too stunned to continue, so Kate spoke up. "The news reports—what's all this stuff about neo-Pentecostals and Evangelicals? The TV networks are interviewing anyone who's ever attended a religious service in Brazil."

"Security forces captured a man," he said without emotion. "He fits the description you gave. He's been traced to an emerging church group in São Paulo. That much has been leaked to the media."

"What else do you know about this guy, *sir*?" Kate asked.

The Brit exchanged a glance with Cardinal Parker, who averted his eyes.

"This man, who apparently uses several names, has refused to say much more—"

"No surprise there," Kate said.

"—unless he can speak to you."

Kate's eyes widened. "Me? Why?"

"Don't go, Kate," Nadia said. "That guy should rot in a dungeon somewhere. Don't give him—any of them—the satisfaction."

Kate observed another silent spat between the Brit and the priest.

"We don't know why he would make such a request, and the Vatican opposes any such meeting," the cardinal began.

"Kate, this is your decision," the Brit interrupted. "You are not required to speak with this man. But I believe something helpful might come from it. He has said nothing about his involvement here and yet makes barely coherent remarks about events that occurred some years ago in Rome. I know your childhood was spent there."

"My childhood was taken from me there," Kate said plainly. "Let's not pretend you don't both know that as well."

Her words turned Cardinal Parker's smile into a grimace. He twisted in his chair and all but buried his face in his folder of documents.

"I'll go," Kate said.

"But Kate, are you sure?" Nadia said. "*Sir* here just said you don't have to go."

"I'll go under one condition," Kate announced. "The guy has to agree to tell me everything. Everything he knows about Rome and everything he knows about—"

"This is an outrage!" Cardinal Parker shot out of his chair. "She doesn't speak for the church. She has no credential or clearance for sensitive information, and he's a criminal. How will we even know if what he says is true?"

"I'll know," Kate said calmly. "But before we go, I want to see Father Maric and Sister Deborah."

The hospital official assigned to Vatican security blocked Kate's path politely but firmly. "I'm sorry, Miss Murphy. Sister Deborah is in surgery, and your priest—let's give him another day or so."

Kate crossed herself. "I'll never forgive myself if—"

The door to the conference room swung open fast, revealing another Vatican security official. "The Brazilian tried to hang himself!"

The Brit's cool interrogator mask cracked. "He what? You imbecile! How could you let this happen?"

"I don't know. I don't know," the man stammered. "They've stabilized him. But he's out of his mind. He keeps screaming that he wants to be shot or—"

"Shot?"

"Yeah. Shot or saved."

"Saved? Saved by whom, Jesus?"

He hesitated, his eyes flickering to Kate. "By the girl from Rome."

◆

THE CONVOY OF security vehicles speeding through the streets of Bethlehem might have been the protective detail of a dignitary, world leader, or celebrity. But behind the shaded windows sat a university freshman, absorbing a rapid briefing before her meeting with a man whose name she didn't know.

"He'll be secured in a chair on the other side of a wide table. You'll have no reason to fear physical harm," the Brit said.

"That's comforting," Kate quipped.

"He speaks several languages, some better than others."

"We have a lot in common," she said with a smile.

"And . . ."

Kate looked at the Brit, who had removed his reading glasses to pinch the bridge of his nose.

"And what?" she encouraged.

"Sorry," he said, running his free hand through his blunt cut blond hair and placing the glasses on his head. "You will not be entitled to share the information he might divulge, to anyone. The Vatican owns this interview, this process, this—"

"It doesn't own me."

"Kate—"

"I prefer Miss Murphy," Kate said. "Unless I can call you Sherlock or double-oh-seven or whatever your name is."

The Brit offered a bittersweet smile, reminiscing about the first time he spotted her as a chubby-cheeked four-year-old dancing on the bridge. Now, he couldn't help but admire what a stunning young woman she had blossomed into. "Steven, and yes, you may use it when addressing me."

Kate grinned. "But never Stevie, I bet."

A chuckle leaked through his humorless demeanor. "Correct. Now, back to business."

Kate's left hand unconsciously soothed the bruises on her pale neck.

Steven paused. "Are you in pain?"

"I'm okay. It looks worse than it feels. It's just . . . I can still feel his hands. How deadly they felt."

"As I've said—" Steven began.

"Yeah, I know. No reason to fear physical harm."

"I understand if this is too traumatic for you."

Kate's mind reeled as images of ecstasy and torment battled for her attention. Steven waited, allowing the silence to lengthen as the caravan sped toward a meeting that might finally give him the proof he needed of a neo-Pentecostal war against the Vatican.

"Kate, are you—?"

"Yes, sorry. I can handle it."

Steven took a deep breath before continuing. "I must stress—and this is very important—promise him nothing."

Kate nodded.

"I'm serious, Kate," he said. "He obviously wants something from you."

"But what do I have to give?" Kate countered.

"My point is, you cannot make a deal of any kind—a pardon, for example, if he wants to trade information. Don't take pity on this man. He is a terrorist, probably an assassin. We are granting his one wish to gain access to his memory."

"But not his soul?"

"We'll lend him a Bible."

◆

IN HIS CAR, Cardinal Parker pressed a phone to his ear and expressed his annoyance. "I don't appreciate the segregation of authority. This is not merely a legal matter or criminal act. This is the business of the Vicar of Christ, the Vatican. A girl who has barely come of age has been given a privilege that, that . . ." He was too perturbed and offended to finish his thought.

Cardinal Dumas, calling from one of several remote, private Vatican offices, responded. "You have yet to make a strong case to His Holiness that would allow him to intervene on your behalf. Remember, he has barely occupied the papal chair for a month. He's taken full command of spiritual doctrine, but he will not reprimand a leader of Vatican security. Not yet. Not now."

"You must impress upon the Pope that there are many layers of risk here," Cardinal Parker advised emphatically.

"Such as?"

"Matters that have been kept separate from every papacy in modern history. He'll be sullied, possibly, and the Church, too, if we don't handle this situation with extreme care."

"As I'm sure Steven Craft is aware. He's not a naïf. Nor is he a power monger," Cardinal Dumas said soothingly.

"But he is thorough. To a fault."

"The reason for his appointment, no doubt. And all to our benefit."

"Not this time." Cardinal Parker struggled to find a way to explain that the babblings of a Brazilian pagan were not his real concern. The man from Brazil could say whatever he wished because he would never again know freedom. But if what he knew about questionable actions taken on the Vatican's behalf more than a decade earlier reached the ears of an unusual girl with an already tense relationship with the Church, it could spell political and spiritual disaster.

"Forgive me, but I must ask, Cardinal Parker. Does all your worry have any connection to your assignment in Brazil back in your youth?"

"How dare you."

"Just a question—"

"How dare you."

"—asked in private."

"The plot against Pope Francis was not my doing. That rumor lingers only because small minds—present company excluded—believe that connecting geographical dots constitutes a conspiracy," Cardinal Parker explained in a tone that sounded well-rehearsed.

How could he explain to the uninitiated that the de facto Supreme Sacred Congregation, the modern-day Roman Inquisition, existed because it still had a role to play in matters of the Church?

To protect the late pope, Cardinal Parker (just before becoming bishop) had been forced to intercede and purge the secret department.

His reward had been a speedy ascension in rank. Yet, with so many familiar faces either retired or replaced, who among the inner circle still fully appreciated his sacrifice?

His assistant leaned in and whispered, "Sir, we're almost there."

With a curt nod of acknowledgment, the priest took a rare approach: he apologized. "Perhaps I've let my temper harm our discourse, Cardinal Dumas."

"Indeed?"

"I certainly value your counsel and trust your judgment in this matter. We're close to our destination. I'll call when I know more."

"Blessings, Cardinal Parker. We are eager to hear back from you."

As the cardinal put away his phone, his assistant spoke again. "Water, sir?"

A deluge would be better, he thought. *Anything to wash away this mess.* "No. Thank you."

Chapter 34

Bethlehem

In a small viewing room, Kate faced a phalanx of stern men and women, including Cardinal Parker and Steven, whom she still thought of as "the Brit." This group would watch the session, which would also be recorded, from behind a one-way window. A technician wired her with an earbud that would allow Steven to suggest questions and provide guidance. Kate did her best to act calm and capable.

The group stirred when the man called Fernando was led to his seat in the adjoining room and strapped to the chair by steel bands at his wrists and ankles. Kate shuddered to see his brutish face marked with fresh cuts and bruises. "Where's the woman he was with?" she asked Steven.

"Killed an officer. Then escaped."

"She scares me more than this guy, and this guy is scary," Kate admitted. "But surely she couldn't have disappeared on her own, right?"

Steven nodded. "It's quite obvious now that they had additional soldiers on-site."

Kate was taken aback. "Why would you call them that?"

"I may be revealing a bit too much, Kate."

"Please trust me," Kate insisted.

"I call them soldiers because one would need trained men to pull off such an audacious extraction," Steven said. "And because these men were clearly taking orders."

Nods and murmurs of agreement were interrupted by a single dissenting voice.

"Charlatans, all of them. They don't deserve any comparison to a military force. They should be exterminated like vermin." Cardinal Parker's vehemence wilted a bit when all eyes turned on him.

"Maybe you're right, Cardinal, uh—what's your name again?" asked Steven, already knowing full well who he was but wanting to stay in control over the room.

The priest turned red but held his tongue.

"It might help to know"—Kate intuitively turned to include the others in the room—"when I listened to the woman talking on the phone, I had the sense that she was speaking to a commandant or general, not some hoodlum. I mean, what were they going to do? Grab a few bags of gold and run?"

"Right. First, they had to verify the discovery," Steven agreed. "Then they had to secure the tomb."

"Or the whole Nativity parish. Even the city," Kate agreed.

Steven added, "Make a statement."

"Make a claim," Kate realized. "Who would dare bomb out a stronghold that held ancient secrets and wealth?"

Grim faces stared back at her. Steven spoke first. "Very nice, Kate. When we're done here, would you consider changing your major to criminology?"

The mood in the room was grave. Even so, a new respect for Kate seemed to spread among the assembled, with the notable exception of the cardinal.

"Give me some space in there, okay, Steven?" she said.

"But not too much," Cardinal Parker interjected. "He's a thug like all the others. A street urchin turned terrorist."

Steven's response was pointed. "And how would you know that, Cardinal? Kate has earned a little leeway." He turned to her in a fatherly way. "Just one reminder—"

"Promise him nothing," Kate parroted.

"Right-o." He placed a hand on Kate's shoulder. "Ready?"

She nodded and was led into the lion's den.

Chapter 35

São Paulo

Fernando was not his real name. He'd had many, over the years, spawned in an urban wasteland: unclaimed, uneducated, and unloved.

He had been betrayed so many times he could no longer draw on any particular reason to live. His survival instinct, once a sharp, useful tool, was now an impediment to his wish to die.

His departure from Rome had been tumultuous. The payment he had demanded from Father Lemski had grown the longer it was delayed. But the Vatican had wanted him gone, and he had ended up on a slow boat to South America.

Back in Brazil, without prospects, he'd crawled through the ensuing years with no compass or ladder to climb. Poor, hungry, and forgotten, years passed like sand through an hourglass.

One day, he wandered into a disused movie theater where an Evangelist promised wealth and prosperity for anyone who would join his parish and accept God.

A new God.

A corporate God.

A God of riches.

A God that rewarded brave, common people for nothing more than pressing their palms together and bowing to the lord of materialism.

A God that, for a price, was attainable by anyone. Even outsiders, pimps, whores, and men of no means like Fernando.

"Do not be fooled, my children. Jesus was an outsider too. Mistreated, scorned. He had nothing when he walked the face of the earth except the kingdom of God. Your kingdom! Your God!" the pastor intoned.

Ecstatic, the crowd wept and shouted, *"Deus é bom! Deus é bom!"*

Soon Fernando was weeping, too, on his knees, overwhelmed by the promise of a glorious ascension that meant bread in his belly and money in his pockets.

After the service ended, a friendly man in a slate-gray suit approached Fernando and asked for a few minutes of his time. "I saw you in there," he said.

"Me?" Fernando asked, looking around nervously.

"Yes, brother. I saw you. I saw a light from above touch you, and . . ."

"What?"

"You have the gift, don't you?"

"The gift?" Fernando's eyes narrowed. He paused. His anger, always close to the surface, was shoved aside by another impulse: pride. He didn't want to appear ignorant. But he'd been tricked too many times.

"Not everybody has it. Not all men glow the way you did. Forgive me, brother. I'm imposing on you."

"No," Fernando said, still suspicious, but softening.

"I can speak freely?" the man said.

"Yes. Tell me."

"I think you should begin your own parish."

"Me?"

"I'm sure of it. Men and women will follow you. They will listen."

"But . . . how?" Fernando was floored and bewildered.

The man spoke at length through cigarette-stained teeth about the changes that were happening in Brazil. Poverty was now a stepping stone, a prerequisite to achieving the kingdom of heaven here on earth. Evangelists everywhere, starting with barely a box to stand on, were claiming their fair share of the power and glory that Christ always delivers. Including money. Lots and lots of money.

"Have you been beaten?" the man said quietly, placing his hand on Fernando's heavy forearm.

Fernando was ashamed to admit he had. He simply nodded.

"Have you wanted for the simplest things in life?"

More shame, averting his eyes.

"Have you chased value, property, women, and acceptance like a dog chases a car? Not knowing, not realizing, that there is no value out there? You are the value. You are the worthy one."

Yes, yes, of course. Fernando could feel it. He'd felt it before. That thing rising from within. The power that thrived on personal recognition and reliability. Hadn't he survived in Rome? Had he not proven his worth countless times only to be wounded by the blindness of others?

"Know your true value, brother. Claim it," the man insisted.

But how? Thankfully, Fernando's new friend, who promised to become his first follower, had a plan.

"You need a teacher. A mentor. Someone who can guide you to the riches within so that you can speak and attract the abundance that God wants for you."

"How do I find this man?" Fernando asked.

"I know someone, but . . ."

"Go on," Fernando said.

"Sacrifice is always required, but you know that."

"I sacrifice. I have sacrificed too much for nothing."

"For the gift, the mentoring—but I can't expect this of you." The man hesitated. "I'm sorry."

"But if I have something—if you see in me . . ." Fernando stammered.

"The light."

"Yes? Then don't be afraid to tell me," Fernando appealed, looking directly into the stranger's eyes.

"The mentor, I believe, would feel blessed meeting you. He has many mouths to feed. His own mission, I mean." The man began to appear distracted.

"He has much work already."

"Exactly," the man agreed. "He wouldn't want to offend."

"No!"

"But he has guided others, and I know he can show you the way." The man's demeanor changed again, hope warming his face.

"Yes?" Fernando urged the man to speak his mind.

"Yes. And a single donation of three hundred dollars will probably be all that is necessary."

Fernando's heart stumbled. The path to peace and happiness was always the same: cash. He had walked the streets of São Paulo where money dangled in the windows and glistened in the neon signs. Everything he had done, in Rome and before, had been for cash, yet he always ended up without, bankrupting his moral self to make more of it.

"Yes," he said simply.

The man implored Fernando to be honest if the offer was in any way crude or an imposition. "Brother," he said, "I mean no disrespect. It is just that this mentor—his responsibilities are already so great."

"I will find the money," Fernando said.

For a week, he fenced stolen narcotics, robbed a rich woman at knifepoint, and took his pleasure with a whore he had seen hiding money from her pimp.

"He'll kill you when he finds you! He'll kill you!" she had shouted. *"Deus é bom."*

Yet he did not advance as he had hoped. Fernando could not catch lightning in a bottle. He could not improvise with the Heavens so that

Christ's words would flow naturally from his lips. Instead, he froze when it was his turn to speak to a group. It was perhaps the only fear he had ever experienced that he could not channel into aggression.

"It's not working," he complained after a long afternoon session.

The mentor encouraged him to continue.

"For how long?" Fernando asked earnestly.

"You are a seeker. The path never ends!" the man said.

"You took my money."

"I did," the man admitted. "And for that, I gave you the knowledge I promised."

"But it's not working!" With those words, Fernando exploded, attacking the man with his bare hands. He tore at the wallpaper, religious ornaments, lamps, and furniture. He bruised and bloodied his teacher's face and ripped at his clothing. His brute strength kept bigger men at a distance, and his tortured cries tore at the ears of his audience, who stood back, fearful and rapt.

The man in the slate-gray suit witnessed everything. He was impressed. As Fernando raced out into the street, he pursued. Fernando didn't seem to know what to do with his hands as he flexed them, released them, and swung them wildly.

"Listen. Just listen to me," the man soothed.

"I listened already!" Fernando roared in response. "How much did you make? What was your cut?"

"I can get your money back," the man said, his hands up to show he had nothing to hide.

"Don't lie to me!" Fernando bellowed.

"Ten times your money back," the man said. "A hundred times and more. You will pay nothing. Your muscle is your salvation. And I guarantee you'll be rewarded for using it."

Fernando's fury did not soften that day. It grew. He would do anything for money. This time, the fist he made found purchase in a wall with peeling paint. His knuckles were scuffed, but his face reflected no pain.

"One more chance. But if you cheat me again . . ." Fernando began, squeezing his fist to make the blood flow.

"You'll kill me?" the man said softly.

"Worse."

But the man was not afraid. "Maybe you'll thank me. Oh, and by the way, when my promise comes true, I'll need a little something. A taste of your glorious good fortune."

Fernando ventured, "God is good?"

"Yes, and for you—war is good."

Chapter 36

Bethlehem

"Can you save me, little girl?"

The question froze Kate before she even made it to her chair in the sterile, brightly lit room. She felt her knees lock and wasn't sure how to answer. If she should answer.

In her ear, Steven advised, "Sit when you are ready, Kate. But you don't have to answer any question you don't like. Remember, you are in charge."

Kate took a good look at the man. She reassured herself that he was, in fact, restrained from getting to her. Then she took her seat, which seemed much too close to the barbaric Brazilian.

"Who are you?" she asked, her voice not projecting as she'd intended.

"You don't know my name?" the man said. The stench of his breath hit Kate in the face.

"Apparently, *you* don't know your name," Kate said, sitting up taller and steadying her voice. "Fernando is only one, it seems."

"Okay."

"Okay what?"

"Call me Fernando."

"All right, Fernando, why did you want to see me?"

He stared at her with a ferocity that seemed etched into his face. It wasn't so much an expression as a daily mask. He began, "I told them about you."

"Okay. Who is *them*?"

"My people."

"Who are your people?"

He stared at her. "You look different," he said. "Not a little girl anymore." He shifted in his seat. "I told them. About you."

"You said that already." Kate took a different tack. "But why? Why do they care about me?"

"I told them about Rome."

This caught Kate in the throat. "What about it?"

"Your dad."

Kate felt anxiety work its way into her extremities. Her fingers, toes, and mind began to tingle. "You know my dad?"

"No."

Relief. "Then why—"

"But I followed him. A priest told me to. He said, 'Just follow the guy.'"

"What was the priest's name?"

"I don't know."

"Then why did you follow his orders?"

"They gave me a—"

"They?" Kate stopped him. "Who are they?"

"*Católicos.*"

Kate sensed he was telling the truth. For the first time, the man broke his intense gaze.

"The Church?"

"The Vatican, I think. They give me a phone. Very good. They pay."

"For the phone?"

"For the phone. And for me too. I get money from them," Fernando explained.

"This isn't making much sense," Kate said.

"You don't like money?" He looked dumbfounded, as if discovering something new and wild about the little girl.

Steven was in her ear again. "Don't let him tie you in knots. Keep pushing for information. Find out about the tomb, the soldiers, the plan."

Kate blurted out, "But he knows something about my dad!" Then she remembered her British guide was not in the room. "Sorry. Sorry," she said.

Fernando thought her apology was for him. He shrugged, and Kate noted that there was not even a fleck of light in his eyes.

◆

IN THE BACK of the viewing room, Cardinal Parker finally could not keep still. "Can't you see she is not equipped to deal with this man or this situation? You've made a major error in judgment, Steven. Pull her out of there and let me in," he said, advancing.

Some of the law-enforcement personnel kept their eyes on Kate and Fernando, while others adjusted their line of sight to watch Steven and Cardinal Parker.

"You seem to forget, Cardinal, that this man did not request a meeting with you."

"He has nothing meaningful to say about the Church," Cardinal Parker spoke quickly. "He's a soldier of fortune."

"Yes, that's possible," Steven admitted. "Though he does seem to have a little something to say about *someone* in the Church."

The men and women attending the interrogation came from various backgrounds: some born and raised in Israel, others from distant ports and cultures. Yet they all understood the push and pull between the cardinal and the Brit.

Cardinal Parker took a deep breath. "I will report your error to the Vatican," he warned.

"And I will be happy to provide His Holiness with a video recording of today's proceedings," Steven responded. "Surely Pope Nelson has a mind of his own."

"If that's a threat . . ."

"Procedure, Cardinal. Just procedure."

◆

KATE TOOK A deep breath and began again.

"Okay. Let's go back to the beginning," she said. "Why did you tell your people about me?"

"They want to win."

"Win what?"

"The war."

"What war?"

Fernando opened his mouth, and a sound emerged that might have passed for laughter. "Show me your gold coins, little girl." His request sounded vulgar.

Steven chimed in again, calm and reassuring: "Good. Keep him focused on the treasure."

"You like gold, Fernando?" Kate said.

"No. I love gold. My people love gold."

"So whoever has the most gold wins the war?" Kate prodded.

Fernando smiled.

"The woman you were with, I bet she loves gold too."

The scowl returned to his face, and Steven sounded pleased. "You've hit a nerve," he advised. "Stay on him."

"What's her name, the woman you were with?"

"Bitch," Fernando spat.

"She must have a name," Kate pushed.

"Djiana is a bitch," Fernando whispered. "She loves only herself."

Fernando's mouth twisted, his head swiveling as if he were looking for options, trying to find a way to give up the imperious woman who had used and betrayed him but somehow also stay loyal to the cause.

"Fernando, is Djiana her real name? Is she the leader?" Kate prodded gently.

"Djiana Gomes! Fucking bitch!" Fernando erupted from his chair. Despite his inability to lunge at her, she felt the table jolt.

◆

"GET IN THERE now!" Steven ordered. Then he snapped his fingers at a thin woman who was taking notes. "The name, the name! Got it? Djiana Gomes. Find her in the database! Now!"

The woman nodded and rushed out of the room.

Steven watched as the two law enforcement personnel charged into the interview room, where Fernando was in a rage. He pulled at his shackles and threw his body in all directions, apparently trying to break free from his restraints.

Kate had fallen backward out of her seat and sat on the linoleum floor for a moment. Steven knew she was rattled but not injured when she scampered to a corner.

The security men ordered Fernando to calm down. "Sit down! Now!"

But Fernando couldn't control himself. "The fucking bitch!" he shouted as he continued to hammer the desk with his fists, stretching his shackles to their limit.

"Get hold of yourself, or this meeting is over!" one of the armed men said. "We'll pull the girl out of here."

"The selfish bitch." This time the curse sounded meek. He seemed timid, almost like he might cry.

"Kate, talk to me," Steven asked gently. "Do you want to come out?"

"Is somebody checking that name?" she asked back, still in the corner but now standing with her arms crossed.

Steven smiled. "Yes, boss," he said. Kate's amused twitch of an eyebrow confirmed that she would stay.

The security men remained in the room until Kate took her seat again and nodded. Fernando was limp, spent. She leaned forward and was surprised and a little ashamed by her instinct to attack his weakness. "Is that why you tried to kill yourself earlier today? Because Djiana gave you up?"

"Can you save me?" Fernando intoned. "I seen you do things. I seen it."

"In Rome, you mean."

"Yeah. Trastevere."

Steven felt a presence behind him. Cardinal Parker, transfixed, had moved closer to the one-way viewing window.

"What about Trastevere, Fernando?"

"I—I can't remember exactly."

Kate was firm. "We have a deal. I come to talk. You tell me everything."

"But—"

"Everything, Fernando, or I leave right now."

"Save me—or shoot me."

Kate stared at the broken man, then glanced over her shoulder at the one-way window. "All right. Start talking, and then I'll save you."

Cardinal Parker protested. "What is she doing?"

Steven quickly reminded Kate of the primary rule. "Promise him nothing."

"Trust me," she whispered. Then she removed the earbud and leaned back in her chair.

◆

KATE KNEW THE door to the interview room could open at any moment and end her time with Fernando. So she began to push hard for answers. "What did you do to my dad?"

"Nothing."

"But something happened to him. Did you do that?"

"I killed him." Fernando sounded defeated.

"Hey, hey! Look at me. You killed who? My dad is alive."

"An old man, I mean."

Kate's body jerked as though arrows had pierced it. She was struck by an onslaught of images and memories: the voices of the *Polizia Giudiziaria*, her father's disgrace at being fired. The powers of hell.

Fernando grinned. "Ah, now you see. I killed the old man and then I told the priest."

"At the Vatican," Kate surmised.

"I think."

"What do you mean, you think? The priest. The guy who gave you the phone and the money, right?"

"But I never met him. Another man paid me. I never knew exactly the priest."

"What was his name?"

"I don't know," Fernando mumbled.

She slammed her hand on the table. "Tell me his damn name!"

"I don't know. It's the truth!"

"But you told him you killed the old man, a beggar in Trastevere, and what did the priest say?"

"Disappear."

"And how did you do that?" Kate continued to keep the pressure on.

"He sent money. Put me on a boat to South America."

Her mind felt as though it might explode. The sound of her mother weeping, her father pleading for his job. "I *should* shoot you!" she said.

Fernando understood. "Okay."

"But not until you tell me everything, Fernando."

He nodded and slowly, finally, delivered the link, the connective tissue. Fernando spoke freely, revealing his failure to become a rich pastor and the success he experienced as a soldier for many illicit causes, a career that eventually led him to a revered man named Edhir Souza.

"I would die for him. God is mean in Rome. God is good in Edhir's church. He gave me strength. More than my body. More than—"

"Gold?" Kate surmised.

Fernando stared at her with black, empty eyes, neither fierce nor friendly. "One day, they recruit me."

"Djiana? For Edhir's Evangelist mission?"

He nodded.

"And?"

"I did good for them. I move up, invited to sit in meetings. One day, three or four years ago, we were planning war against *Católicos,* and I remember you. I wanted Djiana to like me. I say, 'Find the little girl. She knows things.' It took a year. You were in Dublin?"

"For a while."

"They find you. And start to follow you."

Kate bowed her head, realizing the full measure of what she had brought upon her parents. Never once had her father blamed her for the tumult or the career that had been snuffed out before it could truly flourish. Yet it was all her fault.

She heard a pleading voice and looked up as Fernando said, "Shoot me. Please. I am nothing."

"No."

"I don't want to live," Fernando muttered.

Kate pushed away her chair and reached across the wide table so that her slender fingers could touch the shackled, beastly hand of the man who had tried to kill her.

He recoiled as much as possible and begged again, "Shoot me."

"Diligatis invicem. Amatevi l'uno con l'altro."

Confused and frustrated, he asked, "What are you saying?"

Kate stretched out until she lay prone on the table, getting close enough to kiss his hand. Fernando did not move this time—he stared at her, his eyes wide and his body shaking with emotion. She looked into his eyes and spoke three simple words.

With this, tears pooled and then poured from his eyes. Kate had kept her promise. She had saved him.

◆

IN THE VIEWING room, there was a tense silence.

"What did she say?" Cardinal Parker asked, turning around.

Steven confirmed: "She said, 'I forgive you.'"

Chapter 37

Bethlehem

The raids began at dawn. Local police were drafted into the service of Interpol and IDF security forces and assembled into flying squads that rolled down narrow streets in armored vehicles, pulling up in front of nondescript apartment buildings and disgorging heavily armed men encased in body armor.

Commands were given silently, with hand gestures. Up the stairs. Down the hall. That door. Three, two, one. The wood was splintered with steel battering rams, and the men went inside at a run, two by two.

Brazilian men, asleep on floors, were kicked awake and quickly zip-tied at wrists and ankles. They were questioned where they lay on the floor as Interpol officers searched the rest of the apartment. Passports were seized, along with a few guns and slim envelopes containing surprisingly little cash. These men were doing their work for almost nothing.

All told, the police and soldiers rounded up sixteen men from four apartments, all within a mile of the Church of the Nativity. They were brought back to the local police station, where they were redistributed so that no one was in a cell with the other three he'd been living with. Then, the interrogations began.

None of the men could give a convincing account of his reasons for being in the city. They claimed to be tourists but had purchased no souvenirs—indeed, they had almost no possessions at all other than Bibles written in Portuguese and weapons.

Offers of deals were extended, always with the implied threat that if the man in the room didn't take the deal, one of the other men in the cells almost certainly would. But the men cast their eyes down to the table, or up to the ceiling, and prayed in their native language. Every question was met with a three-word response: "*Deus é bom.*"

A more physical, less negotiation-oriented approach met with a similar response. These men could take a punch. Through cracked lips and swollen, half-shut eyes, they continued to pray.

Running their passports was a dead end. They were all natives of southern Brazil and had apparently never traveled outside their home country before. Their names appeared on no international registries, and they had no criminal records outside Brazil.

"What have we got on these guys, really?" one of the officers asked Steven. "They can say they're just religious pilgrims. This city, more than any other, is up to its neck in pilgrims."

"I don't know," he replied. "Keep in mind, we're relying on the testimony of a soldier of fortune. His statements may or may not be credible," Steven said in his clipped, officious way. Perhaps he should let Interpol have these thugs and move on.

Then, a junior officer came into the command center, holding a laptop toward Steven. "Sir, I think I found something," he said.

Steven took the laptop and laid it on the desk. It was open to a social media page belonging to one of the Brazilians. "What am I looking for?"

The soldier clicked on a photo, expanding it to fill the screen. It showed a large group in what looked like some kind of megachurch.

Steven could see at least three of the Brazilians in his custody in the photo, all gathered around a man in some kind of white prayer shawl. The photo had a caption, but he couldn't read Portuguese.

Then Steven noticed one more face in the group. A row behind the man in the shawl and slightly to his right was a woman. She had black hair pulled back in a ponytail or bun and wore bright red lipstick that, honestly, he thought was a little much for church. She was smiling, but not with her eyes.

Based on the descriptions given by Father Maric and Sister Deborah, he knew exactly who she was: Djiana, the woman who had led the invasion of the church in Bethlehem.

"Excellent work," he said to the soldier who'd brought him the laptop. Picking it up off the desk, he took it into the interrogation room.

Answers would be forthcoming. He would make sure of it.

◆

STEVEN ARRANGED A mid-afternoon meeting with Cardinal Parker, held in a conference room down the hall from Father Maric's office. Returning to that office made his hackles rise. Even passing the door brought to mind a badly beaten nun and a frail priest cowed by pain and fear.

Cardinal Parker had barely taken his seat when he announced that Pope Nelson had expressed an interest in seeing the tomb.

"Of course he has," Steven said. "But the area is not yet secure. Tell His Holiness to sit tight until we can be absolutely certain that there aren't more Evangelical cells waiting to pounce."

"We intend to verify the nature and scope of this find," Parker said.

"Well, I hope you've brought some work clothes and have been getting your exercise," Steven said, casting a skeptical glance at the cardinal's soft physique, undisguised by an impractical cassock.

The cardinal ignored the implied insult. "We'll need Professor

Jamira to lead our team to the site as soon as possible," he replied. "I've arranged for younger members of the Vatican staff to be part of that effort."

"Agreed, but with this proviso: Kate is allowed to join us if she wishes. And no more leaks, Cardinal."

"What are you accusing me of, young man?"

"The media were tipped off to the Pentecostal connection as soon as we arrested the Brazilian. That can't happen again. We can't announce a historic discovery of riches until we've had ample time to set up a perimeter of protection. I don't want every pilgrim in the world coming to Bethlehem to pay homage or look for souvenirs until we're in complete control. Is that clear?"

Cardinal Parker snapped, "It is too big. I cannot promise that nothing will leak."

"Then find me someone from your inner circle who can, Cardinal. This is no time for boasts. We have to prepare for the tsunami of interest that this discovery will cause."

Both men took a frustrated moment to gather themselves, but then Cardinal Parker had another demand. "I insist that the transcript of the discussion between Miss Murphy and the Brazilian be edited. Baseless insinuations about so-called Vatican skullduggery should be redacted," the cardinal said.

"Skullduggery, eh? What are you afraid of, Cardinal?"

"A criminal's self-serving claims will set off speculation that will not be in the best interests of this or any pope."

"What was your title back then?" Steven probed.

"What does it matter?"

"Obviously, you're aware of something about Kate's past that has made you defensive since you arrived here."

Cardinal Parker sneered contemptuously, "My concern is for Catholicism, not Kate Murphy."

"That strikes me as cold, Cardinal. Her father—why was he being followed?"

The cardinal made no reply.

"Tell me what was at stake."

Again, no reply.

"One last question."

Finally, a response: "I doubt that."

"For the time being," Steven acknowledged. "Who are you stalking now, and why? And who is approving the activity and paying for it?"

"That's more than one question."

"But I bet there is one good answer." Steven paused, but it was clear that answer was not forthcoming, so he grudgingly returned to logistics. "Let's plan for a visit to the tomb tomorrow. Can your people be ready? Tomorrow early, if the ladies feel up to it."

"Yes, we'd better move before their memories of the route fade," the cardinal agreed.

"If I were you, Cardinal, I would not count on Ms. Murphy's memory fading."

◆

FATHER MARIC AND Sister Deborah were brought to a sitting room in wheelchairs. Kate and Nadia were excited about the reunion, and Kate struggled not to show alarm when they saw how battered and weak the priest and nun appeared.

Despite his pallor, Kate could tell Father Maric was trying to act normally. "There you are," he said. "I'm so relieved you're both okay."

Sister Deborah's greeting was a single word with little inflection: "Hello." Her right eye was patched, and a corner of her head had been shaved for surgery.

Maric reached over and patted her hand. "How are we today, my dear?"

Sister Deborah managed a faint smile.

Kate realized that they seemed like a nice couple. She wondered if either of them had ever imagined something more than the relationship the Church had conferred upon them.

The professor asked a few questions about what they knew of recent events. Unfortunately, the memory of violence was still predominant. Maric was focused on his need to understand how people could be so intentionally cruel.

"And that woman," he said, "even as she berated and struck us, she continued to ask about my sister as if she was genuinely interested. I don't know if I'm more curious or sickened."

"How did she know about your sister?" Nadia asked.

"The photograph on my desk. She kept staring at it, and—I don't know—she seemed intrigued."

"Or jealous," Kate said.

"Of what?"

"Innocence?" she replied. "Obviously, hers is long gone."

"You are a wise child." Maric nodded.

"Just a guess," Kate said. "We'll probably never know what made her the way she is."

"Someone so unremarkable in every way but her mercilessness." Father Maric shook his head. "Suddenly, I miss my sister more than ever. Do you think you could bring me her photograph?"

Nadia took his hand and explained that nothing could be retrieved from police custody until detectives had thoroughly examined the items as evidence. "But I'll ask when they might be able to get it back to you."

"Thank you. Blessings to you both." He looked over at Sister Deborah. "Right, Sister?"

The nun had fallen asleep, her chin resting on her collarbone, her breath slightly crackling from battered ribs.

Kate's heart ached for the woman. She went to the door and signaled a nurse. Two women in white appeared, checked the Sister's vitals, and prepared to wheel her back to her room.

"May I sit with her later, nurse?" Father Maric asked.

"Sure. I'll come get you."

"Thank you."

Kate stopped the nurses. "Excuse me, but is there any chance Sister Deborah and Father Maric could—share a room?"

The nurses exchanged a look and then turned to the priest. Father Maric's face was a mask of surprise, but an almost invisible tension eased from his shoulders. "Well then," he said.

Chapter 38

Bethlehem

The enormity of the challenge was apparent with every step as the priests and engineers followed Nadia and Kate to King David's tomb. Clearing a safe passage for a team of archeologists would be tricky. The eventual visit by Pope Nelson would be another matter entirely.

She was thrilled to be there again, well fed and properly equipped, but Kate's mind was elsewhere. She continuously replayed the telephone conversation she'd had with her parents.

The call to Dublin had not been easy to place. At first, she was excited to share what she'd learned, believing confirmation of the injustice would somehow salve the wounds of their past. Second thoughts, however, made her wonder if such a thing as vindication was even possible. Maybe she should spare her father, who, in his own way, already knew the truth.

Fortunately, the authorities had already contacted Rebecca and Simon. They'd seen the news reports of a shoot-out in Bethlehem and had been frightened for their daughter. Her call home, after meeting with Fernando, started as a chance to catch up. But finally, Kate had to bring up other matters.

"I'm not supposed to talk about this. Vatican security told me to keep my mouth shut," she began.

"Fat chance," Simon laughed.

"I have to ask you to, you know, keep this to yourselves. For your own safety."

"Okay," Rebecca answered with worry in her voice.

Kate outlined the basics—minus the treasure of massive historical and spiritual significance—of how she had come to meet Fernando. She also left out the part about him almost choking her to death. Her bruises would heal before the family could arrange a reunion. Finally, she blurted out what they really needed to know. "You were set up, Dad. The police and that beggar who died, I met the man who did all that. He confessed."

"Set up? How?" he asked.

"The Church was involved. A priest, or group of priests, who ran a secret society within the Vatican. They had money and other resources, and they wanted to hurt you."

"Me? But why?"

This was the hard part. Accepting blame. "Me, Dad. They were threatened by or afraid of the things that came out of my mouth."

"Or the way your words affected everyone in the Church. You were very powerful, even though you were a little girl."

Kate fell silent.

"You're not to blame, Kate. You were a child."

"But everything that happened to you, Dad . . ."

"Blame the bloody priests!"

"Simon!" Rebecca admonished.

"You're still defending them? How much more proof do you need, Rebecca?"

Kate hadn't expected her parents to turn on each other. She put her phone down and cradled her head in her hands.

"Blind faith, Becks. It gets us nowhere!"

"But all religion isn't corrupt, Simon."

"Ask Father Kelly."

"He's still a priest, you know," Rebecca said as calmly as she could manage.

"Yeah, at what price?"

Then, no one spoke.

"Honey?" Simon said. "You still there?"

Hearing the change in tone, Kate picked the phone back up. "Yes?"

"I'm sorry. I . . . you know me. Hot-headed intellectual with a weakness for cannoli and conspiracy theories."

"I get it. You loved Rome, your life as a professor."

"Yes, but mostly I love you."

"Me, too, sweetie," Rebecca added.

Kate's eyes brimmed with tears. "I love you too. You've sacrificed so much for me. But what do we do now?"

Simon answered. "Nothing."

"But—"

"No one at the university would want me back. The past can't be changed."

"B—but . . ." Kate stammered.

"You have an amazing future to pursue. Look ahead, not behind," Simon said.

If you only knew. Kate suddenly agreed. Her parents did not know the full extent of what had transpired. Authorities would not have told them about the discovery, and she was forbidden to tell them. That was just as well because she didn't think she could withstand the endless questions her father would launch.

"But there is one more thing I have to tell you."

"Oh, no, I can't take any more news today," Rebecca said.

"Professor Jamira and I have been summoned to Rome."

"Summoned?" Simon asked cautiously. "That sounds medieval."

"By the pope," Kate said.

"Worse. Summon yourself to run the other way," Simon cried. "Don't go!"

"Simon! Our daughter is going to meet the pope!" an obviously awed Rebecca interjected.

Simon giggled, and for a moment, Kate felt like the little girl who had quickly learned to love her adoptive mummy and daddy, who knew so much and were so in love.

"I'm happy for you, honey, really, I am. Give my regards to Sir Nelson. Or Captain or Astronaut Nelson, or—what's his title again?"

"Sorry, Dad, can't do that."

"Why not?"

"Because you're coming too. Both of you. I insisted that my parents share this moment with me."

What Kate had actually told Steven was, "The Vatican doesn't own me." If the Brit with Vatican security clearance was going to make demands, so was she. "Hey, King David can pick up the tab for a couple of airline tickets from Dublin and a hotel for a week—yes, a week. My parents used to live in Rome. They deserve the chance to go back," she had said.

Rebecca asked, "Share what, exactly? Why have you been invited?"

"Just a thank-you, I think, for—oh, I've got to go!" Kate quickly fibbed, telling her parents to expect a call from Vatican officials to work out the details. "Love you both. *Piccoli baci*—little kisses."

Chapter 39

To Rome

On the flight from Jerusalem to Rome, Nadia and Kate chatted over their in-flight refreshments. Nadia worried about missing more than a week of classes at the university but then laughed giddily when the reason for her absence sank in.

"Oh, wait," she whispered. "I'm meeting the pope."

"Well," said Kate, "it's amazing what a little digging will do for an academic career. Do you have tenure?"

"Of course," Nadia said.

"Wish my dad could say the same."

Kate didn't mean it rudely. It was simply the truth. Simon had admitted to her that he was too old for the tenure track. Universities were like corporations or the priesthood: you climb the ladder early in life. Nothing in those worlds begins at fifty-two.

"I'm looking forward to meeting your dad. I'm sure we'll have lots to talk about," Nadia said.

"May I suggest you prepare yourself for wandering Homeric narratives and numerous bad jokes?"

"Hey, academia could use a little stand-up comedy," Nadia said. "But only if you have a doctorate."

If only Simon had not adopted an abandoned soul named Katie, Kate thought. She made a wry face as Nadia rummaged through her carry-on bag. Kate was about to close her eyes for a nap when she saw a swath of blue cloth appear in the shuffle of belongings.

"You brought it."

"Brought what?" Nadia asked.

"The blue armband—and, in a way, Sister Theresa."

Nadia stopped her search and pulled out the armband, secure in a clear plastic bag. "Do you think . . ." she began. "What do you think of reminding Pope Nelson of these nuns? All they really wanted was to give more of themselves, to serve the Church in new ways."

"Are you going to wear it when we meet His Holiness?" Kate asked with admiration.

Nadia put her reading glasses on before turning to Kate. "I was hoping you would."

"Me?"

"You shouldn't do anything you don't want to do, of course," Nadia said.

"Of course not," Kate agreed.

"And it might seem disrespectful . . ."

"But?"

"But it will fit you better, and I'm not talking about size. Carry the torch, Kate. Answer the call."

"What call?"

Nadia smiled. "If I get a chance, I'm going to tell Pope Nelson that I believe you would make a splendid priest."

Kate felt her insides flutter. "A priest? Ha! You would make a terrible guidance counselor. Seriously, what are you talking about? That's like saying why not become a dolphin or lion? A priest?"

"Yes, a priest, but I'm only going to mention it after I'm sure he has realized how special you are."

Kate turned away. *What good has it done? My "special" qualities ruined my father's career and put other good people in harm's way*, she thought.

Nadia continued, "I'll start by saying, 'I know that you were voted in by the other cardinals because of your conservative views . . .'"

"Oh, boy. Good luck with that one." Kate laughed.

"I'll be nice. I'll remind him that he has chosen the name of arguably the greatest equal-rights activist in the history of the world. Therefore, wouldn't it make sense to authorize the ordination of women?"

"Then he will fall back on the old argument that Jesus was the Son, not the daughter, of God. He will continue with St. Peter." Kate assumed a scholarly, masculine voice. "St. Peter was a man and the first Supreme Pontiff, and Jesus handed him the keys of the Church. Since Jesus selected men to be his disciples, that is what we continue today."

"But why is it inherently wrong?"

"It goes against who we are as people, and it goes against God."

"But, sir, how does a female pope go against God's love for us all?"

Kate was stunned and her voice changed back. "*Pope?* Professor, aren't you getting ahead of yourself? Let's get women ordained before we start talking—"

"Why limit ourselves, Kate?" Nadia said, suddenly serious. "Besides, a woman being ordained as a priest is not the core issue. The root of the problem is that the hierarchy of the Church knows that if they allow female ordination, it means someday a woman could be their supreme pontiff. Discrimination is discrimination, plain and simple. Not to mention—but I will, of course—the Vatican has just been handed the keys to the largest treasure ever known to man, pun fully intended, by two women."

"Money talks, eh?" Kate replied.

"Power and leadership do too. If the fathers of the Church couldn't find this treasure, then how could two women do it? I will ask the Church and the world to question why God and King David chose you.

You will have one of the most powerful female voices in the history of the Christian world once they know it was you who knew the location of the tomb."

Kate's eyes grew wide as the full magnitude of King David's gift struck her. The gold and treasure were awe-inspiring, but she had not fully recognized the spiritual implications until now.

Nadia continued, "The Bible never says that a man is better than a woman. No man should be able to declare that only men hear the call to serve God in the highest stations of life." Nadia pulled the blue armband out of the plastic bag. She held it to her cheek affectionately, sighed, and then returned it to her carry-on bag. "You don't have to decide now."

"I need a nap." Kate reclined her seat and closed her eyes. But she did not sleep.

As she'd matured, premonitions of things to come had continued to join her visions of ancient times. Although most came true in some form, Kate still had not learned to embrace them. Sometimes, movement allowed her to resist them, as she had discovered when she was a little girl whirling in her father's arms. But even if she hadn't been shoehorned into an airplane seat, this onslaught of images—her own private in-flight movie—felt impossible to suppress.

◆

"WE NEED TIME to secure the location before you make an announcement about the discovery," Steven said, arguing his case before Vatican officials.

"We need good news for our followers and the world," they replied, rejecting his appeal.

◆

Father Kelly and his lover Ava were undressed and intertwined, whispering mutual devotion. Kate winced in embarrassment. Then suddenly, they were at an altar, dressed for a wedding.

◆

Cardinal Parker smiled at her and spoke in an unctuous, inappropriate tone.

"You don't remember me, but I remember you."

"Oh?"

"You will not win."

This confused her. "Win what?"

Without answering, her adversary disappeared.

◆

With a warm smile, Father Maric raised a spoonful of soup. Sister Deborah, who lay in an upright hospital bed, opened her mouth.

"Your appetite is improving, Sister."

She swallowed her nourishment and replied, "Mm. Feeling so much better."

"Another roll?"

"Is the bread still warm, Father?"

◆

The pontiff greeted Professor Nadia Jamira. "It is so wonderful to meet the two of you," Pope Nelson said as he extended his right hand. Nadia took his hand and kissed the papal ring, the Ring of the Fisherman.

Then Kate's mother knelt before her spiritual leader and gazed up at him with reverence and gratitude. Her father watched from nearby, enthralled with the history of the Vatican, if not its mandate.

Now Kate saw only the ring and heard Pope Nelson's baritone voice explaining that all popes are successors of St. Peter, the original pope, who had also been a fisherman.

"The ring depicts Peter fishing from a boat and symbolizes that the apostles were fishers of men. I am connected to all the popes who came before me," he said.

Kate heard her voice respond, "As am I." All eyes in the room turned toward her as she asked, "Can you imagine a day when women will be ordained as priests?"

Her mother gasped; her father smiled.

The pope glared. "How did you find King David's tomb?"

"I had a vision."

"Then you tell me. Do you see the day when women will be ordained?"

◆

SAINT PETER CRIED out in pain as his blood spilled. Rome burned. Conflict and bloodshed prevailed.

◆

KATE STARTLED AND sat up in her seat, thirsty and disoriented. She turned and saw that Nadia had fallen asleep.

She knew the professor still had no update on what had befallen her admin assistant, Dafna, and perhaps never would. Kate heard the pilot announce that they were beginning their descent into Rome. Alone with her thoughts, concerns, and a flood of childhood memories, she took a deep calming breath and whispered to herself, "Love one another."

III

THE CALLING

Chapter 40

Rome

The moment Kate and Professor Nadia Jamira touched down in Rome, they were sped along like pebbles in an avalanche. After meeting up with Simon and Rebecca, they were led to a chamber at the Vatican by Cardinal Alain Dumas, a politely reserved man, who opened an ornate door that led to a world of glorious history and tradition. Kate marveled at the frescoes rising a story high on her right and left, bright, detailed, and gilded in gold at the edges. The marble and parquet floors shone as if they had just been polished. Every table, every pedestal, every chair that lined the hallway was carved or gilded or padded in velvet, and Kate sensed the sacred history that filled this place.

Pope Nelson rose from his chair when his guests arrived. He wore a distinguished uniform, even for daily activities: a white skullcap, a short white hooded cape known as a mozetta, a gold pectoral cross, and red shoes. Although the first Black man to sit in the papal chair was sixty-three years old, the smooth texture of his skin suggested someone much younger. A youthful vigor also burst from his bright green eyes and genuine smile.

The cardinal bowed and made the introductions. "Professor Nadia Jamira, Kate Murphy, Simon and Rebecca Murphy, I am pleased to introduce you to His Holiness, Pope Nelson the First."

Pope Nelson welcomed Simon and Rebecca and then turned to the professor and her prize pupil. "So, it is the two of you who have brought the church so much joy and abundance," he said.

"And Father Maric," Kate said. "We could not have found the tomb if he hadn't been willing to try."

"Yes, I intend to visit Father Maric and Sister Deborah when they are feeling better," the pope said, opening his arms. "But for now, I welcome you both and thank you."

The pope extended his right hand to Nadia, who peered at the Ring of the Fisherman and then kissed it. "Thank you, Your Holiness. I have always wanted the chance to kiss this ring."

Kate remembered her vision. Fear ran through her as she looked at the oval-shaped golden signet of the pope's power and responsibility. It shone in the bright overhead lights.

"Yes, out of all the garments and jewelry I must now wear," he confessed, "this is by far my favorite. It makes me feel connected to all of the other popes who came before me."

Nelson turned to Kate, who froze. Nadia nudged her to bow and kiss the ring, but Kate still could not move.

The pope smiled and asked, "Do you know about the Ring of the Fisherman, Ms. Murphy?"

Kate nodded mutely.

Rebecca whispered, "Kate," and gestured toward the pope, who continued to extend his hand, waiting.

"Oh. Yes. I'm sorry!" Kate mentally braced herself, then kissed the ring. Her caution was validated when she was instantly bombarded with images and sensations.

An ocean swell threatened to capsize a wooden boat. A spray of salt water stung her face. She jostled with other men who shouted, hauling in nets as a storm of thunder and lightning exploded overhead and . . .

"My child, are you all right?" the pope inquired with obvious, genuine concern.

Kate felt a firm hand on her shoulder and looked up at the pope. "I'm okay. This whole experience is a bit overwhelming."

Her parents stepped closer, their arms extended as if to catch her in case she fell. Pope Nelson nodded and then, to everyone's amazement, removed the piece of jewelry and handed it to Kate.

"Here you go. Have a good look," he offered. "I've always found that a history lesson is so much better when you are holding the actual artifact."

Kate and Nadia shared an amused smile and Kate's body relaxed a little as they inspected the ring, passing it back and forth.

"Did I say something humorous? Finally." Nelson glanced at the chagrined Cardinal Dumas.

"Actually, your Holiness, Kate knows that one of my trademarks when teaching history is to use actual relics," Nadia responded. "I agree wholeheartedly with you. It's such a wonderful way to keep the students engaged."

"Do you mind if I keep this for my doctoral thesis?" Kate quipped.

While her mother gasped and her father grinned gleefully, Pope Nelson was quick with a rejoinder. "If you don't mind Vatican security surrounding you twenty-four hours a day for the rest of your collegiate life."

Kate laughed and returned the ring. "Thanks anyway, Your Holiness. Not that I don't like Steven Craft, but he keeps pressing me to change my major to law enforcement."

"A worthy choice, I'm sure," the pope said. "But for now, allow me to share a little about the ring. Then please tell me about your blue armband."

Kate had forgotten that she was wearing it and felt completely unprepared. "It's just . . . well, a long story," she stammered and blushed.

The pope raised an eyebrow but did not press her further. "This ring represents the lineage of the pope. All popes are successors of St. Peter."

"The original Supreme Pontiff," Kate joined in.

"Correct. St. Peter was a fisherman, and that's how he is depicted on the ring. The image symbolizes that the apostles were fishers of men."

Kate looked deliberately at the pope.

"Yes?" He encouraged her unspoken question.

"How amazing to be the first Black man to wear this ring," she said.

"Yes. I'm experiencing many firsts. But you and Professor Jamira have provided what I'm sure will be the most extraordinary experience of my time here. The first pope of any race to be shown King David's tomb."

Cardinal Dumas softly interrupted and reminded Pope Nelson of the time.

"Ah, yes. Duty calls. I'm sorry to say that for security reasons I could not reveal one of my reasons for requesting your presence here today. We are on the verge of—what shall we call it, Cardinal Dumas?"

"A momentous announcement."

Kate could feel the immediate tension she shared with her parents and Nadia. The pope gestured for his guests to follow. "Please come sit with me so that I can explain what we have planned. Then afterward, we'll discuss your fashion statement, Ms. Murphy."

Chapter 41

Rome

Kate's parents had often told her that gathering with a crowd in St. Peter's Square for a papal announcement was one of life's greatest thrills. What they could not possibly have described was the sensation of standing with His Holiness on the central balcony of St. Peter's Basilica as he addressed the multitude. Yet, that was what was about to happen.

After being introduced to Pope Nelson, the Murphy family and Nadia had learned that the Vatican intended to announce the discovery of King David's tomb that evening. They also wanted to introduce Kate and Nadia to the world.

As dusk fell upon Rome, a vast crowd gathered in the square for what was vaguely described in the press as an unprecedented event. Rumors swirled, but that was nothing new, and security was as tight as ever.

As Kate took her place behind the pope, she reached out to her parents, who stood on either side of her. Never before had she seen, let alone faced, such an enormous crowd, and she felt humbled by the faces gazing upward.

The supreme pontiff began with a rare apostolic blessing. "To the city of Rome and the entire world, may the Holy Apostles Peter and

Paul, in whose power and authority we have confidence, intercede on our behalf to the Lord."

Everyone in attendance, including a contingent of the College of Cardinals dressed in full regalia, and even Kate's father, murmured, "Amen."

After the blessing, the pope began his remarks. "As most of you are aware, the apostolic blessing is normally only given on Easter and Christmas, but I have my reasons for consecrating it upon us today. Two courageous women, with the help of a priest, have made a discovery that gives Catholics everywhere a new opportunity to rejoice."

Pope Nelson wove an intriguing tale as he prepared his audience for the news. As he built to his finale, the crowd began to grow restless and anxious, and Kate could relate. *Just tell them*, she thought. *Tell them so we can all breathe again.*

As if on cue, he opened his arms and delivered the big reveal. "Now, it is time to rejoice. After nearly three thousand years, King David's gift has finally made it home! We have found King David's tomb!"

Enormous screens projected photos of the sarcophagus and other antiquities. Thunderous cheering shook the square, and cameras began to flash wildly.

"My hope for the world is that this gift from David and his people will bring all of us closer to God and closer to one another, no matter what faith or religion we practice. Be assured, we intend to share the wealth. For all people on earth listening today, King David has returned to renew our understanding of the Old Testament and to remind us where we all have come from."

Kate's parents hugged her from either side.

"I would like to introduce you to the two women responsible for finding the tomb. They are heroes of the Church. From Jerusalem University, Professor of Biblical Archaeology Nadia Jamira, and her student, from Rome, Miss Kate Murphy."

In the months and years to come, Kate would pinpoint this as a moment when her life profoundly changed. Wherever she would travel, she would be recognized. Many times she would wish she had not been born with her cryptic gifts.

Pope Nelson invited the women forward. They walked gingerly to the front of the balcony, their arms linked to bolster each other, and were showered with applause and cheers. The roar was deafening.

"These Catholic pioneers were assisted by Father Lawrence Maric, our priest at the Church of the Nativity in Bethlehem. We thank him for his remarkable contribution and also wish to announce that a portion of the fortune King David left us will be used to establish a mission for the sick and poverty-stricken children of the world. This mission will be named the Sarah Maric Children's Foundation."

Tears filled Kate's eyes. Earlier, she had shared the story of the girl's death, and the pope immediately agreed to Kate's idea of funding the mission in Maric's sister's name. Kate was beginning to believe the pontiff was a man of his word and a man of action.

"Now I would like for you to hear from the two people responsible for locating the tomb. Professor Jamira?"

Pope Nelson had told them that he would ask them to speak briefly. Still, Kate could sense her professor falter before stepping forward, her fear palpable. "Thank you, Pope Nelson, and thanks be to God, Jesus Christ, and King David."

The people in the square erupted again with enthusiastic exultation. Kate glanced at one of the screens and saw wave upon wave of jubilant faces.

"But most of all, I would like to thank Kate Murphy. Without her, we would not be basking in this glory. I admit, I thought she'd lost her mind when she began describing a passage to the tomb. When I finally agreed to work with her, our discovery took mere hours. How can this be? I don't know. Her mind is a mystery to me, but not her heart. I believe God wanted to continue building his temple, and he chose Kate to be the one to renew our faith and ability to keep growing—and believing. Thank you, and God bless you all."

Kate felt her chest swell with gratitude.

Nadia stepped back and gestured Kate forward as the pope spoke to the crowd. "I am sure you would all like to hear from the eighteen-year-old scholar who helped find King David for us."

As Kate approached the podium, her limbs began to twitch, and her eyes fluttered uncontrollably. As she recognized that another onslaught was to come, she was tormented by violent images of bloody human sacrifice. *I am not worthy* hammered in her mind over and over. The crippling pain almost made her pass out, and she gripped the edges of the podium until she was able to speak the words that she knew would calm her.

"In Latin, the phrase is *diligatis invicem.*" She took another slow breath. "In Italian, it is—"

From St. Peter's Square, thousands of people witnessed His Holiness Pope Nelson leaning toward the microphone and completing the young woman's litany. "*Amatevi l'uno con l'altro*—love one another," he said.

◆

THE ROAR OF jubilation was so powerful that a woman in the crowd felt the stone beneath her feet tremble. The outbreak of ecstasy forced her body to sway in unison with the mass of people that surrounded her. She was not pleased.

Her thick black hair was pulled into a ponytail, and large white sunglasses covered her eyes despite the evening shadows. Her lips were ruby red. She pulled a cell phone from her designer handbag and touched the speed dial.

When Djiana Gomes heard the voice of the man she loved, the temperature of her blood rose. "She has won this round, my darling," she murmured. "But there will be other battles, and we will prevail."

"You are a blessing."

"*Deus é bom.*"

"I wonder, my love," he said, "can you tell what she is wearing on her arm?"

"Bad clothes, as usual," Djiana scoffed.

"Yes, but on television it looks like a blue stripe. It must signify something."

"Let me see what I can find out," Djiana replied. She leaned toward the woman in front of her as Kate began speaking again.

"I want to make sure that it is absolutely clear that Jesus is my savior. He is and will always be the real hero. All praise and glory goes to Him."

Djiana was shushed when she asked the woman what Kate's blue armband meant. Anger flooded her body. Reaching into her handbag, she felt the grip of a needle-like knife. Her hand tightened around it as she looked for a quick way out of the crowd. Escape did not seem possible, so she reluctantly dropped the knife back into her purse. She asked others about the blue band, but no one knew anything.

When she heard Kate's tone shift, she looked up at the papal balcony. She cupped the phone close to her mouth. "What did she just say?" she asked.

Her lover replied, "Something about the money not being as important as—"

"Yes. I hear. Stay with me."

Djiana heard Kate say that no amount of gold or silver could compare to the love of Jesus that is eternally within us all.

"And yet, while we are all children of the Universe, and as Nelson Mandela once said, 'There can be no keener revelation of a society's soul than the way in which it treats its children.' It's sad to say, we are not all treated equally by man," Kate said.

Djiana whispered to her lover, "She is about to make a very big mistake. I can feel it." She turned to the screen beside the balcony to watch her young target.

"It's intriguing that after centuries of failure, it was two women who finally found King David's tomb," Kate continued.

Female voices shouted their delight and raised their hands into the cool evening air.

"Yet women are still not allowed to be ordained. Many things in life are complicated. But equal rights are not. Simple, ordinary equal rights should not be controversial for anyone, including the leaders of our Church." Kate looked toward the pope. "With all due respect, Your Holiness."

Djiana could feel the audience stir with confusion. A celebration was tilting toward controversy, or worse, rebellion.

Global broadcast coverage and endless video replay of the next events would contradict what many people in St. Peter's Square swore they saw. Not a high-minded young woman of medium height and average appearance. Instead, the eyes of the faithful were shocked to behold a figure larger than life looming on the balcony with arms spread wide, speaking words that boomed with authority.

"In South Africa, it took a great leader to end apartheid. I'm hoping our pope is worthy of the name he has chosen. Free us, Your Holiness. Free Catholic women. Let us be equal so that we can all truly love one another."

The square exploded. Cheers competed with boos. The announcement of the sensational discovery was forgotten as debates broke out between and within genders and groups. Moments later, the communal joy in St. Peter's Square was torn asunder by jeers and some even started shoving.

On the balcony, members of the Swiss Guard surrounded Pope Nelson and whisked him indoors to safety. Security personnel also escorted Simon, Rebecca, and Nadia away.

But Kate would not move. She clung to the podium, watching the chaos below, repeating her mantra and warning to no avail.

Love one another.

Only one face in the crowd was smiling as she stared up at the balcony. But Djiana hid her glee by pulling a silk scarf across her mouth as she spoke into her phone. "My darling, it appears we have won after all. The girl is a shipwreck."

"We have won nothing!" Edhir reprimanded her. "From witnessing her life thus far, she is the future of Catholicism. If she will not be with us, then I will not allow her to be against us."

Djiana felt jealousy rise in her toward Kate. "I'm sorry, Edhir. Calm down. I understand. Now please tell me, what is next for our friend Fernando?"

"He is no more, my *beleza*. Come home. I miss you."

The crowd began to surge frantically back and forth as though they were at a heavy-metal concert. Djiana wanted out, but she was pinned in place by bodies.

Small conflicts were erupting in various parts of the square. To Djiana's left, a heavyset middle-aged man began to shout at the balcony, accusing Kate of blasphemy; the younger, skinnier man next to him shouted that Kate was right, calling him a pigheaded woman hater. They turned and began shouting at each other, then shoving one another until the overweight man threw a hard punch that landed square in the young man's mouth.

Similar arguments were escalating all around. As the initial combatants wrestled and tried to drag one another to the ground, the friends of the men joined in punching and kicking. Screams could be heard as women and children attempted to get out of the way of the violence; the surges of the crowd became more violent.

Djiana was used to crowds and tightly packed conditions; growing up in the *favelas*, one never expected privacy or open space. But that meant she also knew how fast a crowd could turn into a stampede and how many people could die under such conditions. She had seen it at soccer games and at samba concerts: the innocent trampled along with the idiots who had instigated the panic. She needed to get out.

She pushed the woman to her right, a single sharp shove. The woman glared at her. "Move," Djiana said. The woman moved, and Djiana was one spot closer to escape.

She continued pushing and demanding that people make a space for her. They did, but there were still hundreds of people between her and the nearest side street. Suddenly, the crowd was rushing forward, dragging her along with them. This was bad. Djiana reached into her purse and grabbed her dagger.

Someone gripped her arm. Another hand groped for her purse. No matter the circumstance, when you gathered enough people in one space, some of them were there to rob the others. Djiana knew this from hard experience—on both sides.

She pulled the dagger from her bag and quickly thrust it across her body. It sank into flesh, came back bloody. The hands that had been on her withdrew, and she redoubled her efforts to move out of the crowd, shoving sideways as the masses washed forward like a flood.

It took the longest ten minutes of her life to escape the square. When she was finally free, on a narrow side street, she leaned against the wall, sweaty and panting.

Chapter 42

Bethlehem

Fernando sat in his cell, head in his hands. He was not praying, because he no longer saw the point. He had stared into the girl's eyes, felt her touch, and now he realized that the power of God was not summoned by offerings or by material success; it came from within.

Once she had offered him forgiveness, absolved him for everything he had done to her and her family, he felt a peace he had never felt before. He told her and the police everything he knew about the attempted robbery.

He told them that sixteen of his church brothers were living in Bethlehem. Some of them had been involved in the gunfight that allowed Djiana to escape. Others were merely in place, waiting for orders.

His mission, though, was over. And he had failed. He had been a valuable tool for the church—for two churches. He had worked for the Catholics, then for the Evangelicals. But now he was all alone in the universe. No one wanted him; no one needed him. From dust he had come, and to dust he would return.

He did not know how long he had been in his cell. He had no window, so the only light was a wire-encased fluorescent tube that was never turned off. Food arrived every few hours, but the guards never spoke to him and would not answer questions.

It did not matter to him. He had been in much worse situations for much longer. Physical discomfort was not an issue. But his mind seemed to be out to punish him.

He wanted to see the girl again. Kate. He wanted to look into her eyes again, feel the touch of her hand again, hear her speak to him of forgiveness again. The love he had felt coming off her, like heat from an oven—that was real. He had never felt that from Djiana or anyone in the church. Either church.

He sat in his cell and stared at the floor. He wondered if they needed anything else from him. He wondered if Djiana had been captured yet. He doubted it. She was crafty. She would find a way to escape back to Brazil. As long as the church existed, she would be there, leading it, all the while pretending to be no more than another follower.

He knew that she followed orders, the same as he did, but he also believed that some of the things she was ordered to do had originated with her. Women were like that. They could make you think their ideas were yours. Especially when those ideas came up in conversation in the bedroom.

He looked up suddenly when he heard the scraping of the lock on his cell door. It had not opened since he had been put inside. Food came through a slot in the door. Did they need to ask him more questions?

When the man in the ill-fitting guard's uniform stepped into the cell and shut the door behind him, though, he knew that no one was ever going to ask him anything again.

"*Olá,*" he said without getting up.

"*Deus é bom,*" the man said.

◆

RIO DE JANEIRO

THE FIRST RANKING member of the Catholic Church to publicly condemn Kate was Rolando Azevedo, archbishop of Rio de Janeiro. As a loud, large, and intimidating man, his rise to archbishop had been easy for him. Yet, many Vatican observers questioned his uncompromising conservative views. Was he truly committed to tradition, or was his simplification of complex matters merely a means to an end? Was it a matter of "he who speaks loudest wins"?

Whatever his motives, his blunt and unwavering opposition to the Evangelical movement in his country made him popular with Catholic leadership. One of his most popular proclamations was quoted often among Catholics worldwide: "We may have our share of faults and sins, but I prefer that my Church be founded by the Messiah and not some Evangelist with his hand in my wallet. Our Church will always be the purest path to Christ and his teachings, not the pick-pocket Pentecostals!"

But now he turned his vehemence on the "showboating red-haired heretic with the blue armband." Despite her youth, rising popularity, and miraculous treasure find, the archbishop spared her no mercy.

Minutes after Kate dared to challenge the pope, Azevedo launched a counterattack that went viral and dominated global media. On-camera interviews with broadcast conglomerates ruled the airwaves for several days. His message was a blunt counter to the idea that women must and should ascend.

"I don't care how much gold she finds. Anyone who is invited to speak in St. Peter's Square at His Holiness's personal request, disrespects him, and starts a riot is not a true Catholic. We don't take lightly the cheap shots of renegades."

◆

BETHLEHEM

STEVEN WAS THE first to alert Kate and Professor Nadia Jamira to Azevedo's attack. They were summoned by other high-ranking officials the following day and led to a Vatican office where they could speak with Steven on an encrypted phone line.

"Are you sure you wish to push this agenda, Kate?" Steven asked from Bethlehem, wishing he was at the Vatican at his office at the Corps of Gendarmerie.

Kate was firm. "I'm sure I wish to speak the truth."

"Then expect a lot of recrimination."

"Okay."

"Okay? Have you no sense of what you've stirred up?" Steven's frustration was born of concern for the charismatic young woman. "Kate, please know that I'll do everything in my power to protect you, but I am an employee of the Vatican. My duty here must always come first. However, I can tell you that Archbishop Azevedo and Cardinal Parker are not the only high-ranking Catholics who oppose you and your beliefs."

"Why?"

"They are all now very aware of your childhood here in Rome, and you are threatening the hierarchy. You are threatening—"

"Men of power."

"Power is the operative word. And political leaders around the world are assassinated for a lot less than what you have done," Steven warned.

"But I have no political philosophy," Kate insisted.

"That's what makes you so dangerous. Have you spoken to His Holiness since your speech?"

"Yes."

"And?"

"It was, uh, tense."

For the first time, Steven laughed. "Well, I should imagine so. You ambushed him, and he hasn't been sitting in the big chair for long. You cannot underestimate what your comments have put into play. You are reviled and yet loved, and in my experience, that is the most dangerous combination."

"Then what should we do?" Kate asked earnestly.

"We?"

"Professor Jamira is on my side."

"Great. An undergrad and a teacher against a tidal wave of tradition." Steven sighed.

◆

ROME

KATE HEARD OTHER voices in the background interrupt Steven. An argument escalated. Then she heard silence and thought the phone line had gone dead. As she was about to hang up, a brusque Steven returned and said, "Stay where you are. I'll have to call you back."

When Kate ended the call, Nadia inquired, "What happened?"

Kate explained what she'd heard and then imagined Steven taking deep breaths, the method of self-governance and control he had used after the interview with Fernando.

"Carlitos," she murmured.

"Fernando, you mean?" asked Nadia.

"Yeah. His name was Carlitos when his leaders framed my dad."

"What about him?"

Kate could not explain her sense of foreboding. When the phone rang, she stared intensely at it before lifting the receiver. She didn't bother with formalities.

"He's dead, isn't he?"

The security chief was stunned. "How did you know?"

She wasn't prepared to explain but instead asked, "When did he die?"

"We're not sure of the timeline yet."

"How?"

"We think poison in his food or maybe in his water. We won't know until—"

Kate interrupted, "In a high-security jail? How could this happen?"

"I know you're upset, but—"

"Of course, I'm upset, Steven. You're not telling me everything."

"I've hardly been given the chance," Steven answered calmly.

Nadia put a hand on Kate's arm.

"There's something else, isn't there?" Kate pushed.

She heard deep breaths from Steven and then a blunt preamble.

"Yes. This is why I want you to listen to reason. Will you do that, Kate?"

"Reason seems like a rare item lately, but I will try."

"When Fernando was found in his cell, he was on his knees with his head resting on the bed."

Kate attempted to make sense of this. "Praying?"

"That's what it looked like, which may be why we didn't discover his condition sooner. But when he was lifted onto the bunk . . ."

Kate had no patience for the pauses. "Tell me. I'm not a child!"

Another deep breath. "There was a photo."

Kate's stomach dropped. "Okay."

"Under his head. He was lying on it."

"Of?"

"You and Professor Jamira . . . as you entered the Vatican for your meeting with Pope Nelson."

Stunned, Kate whispered, "Someone inside the Vatican took the photo?"

Steven chose his words carefully: "For now, let's assume that is true."

"How else could it have happened?"

Thinking out loud, he answered, "More to the point, who took the picture, and was their intent malicious, or was the image pulled from . . ." He stopped. "Is Professor Jamira with you now?"

"Yes."

"You must never be alone, Kate. Never."

"Why?" She heard his hesitation. "Steven?"

"A message was scrawled on the back of the photo. It said, 'Stop searching for us now or the gifted one is next.'"

Chapter 43

Rome

In the days that followed, Kate and Nadia were not afraid. They chose to grant nearly every television interview request they received so they could rebut Archbishop Azevedo and defend their position on female ordination. For viewers, it was as if they were watching an edited version of a live debate.

On one news channel, Azevedo argued, "These women seem unable to take no for an answer."

Turn the channel, and Nadia was responding, "If we had taken no for an answer from men throughout history, we still would not be able to own property, vote, or free ourselves from abusive relationships. 'No' is not an acceptable answer to this issue any longer. In 1870, White men in the US granted African American men the right to vote, excluding women." She paused for emphasis, "I truly admire Susan B. Anthony for voting anyway and defiantly telling the judge to stick his $100 fine where the sun doesn't shine."

"Despite her courageous efforts, all women in the US did not gain the right to vote until 1965. Fast-forward to 2023, and it was only then that men in the church finally allowed women some limited voting rights. Yet, even this concession is flawed. The votes women cast in the Church synod that Pope Francis created do not give them equal rights or any real power; instead, they merely offer suggestions to male leaders. Ultimately, these leaders still decide on all significant rules without female votes. The continued refusal of the Church's male leaders to grant women equal rights is truly astonishing."

Azevedo: "Women can protest all they wish, but the writings of the early Christians say that women cannot be ordained. As Pope Leo said, 'It isn't as simple as saying, "You know, at this stage we're going to change the tradition of the Church after 2,000 years on any one of those points."'"

Kate: "Those are the writings of only early Christian men. Please do not group all early Christians together. The women of the time might have had a different opinion about whether they were worthy of ordination had they been allowed one. Furthermore, in regards to Pope Leo and 2000 years of tradition, as if it's frozen in time, tradition is a living thing, guided by the Spirit! The Church's understanding has grown on so many things—slavery, religious freedom. We're not breaking tradition; we're living its deepest meaning now. History itself shows women had vital roles, even deaconesses. Fidelity isn't rigid repetition, it's dynamic faithfulness to the Gospel in this age."

Nadia: "The archbishop's comments reflect a troubling parallel to historical claims of superiority. Much like assertions that Christians are better than Jews or that Black people exist to serve Whites. Throughout history, those who assert they know God's will have created countless wars by propagating such divisive narratives. It is heartbreaking to watch the men of my faith continue to run the Church into the ground. They must wake up and realize that, for the future sake of the Church, women must be given equal opportunities. Due to the current gender bias rules, the decline of nuns in the Western world has plummeted by over 70 percent. Only 1 percent of nuns in America are under 40, while the average age of a nun hovers around 80. The repercussions are catastrophic, affecting our schools and ministries as fewer nuns and women are willing to serve and be treated as second-class citizens. Convents are being forced to close their doors. Unless women are finally given the respect they deserve, the Bride of Christ may not survive. If it doesn't, then it will be because of the archaic sex discrimination laws of stubborn old men. As Catholics, we can do better and love one another

equally. When the change does come, when all members are valued and empowered, we will watch the glorious growth of Catholics world-wide. Jesus's flock will flourish once again. The time is now!"

Kate: "The Universe's gifts know no limits or gender. If God gives spiritual gifts for building up the Church as the Bible says It does in Corinthians, are we saying the Spirit holds back certain gifts based on whether you're a man or a woman? To limit who God can call, who the community can discern, based only on gender—that's putting human limits on divine power. Spiritual equality means the potential for all forms of service is open, if God calls and the Church discerns. If I had the chance, I would ask Archbishop Azevedo this question: Because you are a man, are you spiritually superior to a woman? That seems to be his basic argument."

Consciously or not, Kate had suggested a showdown. News organizations immediately offered to sponsor a debate. Steven had insisted on keeping Kate's parents in Rome for security reasons, so Simon became his daughter's de facto agent, negotiating to find the ideal date and venue, and Simon and Rebecca's hotel room became his office.

Kate balked. "I'm really not the best spokesperson for this. Nadia or any number of active Catholic women would do so much better."

"My dear, I believe you asked for it. You said, 'If I had the chance...'"

"Dad, isn't that what you call a rhetorical comment?"

"These days, it's considered taunting."

"But Professor Jamira is the expert here." Kate paced in indecision. Her parents didn't know about the death threat, and she'd made Steven and Nadia promise to keep it a secret.

Nadia had some ideas about how the debate might be structured. She also admitted that the idea of tearing apart the old guard of Catholic thought on television was highly appealing.

Rebecca gasped. "This is serious business."

"Yes, it is," Nadia agreed. "But it's also theater, and the audience will be much larger if the Girl Wonder debates the Archbishop of Rio."

Kate groaned.

"I'll coach you, Kate, and I'm sure your father can negotiate debate terms that favor your strengths."

"What strengths? What if I have a panic attack or another vision—on live TV?"

Simon grinned. "You're right, hon. We should insist that this be promoted as a pay-per-view event like the pro fighters. Now that's great TV!"

Kate shrieked and attacked her father. "I'll wrestle *you*!" They laughed and grappled until both teetered and fell onto the brocade couch.

Nadia couldn't help smiling, but she wondered what was in store for this remarkable yet vulnerable young woman as Kate wound down, resting her head against Simon and curling up like a little girl.

Simon stroked Kate's forehead. "Don't worry. We'll prep you."

◆

Preparing for her televised debate with the Archbishop, Kate's priority was some serious brushing up on history. Yet Nadia insisted on taking Kate shopping.

"I can't believe you stood on the balcony next to the supreme pontiff in a T-shirt and jeans," the professor said, tempering the comment with a smile. "Now that you're famous, we're going to have to get you properly dressed."

Kate protested that it was her ideas that mattered, not the person conveying them, and especially not her clothes, but Nadia was having none of it.

"If you decide to take vows someday, you can disappear under your habit. But for now, you're going on television to be seen across the globe, and you will dress accordingly. This is Rome, Kate. If you can't find something to accentuate your natural beauty here . . ."

Kate looked to her parents for support, but her mother nodded. "Professor Jamira's right, dear. You really do need to present yourself better. Go."

The two women were accompanied by two of Steven's security guards, but the men kept a reasonable distance. Kate and Nadia were able to shop Rome in relative peace.

Kate's one condition was that she not be swathed in designer luxury; she was willing to dress up, but she wanted to retain her essential humility. Nadia agreed, and they avoided the high-end boutiques in favor of small shops on side streets.

Kate tried on piece after piece, but none seemed to feel right.

"You're sure I can't wear a T-shirt and jeans?" she groaned.

"Absolutely not. You're a grown-up now, and you have to start dressing like one. Who knows? Pick the right outfit and you might even get a date after this."

Kate blushed. "I haven't got time for dating."

"Have you ever tried to make time? I never saw you talking to anyone on campus. Well, there was that one guy the day the whole classroom erupted."

"Okay. What was his name? Jerry?"

"James," Nadia replied. "Did you two get along?"

"He didn't seem to take my ideas seriously," Kate replied.

"Nobody takes anyone's ideas seriously when they're flirting, Kate. It's part of the dance. You tease, you joke, you see if there's an attraction."

"I'm not interested in guys right now. I would rather stay focused."

"Well, there may come a time when your priorities change or at least expand. And you're going to want to have a nice outfit or two when it happens."

Kate noticed the shift from might-happen to will-happen but let it go. She'd found something that appealed to her. It was a deep-brown sheath that reminded her of a monk's robe but also flattered her body and complemented her hair. She modeled it for Nadia's approval.

"That's great! Now let's find you some shoes."

Chapter 44

Venice

Still unsure what to do with himself after receiving his university degree, DeBray Ayalaz had taken a clerk's job at the Casa Trovaso Hotel in Venice. It was good to stay in Europe while also keeping some distance between him and his family, who lived just outside of Barcelona.

Despite its tawdry interior and mediocre accommodations, the Casa Trovaso was a haven for DeBray because it was popular among students. Many were studying abroad for a semester, but more importantly to DeBray, many were seminary students. As the tenants came and went, DeBray engaged them with philosophical questions and offered advice for navigating the city. He also showed them the small watercolor paintings, mostly depictions of baby Jesus and Mother Mary, that he created at night.

"They are lovely, DeBray."

"You have a gift, DeBray."

"May I buy one for my room?"

The compliments lifted his otherwise low spirits. He never wanted to sell his art because, for him, each painting was a prayer. So he gave them away.

None of the young women passing through the hotel truly captivated him—he felt like he could see right through them. Still, he often wondered if he could forsake romantic love for the priest he desired to be if the right woman came along. But if he married, how could he avoid becoming the brute his father and grandfather were? Every day, he thought himself in circles and asked for advice from the seminarians who stopped at his counter.

"It's normal to be tempted," one student said. "If there is no temptation, there is no sacrifice."

Hendrik admitted he'd recently met a girl at his brother's wedding and couldn't concentrate on his studies or even pray for a week. She was always in his head. "But it was good because I had to reconsider my choices. Obviously, I chose God."

"No," DeBray protested. "You chose the Church. God is for everyone."

Hendrik smiled. "You'd make a good priest."

"Maybe."

On this night, though, DeBray was mesmerized by a televised debate between Archbishop Rolando Azevedo and a newly famous young lady wearing a simple but stylish brown outfit and minimal make-up, with her hair pinned up in barely contained waves.

Azevedo, whom DeBray knew was one of the Church's intellectual powerhouses, began with an oily smoothness. "First, Miss Murphy, I would be remiss if I didn't express my gratitude for having the tomb's contents go to the church. They will be utilized appropriately. However, after everything I have read and heard from others regarding your past, I feel compelled to ask: Are you a true Catholic?"

Kate responded, her voice laced with disbelief, "Wow! You come right out of the gate with sheer chauvinism. You would never dare pose such a disrespectful question if I were a man." She continued, her intensity growing, "You thank me for tripling the Church's worth, yet you question my faith?"

"Someone has to address it, Miss Murphy. Your past leaves much to be questioned."

Kate replied thoughtfully, her voice filled with conviction, "If this were a private conversation, I would not answer such an audacious question. Yet, for the public to understand my beliefs, I will respond. Yes, I am Catholic. To be more specific, I identify as a mystic, much like others you may have heard of, including Jesus and the apostles." She paused momentarily, her gaze steady as she added, "This includes the first apostle, Mary Magdalene, who holds a distinguished place among them—equal to, and in many respects even more influential than, the twelve male apostles. Later, the likes of Saint Teresa of Avila, Saint Francis, Meister Eckhart, Thomas Merton, Amma, and Gabby Bernstein, to name a few. Mysticism emphasizes achieving a direct connection with the Universe."

"I am familiar with mysticism, Miss Murphy. No need for a lecture," Azevedo interjected.

"As I mentioned earlier, Cardinal, my answer is for the viewers. May I finish?"

Azevedo nodded.

"Christian mysticism also aligns harmoniously with Kabbalah Judaism, Zen Buddhism, and Sufi Islam—home to two of my favorite poets, Rumi and Hafiz. It also shares common ground with Vedanta Hinduism and all traditions that guide us in connecting with the eternal love, peace, and joy that the Universe embodies." In that moment, her fervor brought the essence of her faith to life, weaving a rich tapestry of beliefs that resonated deeply. "Thank you, Cardinal, for allowing me to elaborate. Now, I have a question for you. Why do you think it is inherently wrong for a female to serve as a priest?"

Azevedo cleared his throat and sat up straight in his chair. "The late Pope Francis put an end to all of this when he said no to women's ordination and explained the Marian principle that the Church is a woman and spouse."

In response, Kate asserted passionately, "First, there is never an end to equal rights until they are fully realized. While Pope Francis contributed positively in many areas, his comments on the Marian principle ultimately reinforced harmful and outdated views of women's roles in the Church, aligning with the very structures of misogyny that we strive to dismantle." She continued, emphasizing her point, "By presenting women's dignity solely in relation to the Church—as mere reflections of its feminine aspect—he diminishes their status and autonomy. This echoes the limitations imposed by chauvinism, which confines women to traditional roles and which Jesus directly stated in Luke 10:42 were not a woman's highest calling. Instead, Jesus emphasized the importance of spiritual fulfillment for women and, consequently, their leadership."

Kate paused for effect before declaring, "A true theology of women should not confine them to supportive roles; rather, it must recognize them as equal participants in all aspects of church life, including leadership. Progress demands dismantling these restrictive concepts and celebrating women's unique contributions without the constraints of patriarchal glass ceilings. Only then can we create a genuinely inclusive Church where all voices are valued equally."

She concluded her powerful statement with conviction, "An authentic spousal relationship is one rooted in equality at every level, where both partners, regardless of gender, are empowered to lead."

Cardinal Azevedo stated firmly, "The Bible does not say a man is better than a woman, and I do not believe they are better or less, only different."

His young challenger tilted her head thoughtfully. "Different. Interesting. In what way, sir?"

"Well, obviously, there is a physical difference."

The young lady offered a light, conciliatory laugh, "Thank you for noticing. And . . .?"

With a smirk that suggested an air of superiority, he continued, "Emotionally, men are different from women."

"In what way?" Kate repeated.

"Women are generally much more emotional than men. It's a fact of life."

"Hmm. I think you're referring to emotional intelligence, and women often have more of it than men. But wouldn't that characteristic serve as a powerful asset in leadership? If women possess different skills, talents, and perspectives than men, wouldn't the Catholic Church benefit from including women in the priesthood?"

Azevedo stuttered, "That's—that's not what I'm talking about. Women make more emotional decisions. Men make more logical decisions."

Kate tilted her head once more. "So, you and I are saying the same thing differently. Just as men and women worldwide seek love and connection to the Universe—but sometimes approach these goals differently."

"Your Universe sounds distinct from my God. A female priest goes against God's design. God made Man in His image, and he created Eve to give Adam a companion—not a spiritual leader."

Kate shook her head, her tone assertive. "It seems that your concept of God is still that of an elderly man with flowing white hair, perched above us in the clouds, passing judgment. Did we not evolve beyond the lower-level consciousness of Zeus and the Greek pantheon a few thousand years ago? My Universe aligns with the God Jesus spoke of when he said in John 4:8, 'Anyone who does not love does not know God because God is love.' Jesus taught us that God embodies eternal life and love. Just because he occasionally used masculine pronouns to describe the indescribable doesn't imply that he envisioned a man in the sky. By defining God as love, as Jesus clearly did, that includes both males and females equally."

DeBray felt an exhilarating rush of clarity as he watched Kate radiate from the screen. "The Baptismal truth is that it is not about conforming to the world, but to Christ! Paul said in Galatians, 'there is neither male nor female, for you are all one in Christ Jesus.' Our real equality, the spiritual kind, is given at baptism. As the Bible says in Corinthians, we are all equally God's children, equally temples of the Holy Spirit. How can that fundamental truth not extend to any service God might call us to?"

After waiting for a response from Azevedo that never came, the young woman pivoted the conversation. "I value both logic and emotion. Let's discuss how the top ten percent of business leaders worldwide comprise men and women, all equally gifted in stamina, emotional maturity, intellect, and spirituality. Shall we debate a woman's true capacity for and rightful place in leadership, whether a CEO, president, or pontiff, or must we limit our conversation to the one endowment that allows you—but not me—to don priestly robes?"

"And what would that be?" Azevedo finally sputtered.

Kate Murphy, whose name was accompanied on screen with the tagline "Discovered King David's Tomb," replied coolly, "A penis."

DeBray's gasp was so loud that Hendrik, who had come in for the night, rushed over. "Are you all right, DeBray?"

"No!"

"What is it? Should I get help?"

DeBray was laughing too hard to answer. He watched Azevedo squirm in his chair and protest about disrespectful language, only to hear Miss Murphy reply, "Now, now, Archbishop. 'Penis' is only a word. Let's not get all emotional about it. The simple fact is that genitalia has absolutely nothing to do with spirituality."

"Oh. It's the treasure-hunting heretic," Hendrik said after coming around the counter to see what had amused DeBray.

He sat up straight to turn his attention to Hendrik. "Why do you call her a heretic?"

"The girl who would be queen—or pope! More like a has-been, soon enough."

"Dude. She's just arguing that women should be ordained as priests."

"And then what?"

"Uh—world peace?"

Hendrik chuckled. "But if they ordain women, what's next? Priests being allowed to marry?"

For the second time tonight, DeBray had a realization that swept through his whole body. "I'm all for that."

"But—"

"But what, Hendrik? You could date that woman you met at your brother's wedding. She could have your children."

Hendrik shrugged, looking distinctly uncomfortable. "I don't know, DeBray. It's so foreign to me. Suddenly, I can have the thing that I've had to completely resist all these years?"

"What years? You've just started seminary."

"Yeah, but it's hard to throw away the tradition. The calling. The—"

"Unnecessary need to abstain from sex?"

"Conjugal marriage."

"Love that word."

"Conjugal?" asked Hendrik.

"No, marriage. I mean, really, why are you a better priest for not knowing what it is like to be a marriage partner and love a woman and maybe even have children of your own? You could be a Father to your parish *and* a father to your children."

"DeBray, you are talking about changing serious tradition. Anyway, some priests had girlfriends and—you know—before they joined the priesthood."

"Really? Can you tell me who they are?"

"DeBray!"

"I am being serious. I need to talk to them. I need to understand how they could give that up."

Hendrik shook his head and waved off more questions from DeBray.

"But, Hendrik, can't you be holy and in love?"

"Only in a pop song."

DeBray pointed to the television. "But listen to her. She's kicking his butt. The archbishop is no match."

"Oh, heavens, no. Don't tell me you've fallen for a girl on TV!"

A spark was igniting in DeBray's mind. "I want both, Hendrik. Love and sanctity. That's all I know."

"DeBray, the way you dress, look, and paint, you will have plenty of opportunity for romance. But you have to choose one or the other and be happy with your choice."

His chest tightening, DeBray looked at the floor as a voice inside himself scolded, *You'd end up hurting her anyway. Just go and be a priest already.*

Chapter 45

Venice

Kate enjoyed the heat of the television studio lights on her skin. She could feel it all the way into her bones. It reminded her of Jerusalem, and it helped her focus in a way that she hadn't expected.

"But how do you intend to hold the Vatican to any kind of response or deadline?" the female news anchor asked.

Kate smiled with all the gentleness she could muster. "It's not me who is making demands. It's Catholics around the world. It is this epoch, this time of heightened consciousness that calls for change in canon law."

"Then how realistic is it to expect that your effort, and the effort of so many others, can influence a revision of centuries-old thought?"

Kate countered, "Was Christ's mission realistic?"

Off camera, Nadia bounced her head and elbowed Simon, who contained the urge to applaud. Rebecca put her fist in the air as she always loved when her daughter spoke about Jesus.

Predictably, the interviewer asked, "So, you compare yourself to Christ?"

"We should all compare ourselves to Christ, even if we always come up short. No one might ever match Him, but He still remains our model, our guide for striving to do better. The Catholic Church can do better."

"So you'll just wait."

"Wait?"

"If you have no expectations of Vatican officials . . ."

"Respect is the expectation," insisted Kate.

"Fine. But here in Venezia, we know that the Vatican would lose a foot race with a glacier. Why bother imploring Pope Nelson to do the right thing without some sort of—I'm grasping here—pressure?"

For the first time, Kate paused, appearing stumped. As the silence grew longer, she glanced off-camera at her professor. Then a smile flickered across her face. Nadia sat up straighter.

Kate returned her focus to the woman who sat across from her. "Oh, yes, I thought you knew."

Nadia tensed.

The interviewer asked, "Knew what?"

"If the Vatican does not respond soon by agreeing to convene the College of Cardinals to consider our request, women and all the friends of the women of the world are invited to join me in St. Peter's Square to let Pope Nelson know exactly how we feel."

In the control room, the program director knew breaking news when he heard it. He shouted orders, and his technicians began to attack their keyboards.

"Stream it across the screen: 'Women to gather at St. Peter's Square to challenge Pope Nelson'!"

In the studio, the interviewer's earpiece burned with instructions. She leaned toward Kate and went for the kill. "You're saying, unequivocally, that you'll challenge the pope in Rome—but when?"

"Not me."

"Kate, you just said—"

"Not me. Not alone. I'm inviting women and friends of women who want change to gather in St Peter's Square," Kate stammered for an instant, then accelerated, "in one month, to denounce the inability of the establishment to understand that none of us can be free until women have the same rights as men. To love another means to recognize oneself in another. It is time the male hierarchy of the Church proved their love for women, and this means recognizing women as equals. Specifically, spiritual equals."

"By what authority are you organizing a global assault on the Vatican?"

"The word 'assault' is inappropriate, as this will be a peaceful protest. The blue armband is our authority. Everyone who attends will be given an armband. Bring your daughters, your sisters, your grandmothers, brothers, and husbands. Bring anyone and everyone who believes women are the foundation and the future of the Catholic faith!"

Chapter 46

Countryside near Lumphat

The day was unbearably hot and thick with humidity. Father Justin Kelly was thankful for the shade of his parish office, blessedly sheltered and cooled by the grass roof that swished in the strong breeze. He had slept poorly the night before and woken early to the sound of the river, the high-pitched tweets of the kingfishers. He rolled from his bed where Ava had been only hours before, her warm skin on his. She'd left his raised hut sometime in the night, an expert at quiet steps down the wooden planks and along the dirt paths.

Now, Father Kelly sat in the mission at the desk one of his parishioners had fashioned for him from local rosewood, going over his sermon for Sunday. He enjoyed these quiet moments alone, happy for a chance to plan and ponder. But the silence was broken when he heard footsteps, and a stocky, gray-haired man appeared in the doorway.

"Sorry to intrude—and so early, Father—but may I beg a word? I'm here to offer help. I'd like to volunteer."

Father Kelly was shocked and instantly suspicious. Europeans did not often traipse through the Cambodian countryside, stumble onto a Catholic outpost, and express a wish to volunteer. He wondered if this was a ruse—a man sent to spy or call him out.

"What is your name?" Father Kelly asked him.

"Wicus."

"Well, friend, how long do you plan to stay?"

"How long will you have me?"

Father Kelly's stomach turned. "Are you a tourist?"

"I'm a seeker, Father."

"Raised Catholic?"

"Born Catholic."

The back-and-forth went on for some time, giving Father Kelly little information but no real reason to deny the man shelter.

Although it had been well over a year since Kate's visit, he had kept her admonition in mind about being caught by the Vatican and punished. So he and Ava were careful in public, taking nothing for granted. This meant not even holding hands on their evening walks. Their devotion was private and had to remain so unless the Church changed its stance.

But as time went on, Wicus seemed to prove his devotion, working hard, eagerly taking on any chore, capable of patiently assisting church members in their quest to become devout Catholics. It was the parish's practice not to inquire about the past of a person whose servant's heart was strong enough to venture this far into the wilderness. Who would work so hard to do harm? The Vatican might, Father Kelly thought, but he did not press Wicus for more detail. Instead, Father Kelly watched him closely, finding him seemingly innocent of malicious intent.

Several weeks after the seeker's arrival, Father Kelly overheard him counseling a mother who wanted to raise her children in the Church. Not only did the man have a detailed understanding of the baptismal ritual but his manner of speech suggested seminary training.

When Ava appeared, Father Kelly quickly moved her into another room.

"Is something wrong?"

"No, no. I was just thinking. I've been wanting to, I don't know—improve the children's playroom. When Wicus has finished his meeting, would you mind asking him to help you?"

"Help with . . .?" She looked around at the bare space.

"The benches—if they were rearranged. Let's go back to having them in a circle."

"But last week you asked for—"

"Ava. Darling. Keep Wicus occupied. I'll explain later."

"Something is wrong."

"It's just me. I have to . . . I'll be back soon. I promise."

Father Kelly exited the church and moved across the grounds to a smaller structure that had been built for guests. He entered, knowing the rooms would be empty. He did not like what he was about to do. He bowed his head, crossed himself, requested forgiveness, and walked through the doorway.

The room was barely large enough for a bed, chair, and small shelving unit. The single piece of luggage Wicus had brought was in the corner. Father Kelly knew he had no right to open it.

Kneeling, he laid the suitcase flat on the floor and flipped open the latches. Nervous, he asked forgiveness one more time before lifting the top. Inside, he found what looked like a black leather wallet. He opened it and felt his heart implode. There it was, staring at him: proof that his worst fear had come true.

"I guess you are a seeker, too, Father."

Father Kelly started and fell back against the wall. He looked up to find Wicus staring down at him. "Who are you?"

"Don't you already know, Justin?"

"You lied about your name!"

"No. Wicus is my middle name. Henryk Wicus Lemski."

Father Kelly stared at the ID card in its leather sleeve. It was an improvement over the bishop's letter of introduction that priests used to carry when traveling. The identification proved the holder was in good standing with the Church and entitled to celebrate the sacraments.

"Why didn't you tell me you are a priest?"

"Because I am not."

"Don't lie to me! This is proof that you are."

Lemski was unperturbed when he reached for the ID. "May I?" He took the document, perused it with a sigh, and then pointed to a spot on the card and held it close to the younger man's face. "Please note the date, Father."

Father Kelly flushed. "Expired?"

"Yes. I'm a former priest."

"Then why carry the ID?"

When Lemski answered, his words were carefully chosen. "It is still who I am. I can't separate myself from the mission of Christ. Call me Father Lemski or call me—actually, I've been called many names in recent years. But why worry about it now? If you were still in Rome, wouldn't you welcome the help of another member of the clergy?"

Father Kelly still felt vulnerable. How did Lemski know his résumé? What did he know about the sudden departure from Basilica di Santa Maria in Trastevere?

"You don't need to answer, Father Kelly. I have not come here to hurt you."

"Then why are you here?"

"To beg your forgiveness."

"For what? I don't even know you. Don't play with me, Wicus!"

The older man nodded. "I understand your anger. I'll explain every-thing. But perhaps Ava should also hear what I have to say." Lemski held out his hand to help Father Kelly to his feet.

Father Kelly hesitated.

"She is lovely, Father. A good soul. Hold on to her."

Dumbfounded again, the priest watched as Lemski dropped the ID into the suitcase and paused for a moment with head bowed and eyes closed. After he lowered the lid with his foot, he turned toward the door.

"Ready?"

Chapter 47

Rome

It was not unusual to see two influential members of the Church strolling the winding paths of Giardini Vaticani. Created during the Renaissance and Baroque eras, the Gardens of the Vatican were an oasis of flora adorned with fountains and statues that, no doubt, had overheard many a secret exchange through the ages. Archbishop Rolando Azevedo and Cardinal Daniel Parker felt comfortable conversing candidly in their lush surroundings.

"Blue armbands," Parker scoffed. "She is not even twenty years old. Could we be overreacting?"

"Yes, of course we are. We have no choice. That's why I immediately scheduled a flight. You remember what happened with Pope Francis. All the swelling of love, emotion, and demand for change. Then, Pope Leo and his 'building bridges with dialogue.'"

"A couple of hot-air balloons that didn't reach their full flight."

"Not without help," Azevedo stated, with a definite note of implication.

Parker flushed as the archbishop eyed him. He did not appreciate the tone. Francis and Leo were gone. Good riddance. Parker had only done what he was told back then, and he had done it on behalf of men like Azevedo. Yet occasionally, they seemed to forget his loyal diligence.

The archbishop sat on a marble bench, smiling as though he were admiring the emerald surroundings. "More must be done now, Cardinal. But what? You might ask, and I ask the same question. More, certainly, but quietly. We cannot unwittingly set off a backlash or unexpected consequences."

"She won't win."

"Maybe not this year. But we must always be ready and look down the road. We must now know what impact these rumblings might have on a man from Rio who wishes to be pope."

Parker could not suppress a snicker. "Pope Nelson has barely etched his name in the history books, Rolando. Isn't it a bit early to be throwing your hat into the ring?"

"He's a young man, relatively. I'll have to wait my turn. But my time will come if I have properly tilled the soil. Now, what is this new wrinkle you fear so?"

The cardinal sat. His career had taken so many unexpected turns that he sometimes wished he could simply retire to a vineyard somewhere and sip rare vintages as the world went to rot. He was either in a position of knowing too much or much too little.

"To begin, Steven Craft . . ."

"Friend or foe?"

"Shrewd is the best way to describe him. He's not to be dismissed or categorized. He behaves, at times, like my ally and at other times . . ." Parker shrugged.

"Yes, all right, go on."

"Years ago, we employed a hoodlum, an idiot actually, who killed a man and made things very tense for us. We escorted him out of the country, only to see him emerge in recent weeks as a soldier in the Evangelical movement."

"The fellow who caused so much distress in Bethlehem?"

Parker nodded. "He was incarcerated and placed under heavy guard in Israel."

"So he is under control."

"He's dead."

The archbishop raised an eyebrow. "Natural causes?"

"You might say."

"Meaning?"

"It is natural to die after a toxic pharmaceutical cocktail enters your bloodstream." Azevedo clearly had no tears to shed for an enemy soldier, and Parker continued his report. "He had much to say about our adversaries in Brazil. Steven had begun an interrogation strategy that might have exposed Edhir Souza and his organization."

"So we know who served the cocktail."

"They may offer another round soon." The archbishop raised an eyebrow, and Parker explained, "The girl. She may be next."

"But why? She's playing into their hands. Our older conservative flock would run to Evangelists if we modernize and let women become priests."

"I can't say what their strategy is. I find it odd that they would make such a threat known."

Azevedo stood and paced, considering the ramifications of an assassination. Popularity came and went. Veneration was another matter. Its tentacles might stretch for decades. He turned on Parker.

"We cannot let her or anybody else in this *cause célèbre* become a martyr. We have to stop Edhir."

"Tell me how."

"Find a way, Cardinal! Reach out to her."

"I can't do that."

"You'll do it if I tell you to do it."

"What am I supposed to do, Rolando—take a bullet for her? Come to your senses. There's only so much we can control around here."

The archbishop shook his head in disgust. "We have to keep her alive. Let her fail on the great stage. Let her slink away bloodied and wounded. But we will not allow her to become a modern-day Joan of Arc!"

Parker felt weary and helpless. As he stood, his cell phone chimed. He quieted it and continued to speak, but it immediately rang again twice while Azevedo continued to insist that Parker had to work with Kate Murphy to protect her. When a fourth call came in, both men cursed.

"Answer the stupid thing, Parker!"

The cardinal pulled the phone from his cassock and barked, "What?"

The voice at the other end was apologetic. "Have I caught you at a bad time, Cardinal?"

"Who is this?"

"You're busy. I'll come to the point."

As he listened, Parker's eyes widened with disbelief. He quickly walked away from the archbishop for privacy, occasionally barking threats that he would hang up—and yet he did not. *Why is this happening?* he thought. *Why now?*

Oblivious to his location, he stopped when he came to a round marble foundation. His jaw tensed as he lowered his voice to a harsh hiss. "I won't meet with you."

He turned and saw Azevedo peering at him with narrowed eyes.

"But you will," the caller said.

"You don't frighten me."

"Then you have no reason to ignore my request."

Parker turned his back to the archbishop, gazed upward, and discovered that he was standing before a bronze sculpture of Saint Michael the Archangel. He froze as a chill crept up his spine. He recalled seeing it for the first time in his youth. It was the day the statue was blessed by the late Pope Francis. The pontiff had followed a tradition of asking the patron saint to defend Vatican City against poverty, opportunism—and corruption.

The caller pushed on. "There is ample proof. But you must know that already."

"Your so-called evidence can disappear. Digital files can be destroyed."

"Only if you know where to find them, Cardinal."

Parker tottered and was forced to sit at St. Michael's feet. "All right, all right. Tell me where, and when."

"Now."

◆

STEVEN CRAFT UNLEASHED his frustration with Kate, scolding the young woman for jeopardizing his agency's efforts to keep her secure. She, her parents, and Nadia had been summoned to the Vatican, and they sat lined up on a low couch beneath a towering portrait of the pope like students in the principal's office.

"When will you stop and think about the ramifications of your statements? When will you realize you risk more than your own life? You've endangered anyone who is now making plans to join your party in St. Peter's Square. You've endangered Pope Nelson and Vatican City!"

He broke down the intelligence that had been gathered in the wake of the death threat scrawled on the photo in Fernando's cell. He pointed out that his search for the origins of the image demanded scrutiny of Vatican staff, a delicate operation. "You are an arrogant child! I should lock you up for your own good and the good of everyone around you!" he shouted.

No one dared respond as Steven fumed. Kate sat on a sofa between her parents, apologetic and quiet. She didn't look up or challenge Steven.

Rebecca prompted her daughter. "Do you have anything to say, honey?"

Kate nodded and looked at Steven. "Sacrifice."

The others stared at the young woman, waiting for her to say more. Finally, she did.

"I apologize, Steven. All that you say is true. I'm arrogant, egotistical, and foolish. I may be harmed by my own actions and words, and a lot of other people may be harmed as well."

The tension in the room eased. Steven sat on the edge of a desk as his face softened. But the calm didn't last long.

"But I won't back down."

"Katie!" Rebecca begged.

"Mom, you can't stop a runaway train by standing in its path. Something larger than us is moving now. Something we never could have imagined only a few weeks or months ago. If I die for my beliefs, that doesn't really matter. Millions of others will take up the cause. They already have. The inquiries and letters to the Vatican. The news coverage. Social media. The world is burning with this. What difference does it make if one life is sacrificed?"

"We don't want to lose you, love," Simon said. "You can't expect us to stand by and watch . . ."

Kate looked at her father. Even he was against this. "Don't stand by. Go home. I don't want to lose you either, Dad. But I also can't let this go."

Nadia looked to Steven, who brushed off Kate's pronouncement.

"Vatican security won't allow it. *Carabinieri* will shut down the square. Rome will come to a standstill if hundreds of thousands enter the city expecting to congregate for this. You will cause more harm, and therefore, you will fail."

Cardinal Dumas had entered and was waiting patiently.

"Didn't mean to ignore you, Cardinal," Steven said.

Kate and her entourage turned to see the priest nod and tap his wristwatch. "Forgive my interruption, Mr. Craft, but your meeting with the pontiff started ten minutes ago. Shall we reschedule?"

Kate smiled. "You should go."

"Not until you respond to what I've just said, young lady."

Kate closed her eyes and took a deep breath; a forceful energy swept through her body. She spoke in a heavy voice. "Sanctify the Lord God in your hearts, and always be ready to give an answer to every man that asks you a reason for the hope that is in you."

"Ah, how lovely to hear our youth quote the Bible," Cardinal Dumas interrupted. "However, darling, our beloved St. Peter actually ends that line by saying, 'with modesty and fear.'"

The room fell silent as Kate and the cardinal interrogated each other with their eyes until Rebecca placed her hand gently on Kate's arm.

"Don't worry, Mom. It took Edison over ten thousand attempts to create the light bulb. No great success was ever achieved without failure."

Nadia had been jittery during this whole confrontation, her crossed leg swinging forward and back. Suddenly, she rose from her chair and spoke calmly, but with an edge: "If mayhem and bullets or poison or bombs do not scare you, Kate, there is another matter that might," she began. With her hand on her forehead and the timing of a stand-up comic, Nadia moaned, "Where are we going to get all the blue armbands?"

Chapter 48

Rome

From the shadows of a cafe near Piazza Santa Maria, Henryk Lemski sipped his frothed cappuccino and nibbled at the pastry he had ordered more for show than appetite. He was a tourist in colorful, flowing clothes and a floppy, broad-brimmed hat, enjoying the historic site of Basilica di Santa Maria in Trastevere.

His early arrival gave him ample time to enjoy the view of the square, check the rear exit through the kitchen where he might make a quick departure, and reminisce. Mostly, he thought of Stefan. But he also imagined what he must have looked like sprinting from the church following the little girl's baptismal catastrophe.

He considered the havoc his actions had wreaked upon the Murphy family and Father Kelly. In Cambodia, Lemski had confessed his involvement in the strategy designed to discredit the child, her parents, and a young priest whose only crimes had been kindness and intellectual curiosity.

"I am responsible, in large part, for your reassignment far from Rome," he had told Father Kelly. Father Kelly had remained mystified, unable to make the connection. Lemski was forced to offer many painful details of his overzealous management of his secret Vatican department. He also found himself telling Father Kelly and Ava about his attraction to the young artist, fiscal improprieties, and the affair that eventually was used to oust him from his position and the priesthood.

"Why did you wait so long to tell me all this?" Father Kelly had finally demanded.

"I lacked the courage."

This was partially true. When he had arrived at the rural parish, he could not bring himself to confess. He took on chores and worked tirelessly with the hope that penance alone would be enough.

But even before this pilgrimage, other obstacles had stopped him from facing his sins. He had been consumed by his relationship with Stefan, which had eventually succumbed to his inability to transcend his strict Catholic upbringing.

"Where is the young man now?" Ava had asked.

"In high-level security and no doubt in the arms of another man. I had no experience with love of this kind. I was jealous and then demanding. Strict and yet helpless. Losing my position at the Vatican was crushing. Losing Stefan was . . . God's punishment, and much deserved."

Father Kelly interrupted. "God does not punish, Henryk. Love is not a sin."

They debated many strictures and challenged one another's viewpoints and choices. At times, the former priest from Gdańsk felt that he was being attacked, and rightly so. Strangely, he also felt embraced, which made him appreciate Father Kelly and realize why he had been such a bright prospect so many years ago in Rome.

Then Lemski made a mistake. He offered to help the couple in any way that he could.

Father Kelly erupted. "No! We don't need your help."

Ava protested. "You're being rude, Justin."

"The damage has been done. I can't be reinstated."

"He's just bared his soul," Ava said.

"Then let him help Kate. She's taken on too much. I'm afraid for her. Do you still know people in Rome, Henryk?"

"More importantly, I know *about* people in Rome. Including your former mentor."

"Bishop Parker?"

"Cardinal Parker. He's a member of an inner circle that uses bureaucracy—and other methods—to stalemate progress."

"You know how to reach him?"

Lemski nodded. "And others."

Kelly paused, deep in thought. "Kate and the blue-armband movement are doing Christ's work. Make their goals happen, and you owe me nothing."

"And if I don't succeed?"

Ava looked at her companion with pleading eyes.

"If your effort is genuine, you will earn my forgiveness."

◆

CARDINAL PARKER DID not like waiting. He felt vulnerable sitting on a bench in the piazza, not knowing if he would even recognize his adversary. Then he heard the voice.

"Is this seat taken?"

Parker turned to see Henryk Lemski, disguised as a tourist, at the opposite end of the bench. Both men pretended not to know each other. Strangers chatting on a sunny afternoon.

"You won't win, you know," Parker said.

"That's exactly what they said to the first Christians," Lemski replied as he slid a piece of paper across the bench. "I'm sure you're familiar with these names. Members of the hierarchy who were sympathetic to your anti-Francis campaign. Vatican journalists. Security personnel."

"No one will believe you."

"They won't have to. The documents I possess will tell the tale."

"Why are you doing this?" Parker demanded.

"One bad turn deserves another, Cardinal. Too many people have been hurt and continue to nurse serious wounds. For what? Doctrine? Dogma?"

"The little girl is going to save us all from oblivion, is that it?" the Cardinal sneered.

"You put far too much emphasis on her. There are millions of people who have awakened to new possibilities of faith. That's what frightens you. That someone else will be in control. Someone with ideas that differ from your own. This is why Francis was such a threat, was it not?"

"He was a poseur for change. Better that he fade away so real leadership could guide the Vatican. You want me to believe that you shed one tear for that man?" Parker scowled. "I can't help you. Ruin me, if you must. But then what, Henryk?"

"Ruining you is not the point. Though I suggest you not be so blithe about your downfall. You won't like it, Cardinal."

"I'm sure you could educate me."

"I'll send you my memoirs. Now, back to business." Lemski carefully laid out the plan, his expectations, and the manner in which Parker might proceed. As he did so, he dropped names with a suggestiveness that could not be misinterpreted. Finally, the former priest offered his final directive.

"You will advise Pope Nelson to convene the College of Cardinals to consider this historic change in canon law. But do not fear sounding like a fool on the hill. By then, many others will also be showing signs of capitulation. There will be whispers and news stories provided by Vatican observers and blogs. You'll only feel alone if you insist on blocking what by then will be inevitable. In that case, you will be destroyed. Catholics everywhere will know you for who and what you truly are—a conspirator."

"Are you out of your mind? Have you thought this through, the calamity that the ordination of women would thrust upon the Church?"

"You'd rather tear down the Church than allow it to grow, and you think *I'm* mad?"

Lemski stood, ignoring Parker's protestations, and let his eyes sweep the piazza. From the collar of his shirt, he drew a silk cord that held a silver cross and a small flash drive. He detached the device and tossed it to Parker.

"I made you a copy. Did you really think I'd let you vultures feed on me without taking a few souvenirs of my precious time here?"

Parker was outraged. "You're an incompetent. You bungled the whole thing. Carlitos, the Murphy family. If not for my intervention—"

"It won't take much effort to send copies to members of the press and the pope himself. So you don't have much time to get started. Be glad I've given you a way to get out in front of this."

Parker tried to interrupt, but Lemski continued.

"Don't try to reach me. Don't worry. I'll be watching. *Ciao.*"

◆

As he disappeared from the square, Lemski removed his hat and gaudy shirt and handed them to a beggar. The modest black shirt underneath matched well with his trousers and the hat he purchased down the street. He felt a sense of possibility and hope—something he had lacked for so long now. He knew again the joy of serving a God of love rather than fear. As he turned down another cobbled path, he left his priesthood behind. The fallen man of God looked like a debonair native of Rome.

Chapter 49

Barcelona

DeBray had flown home to surprise his parents and tell them his news. He arrived in the afternoon, flush with hopeful anticipation. But upon entering the kitchen, he quickly knew something was wrong. He saw a half-empty bottle of vodka on the counter and could hear whimpering coming from the living room. There, her found his mother curled in a ball on the floor, crying, and his dad standing over her with a clenched fist.

"Dad!" he yelled, heat rising quickly to the top of his head. His poor mother, subject to the evil that ran in his father's veins. "That is *it*!" DeBray sprinted across the room and struck his father in the face with full force, his hand instantly on fire. His father flew against the wall and crumpled to the ground.

"DeBray! No!" his mother yelled. Blood dripped from her nose onto the carpet, and one eye was already swelling, red, and quickly turning blue. He wondered at her willingness to stay. At women's willingness to remain subject to a man's authority when that authority was so clearly abused. When the one in power had only his own interests at heart and used his power to rule over another human rather than lead with integrity. He thought of the Church that he loved so well; of God, who he did not believe meant for women to suffer as they did; and he felt pity and horror for his mother, lying on the rug, still defending the man who'd caused such pain. He wanted to change the system, and that change started here, in his own home, with his own dysfunctional family.

Bleeding from his nose and mouth, the disheveled alcohol addict glared up at DeBray. "You call yourself a man of God?"

"No, Dad, right now, I call myself *done* dealing with *you*." DeBray stumbled toward him, his body shaking now from the trauma of the moment. "I am going to *learn* how to be a man of God." DeBray pulled his seminary-school acceptance letter from his pocket, threw it at his father, the paper falling open on his chest, and stormed out the door.

◆

VENICE

BACK IN VENICE, Hendrik pointed at the gold school emblem now secured on DeBray's left lapel. "You've made the right decision. I believe you will make a magnificent priest."

DeBray shrugged his shoulders and scrutinized the other seminary students in the café. "Or a very good heretic. I'm going to Rome this weekend."

Hendrik's smile disappeared.

"And what do you plan to do there?"

"Haven't you heard? The Vatican is in Rome."

"Very funny."

"Don't worry. I have not planned a rendezvous with a beautiful woman."

"Good. You've made your choice, my friend. No affairs."

"But activism is okay, right?"

Hendrik turned pink.

"DeBray, please, no. You will ruin your career."

"Not if she wins."

"Seriously, DeBray!"

"Don't worry, Hendrik, I'll put in a good word for you."

Kate Murphy had inspired DeBray to embrace a church that was on the verge of historic change. Her intellectual vigor and insight drew him to respond to the call to protest at the Vatican. He prayed that he could expect the same vision from his current pope.

The outcry against Kate troubled him. He couldn't predict what the pontiff or the College of Cardinals might do, but he chose to begin seminary while also advocating for progress.

As Hendrik continued to lobby for conformity, DeBray pretended to listen, even though he had already made up his mind. *Make a difference or make my way to the grave*, he thought.

◆

TO VENICE

HEADED TO VENICE for another TV interview, Kate and Nadia spent the train ride calling their most avid supporters. The countryside rushed by outside the wide windows as they both chattered into their phones and checked off their long lists.

At one point, Kate stopped and peered out at the passing fields and trees, wishing she could stop for a moment to enjoy the peaceful surroundings before descending once again into a bustling city and so much attention pointed her way. But the movement she had begun was bigger than her; people wanted to participate in whatever way they could. Many didn't have a clue as to how they might help. Father Maric and Sister Deborah were the first to offer hope.

"Members of our church have already made twenty blue armbands." The priest also reported that he and his favorite nun were back at their church and feeling much better. "I know it is only a drop in the ocean. But we've made twenty, and we'll make more."

"Thank you, Father, but can't we just order them online?"

"Yes, of course, my dear, but more to the point, we need to make this a worldwide affair, not just to have enough armbands, but to give Catholics who can't go to Rome with you a way to be involved. Let's get word out in every way we can. Be sure to mention you need help in all of your interviews."

"Will do, Father. I love your enthusiasm for this. You are the best."

"I'm taking a page from your playbook, my dear. Also, you'll need a place in Rome where all the armbands can be sent. Let me give you some names to jot down. They may have temporary spaces you can use, as well as a mailing address."

When the priest had signed off, Kate shared her glee with Nadia.

"Ask and thou shall receive, Professor!"

"What do you mean?"

"Father Maric and Sister Deborah are going to rally everyone to make homemade armbands."

"It's not enough."

"Part the sea. Hold that thought."

Chapter 50

Venice

The peal of Kate's alarm clock startled her at 6:30 a.m. Momentarily forgetting that she was in a new town, she lay in bed and was surprised by a song floating through her window.

'O sole mio sta nfronte a te!

'O sole o sole mio

Sta nfronte a te, sta nfronte a te.

With a blanket wrapped around her, she opened the doors of her balcony and took a peek outside. The sun was rising over the buildings across the Grand Canal, and a singing gondolier was slowly rowing by. The light shone on the small waves of the canal as they slapped gently against the buildings.

She took a deep breath, and contentment permeated her for the first time in months. She listened until both boat and song faded away as the boat floated on. There was a wet chill in the air, so she closed the doors. Deciding not to wake Nadia, she dressed for a morning stroll. Nadia had agreed to let her explore the city as long as the security guard assigned to her could follow along. He stood right outside the building, waiting for her to emerge.

She opted for old baggy jeans, a hoodie, and tennis shoes. As she exited her room she stuffed her hair under a baseball cap and turned the corner to the wide marble staircase.

"Santa Maria!" she cried. The entire bottom floor was covered in a foot of water.

She had heard that Venice was sinking and had seen the water levels high, but never like this. As she made her way to the bottom two stairs where the water line began, she looked out across the lobby and tried to figure out how to deal with the situation.

The clerk was reading a book and looked up. He disappeared behind the desk and reappeared with a pair of galoshes.

"*Avrete bisogno di questi oggi*—you will need these today," he said in broken Italian that sounded more like Spanish, which Kate picked up on.

"*Muchas gracias, señor*," Kate replied then began laughing as she watched him slosh through the water.

"Am I amusing you?"

"Yes, you are." Kate noticed that he was dressed incredibly well, all the way down to his designer galoshes.

Wow, he is handsome, Kate mused as he came into her full view. Suddenly, his left boot—made more for fashion than for serious use— tore at the ankle. As water rushed inside, the weight of it made him stumble. He tried to brace himself with his other leg, but it was too late, and he fell forward, stumbling into the water with a strangled cry.

Frigid water splashed Kate from waist to toe. She shrieked as she held her hands out in a fruitless attempt to block the splash.

He rolled back onto his feet and bounced up with her boots in his hands. "I'm so sorry." He tucked both boots under his left arm and put his right hand out. "I'm DeBray."

Kate shook the water from her hand, then held it out and looked down at him. "Kate."

"Kate? Kate!" The voice was high and excited.

She smiled. "DeBray. Do I know you?" She wasn't used to people recognizing her.

DeBray grinned. "Me? No. But, you're famous—hold on. I'll get you a towel."

As he trudged back through the water, Kate asked, "You are from Spain, yes? Let me guess, Madrid?"

"Wow, so close. Barcelona. Is my accent really that thick?" He reached behind the desk again and pulled out large towels for Kate and himself.

"You have all kinds of goodies behind that desk, don't you?"

"*Sí.* We have these for the days with the high tides. Venice was due for an extremely high tide any day. They say that a person better be a strong swimmer or know someone with a boat on days like today."

"The twelfth of never would be nice for the next one," Kate grumbled as she attempted to dry herself. "How do people get around town and go to work when it is like this? And how long does the high tide last?"

"About three hours. Most people stay home until the water recedes. But since I went through all the trouble of getting you wet, you might as well go enjoy the morning. It's actually kind of fun. How often do you get to walk around a city that is under water when the sky is bright, and it hasn't rained a drop?"

"That's a good point. It is a perfect day for soaking others!" Kate reached down to the water and splashed DeBray.

"*¡Ay caramba! ¡Es frío!*"

"Uh, yeah it's cold—you didn't notice that when you were rolling around in it a minute ago?"

"No, I guess I was more worried about you and your boots."

"So chivalrous of you, kind sir," Kate said in a mock English accent, then tugged at the galoshes. "So, how long have you worked here?"

"Not long, only a few months." DeBray slapped his forehead. "I can't believe you are here at my hotel."

She pointed at the school pin on his lapel. "Are you also going to seminary?"

DeBray gazed down at the pin and touched it. "Yeah, I just started. What about you—why are you here in Venice?"

Just then, the security guard came in the front door of the building, his own boots sloshing through the calf-high water. "Miss Murphy, you all right in here?"

"Yes, Benito, I'm fine. I'll be out in a minute."

He nodded and stepped back outside, but not before eyeing DeBray for a full five seconds with a serious stare.

"Whoa," DeBray said, his eyes wide. "Who's Benito?"

"He's security. I'm apparently a *giant threat to humanity*, and them to me," Kate said, waving her hands around dramatically. "I'm here for an interview."

◆

"AH, RIGHT, I saw your debate with the archbishop," he said. "You were amazing."

Kate blushed, they met each other's eyes, and they both felt the electricity that ran between them.

"It is really nice to have you in my hotel, *Miss Murphy*."

"Miss Murphy? So formal. Okay, what's your last name?"

"Ayalaz."

"It is very nice to be in your hotel Señor Ayalaz." She curtseyed.

DeBray had never been affected by a girl this way before. His heart was beating fast and his knees felt weak. He worked to maintain his composure.

Ask her out, you fool! But you can't, remember—he touched the pin—*you have already made your choice.* "Uhh—I owe you a cup of coffee for getting you wet. Will you do me the honor of accompanying me? My shift is almost over, and the place around the corner makes an excellent cappuccino."

Kate replied again in the English accent, "Thank you so much, Señor Ayalaz. That would be lovely."

"Allow me!" cried DeBray. Kate gasped as he swept her up in his arms and began carrying her through the flooded lobby. "You should really think about dropping . . ." He let go of her for a split second. Kate let out a yelp. As he caught her and lifted her again, he continued, "That awful English accent."

◆

AFTER COFFEE, KATE and DeBray spent the day touring Venice, with Benito a respectable distance behind. DeBray knew all of the ins and outs of the labyrinthine city—the best *sotoporteghi* to explore, the hidden cafés, and the most worthwhile tourist stops. He soon became used to Benito's presence and let him do his job while they enjoyed the glorious day.

They strolled through churches, opera houses, and art museums. Kate found an old silliness returning to her that she hadn't felt since she was a child—the play and enjoyment of the moment that could shut everything else out. Everything seemed to flow with natural ease.

"Thank you for showing me so much of the beauty of Venice," Kate said.

"My pleasure. It is rare that I meet someone who is not an artist but is so knowledgeable about art. You said your dad taught you?"

"Yes, for big parts of my childhood, we were in the ancient section of Rome, and he would tell me about each piece on a daily basis, even if I pretended not to care. I have heard fourteen different stories about one bridge. Come to think of it, I am still not sure what the actual history of that bridge is!"

"Ha! I can hardly imagine how incredible it would have been to have an art history professor for a father."

"Yes, he is incredible," Kate mused. "But what about you—what got you interested in art?"

"Well, I'm not just a hotel clerk and a seminary student. My real passion is painting. Back home, they call me *el pintor de Dios*—the painter of God."

"May I see some of your paintings?" Kate asked.

"Another time." DeBray pulled two tickets from his pocket and waved them in the air. "This evening, we are going back to the Teatro La Fenice opera house for this evening's showing of *La Boheme*."

Kate's eyes lit up. "How . . . and when did you get those?"

"Easy. While we were on the architecture tour of the opera house, you were gushing about wanting to see *La Boheme*, so I ran up to the ticket window while you were in the restroom."

Kate bounced up and down, clapped her hands, and hugged DeBray. "*Es una fiesta* DeBray! *Gracias!*"

"You're welcome. It's already worth it just to hear you speak Spanish to me."

Kate looked down at her clothes and shoes and put her finger to her chin. "Umm, are we going to need to get dressed up?"

"But of course, there is no other way to go to one of the most beautiful opera houses in the world than formally dressed."

"Well, I don't think my clothes will suit."

"You look wonderful, but don't worry. My mother is a shoe designer and has some connections here. I will have one of the boutiques send some options to your room."

Kate smiled and softly touched his shoulder. "You are so thoughtful."

DeBray glanced up at St. Mark's gold and marble clock tower. "It is almost four o'clock now. We have time for one more museum. I have been saving my favorite for last, and since you like modern art, I think you will enjoy it too." He pointed across the canal. "Just over the bridge is the Guggenheim. They have a Miró exhibit going on right now."

"Miró? He is my favorite."

"I had a feeling you would like him. Living in Barcelona most of my life, I grew up amongst his sculptures and paintings. When I was ten, my mom and I rode a train to a small town on the island of Mallorca, where Miró once lived. In the train station, there is a world-class Miró and Picasso installation. Picasso is my mom's favorite artist, and that day, Miró became mine."

"I've only seen his work in books before! But even in books, I could feel his sense of joy and celebration. The way he expresses ideas of freedom and happiness is awe-inspiring, especially in times of unimaginable war. So, I guess for me, it's about what his art symbolizes. But his Surrealist shapes and colors were fascinating to look at, even before I understood the symbolism."

As Kate spoke, he was drowning in the deep blue of her eyes. A heavy, nervous feeling came into his chest, and he couldn't breathe. *What is this? She's so normal, yet so . . .*

"DeBray? Did you hear me?"

"Uh-huh."

"What are you thinking about? I think I lost you there for a moment."

"I—Uh, nothing. I was just appreciating you—I mean, your—your description of Miró."

That evening, DeBray sat in a brown leather chair as he waited for Kate to come down from her room. Nadia had agreed if, again, Benito came along, waiting in the shadows of the opera house, watching for any threats. When Kate appeared at the top of the staircase, DeBray's mouth dropped open, his eyes widened, and he instinctively stood up straight.

She wore a modest yet chic black dress with simple, delicate jewelry that accentuated the sparkle in her eyes. Her heels looked as though they were a simple continuation of her lean calves.

A light breeze swirled through an open window, catching Kate's curls and making them dance like flames, while her cheeks grew rosy. She stumbled slightly on a step, and he leaped in her direction. "Careful, Kate, we don't want any broken limbs."

"Yeah, I have not worn these torture devices they call heels much at all." Kate grimaced. Then she looked over DeBray's sleek black tuxedo. "Oh my, you look like a classic movie star."

"Why, thank you." DeBray leaned in and kissed both her cheeks. "So do you. Maybe we should fly to Hollywood and go to the Oscars instead."

"Oh no. Too many egos for me." Kate stood up straight and looked DeBray in the eyes. "There is nowhere else I would rather go this evening than to the opera with you."

"Perfect," DeBray managed to say around the sudden tightness in his throat. "Right this way. Your serenading gondolier awaits."

"We're taking a gondola to the opera?"

"Yes. How else would we go looking like this?"

"Oh, DeBray, thank you. I was prepared for a torturous walk over cracked cobblestones with these gorgeous things on my feet."

DeBray looked at the shoes his mother had designed and smiled. "As entertaining as that would be, there are not enough cobblers or emergency rooms in Venice for us to do that."

Chapter 51

São Paulo

"Do you want money?" Edhir Souza's voice echoed through the massive sound system as he raised his arms and looked to the ceiling of his enormous church. "God wants you to have it all! He is calling you today to stand up"—the congregation of over ten thousand immediately stood—"and know that you are worthy of all the gold in heaven!"

His disciples roared and applauded.

"Now, as God plainly said: as you give, you will receive tenfold in return." The ushers began passing around the offering baskets. The impoverished Brazilians quickly began reaching into their wallets and purses, in desperate desire for the new life Souza promised.

Edhir leered at the people and began singing softly, slowly, in an eerie tone: "Jesus loves me, this I know, for the Bible tells me so. Little ones to Him belong." He pointed at his flock and boomed into the microphone, "You are weak!" then slowly and softly again sang, "but he is strong. Yes, Jesus loves me. Yes, Jesus loves me."

Two hours later, in his luxe private jet high above the filth and frenzy of São Paulo, Edhir toyed with the top button of Djiana's tailored silk blouse. The nearness of her never ceased to excite him, particularly after an extended absence.

"You see, my darling, we don't need her alive anymore. You have done an incredible job finding and following her. But the whole sordid ordeal made me realize how foolish I was to let you risk your life in Bethlehem and Rome."

"But it was my wish. Live or die."

Her devotion stimulated his desire. He searched Djiana's dark eyes and then leaned over to inhale her scent. She purred, and it took great restraint on his part not to devour her right then and there.

"It is the little girl who must die for the cause, not you," he said. "She is a major key, and we have always known that, but I don't want her to enrich the Vatican any more than she already has. We'll never keep up with that kind of money. How shortsighted of me to think we could seize the tomb. There was no need for that."

Djiana's top slid open, revealing her smooth, tanned shoulders. "But I thought you needed the Vatican's wealth for our church."

"Yes, of course, but I have realized that the road to glory is not that of a thief who runs off in the night with a bag of jewels. We don't need to steal resources. We must instead gain control." He slowly caressed her shoulder with his thumb.

"But how, Edhir?"

"Jesus always taught that true joy comes from within. We must recruit someone in the upper echelon of the church. Then put our resources behind him so that he knows we have the power to fulfill his ultimate goal."

"His goal?"

"To become pope. Listen to me, my darling," he whispered as he nibbled her ear.

She gave a throaty giggle and wrapped her arms around his neck.

"You see, no one actually needs to know that the Vatican is ours. Not at first. The pope we select to sponsor will be our marionette. Their wealth and power will be our very own treasure chest that we'll draw on to fund our plans and gain more influence."

They both sank onto the couch. Edhir pinned Djiana's arms and nuzzled her neck.

"I want true joy," Djiana purred.

"You will have it, but we don't need to tear down the Vatican."

"No?" Djiana questioned.

"We just need to own it. All of it."

"Yes!" Djiana threw her head back. "All of it! But why . . ." She moaned with desire.

Edhir held back. "Ask your question."

"Why did you tell them you'd kill the little girl?"

"I told them to prove that there is nothing—nothing they can do to stop me!"

◆

THEY BURNED IN a flame of mutual ambition, and Edhir lost himself to the pleasure of Djiana, fully engrossed. But the Brazilian beauty felt her star rise. The risks had been worth it, making her rich and even secure in a precarious world. Yet a knot of anxiety and insecurity remained. Perhaps her plans to gain more influence—to be more than a mistress—would finally make her feel safe.

◆

ROME

AT FIRST, THE gymnasium in an abandoned school in a forgotten corner of the city seemed ridiculously large and unnecessary. Kate, Professor Nadia Jamira, and a volunteer web designer set up a single table for a computer in the echoing, high-ceilinged room.

Then, boxes of various sizes began arriving from around the world, from schoolchildren, teachers, priests, and nuns. Each box contained heart-warming drawings or messages of support. The Leadership Conference of

Women Religious, the same organization that originally wore them, made the majority of the armbands. Over fifty thousand nuns made at least twenty armbands each, exceeding one million in total.

Postal authorities approved multiple daily deliveries so that they could clear the deluge from their facilities.

"Good heavens, we'll be buried!" Nadia said, quickly adding, "But I'm not complaining."

Simon posted in the online message boards of schools in Rome where he had taught: "Many of you may not remember me, but my daughter Kate Murphy, who I am sure you now know, needs your help. Please contact us to volunteer."

Old students and former colleagues poured through the gym doors. Simon embraced each one and seemed whole again for the first time in years.

Many of Kate's high school classmates helped in various ways. Rebecca and Dr. Maly Rin called upon their network from Bambino Gesù Hospital.

"You make us proud, Kate," Maly said when Rebecca and Kate called her.

"I'm here because of you, Dr. Rin. You gave me the gift of my wonderful parents."

"Yes, it has been so good to spend time with them again."

"More and more, I hope." Kate smiled. "They love Rome so much. They're like kids here. Wait. Were they ever really kids?"

"Your father still is," Maly teased.

The women laughed, and Maly promised to spread the word and to walk with Kate and her parents at the front of the march.

Concerned, Rebecca looked at Kate after the call. "I know we are enjoying this camaraderie right now, but you know that this is extremely dangerous."

"Yes, Mum. We have been through this ten times now."

"I know, I know. I stay up late every night worrying about you, regret it every morning, then do it all over again. I am your mum, and a daughter is just a little girl who one day grows up to be your best friend."

Mum and daughter embraced. "I love you, Mum."

"I love you, too. And I want to keep loving you beyond next week. In the flesh, I mean. Keep in mind that you can quit anytime you want. We will certainly understand."

"I know," Kate said. "I know you will."

◆

Steven Craft was less than enthusiastic about the gymnasium arrangements. The neighborhood was tough and sparsely populated—a nightmare even for the extra security personnel he had assigned.

"Identification, please."

The two burly guards had allowed numerous women to join the merry workers without interference, but the first man to arrive was suspect.

"What brings you here?"

"I'd like to volunteer."

"Are you a friend of anyone in the organization?"

"Uh, yes. I think you could consider us friends."

"Do you have references?"

"I need references to volunteer?"

"Two forms of identification, please. One with a photo."

Kate looked up from her work when she overheard the interrogation. She walked toward the entrance to learn who was causing the fuss. She arrived in time to hear a guard ask, "You're from Barcelona?"

Kate was thrilled. "DeBray?" she called.

The well-groomed young man turned with a grin. He held out his hand as he bowed at the waist. "Miss Murphy. Such a pleasure to see you again."

Kate quickly pushed his hand out of the way and flung her arms around him. In her short life, she had been rocked by revelations, invasive voices, hallucinations, and intuitions that bordered on madness. Until this moment, the one thing she had not experienced was an overwhelming physical attraction to a man. She blushed as the feeling swept over her.

When she had left Venice, they had both hesitated to say goodbye, and she thought she felt the same regret in him that she felt at leaving him behind. She knew she had work to do but felt a pull to stay by his side too. *Why was everything so confusing,* she wondered.

"Gentlemen," she asked, "is there any reason we should not allow DeBray to enter the fray?"

The guards smiled and shrugged. "But everybody has to sign in. We're conducting background checks," one said.

"Me? A background check?"

"Especially you," Kate teased.

"Interesting," DeBray said. "I've never been suspected of anything except being too compulsive."

Kate smiled and pulled him into the gym. Once they were out of earshot of security, DeBray confided, "I hope they tell me what they find. I don't think I *have* a background."

She laughed giddily. *Get a grip!* she told herself.

"We have a lot of work to do," Kate told him. "But before you leave today, I want to know everything about seminary."

"Yes, of course. After all, we'll be classmates soon."

The remark delighted her. Here was a man who welcomed the possibility without being defensive or dismissive.

That was when it struck her. Until then, the ordination movement had largely been a call for change, with the idea of helping current nuns rise in the Church hierarchy. The benefits that would eventually come to women of her own generation were more like a mirage than a destination. *Seminary.* Kate liked the sound of that. When she looked up at DeBray, her eyes were glistening with tears.

"Oh, I'm sorry. I often make women cry. I'm trying to work on that."

"Oh. Love 'em and leave 'em, then?"

"Ah, well . . . anyway, the seminary frowns on dating. Why, I don't know."

They grinned at each other and Kate pulled away from her unexpected feelings to focus on her work.

◆

EDHIR SOUZA COULD be smooth even when he was angry. On those occasions, he kept his voice low and even, allowing his words, not his temper, to deliver the message.

Djiana listened to his telephone conversation, knowing she would never master the same kind of emotional governance. When she did not get her way, she became demanding and irate.

Edhir's method appeared more respectful and, as Djiana was learning, far more effective. He had put the call on speakerphone so that she could listen and understand what he expected of the Vatican functionary who had been brought into the fold.

"It's a very simple request, actually," Edhir said.

"No. It's dangerous. I cannot be compromised."

"Of course. We know this."

"Yet what you've suggested places me in the limelight. It puts me in the middle of a spectacle that will—"

"No one will blame a man of grace and fairness. Your decision to honor the girl's request will be a mere formality that leads to a disaster you could not have predicted." Edhir lulled the listener into compliance.

Still hesitant, the man on the other end of the line said, "I don't understand why she must die."

Edhir glanced at Djiana, who was dressed for a night on the town. He winked and smiled. "Because it is God's will."

"Why so close to the Vatican?"

"The Vatican must take responsibility. An assassination in an abandoned gymnasium is tawdry and much too simple. It's a day's headline on the evening news and nothing more." Djiana was witnessing Edhir's persuasive powers.

"But suddenly, there are things happening here that don't make sense. Requests to see His Holiness to discuss ordination of women."

"Good. This is good."

"But it's cardinals and bishops, not nuns," the caller said, agitation in his voice.

"Even better."

"Doesn't it strike you as odd?"

"We Evangelicals count our blessings, Cardinal. We are not surprised when the world works for us. Now, let's go over the plan again."

Chapter 52

Rome

Kate missed DeBray. She thought back to a few days earlier, in front of his easel, when he had turned to her and said, "I will paint something that will speak louder than words. The brush is mightier than the pen or the sword."

"I bet you use artsy lines like that on all the girls." Kate smirked.

DeBray had gently brushed blue paint on Kate's left cheek. "Only the perfectly gorgeous ones."

She blushed. "How many have you met?"

"One."

DeBray had promised he would return to Rome each weekend to prepare for the blue-armband march to St. Peter's Square, but that didn't make his absence easier for Kate. When a package from Venice arrived on Wednesday, it made matters worse. DeBray had included a watercolor of Mother Mary and Child, with a new variation: they each wore blue armbands. There was also a single red rose placed gently on top of the painting.

Kate smiled through watery eyes. By Friday, she was so dreamy she no longer heard the voices of Nadia and the volunteers.

"Kate. Kate?"

She jumped when Nadia tapped her on the shoulder.

"You didn't hear me call?"

"Sorry."

"I have a few questions about these new packages."

Kate walked with Nadia to the far end of the gym. For a moment, they watched as dozens of volunteers chattered happily while sorting through box after box of armbands.

Nadia turned and spoke softly. "What's going on? You're not yourself."

Kate tried to deflect her mentor with a wisecrack. "I'm not sure I even know who *myself* is."

"Come on, Kate. What is going on?"

"Is this when we have one of those girl-talk moments?"

"It could be. Do you still want all this to happen?"

Kate squirmed, looked around helplessly, and pulled Nadia into an adjacent locker room where they could talk more privately. She paced a bit before blurting out, "How can everything suddenly seem so strange?"

"Strange?"

"This place. The women here, the armbands, the . . . I'm spinning. I'm being pulled away. I'm not really here half the time."

"Then where are you?"

Kate's frightened eyes and anxious expression were reflected in Nadia, who clearly feared she was about to hear very bad news. "DeBray."

"Oh, the painter?"

"Yes. I keep thinking about him."

"And . . .?"

"With all that's going on in my life, and after only knowing him for a short time, why is it that the main thing I think about these days is when I'll see him again?"

"Ha!" Nadia laughed and threw her arms around Kate. "Now I get it. I think you may have your first crush, my dear."

"Oh no," Kate said, shaking her head. "What? No."

"Haven't you ever felt this way before?"

"No. Nothing even close to it. He's so . . . I can't stop thinking about him."

"Oh, Kate. It's a rite of passage. And, I mean, he's really good-looking."

"So I have good taste?" Kate asked with a grin.

"Well, I approve. But beauty is in the eye of the—"

"Shipwrecked?"

"Beholder. So when will you see him again?"

"Tomorrow. Even as busy as we are, this has been the slowest week of my life. And Professor . . ." She groped for the right words and the courage to say them. "I would really like to spend some time alone with him."

Nadia put her hands on Kate's shoulders. "Look, you're under a lot of pressure. Maybe you need a break."

"Exactly. With DeBray."

"I meant maybe taking a walk or something." Nadia grinned. "There's still a lot to do, but you definitely need to clear your head and just be a human being for a little while."

"Steven's people follow me everywhere. I have no peace."

But escaping wasn't as hard as she had thought. After returning to the gym, Kate saw that both guards were distracted by one very pretty volunteer. She made a dash for the door, and within seconds, found herself on the street in front of the abandoned school.

She chose the only side street that looked interesting and walked briskly. Soon, she was winding her way through an old neighborhood of apartment buildings intermingled with abandoned storefronts. For a time, she shared the cobbled byways with residents and Vespas, but she found solitude after turning a corner and discovering a passageway not much wider than her outstretched arms. Her bliss was short-lived, however, as she realized she was being followed.

The woman who pursued her had shrouded her face with an emerald scarf with black markings and gold trim. She also carried a shoulder bag that concealed her right hand.

Kate began to panic. Steven had warned her about brash decisions. Now, she was trapped in a narrow back alley that was fast leading to what must be the Tiber River. *Jesus, please help me. Where are the angels? Why aren't they here?*

The sound of the woman's boots on the pavement quickened. Then she called, "Stop!"

Stopping would mean death. Kate was sure of it.

"Stop! Wait!"

Kate burst into a sprint, which only brought her more quickly to the end of the alley, where the water blocked her escape. She leaned over and thought about diving in, then pressed her forehead against the wall next to her. She gritted her teeth in anticipation of the attack. Would it hurt? Could she survive a blow to the head or a bullet? Outraged by her own cowardice, Kate spun to confront her fate.

"Who are you? Tell me who you are!"

Stunned, the shrouded woman stopped. But she reached into her shoulder bag so fast Kate was convinced she would soon be riddled with bullets. She had no choice. She turned and went to dive into the river.

"Wait! What are you doing?" the woman yelled.

Kate was prepared to jump; then she heard the thudding sound of a man's boots running with such speed and abandon that Kate couldn't help but turn. He approached the shrouded woman.

"Don't hurt me!" the woman screamed, cowering and covering her face. "Please don't hurt me!"

The man ignored her completely. He sprinted past her and dragged Kate from the water's edge. Strong arms wrapped around her body.

"Kate. Are you all right?"

"DeBray!" She was overjoyed to see him. Then panic swept through her again. "She's got a gun!"

The woman was now standing at the ledge, and she pulled her hand from her shoulder bag. Both DeBray and Kate took a moment to realize that the woman was not holding a weapon. Dangling from her thin, white fingers was a piece of paper.

"Kate. It's me, Meghan. Remember this photo?"

◆

WHEN THE ESPRESSO and biscotti were served, the three were still chattering from their shaken nerves.

After apologies were made on all sides, DeBray had driven them to a small café on the other side of the river. The car was on loan from a friend just outside of Venice. By way of explanation, he opened the passenger door and whispered, "I couldn't wait until Saturday."

Kate lowered her voice. "Neither could I."

Inside the café, the rich smell of tomato sauce and starch filled the room. The customers at the next table spoke in animated Italian, their hands moving as if they were conducting a symphony. Meghan sipped hot coffee and smiled weakly. "I'm sorry, Kate. I'd read so much about you that I wanted to come and volunteer. When I was about a block away from the school, I saw a woman skip down the steps. Something about the way you moved—and, of course, your hair—told me it was you, so I followed. You were always a fast girl. You take such big steps. Lord."

Kate smiled. "I needed to get away for a while."

She stole a glance at DeBray, who looked concerned. Kate turned her attention back to her old friend, whom she hadn't seen in years. "I wasn't sure you'd ever forgive me, Meg."

"Ah. We were children." Meghan pointed at the photo Kate was now holding. It showed two seven-year-old girls posing in front of a Dublin sign. "Then your family moved away. But watching you on the telly made me realize that back then, you were probably just discovering your gift."

"Or curse."

"Or destiny," DeBray offered, though not entirely sure what the two women were discussing. Then he turned to Meghan. "Maybe someday you'll forgive me too. I'll need it to complete my studies at the seminary, you know."

Meghan's laugh was spontaneous and soft. "I forgive you today. Now. As I sip this delicious coffee."

He bowed his head with a smile, then turned his attention back to Kate. "What did you do that needs forgiveness?"

The young women shared a look with eyebrows raised.

"Who should tell him, Meg?"

"Only you know what truly happened the day we made the wooden cross, Kate."

DeBray's eyes grew wide as he listened to Kate's childhood crucifixion story. "Then what happened?"

"Well, Meg's dad shook me back into reality. He told my parents that I was standing there in a trance, staring at Meghan on the cross while she screamed and begged me to let her down. I don't remember anything. I was gone. Totally. In another realm." She had learned to keep things to herself unless she felt safe.

"But how did your parents respond to my dad and everything?"

"They just tried to get me to share my feelings about it and help me. Besides my parents, I have never told anyone else what happened." Kate caught herself. "Until now, of course."

DeBray reached across the table and held Kate's hand. "Thank you for sharing that with us."

The three sat in silence for a long moment. Suddenly, sirens blared. All three looked up to see three armored security vehicles screeching to a stop in front of the café. Guards rushed into the shop, weapons pointed at DeBray. A moment later, Steven Craft strode in with an icy expression.

"Enjoying your coffee, Kate?"

"Stevie!"

It was the wrong moment to joke with the security chief. He pointed at DeBray, who was lifted out of his chair for interrogation.

"Hey!" Kate stood to confront Steven. "I don't need you here. How did you even find us? GPS in my pocket?"

"Sir," Steven growled, "is that your car parked outside?"

"Uh, actually, no."

"Do not play with me."

"No, I mean, a friend loaned it to me and—"

"He's with me! This is ridiculous!" Kate yelled.

Steven was firm. "Listen to me, Kate."

"No, you listen." Kate's authoritative tone turned heads throughout the cafe. "You're suffocating me. I can't live like this."

"You know why it has to be this way."

"Threatening my friends? No, it doesn't have to be that way!"

Meghan remained in her seat but began to cry. Steven glanced at her and turned back to DeBray. "Why did you leave the school without consulting with the guards?"

"Consult?" DeBray asked, raising his eyebrows. "I had a hunch."

"Conspiracy charges would crush your seminary plans. But that's an alias, anyway, right? Or we could hit you with kidnapping. Does that sound like a good future?"

DeBray, speechless and pale, stared at his interrogator and then at Kate.

"Steven . . . he . . . DeBray doesn't know."

"Know what?" DeBray asked.

Steven cursed and glanced around, motioning for the guards to move the café proprietor out of earshot. "Young man, this woman's life has been threatened. We take it very seriously, even if she does not."

DeBray turned to Kate in dismay. "Kate, why didn't you tell me?"

Steven answered. "She was ordered not to—the one request she has apparently respected. This cannot become public knowledge. Do you understand?"

"Of course."

Steven turned to Meghan. "Miss. Understood?"

She nodded, too, and crossed herself.

Chapter 53

Vatican City

"Why do you persist? And why now? You're caving in to the demands of a girl? Centuries of history and tradition should be suddenly swept into the Vatican rubbish bin?"

Cardinal Dumas was clearly annoyed with his visitor, along with all the other urgent requests for meetings with Pope Nelson.

Cardinal Parker was undeterred. He explained again his evolving belief that quashing the movement for female ordination might cause more harm than good. "Let's go over it again."

"Let's not."

"By yielding, we actually gain control."

"Of what? When the dominoes begin to fall, we won't be able to measure their speed or true impact. What has happened to your mind, your faith?"

"My faith is in God's plan. My logic is that we strengthen this movement by resisting it," Parker contended. "Let them enter. Let them struggle within their own rabble. They think it will be smooth? Suddenly everything in the Vatican will be easy and sweet? I don't think so."

"I will not allow you and others—"

"Others?"

"You must know that you are not alone in your request to convene the College of Cardinals. I will not allow you to lead this new pope into the quagmire."

Parker was not surprised by Dumas's rigidity. It had served him well through the years, fueling a slow but steady ascent. He decided to reverse course. "You're right, Alain. Protect His Holiness. Ignore the protest. The noise will go away, and Pope Nelson will appear strong—even if he is not."

"Not? I beg your pardon?"

"Abe Lincoln, an American president—"

"I do not need to be educated about your nation's history."

"He invited many of his political enemies to be part of his cabinet. 'Keep your friends close and your enemies closer.' That sort of thing."

Dumas narrowed his eyes, then stood up, turning his back on the visitor. Parker noted the grimace that flashed across Dumas's face and changed course once again.

"Convening the college does not mean a vote on female ordination will succeed, but it would show the world that Pope Nelson has an open mind, a willingness to consider both sides of complex issues. He'll be remembered for that, no matter what the outcome."

Dumas turned on his visitor. "What is your cause?"

Feigning innocence, Parker replied, "Cause?"

"What do you gain by this course of action?"

"How dare you." Parker breathed. "I broached this subject when you were in Jerusalem overseeing—or interrupting, as the case may be—the criminal events at the Church of the Nativity. You had an agenda then, and you had one in Brazil—"

"You shut your mouth!" Dumas rushed toward Parker, his finger raised, his voice low but hostile. "We all know, Parker." He jabbed his finger into the larger man's chest. "We know who you are and what you are capable of. Deny it in your private chambers, but do not deny it to me, here, now. You want something. Tell me what it is."

Parker felt the blood rush to his face. He held his position and restrained his impulse to crush the accusing cardinal.

Dumas moved even closer, invading Parker's space. "I need an answer to my question."

"I want nothing." Parker spun to leave.

Dumas did not try to stop him. But he had parting words. "Your American president, your Lincoln, would never have survived the Vatican."

"He'd own the place," Parker replied flippantly.

Dumas's eyes grew wide. "Own it? You can't keep your enemies close—"

"I'm going."

"—if you don't know who they are!"

◆

ROME

Archbishop Azevedo was waiting patiently in a television studio in Rome when his phone chirped. He reached inside his garment, wondering if he dared answer before being ushered in front of the cameras to once again denounce the march on St. Peter's Square.

"I only have a minute."

Parker's voice lacked its usual smoothness. In a rush, he tried to explain his suspicions, but the stage manager was rushing toward Azevedo and tapping his watch. "Stop with the guessing games, and tell me what you think it means."

"Something is going on with Dumas."

◆

VATICAN CITY

Cardinal Dumas sat quietly at his desk for many minutes after Parker's visit, doing everything in his power to avoid his most disturbing thoughts. The knock on the door startled him. "Yes. Come in."

An administrative assistant shuffled forward with a small box. "This arrived for you today, Cardinal."

"A treat, I hope. Thank you."

The factotum nodded and exited as Dumas retrieved scissors from his desk drawer and sliced the translucent tape. When he pulled away the layers of packing material inside, his breath stopped. A black Glock handgun lay on its side with an envelope underneath.

His hand trembled as he opened the greeting card. The handwritten note was short but not at all sweet:

Do—or die.

Chapter 54

Rome

There were no design specs for the blue armbands. Each parish, household, or club created its own version, and Kate loved the uniqueness of each group's contribution. The volunteers marveled at the many styles that continued to flow into the gymnasium. Materials ranged from paper to velvet. Shades of blue were equally various, and attachment methods included elastic, tie-ons, and even plastic snaps.

DeBray's oil painting, depicting Mother Mary and the Christ child wearing blue armbands, had been scanned and posted online. It had gone viral quickly. Only two days later, vendors were hawking T-shirts with silk-screen reproductions of the piece. Soon, the blue armbands became ubiquitous throughout the world.

◆

AFTER SENDING OFF the last box, Kate pulled DeBray aside. "When we begin the march, I want you to join me at the front with my parents, Professor Jamira, and Meghan."

"Are you sure?"

"Why would I ask you if I wasn't sure?"

His eyes crinkled. "Then I'm honored."

"Good. But listen, there will be a lot of media out there. So try not to hog the camera, okay?"

DeBray laughed. "Why me? Why allow me to walk with you?"

"*Tranquilidad*." Kate shrugged.

He cocked his head, unsure of her meaning.

"That's how you make me feel, DeBray. Tranquil. Calm."

He liked the way this conversation was going but realized that she knew nothing about his inner turmoil. *I am anything but tranquil around you, Kate Murphy*, he thought.

"How nervous are you, really?" he asked.

"More excited than scared," she admitted. "I probably won't sleep at all tomorrow night."

"Yeah, I know. Me too."

Kate waited, sensing DeBray had more to say. "Is something wrong?"

"No. I . . . Yes. No. It's just that . . . I realized that after this week, I won't necessarily have an excuse to visit Rome on the weekends."

"Museums, the Pantheon, La Maddalena?" Kate poked.

"You love to tease."

"I get it from my dad. We are both socially inept."

"You should get a second opinion."

"What's your opinion?"

DeBray knew what he wanted to say. He was terrified to say it. And he knew that if he did not seize the moment, he would regret it forever.

"You are not socially inept. You're incredible, and full of amazing things to say. You are like no one I've ever met, and I . . . I mean . . . I'm going to miss you. A lot."

As he watched the light dance on her face, he did not care if his secret wish went against his new vow. He wanted to wrap his arms around her body and pull her close. So that was exactly what he did. Their embrace was long. DeBray noticed his lips touching Kate's neck and he reluctantly pulled away.

Chapter 55

Rome

Long past midnight, Kate startled awake and sat up. She felt a presence in her room but could see nothing. Cool air blew through her hair, and a crowd of voices began to speak. Warnings and condolences, accolades, and cheers all competed for her ear as she continued to search the dark for a specter or intruder.

"Who are you?"

The answer came not in words but in vibrations. She felt wrapped in revolving spheres and aural sensations that were as familiar and confounding as her recurring dreams. Then, the sensation of embrace was pulled away, and she felt vulnerable and alone.

"Will I survive what I've started? Will I live?"

She waited for an answer that never came. Near dawn, she finally fell back asleep, only to be awakened minutes later by her alarm clock. It was time to visit with the pope.

◆

VATICAN CITY

"Miss Murphy, thank you for visiting me today. Have you found me any more ancient tombs or holy treasure?"

The summer sunshine cascaded through the windows of Pope Nelson's apartment. It was simple in comparison to the ornate furnishings that filled the rest of the building but tasteful. A full-size bed with white linens and an antique brass frame sat against one wall, and a large, beautifully carved wardrobe rose in the corner. There was a mahogany desk at the end of the room with two neat stacks of paper and a lovely marble pen stand. The desk was angled toward the windows to catch the light. And against the other wall was a small sitting area, with a long leather couch, a coffee table, and a deep-set upholstered chair, where the pope sat now.

Kate grinned from the couch. "Always wanting more, eh, Your Holiness?"

"Of course. You know we popes are never satisfied."

"Thank you from the bottom of my heart for respecting our march tomorrow. I may have some ideas on more treasure for you, but I can't think of anything that the women of the Church need more right now than to be made equal. Perhaps allowing priests to marry?"

"Ha! It seems that you are never satisfied either. You could make a good pope someday."

Kate smiled but was taken aback by his suggestion. Was he joking? Poking fun at the reason for the protest? Or serious?

"Kate, I asked you here because I have a few questions for you. But first, may I tell you a story?"

"Yes, please do."

"When I was about seven years old in Cape Town, my class took a field trip to Robben Island. I had never seen or heard anything about Robben Island prior to our trip. But as soon as I saw the lighthouse from the top deck of our boat, I instantly knew everything about it. I knew where all of the buildings were located. I knew exactly what the jail cells looked like. When I walked into one of the cells, my mind was filled with a vision of men sleeping on the floor on thin mats with old gray wool blankets. The tour bus drove us to the rock quarry where the inmates used to work daily. As we toured the quarry, the dense dust particles that filled our lungs had a familiar scent, and I already knew how to handle the tools and break the rocks in the way the tour guides instructed us. There was no doubt in my mind that I had been to this place before."

"Wow," Kate said, forming a new sort of respect for and bond with the fledgling pontiff, but not feeling safe enough to comment more or ask any questions.

"My point is, because of this experience, I believe in old souls. And as any learned theologian knows, almost all religions at some point in their history have held a similar belief—even us Catholics."

"Yes." Kate nodded.

"I have heard your story in detail so many times, how you saw a vision of the location of King David's tomb. I have tried my best to respect your privacy regarding this very personal experience, but I have reached a point where the questions must be asked. Please also understand that no one else will ever know of our conversation."

Pope Nelson paused, and Kate could tell he was pensive about what he was about to ask. She knew that his influence could determine whether she was exalted or cast off by the Holy See, whether her cause would be taken seriously or diminished, even crushed. He looked at her intently, clearly hoping for a glimpse into the true depth of her soul. And then he proceeded.

"Who was your guide to the birthplace of Christ and then through the tunnel to King David's tomb?"

Kate's face glowed with a youthful serenity. "I always knew that the person who first asked me that question would already know the answer."

"Jesus?"

"Yes." Kate nodded and continued to smile.

Pope Nelson bowed gratefully. "Thank you. I promise I will not tell anyone else about this." He stared at the Fisherman's Ring on his right hand. "I want to show you something. Let's go on a little field trip."

Eight Swiss Guards awaited them outside the pope's door. On the walk to St. Peter's Basilica, they encountered hordes of tourists. Kate knew the pope could have easily requested a private walk or an incognito vehicle. Every phone captured photos of the two walking together. When the pope stopped to bless people in the crowd, Kate signed items people handed her.

"You have become as popular as me," Nelson said as they walked.

"I guess it is my cross to bear now."

"Yes, a glorious, bright burden that you should bear to the world as much as possible."

Kate nodded, grateful for his respect.

They finally reached a small stairwell with a simple sign above that read *Necropoli Vaticana*. The Swiss Guard stood at attention and forced the mob of people behind them to come to a halt.

"Here we are, the back entrance. Good day, Mr. Craft," Pope Nelson said.

"Stevie!" Kate grinned. Despite their disagreements, she always appreciated Craft's presence.

Steven looked at the pope over Kate's shoulder. "Good day, Your Holiness. And you, Miss Murphy."

Before Kate could tease Steven about not being able to get away from him, he bowed his head and said, "Your Holiness, we have secured the area, and the necropolis is now completely private."

Kate turned to the pope. "He is always the consummate professional."

Steven smiled at her, then opened the gate to the stairwell. "Enjoy your tour."

"Thank you, Mr. Craft," Pope Nelson acknowledged.

As they descended, Kate felt the humidity rise and the temperature drop. "A private tour with the pope is incredible."

"I'm happy that you want to see it with me. The walk through the ancient city of the dead is a journey through the centuries. It allows us to drink in the faith and emotions that the first Christians experienced."

At the bottom of the stairs, white marble tombs surrounded them. Kate felt a rush of anxiety as nightmares of crucified bodies began invading her mind. She drew long, deep breaths and exhaled slowly. She felt that she might finally be learning how to manage the mysterious awareness that had been with her since childhood.

"Are you all right, my dear?"

"Yes, I just . . . the air down here is so much more"—Kate took another deep breath—"dense."

"Oh yes, much more humid from the wet earth. We have to hermetically seal many of the items so they will be preserved."

Pope Nelson guided Kate through the long, dark hallways. He related the history of the relics and tombs with heartfelt passion. "Imagine that you are one of the first Christians carrying the body of St. Peter to his burial."

Kate felt a pressure in her chest and attempted to take a deep breath but could not.

"Go back with me now." Pope Nelson continued to walk and talk. "To the family, disciples, and friends of St. Peter, it was a horrific time of mourning. They had just seen him crucified upside down in public. Then, they had to carry his bloody body through these streets to bury him. He was the best friend of Jesus, and the closest they would ever be to Jesus until they too died."

A searing pain shot into Kate's hands and feet. She glanced down to see large, thick nails being hammered through her flesh and bones until blood gushed from the holes. Soldiers stood over her, spitting on her and shouting, "Die! Friend of the King of the Jews! Die!" Kate's eyes were completely glazed over, and she no longer knew where or who she was.

The Vicar of Christ did not see her face or detect her failing attempts to keep pace with him in the dim cavern. "It had to be just as hard for these early Christians to bury Peter as it was for the family and disciples of Jesus to bury him. Yet, not many stories are told about St. Peter. Was he resurrected? For me, he is the eternal brother sitting at the right hand of Jesus."

Kate collapsed to the ground.

"Kate! Are you all right?" The pope kneeled to pull her into his arms. "Kate. Kate!"

Her chest heaved as her lungs strained for oxygen.

"I have you. Kate, can you hear me? Breathe! Breathe!"

From a deep abyss, beyond any grave, Kate heard Pope Nelson's voice and felt him rocking her back and forth in his arms. She felt her lips move as Latin poured from them.

"What?" Nelson leaned in to listen. "Come back to me, Kate. Breathe. There you go. Just breathe. You are fine. Yes, just breathe now." The pope gently brushed her hair from her forehead.

Kate had the same semiconscious waking sensation she'd felt many times as a child, being rocked awake in her parents' arms. "I love you, Dad," she mumbled.

Pope Nelson was taken aback, then smiled down into her eyes. "I love you too, my child."

He continued to rock her in his arms. The two of them sat in silence until her breathing became normal again.

"Do you want me to get you a doctor?"

"No."

"Do you want me to get someone else to help bring you out?"

"No."

"Okay. We can go slowly, but we are only about halfway through."

"I will be fine. Thank you."

Kate regained her awareness and strength as they walked slowly.

"What happened? Do you have health problems?" Pope Nelson asked.

"I don't." Kate didn't want to be cryptic when the pope had so recently confided in her, but she knew it was much better to process a vision before telling anyone else about it.

After a long pause that Kate clearly refused to break, the pope tried a different tack. "I didn't know you spoke Latin."

"Oh. Yes. But why do you ask?"

"You seemed to be writhing in pain and started speaking in Latin. The words I could make out were *diligatis invicem, ignosce*. Love one another, forgive."

Kate made a noncommittal noise.

"Well, I am relieved that you are feeling better. I would hate to have lost you, especially on my watch."

Kate cracked a smile. "No kidding. Can you imagine what the media would have said?"

They approached a large, red-painted wall, but Nelson pointed toward the exit and led her toward it. "Come this way, my dear. The exit is over here. Let's get you to a doctor."

"But wait. Isn't this the gravesite of St. Peter?"

"Yes, but we can come again some other time."

"No, please. I'm fine, I promise. Please, show me the tomb."

"Are you sure?"

"Yes, please."

He peered at her carefully. "Okay. But we won't stay too long." They walked along the large red wall, and he flipped a switch that beamed light onto the inscription βράχος είναι μέσα. "It says, 'Rock is within.'"

Kate nodded her head. She could feel the pope staring at her, considering whether to speak, what to say.

"Earlier, you told me that Jesus was your guide to King David's tomb." He inched closer to see Kate's face. "Now please, Kate, know that you are safe with me. My other question is—who were you?"

Kate's gaze dropped to the floor as she instinctively clutched the small silver cross that hung from her neck. In the silence that followed, she was barely conscious of her fingers' slow, subtle twisting of the cross or the faint whisper that escaped her lips in a baritone, the Latin words inaudible to all but the two angels sitting on the grave:

"*Nunc coepi.*" Now I begin.

The pope's eyes grew wide, and his body stiffened. He paused in silence, then nodded his head and embraced her.

Chapter 56

Rome

The day began like any other: Kate opened her eyes. The sun was just coming up, the slanted light streaming in through her window, and she could hear the sound of the world waking outside. She lay breathing quietly in her bed for a few moments, and then immediately, as if hit by a wave, she could feel that things were different. The air itself was full of electricity, the whole world's energy pointed at one place: Rome.

When Kate arrived at the beginning point of the march with her parents, Professor Jamira, Meghan, and DeBray, followed by her security detail, they were greeted by members of the Corps of Gendarmerie, dressed in their sharp blue uniforms, each looking serious and tense. She turned and looked behind her, where the line already reached three full blocks, even at 8 a.m. Things had only begun; it would be a very long day for these security guards, she thought.

DeBray squeezed her hand after they passed through. "Step one, get manhandled by burly guard. Check," he said and smiled. They looked down the long stretch of road before them, which led to the Via della Conciliazione, which itself led to St. Peter's Square, and sighed in unison. The entire road was lined with barricades to hold back the crowds not planning to march, only observe.

"You ready for this?" she asked.

DeBray nodded and squeezed her hand again. "Lead the way, boss."

By 10 a.m. the number of people overflowing through the streets of ancient Rome was estimated at just over 1.5 million, which was 500,000 more than any Vatican crowd before. The pressure was mounting on Kate's shoulders, as if she could feel the weight of each additional person who joined the protest, each soul's hopes and dreams placed in her hands. At the same time, she felt their power urging her on. It was a responsibility and an honor, she realized. She would have to bear them both. She wore a microphone for the speakers they had placed throughout the streets and held a bullhorn. It shook in her hand then stilled, her resolve growing, giving her strength. She raised her hand, and slowly the crowd quieted, the silence starting at the front and rippling like a tide backward. When only the typical sounds of midday Rome surrounded her, she let the first words of the protest soar above the multitude.

"Jesus loves all of his children, men and women equally!" The sea of protesters roared at the sound of her voice and then stayed quiet, waiting, trying to hear, and her tone began to grow. "We are here today in support of half of the world who has been held back, held down, made to feel like second-class members of Jesus's Church." Murmurings began. Her timbre grew louder still. "We want equal rights for women. Let us serve Him. Let us lead." And then she shouted: "Set us free!" At this, the crowd erupted into chanting, "Set us free! Set us free!" Energy charged through the mass of optimistic activists. Blue bands and fists were held high. A dynamic JEFFK & Sandy Legal remix of Aretha Franklin's legendary anthem "Respect" erupted through the speakers, filling the air with bass, energy, and excitement as the dancing march began.

Chapter 57

Vatican City

The surge of humanity that marched toward the police barricade at St. Peter's Square astounded onlookers and media alike. The procession wound along main roads for over a mile, then down Via della Conciliazione, and news outlets estimated over one million participants, most of whom wore either a blue armband or a T-shirt displaying DeBray's now-famous image of mother and child. People carried signs with slogans like "Equal Rights Now," "Kate Is My Hero," and "A Woman's Place Is in the Vatican."

Inside the Vatican, Cardinal Dumas and Pope Nelson watched television broadcasts that included aerial views from helicopters and drones. The enormity of the event gave them pause, as did the chants and placards.

"I feel under siege, Alain."

The cardinal nodded, his phone to his ear. He was receiving constant updates and details of the march from the Carabinieri and Steven Craft's security team. Now that the throng had reached the square, he did not like what he was hearing.

"Sir, the Murphy girl and her associates are making demands."

"Such as?"

"They insist on an audience."

The pope pointed to the television wryly. "Larger than the one they've got?"

Oblivious to the double meaning, Dumas clarified, "An audience with you or other Vatican leaders. It appears that they don't wish merely to make a spectacle, they also want assurances that the ordination issue will be taken up by the College of Cardinals."

"I am the Supreme Legislator, and only I have the true authority to change Canon Law 1024," Pope Nelson said sternly as he pulled a large, rolled document out of his desk. "Kate will get her wish." He poured a dab of red wax and used his Ring of the Fisherman to seal it. "But we will not deliver this today. Not like this. I will not have it seem as though I gave in to the pressure of a mob."

Dumas continued to listen intently to updates via his phone until his other phone vibrated. He excused himself, accepted the call, and heard the deep voice of Edhir Rene Souza.

"I hope you have received our package."

"How thoughtful of you."

"A friendly reminder of our agreement."

Cardinal Dumas gritted his teeth and returned to the chamber as the pontiff fretted at the television. "I hope she knows what she's doing. What if they surge past the barricade? The police can't hold them back!"

"Sir, there may be a way to appease their leadership."

◆

ROME

IN A HOTEL room in Rome, Henryk Lemski watched the television broadcasts while holding his phone away from his ear. Cardinal Parker no longer seemed capable of conducting a conversation without shouting.

"I've done everything that I can! Stop calling. You can't expect me to move mountains," Cardinal Parker yelled.

"Of course not. I merely ask that you move cardinals. Do you know who is always referred to as just 'the Monsignor' and 'the Cardinal-Deacon'?"

"Who?"

"Of course not." Lemski smirked. "These are the vague pseud-onyms used by the Vatican officials who recruited me to run the de facto Supreme Sacred Congregation. I will give you their real names and contact information."

"Why?"

"You will call them to deliver a message."

The former priest's words sent Parker into another rant. After it died out, Lemski pressed on. "Write it down, Cardinal. 'Henryk Wicus Lemski remembers everything.' And then hang up. Simple assignment. Thank you for your effort."

He ended the call as a newscaster announced that a Vatican official had agreed to speak with Kate Murphy and Professor Nadia Jamira and was now crossing St. Peter's Square.

The helicopter TV cameras followed a dignitary in robes whose gait was slow but steady. Lemski sat and watched with keen interest. *Speak of the devil*, he thought. The familiar face was none other than the Monsignor, otherwise known as Cardinal Alain Dumas.

◆

VATICAN CITY

KATE'S SIGN BORE a large photo of Nelson Mandela above his famous quote, "We can change the world and make it a better place. It is in your hands to make a difference."

Kate's supporters were mocked and ridiculed by groups of counter-protestors as Cardinal Dumas approached the police barricade. She passed the sign to her mom and steadied herself by linking arms with Meghan on her right and DeBray on her left.

Simon conferred with Professor Nadia Jamira and Dr. Maly Rin. The webmaster who'd helped set up operations at the gym was nearby, working feverishly to update social media with real-time reportage and quotes. Steven's security forces were deployed to maintain a protective membrane between Kate's entourage and the masses.

The cardinal stopped and nodded to Kate.

"Miss Murphy, there will be no audience today with Pope Nelson or any other Vatican officials. We cannot and will not negotiate with a mob. But His Holiness has asked me to express his concern for the issue that is clearly so important to you."

"Thank you. But concern is really not enough. Do you see how many people have come to Rome to support this cause?"

Nadia and Simon nodded emphatically. Other voices in the vicinity shouted their support for Kate.

"We understand. For this reason, His Holiness has granted you, and only you, the opportunity to step past police and place an armband near the foot of the obelisk. Kneel if you wish. Take time for a prayer, if that suits you. Do not feel rushed. But within fifteen minutes, if you have not returned here, we'll instruct police to escort you off the square. Agreed?"

Kate consulted her parents and Nadia. They spoke rapidly, suggesting variations on the invitation that the cardinal quickly declined.

"What do you think, DeBray?"

His mind was clearly a battlefield of conflicting thoughts. "It sounds like a good offer, but something doesn't feel right."

He scanned the square. Kate followed his gaze and came to her own conclusion. "I'm going."

Cardinal Dumas nodded and began his walk back to the pontiff's chambers.

The webmaster announced Kate's decision via a live feed that others in the crowd soon noticed.

"How many nuns were at the original protest in 1979?" Kate yelled. Nadia was only a few meters from her, but the crowd chanting "Equality for all!" was deafening.

"Fifty!" Nadia yelled back.

"Give me fifty armbands. They are coming with me."

The helicopters overhead roared so loudly over the square that Kate felt as though the sky was pressing down on her. Even so, she took her time walking alone toward the obelisk. She wanted to remember this journey: the roar of the crowd, the sun on her back, the energy she felt flowing to her, above and around her. She carried the goodwill of so many people who believed, as she did, that the time had come for equality for women within the Church.

Suddenly, Kate heard the crowd behind her erupt in thunderous applause. Initially she thought it was for her.

"Pink smoke! Pink smoke! Kate! Look! Look up! The chapel!" She turned to see DeBray shouting, and as she looked at him, she saw the entire sea of people pointing upward.

She looked in the direction they were pointing, past the giant obelisk into the distance. There it was, an immense quantity of vibrant pink smoke spilling from the Sistine Chapel fireplace. Typically, the sight of white smoke signaled the solemn election of a new pontiff steeped in ancient rituals. But this was a declaration unlike any other.

Chills surged over Kate's body.

"Yes! Yes!" Kate yelled and pumped the bag full of armbands into the air at the pink smoke. Then she thought, *Who could do that, and how?*

A Vatican helicopter began to hover ominously over the chapel fireplace. A chorus of boos rang out from the crowd. Suddenly, hundreds of small fires burst to life throughout the crowd billowing pink smoke as well. She had heard the murmurs of women's rights activists lighting pink fires in the square whenever a new pope was elected, a subversive act meant to overshadow the solemnity of tradition.

The helicopter rotors churned the air as it fought to disperse the thickening smoke that poured from the chimney and up from the immense crowd. Instead of dispersing the rose-colored smoke high into the sky, it had the opposite effect, pushing it down, blanketing St. Peter's Square in a surreal fog that crept insidiously into the very heart of the Vatican.

This was a revolutionary realm of rebellion—an overwhelming wave of pink enveloped the crowd and twisted its way into the sacred spaces not meant for such audacious displays. The scene was a passionate riot of color that transformed the square into a theater of defiance as the intoxicating haze surged through the air like a living entity.

With each breath, the air crackled with enthusiasm, heavy with the scent of evolution. The pink fog covered everything, permeating the walls of the Vatican as if challenging the very foundation of the institution. In that moment, the complex tapestry of the old order and the fresh surge of transformation collided violently, capturing a timeless struggle that resonated through history like a powerful anthem for those who dared to defy.

Near the obelisk, Kate knelt. She placed one hand on the soft pile of armbands and stared up at the magnificent Egyptian structure she'd first seen with her parents. Images of that day began to bombard her—Father Kelly, the Mass in the Basilica, the two white angels who held a red marble font of holy water.

Her reminiscence ended abruptly when she felt something at her back. She stiffened with fear as she had done when awakened suddenly in the wee hours. She stood and slowly turned. A shaft of sunlight broke through the pink smoke. She did not turn away. Instead, she lifted her face toward it, embraced it, and raised her arms. She took a deep calming breath and heard a thunderous voice.

Her own.

"In Latin, the phrase is *diligatis invicem*."

The helicopters howled.

"In Italian, it is *amatevi l'uno con l'altro*."

The angels descended and sang to her.

"In English, the phrase is . . ."

◆

POPE NELSON LOOKED away from the television and noticed that Cardinal Dumas was sweating and shivering. "Alain, are you well? You seem terribly anxious."

"My only concern is for you, Your Holiness."

"Not even a little worry for the girl?"

"Worry for her? What could happen to her?" Dumas collapsed into a chair, thinking, *What have I done?*

◆

ON HIS ROOFTOP perch, Dumas's sniper had his crosshairs firmly focused on Kate's forehead when the scope filled with pink smoke.

◆

DEBRAY FELT SOME relief when Kate kneeled at the obelisk. But then something had caused her to stand. Now, he watched as she spread her arms to the heavens, making her an easy target. He looked to the rooftops behind him and saw a flash of light reflect off the sniper's scope.

"It's a trap!" he screamed.

Simon turned to him. "What did you say?"

"Call her back, Mr. Murphy. Call her back!"

"What are you talking about? She's fulfilling her—"

"It's a trap! She's target practice out there!"

DeBray launched himself at a policeman and demanded that Kate be warned. "Tell her to get down! She's not safe!"

DeBray slipped to the stone pavement, rolling, standing again, and dashing past the barricade. He sprinted toward Kate, wailing and waving. "Kate! Kate, get down!"

◆

THE SOUND OF her name jolted Kate out of her reverie. She turned to see DeBray throw his body at her. She yelped as his momentum took them to the ground, but it was a shrill howl of pain that told them something awful had occurred. A dark red stain began to spread upon the white stone.

Another shot zipped by and ricocheted off the pavement, causing police to scatter and begin searching the rooftops.

◆

IN THE VATICAN command room, Steven Craft was riveted to the wall of monitors, dumbfounded by the chaos on the square and the tsunami of panic that had turned Via della Conciliazione into a stampede.

"What in the hell is going on out there?"

◆

POPE NELSON WAS watching the television intently, trying to see through the pink smoke. Behind him, sweating profusely and hyperventilating, Cardinal Dumas reached into his pocket and gripped Edhir's gift.

Staring blankly at Pope Nelson, he pulled the gun out and examined it. "Your Holiness." He stopped speaking when he saw the pope turn around to look at him.

"Alain! What are you doing?"

The cardinal raised the gun and pointed it at the supreme pontiff's chest. Tears welled in the cardinal's eyes, his nostrils flared, and his upper lip began to quiver. Then, in a swift movement, Dumas pressed the barrel to his temple and mumbled, "Please forgive me. I have failed."

◆

THE GUN WENT off. Dumas's lifeless body tumbled to the floor, his blood slowly soaking into the exquisite wool rug.

Two Vatican security guards burst in from the next room, sprinting toward the pope. They grabbed him under each arm and dragged him away to a secure, hidden chamber.

The pope sat in a padded armchair tucked into a pool of shadow in the corner. One of the guards stood by the door, while the other stayed by his side, speaking quickly into his collar-mounted microphone and listening intently to the responses coming through his earpiece.

"You go," he said to the guard by the door. "I will wait for the others." The guard at the door nodded and disappeared into the outer room.

The pope closed his eyes, folded his hands, and began to pray. For Cardinal Dumas, for Kate Murphy, and for the whole world, so plagued by violence and confusion. He did not notice the guard stepping closer to him or pulling a syrette from his shirt pocket. It was only when he felt the pinch of the needle going into his neck that he opened his eyes, gazing in horror at the guard, who was already stepping away again, his task complete.

"Why?" the pope asked as the injection began to work its way through his system.

"*Deus é bom*," the man said and smiled.

◆

WHEN CRAFT AND four other Vatican security guards burst into the room, they found him kneeling over the pope's limp body.

"He's had some kind of seizure!" the guard cried. "I don't know what happened!"

He stood up as they advanced, and as they huddled around the Holy Father where he lay, he slowly backed toward the doorway. When he saw that they were no longer aware of him, he slipped out the door and was gone.

◆

ROME

LEMSKI LEAPED FROM his chair when the chaos erupted. His phone began chirping, but he ignored it. He shouted at the screen, demanding that the cameras stop chasing every stray police officer and return to his sole concern.

"Show me Kate! Where is Kate?"

Finally, the cameras began to follow a descending police helicopter and soon lowered their lenses to the young woman weeping and reaching out for help as she cradled DeBray's head in her lap.

Lemski fell to his knees, crossed himself, and began to pray.

Chapter 58

Vatican City

Kate's tears fell onto DeBray's chest. Once he had fallen, he had passed out, and he remained unconscious. He was breathing but slowly, and blood spilled from his leg onto the dark cobblestones.

When the crowd's shock and confusion had lifted, many of those in the crowd began to surge forward, its heroine and her friend in trouble. Police ran up and down the barricades, attempting to hold them back, but the farthest spot was left unguarded for a moment, and they poured through. Others ran from the square, screaming and crying, spreading through the streets of the city as they escaped harm. From those who remained, cries for justice—against the pope, the Vatican, the police themselves—rose from every corner of the square, fists raised, the anger in the air palpable.

Kate was oblivious to this, however, as her only concern now was the young man in her lap. She felt as if time stopped and the world dropped away. She wiped the hair from his eyes, rocked him slowly, cried, and called for someone to please, please save him. After some moments, DeBray opened his eyes and looked into Kate's.

"Oh, DeBray, I'm so sorry."

His eyes swam with confusion then, looking at himself on the ground, at Kate's tear-filled eyes, at the world erupted in chaos around him.

"You've been shot," Kate said. "You've been shot, and it's all my fault."

DeBray sat up slightly and looked at his leg. "Whoa," he said, then lay back down.

"I'm so sorry, I'm so sorry, I'm so sorry," Kate repeated, shaking her head.

"No," DeBray said. Then he took her hand and kissed it. "No need. You're here, you're safe. That's all that matters."

Just then, the police dispersed the crowd gathered around them as an ambulance backed up to the scene. After that, everything was a blur; time sped up again. As they lifted DeBray onto the gurney, Steven's security team swarmed Kate, a circle of bodies around her, and she could no longer see DeBray. She yelled for him but could hear nothing in return. Finally, she could see the ambulance leaving, the lights flashing and the terrible sound of the sirens fading as they sped off. The security team whisked her to a waiting vehicle, and when they closed the doors, the world went quiet, all the sounds from outside muffled, then gone.

The last thing she remembered was the sound of bells in the distance, tolling from a church somewhere—the sound of joy or sadness, depending on the occasion. Today, the sadness overwhelmed her, and she collapsed on the seat, a blue armband gripped in her hand.

Chapter 59

Rome

Hendrik sat beside DeBray's hospital bed. He was overjoyed to find his friend weary but coherent. The leg that had taken the bullet was heavily bandaged. The bullet had gone straight through above the knee, miraculously missing muscle and bone but damaging tissue and nerves. Numbness came and went in his thigh, and because of the velocity of the sniper's bullet, there was healing to be done, but they expected a full recovery.

On the news, pundits theorized that the young Spaniard had gained the confidence of the remarkable but naive woman with the intent to do her harm. It was rumored that he must have known something, because only he had understood the grave danger Kate Murphy had faced in St Peter's Square.

Hendrik defended his friend at every opportunity. He knew DeBray had no ties to political groups or to Evangelists, nor to Dumas, the alleged mastermind of the assassination. "He's a painter, a romantic who just devoted his life to God. He would never knowingly or willingly harm anyone," he had told the authorities, who'd seized on him as soon as he'd revealed that he was DeBray's friend.

To his astonishment, Hendrik also became the focus of rumors. A grainy photo of him had been captioned, "Mystery accomplice pressured by police." The garbage reportage had consequences. He'd been forced to defend himself to DeBray's father, who was looking for any undue influences that could be blamed for DeBray's decision to enroll in seminary.

Their first visit was short.

"You look happy," Hendrik said.

DeBray averted his eyes. "Well, at least I'm alive."

"You're all anyone talks about at seminary," Hendrik relayed. "They may build a statue."

"I thought activism was frowned upon?"

"Apparently, not anymore. But affairs with world-famous redhaired . . .?"

"I haven't even kissed her, Hendrik."

"Really? Good, let's keep it that way."

DeBray's face darkened, and he turned away.

"Have you thought about when you'll come back to school?"

"Yes. And no."

"Why can't you choose, DeBray?"

"Tell me again what my choices are."

"Her or—"

When Hendrik wasn't quite sure how to finish, DeBray filled in the blank. "Or the priesthood."

"Sounds rather dry when you put it that way." Hendrik perched on the arm of the hospital chair. "Don't you love God?"

"Of course, but . . . how does He look in a dress?" DeBray grinned briefly before returning to his somber mood. "Hendrik, she's a real spiritual woman, not some screwball prophet trying to make headlines."

Hendrik was truly sad for his friend. DeBray was enthralled, and his dabbling with love would eventually end badly. "Sounds like you've already made your choice."

"Pray for me?"

Hendrik closed his eyes and thought deeply for a moment, then put his hand on DeBray's.

"Lord, hear our prayer. It is our will to surrender to You everything that we are and everything that we are striving to be. We open the deepest recesses of our hearts and invite your Holy Spirit to dwell inside of us."

DeBray whispered, "Amen."

Silence permeated the room. Then Hendrik stood to leave. "Oh, I almost forgot. Have you heard the news?"

DeBray grimaced. "Now what?"

"Pope Nelson's last official act was changing Canon Law 1024. Her persistence prevailed."

Chapter 60

Countryside near Lumphat

Henryk Lemski made the seventeen-hour flight, two-hour bus ride, and thirty-minute tuk-tuk journey to Father Kelly's parish office, as he'd done months before, but this time having made tangible penance about his long-present guilt. He was exhausted from jet lag and weary from watching the horror erupt on his television screen, but he felt buoyed by the hope of forgiveness.

He found Father Kelly in his office, at the same oiled rosewood desk, the same sheltering quiet surrounding him so far away from the drama of Rome. As Lemski stepped through the door, Father Kelly looked up, his hair showing some gray now, Lemski noticed—a life given to service, a life forced to hold secrets. Lemski saw Father Kelly's familiar, gentle grin spread over his face and felt relief.

"Am I forgiven?" he asked before even reaching Father Kelly's desk. He dropped his bags on the dusty floor.

"More than forgiven," Father Kelly said, standing and opening his arms to embrace Lemski. "Admired, my friend."

"Thank you, Father."

"'Well done, good and faithful servant.' I believe Christ would say those very words to you in this moment." He gestured for Lemski to sit. "The One whom we serve, despite the arrogance and greed of humans."

Lemski sat. "Not all humans."

"Not all."

"Did you enjoy your pink smoke?" Lemski asked.

"More than you will ever know, Wicus," he said with a huge smile thinking about how much it had helped his daughter's cause and possibly even saved her life.

That evening, the men walked with Ava along the banks of the river, and Lemski recounted to them all that he'd witnessed in Rome. Father Kelly grew visibly shaken when he came to the moment Lemski believed Kate had been shot.

"I thought, surely not. Surely, it can't end this way. Was it all—everything—for nothing? But of course, it wasn't. Of course, that miraculous girl was kept safe." He smiled. "And by a boy who supposedly intends to enter the priesthood, no less." Lemski winked. "We'll see how things progress. The boy seemed *doubly devout* to me, if you know what I mean."

"I surely do," said Father Kelly, glancing at Ava.

"May His Holiness Pope Nelson rest in eternal peace," Lemski said, lowering his head, and the other two followed.

Father Kelly held out an arm, directing Lemski and Ava to stop. "A moment of silence," he said. They stood, listening to the water rush by, watching it swirl and flow. The sounds of nighttime were erupting around them—crickets and birds, the jungle settling in or waking up, depending.

"Look at that," Father Kelly said. "That stick there." He pointed at a two-foot piece of wood caught in an eddy. "Look, it seems like . . . yes . . . it's about to be set free," he said, and they watched as the stick turned one last time before it washed back into the current, unencumbered. "I sat here with Kate once, before all of this. Worried for her, for me . . . *us.*" He looked at Ava. "For the Church. But now . . ." He smiled, and Lemski knew what he saw there: the future. The freedoms that Pope Nelson had put in place before his death. A new day coming.

Lemski wanted to hope along with him, but he had seen too much of the inner workings. He knew not all humans were full of greed and arrogance, but there were enough to do a great deal of damage. Yet, he had changed so much that he now felt others could too, and he knew they weren't finished.

Chapter 61

São Paulo

"Are you kidding me? How hard is it for two men to kidnap a woman?" Djiana yelled at the men standing over Edhir Souza's wife, who was sitting in a chair with a blood-soaked towel covering her face. "Move the hell out of the way, dumbasses. How bad is it?"

"The knife, it, uh, slipped."

Djiana pulled the towel away from Edhir's wife. "Oh, *meu Deus*! You butchered her."

Djiana imagined Edhir seeing his wife with a massive scar across her face from her eye to her mouth. She was flooded by fear of what he would do to her out of retaliation. "Get the box. We have to dispose of her."

Bloodshot eyes looked up in horror from behind the towel.

"What's the problem?" Djiana asked as she began running her fingers through the blonde woman's blood-soaked hair. "Poor little miss who becomes a multibillionaire as a teenager finally has an adult problem?"

Edhir's wife sobbed and mumbled incoherently.

"He only married you because you have money. I grew up in a disease-infested *favela*, being raped by my uncle. And yet, Edhir loves me more than he ever loved you, with all your money and your private island."

"But, I—I never—"

Djiana scowled into the mangled woman's eyes. "You never what?"

"I never wanted money."

"Ha, ha! So predictable! You hear that, boys? It always makes me laugh when rich people say they never wanted money. Take her to the box. Now! *Idiotas!*"

Chapter 62

Rome

The room was too Baroque to feel cozy and too large to feel safe. Tall windows invited the Italian sun, sky, and angels to teem in without ceremony or reserve. They surrounded Kate and wrapped her in an ethereal, unswerving devotion that did little to calm her nerves or her grief.

She had been sequestered in an apartment of the Domus Sanctae Marthae after the attempted shooting, along with her parents and Professor Nadia Jamira, and in that time, she had felt more alone than ever before.

She lay in the fetal position on a red velvet couch, twisting strands of her hair into tangles. "It's all too much. I can't handle it anymore. I can't. I won't," she whispered.

Another voice responded. It arrived from somewhere deep within, more of a vibration than a sound. Commanding yet calm, firm yet compassionate, the voice refused to let her give up.

You can't, you won't, but you will. It is your—

"Destiny is a choice."

Not entirely.

"Then I don't want destiny! I want—"

She heard the door push open behind her. She did not need to look to know who had arrived. DeBray. *Tranquilo.* Her gorgeous, graceful savior. The man she adored but could not face. Not now.

"Who are you talking to?" he asked.

Kate did not sit up. The back of the couch was her rampart. She knew that it was time to explain everything; that she could no longer hide the truth.

He crutched over to her and she felt his shadow upon her. Opening her eyes, she finally answered, "No one."

"But I heard two voices."

"Yes. I'm sure you did."

Her half-smile and her long curls blanketed the sofa like the sun setting on a sprawling red sea.

Kate sat up and tried to laugh, but this was not a joke, and tears began to run down her cheeks.

"What is it?" He moved closer.

Helpless, she shook her head. DeBray had been patient. A saint, she thought. But how long would his goodness be able to withstand her inability or unwillingness to trust him with her whole story?

"I've been waiting for you. I thought we were going to talk about—" He let his thought hang in the air. "Our future."

She only nodded because more tears began to choke her.

"I feel . . . I think that . . . I may be falling for you, Kate."

"And I care tremendously for you, DeBray."

Kate's whisper was too quiet, and she continued to stare at the floor, and not out of modesty. There was no way for him to avoid the obvious any longer. He had to ask. "Kate, is there another man?"

The longer he waited for an answer, the lower his face sank.

Kate felt trapped, with no way forward. "Not another man. Another . . . I don't know how to explain it."

"Sounds like another man to me."

"No."

"Then explain it to me. Please."

Kate curled her legs beneath her and looked at her tranquil beau. "It drives me."

"Crazy?"

"Beyond crazy. It makes me want to do things, all kinds of things, that are frightening and . . . the kinds of things that have put me in this awful situation."

"What's so awful about helping the Church evolve?"

"It's not that." Kate turned away.

"Then I don't know what you're talking about. If you care for me—"

"I do! But—"

DeBray sat next to her on the couch giving her a hug; his large hands cradling her back. Angels hovering in the dusty light burst into motion like a flock of birds, jubilant and envious.

Kate was both submissive and resistant. Her two minds wrestled until she broke from DeBray's arms. She stumbled to the floor on her knees beside the couch, doubled over, held her head in her hands and said in a sad soft tone, "I can't be what you want me to be!"

DeBray reached out gently. "I probably can't be what you want me to be either."

She deflected his hands. "I know, you are a priest."

"I am a seminary student."

"Studying to be a priest, DeBray."

"I'll quit."

"Not for me."

"For us."

"No!"

"But why?"

"Because maybe I want to be a priest too!"

Her conviction had returned, but only briefly.

DeBray's concern showed in his voice, but he spoke with respect and reserve. "And you can be. The world is changing, fast, really fast, and it is all because of you."

"No. Not me."

"Yes, you. The whole world knows your name. That's why you and other women can now be ordained. You'll have the power to make other changes, and very soon, I believe, you'll have the right to be married. As a priest!"

She wiped her eyes and sat back up on the couch. The courage and clarity that had brought her through the last weeks was starting to return. "Soon I'll have the right to *choose* to be married."

◆

DeBray sat next to his dearest, but suddenly, he sensed a chasm open between them, unseen but clearly felt. A chill rose from its shadowy depths. Slowly, a third being emerged.

Invisible yet vibrant, the force Kate had failed to describe made itself known, and DeBray's eyes widened while his heart began racing as he watched Kate grow more luminous and resolute. She seemed to grow in power, inhabited by something spectral and magnificent.

Her lips moved, yet her words were spoken in the second voice DeBray had heard before entering the room.

"Kate," he gasped.

"The gates of hell shall not prevail."

He tried to reach for her, then pulled his arm back, afraid. "What? Kate, what is happening?"

But she wouldn't—couldn't—answer. More statements issued forth until the timbre of the voice resonated so profoundly that the floor began to tremble. DeBray felt like a sapling in a heavy wind, but he loved her. He had to reach her somehow. When he believed that his very being might be uprooted, he shouted into the void with all his mortal might: "It's a new world, Kate! Let's make a life we want!"

Kate cried out, but all DeBray could hear was a howling gale that invaded the room and then exited, leaving behind a ringing silence.

Paralyzed, DeBray found himself laying on his back staring upward, numb and unaware of the angels that swirled around him and grazed his face. He could not see Kate either, until he felt her touch. He found her collapsed at his feet on the floor next to the couch, her pale, perfect hand reaching toward him.

He reached down, pulled her up to him, and whispered, "Even hell would feel like heaven if I'm with you. I will not leave you." He kissed her first with tenderness; then, as she came alive in his arms, with a passion that roared from the depths of his soul.

The angels swooned and sheltered their eyes with their wings.

Chapter 63

São Paulo

"I know what you did to her," Edhir growled as he choked Djiana, lifting her completely off the floor.

Her larynx closed as his hands squeezed her neck tighter. Her body started to shake. He let her dangle in fear and pain.

"Never go behind my back again!"

He released her and threw her down. He stood over her as she lay coughing and rubbing her neck, then slowly lowered himself and placed his arm around her shoulders, gentle again, tender. "But it is done," he said softly, whispering in her ear. "My wife served her purpose." Then he stood and held out his hand. "Now it is time we start sizing a finger that will fit the most powerful ring on earth. Come with me, the archbishop is waiting."

Chapter 64

Rome

The crowds had been gathering in St. Peter's Square every day since Pope Nelson's funeral nearly three weeks before, watching for the white smoke that would signal the election of his successor. The shocking circumstances of Nelson's death had caused the Vatican to institute a total press blackout, but the ever-present and irrepressible rumors had settled on three candidates who were allegedly being seriously considered: an American, a German, and a Brazilian. Still, no one knew anything.

No one, that is, except two wealthy-looking tourists who stood in the middle of the crowd, conversing affectionately in soft Portuguese. The man was middle-aged, with thinning hair and an impeccably tailored white suit; the woman was younger, though plastic surgery had made her actual age difficult to determine. She had lustrous black hair pulled into a tight bun and wore large dark sunglasses and bright red lipstick. Her blazer, skirt, and heels were also white, and ostentatiously expensive.

"Today is the day," he murmured into her ear.

"It's confirmed? It's done?"

"The votes are ours. There is no question."

Suddenly, a roar went through the crowd. Fingers pointed in the direction of the smokestack atop the Sistine Chapel. Everyone gazed upward at the first coils emerging from the pipe. It was gray. Light gray, but still gray. But then the tint lightened, and suddenly great puffs of white smoke issued forth and continued in a thick stream.

The cheering was deafening, but it was soon overtaken by frantic discussion about whom the conclave might have chosen. The rich tourists in the middle of the crowd smiled and said nothing to each other or their neighbors.

The interval between the release of the smoke and the new pope's appearance seemed to stretch into eternity. Finally, the announcement came over the public address system: "*Annuntio vobis gaudium magnum. Habemus papam!* I announce to you a great joy. We have a pope!"

The heavy red curtains parted, and a procession reached the balcony's edge. First, a priest carrying a tall crucifix, then three more men: two cardinals and the new supreme pontiff. His eyes were dark and sharp like an eagle's, while his smile hinted at craftiness and patience. Towering above all with an imposing presence, he loomed like a specter draped in an opalescent cloak that fluttered ominously in the breeze. His broad shoulders bore the weight of authority, while the towering mitre perched atop his head gave him an almost supernatural stature.

In that moment, he resembled not a frail pope of ages past, but rather an unsettling incarnation of dark power—like a sinister Darth Vader cloaked in the ghostly guise of white. The air around him crackled with an unspoken dread, leaving the crowd both entranced and fearful as if they stood before a harbinger of impending doom.

The senior cardinal introduced him as Pope Mercellus III. Although his speech was in Italian with a heavy Brazilian accent, he could still be understood, even through the layers of echo as the speakers pumped his words through St. Peter's Square.

After his speech, he gazed down at the newly placed ring on his finger. He kissed it, then raised the Fisherman high above his head with a clenched fist.

"The Church will thrive by strengthening its embrace of tradition, not changing to suit the demands of the modern secular world," he declared.

As he turned his back on the crowd, he murmured, *"Deus é bom."*

To be continued . . .

About the Author

DUSTIN DUNBAR is an author deeply committed to championing equal rights for women, a passion rooted in his upbringing in a household filled with strong, loving women. Drawing inspiration from their resilience, he crafts powerful narratives that illuminate the journeys of women striving for equality in a world that often seeks to silence them. In his latest work, *Her Holiness*, Dunbar explores the complexities of societal tradition and inequality, shedding light on the struggles, triumphs, and unwavering spirit of women who dare to raise their voices. This poignant narrative serves as a compelling reminder of the strength found in solidarity and the urgent need for gender equality. With a firm belief in the importance of amplifying women's voices, Dunbar encourages readers to reflect on their own roles in the ongoing fight for equal rights, inspiring them to join the movement for meaningful change.